THE PR...
P...

BRENDA HARLEN

AND

HOPE'S CHILD
BY
HELEN R MYERS

MILLS & BOON

Dear Reader,

Every woman remembers her first love—and her first heartbreak. Cameron Turcotte was both for Ashley Roarke, and when he left town, she was sure she'd never love anyone as much as she'd loved him.

Of course, a lot can change in twelve years, and when Cam comes back after that time, Ashley has no intention of picking up where they left off.

But Cam knows the one thing that hasn't changed is the chemistry between Ashley and him—if only he can convince her that first love sometimes deserves a second chance.

I hope you enjoy their story.

All the best,

Brenda Harlen

THE PREGNANCY PLAN

BY
BRENDA HARLEN

First published in Great Britain 2011
Harlequin Mills & Boon Limited,
Eton House, 18-24 Paradise Road, Richmond, Surrey TW9 1SR

© Brenda Harlen 2010

ISBN: 978 0 263 88871 3

23-0311

Harlequin Mills & Boon policy is to use papers that are natural, renewable and recyclable products and made from wood grown in sustainable forests. The logging and manufacturing processes conform to the legal environmental regulations of the country of origin.

Printed and bound in Spain
by Litografía Rosés S.A., Barcelona

Brenda Harlen grew up in a small town surrounded by books and imaginary friends. Although she always dreamed of being a writer, she chose to follow a more traditional career path first. After two years of practicing as a lawyer (including an appearance in front of the Supreme Court of Canada), she gave up her "real" job to be a mom and to try her hand at writing books. Three years, five manuscripts and another baby later, she sold her first book—an RWA Golden Heart winner.

Brenda lives in southern Ontario with her real-life husband/hero, two heroes-in-training and two neurotic dogs. She is still surrounded by books ("too many books," according to her children) and imaginary friends, but she also enjoys communicating with "real" people. Readers can contact Brenda by e-mail at brendaharlen@yahoo.com.

To Shelly & Brett—
High school sweethearts who, twenty-three
years later, are still going strong.

Thanks for the example and the inspiration.

Chapter One

"**I**'m going to have a baby."

Ashley Roarke's statement, made to her sister and her cousin over Sunday brunch, was met by silence.

She glanced from Megan to Paige and back again, but she couldn't tell what either of them was thinking.

Paige Wilder, a family law attorney who was accustomed to responding quickly to unexpected revelations in court, recovered first. "You're pregnant?"

"Not yet."

Megan Richmond, a research scientist, took a moment to absorb the news and consider before she said, "I didn't even know you were dating anyone."

Ashley swirled a piece of French toast in the maple syrup on her plate, focusing all of her attention on the task. "I'm not."

"Then you're going to have to explain this to me," her sister—recently and very happily married—said.

Ashley nibbled on the sweet bread while she considered her response.

Megan and Paige weren't just family, they were her best friends, and she'd always been able to count on their unequivocal support in whatever she chose to do. Though she wasn't sure they would support her in this, she also wouldn't be dissuaded.

"I made an appointment at PARC," she finally said, using the acronym for the Pinehurst Assisted Reproduction Clinic.

Megan set her cup down and turned to Paige. "This is all your fault."

"What did I do?"

"You were the one who insisted she didn't need a husband to have a baby."

"Well, she doesn't. And she certainly doesn't need a husband like CBB," her cousin said, invoking the nickname she'd bestowed upon Ashley's ex-fiancé.

His real name was Trevor, but after the breakup of their engagement, he'd been referred to as Cheating Bastard Byden, and the initials had stuck.

It was Paige who'd discovered that Trevor was cheating. She'd seen him cozied up in a booth at a restaurant with a colleague, and while she didn't want to believe he would be unfaithful to his fiancée, the evidence had been irrefutable. Ashley knew that Paige hated telling her, but she would have hated even more for the deception to continue.

Of course, Ashley had refused to believe her. She'd even—she was embarrassed to admit now—accused Paige of being jealous of her happiness. In fact, she'd been so positive that her cousin was wrong, she'd gone straight to Trevor.

She'd expected him to reassure her of his love and fidelity. And while he did insist that he loved her, and that he'd never felt about anyone else the way he felt about her, he'd also admitted that he'd been with other women.

Not another woman—singular, but other women—plural.

And Ashley had felt as if the ground had crumbled beneath her feet.

He'd tried to explain that he'd been feeling a little uncertain since their engagement, and that every woman he'd been with since had reassured him that he was marrying the only woman he would ever love, and he promised her that he would never even look at another woman after they were married.

Ashley was not reassured. As far as she was concerned, he'd made a vow when he'd asked her to marry him, and if he couldn't honor that vow before the wedding, she knew nothing would change afterward.

She didn't regret ending their relationship, but she'd been looking forward to her wedding day since she was a little girl. As she'd grown older, her dreams had taken on a more specific focus. It wasn't just that she wanted a wedding, she wanted to be married. She wanted to fall in love and build a future—and a family—with a man who loved her, too.

She'd thought Trevor was that man. And when she'd handed back his ring, she'd relinquished some of her dreams, too.

That had been almost four months ago. Since then, she'd given the matter a lot of thought. The more she thought about it, the more she resented having to put her life on hold because she'd been wrong about Trevor.

And she'd decided she wasn't going to put her life on hold any longer.

"You can't blame Paige for this," Ashley told her sister now. "I would have thought about artificial insemination on my own if I hadn't been so preoccupied with planning my wedding."

Paige wrinkled her nose. "Anything 'artificial' can't be very much fun."

"I'm not doing it for fun. I'm doing it to have a baby."

"Just because CBB turned out to be a first-class CB doesn't

mean you should give up hope of finding a wonderful man to father your children," Megan said.

"I haven't given up," Ashley denied, though she wasn't entirely sure it was true. Two broken hearts in one lifetime were too many for her. "But I'm tired of waiting."

"You're not even thirty yet," Paige reminded her.

"But I'm no closer to having a husband and a baby than I was at twenty," she pointed out to both of them. "I was devastated when I found out that Trevor was cheating on me. But I'm not sure if I was really heartbroken by his betrayal or because he derailed my hopes of having a child. And I began to wonder if one of the reasons I accepted Trevor's proposal in the first place was that he seemed to want marriage and a family as much as I do."

"That doesn't excuse what he did," Paige said fiercely.

"No, it doesn't," Ashley agreed. "But it made me realize that I want a baby more than I want a husband."

"But your engagement only ended four months ago," Megan said gently. "You have to give your heart time to heal."

"How much time?" Ashley wanted to know. "How long am I supposed to wait until you'll trust that I've considered all the angles, that this is what I really want to do?"

"More than four months," her sister told her.

"We know how much you want a child of your own," Paige chimed in. "And how much love you have to give. But I think we're both concerned that this is an impulse, an emotional response to the breakup of your engagement."

"I'm going to have a baby, and nothing either of you say is going to change my mind now," Ashley assured her.

"I don't want to change your mind," Paige said. "I just want you to rethink your options."

"The Pinehurst clinic has a reputation for excellence and a record of success."

"I know it does," her cousin admitted. "But did you know that Cameron Turcotte is back in town?"

Her cousin's question seemed to come from out of the blue, but Ashley knew the remark wasn't unintentional. Because even after twelve years, just the mention of his name was enough to make her heart skip a beat, but she wouldn't—couldn't—let Paige know it.

"Who?" she said instead.

"I know you saw him at the reunion," Paige said, referring to the high school reunion they'd all attended a few months earlier. Although Cam had been two years ahead of Ashley in school, the party had been open to all former graduates in celebration of Hill Park High School's one hundredth year anniversary.

She shrugged. "So we talked."

"And maybe your…talk…had something to do with his decision to come back to Pinehurst."

Megan frowned, and Ashley knew her sister had concerns about Cameron's return—specifically how it would affect Ashley.

"Is it true, then, that he's going to be working with Elijah Alexander?" Megan asked.

Paige nodded.

"So Cam's back," Ashley said. "So what? What does that have to do with anything?"

"It just seems to me that someone who spent so many years in medical school would have a pretty good idea about how to make a baby," Paige teased.

Ashley didn't doubt that it was true, but she had no intention of letting her mind wander down that dead-end path.

Cameron Turcotte had been her first love, her first lover, and even way back when they were both in high school, he'd been a creative and considerate partner. He'd also broken her heart, and she wasn't going to forget that for a few horizontal thrills. Not even if he'd given her any indication that he was interested in a reunion of that kind, which he hadn't.

"You seem to be forgetting that one of the reasons Cam and I split up was that I wanted to have kids and he didn't."

"He didn't want a baby twelve years ago," Paige pointed out. "I wouldn't be surprised if he's changed his mind since then."

"Well, I've changed mine, too," Ashley said. "I'm no longer looking for a marriage proposal or even a relationship. All I want is a sperm donor."

"You're really not interested?" Megan asked skeptically.

"I'm really not interested."

But while Ashley's voice rang with conviction, her heart wasn't quite so certain.

When Cameron Turcotte first contacted the real estate company, it was to inquire about available rental properties in the area. Since he wasn't convinced that the move back to Pinehurst would be a permanent one, it seemed logical to rent rather than buy. But he didn't want an apartment; he wanted a house, a place to go at the end of the day that was his alone without neighbors above and below him. Unfortunately, house rentals were apparently rare in the area and Tina Stilwell hadn't sounded optimistic about his prospects.

But she'd called earlier in the day to let him know that the owners of a house she had listed might be willing to consider a one-year lease in the hopes that the housing market would pick up within that time and ultimately result in a higher sale price for the home.

Since Cam had committed to a one-year contract with Elijah Alexander—a trial period for both of them, with the possibility of buying into the practice at the end of that term if it was what they wanted—he figured a housing lease for the same amount of time would be ideal. So it was that after a ten-hour day, he wasn't heading back to his parents' retirement community bungalow, where he'd temporarily taken up residence, but following a much too perky real estate agent through the front door of a gorgeous stone and brick two-story.

"It's a wonderful neighborhood, close to the local schools and parks, convenient to shopping, entertainment, and pretty much anything else you'd want," she told him.

And only a short drive from Dr. Alexander's offices, he'd noted.

"I can walk through with you, if you want," Tina said, as she led him from the living room through the dining room to the kitchen at the back of the house, from plush carpet to glossy hardwood to cool travertine. "But I find a lot of clients prefer to look around on their own."

"I'll wander, and let you know if I have any questions," he said, accepting the spec sheet she'd taken from the upright display on the long granite counter in the kitchen.

The agent nodded, pulling out her BlackBerry as she settled at one of the high-backed stools lined up by the breakfast bar.

He exited the kitchen through another doorway, passing a family room and den as he made his way toward the stairs. On the upper level he found four bedrooms, all of them generously sized with lots of windows to ensure plenty of natural light.

The master bedroom at the back of the house was enormous—or maybe it just seemed so because it was devoid of furniture, as were all the other rooms in the house—with a huge walk-in closet and a four-piece ensuite bath of gleaming marble and glistening chrome. Returning to the main part of the room, he wandered over to the pair of wide windows overlooking a professionally landscaped backyard complete with a stone patio, pond, and decorative beds filled with colorful blooms and greenery.

Best of all, there was still a lot of open space, enough room for a child to run around. Several children even, he thought, and sighed with regret that his marriage hadn't worked out quite the way he'd planned.

When he'd proposed to Danica Carrington, he'd known that she was focused on her career to the exclusion of all else; she'd made no secret of the fact that children weren't part of her plan. He'd married her anyway, certain that she would change her mind when she held their baby in her arms. But it hadn't happened that way at all, and after three years of desperately trying to make their marriage work, he'd finally given up and she'd eagerly walked away.

He pushed aside the disappointments and continued his tour. There was no reason to think of Danica now, to continue to mourn what had never been anything more than an illusion. He was determined to put the past behind him and make a fresh start in Pinehurst, to make a new life with Madeline.

And one of the most attractive features of this home, from his point of view, was its move-in condition. The walls were freshly painted in neutral colors, the carpets were pristine, the hardwood unmarked and the cherry kitchen was a chef's paradise.

Not that he was a chef, by any stretch of the imagination, but he enjoyed experimenting in the kitchen. And he knew he would enjoy experimenting in that kitchen, with its top-of-the-line stainless steel appliances, luxurious island and two sets of French doors opening onto a cedar deck.

Tina tucked her BlackBerry away when he paused at those doors to survey the backyard more closely.

"Any thoughts?" she asked him.

I want it, was the first thought that came to mind.

"It's probably a lot more space than I need," he said instead.

"It is spacious," she agreed, choosing to put a positive spin on his negative comment. "More suited to a family than a single man, but definitely a good investment."

"It's certainly been immaculately maintained."

"It's a three-year-old custom-design by Armstrong & Sullivan, built by Carson Construction," she said. "The owners are both young professionals who, from what I understand, spent more time at their jobs than at home."

He knew what that kind of life was like—and the toll it could take on a marriage. But all he said was, "Either they've taken minimalist decorating to a new level or they've already moved out."

"Moved out," she admitted, with a smile. "The wife got transferred to New York City, the husband took a job offer in Los Angeles, and they left me in charge of the house."

And Cam would bet the proceeds were to be split down the middle, along with all their other shared possessions, with a significant chunk from each side going to their respective bloodsucking lawyers.

Yeah, he'd been there, done that, too.

Of course, when he'd met Danica he'd thought she was the type of woman he wanted, someone who had ambitions and dreams, who wanted more than to be a wife and a mother.

Someone who didn't remind him of Ashley Roarke.

Since he'd been back in Pinehurst, it seemed as if everything reminded him of Ashley. Every street and shop and landmark brought back memories of times they'd spent together.

When he'd left town more than a dozen years ago, he'd left his high school sweetheart behind. He could have chosen a college closer to home and had, in fact, been far more tempted to do just that. Instead, he'd opted to put some serious distance between them, so that he wouldn't be able to come home on a long weekend, so that he wouldn't end up sacrificing his own dreams just because he was in love.

During his first few years away, he'd dated only occasionally, and the girls he had dated were usually blue-eyed blondes who reminded him of Ashley in some way. Not surprisingly, none of those relationships ever went very far.

An initial attraction sparked by a superficial resemblance to the girl he'd left behind inevitably fizzled when he finally accepted that no one else was Ashley. No one else's eyes were as bright, no one else's smile was so warm, no one else's touch felt so right.

And then he met a dark-haired, dark-eyed first-year law student who didn't resemble Ashley in any way.

Danica wasn't looking to get married; she didn't want to tie herself down. She had plans for her life and she wasn't going to let anything—or anyone—stand in the way of fulfilling them.

She was, it had seemed to him then, his perfect match.

It had taken him a long time to realize what a mistake he'd made.

He sometimes wondered how differently his life might have turned out if he'd never gone away. If he'd never said goodbye to Ashley. But wondering and wishing couldn't change the past, and though there had been more bumps in the road than he'd have chosen, he couldn't regret where he was now.

Now he had Madeline, and she was the reason for everything he did, for everything he was. She would probably expect him to consult with her before making a decision on their housing situation since it would impact her future, too. But she wouldn't be back from London for three more weeks and he didn't want to wait that long.

He needed to move into a place of his own. He loved his parents dearly—in fact, being closer to them was one of the reasons he'd decided to move out of Seattle and look for a job in the area. But he was too old to be sleeping on living room furniture, and he certainly couldn't share the couch with Madeline.

He considered calling her now, not just to tell her about the house but to hear her voice. But with the five-hour time difference, it was likely that she was already in bed.

He glanced at the spec sheet he still had in hand, then up at Tina. "What are they asking for rent?"

She told him the amount. "Plus utilities," she said, sounding apologetic.

"It would almost be cheaper to buy it," he noted.

"I think that's the point. They are willing to rent, but they'd rather sell."

Cam hesitated. He hadn't considered buying a house. On the other hand, real estate was generally a good investment and he had no doubt his mortgage payments would be less than the quoted rental fee.

"I know you were adamant about wanting a house," she said. "But I did find a couple of condos available for rent, and I've got the details with me if you want to take a look at those instead."

He wasn't usually impulsive, but something about this house just felt right. As if he and Madeline belonged there.

As if they'd finally come home.

And if it crossed his mind that being back in Pinehurst meant being near Ashley Roarke again, well, he pushed that thought aside.

Chapter Two

Ashley was a big fan of retail therapy. A great pair of shoes could put a smile on her face on the gloomiest of days, and she was positively beaming when she pulled onto Chetwood Street heading home after her shopping expedition Thursday afternoon.

Only two and a half weeks until the first day of school, and she was as excited as any of the first graders who would be entering her class.

She'd enjoyed the summer break and had, in fact, needed both the time away from the classroom and the solitude to let her bruised and battered heart heal. But six weeks of intense rest and relaxation along with some quality time spent with Marg & Rita had her feeling a lot better about herself and her future. Okay, so maybe she'd wallowed a little, but she'd eventually pulled herself out of the funk and now she wasn't just ready but eager to move forward. Deciding to have a baby was a big step forward, but one she was more than ready to take.

Her already high spirits got another lift when she spotted the SOLD sign down the street. She hadn't known the previous owners except to say hello in passing, but she'd heard that they were newlyweds when they'd first moved in and now, three years later, newly divorced. Maybe that was part of the reason she'd felt inexplicably saddened when they'd packed up, or maybe she'd just hated to think that the beautiful home had been abandoned, but today, the SOLD sign seemed to her another beacon of hope.

She pulled into her driveway already speculating about the new owners, wondering where they were from and when they'd move in. Were they another newlywed couple? Empty nesters? A family with kids? The neighborhood was an eclectic collection of each, including a few singles like herself.

Because she was thinking about her potential neighbors, she didn't see the package propped up against the door until she was sliding her key into the lock. It was wrapped in brown paper and blended in with the paint, suggesting that she really should repaint the door to give the outside a little boost of color and a more welcoming feel. Since she wasn't getting married and moving any time in the near future, she should consider adding some personal touches to make the house more distinctly her own.

She felt a slight pang when she thought of the wedding that wouldn't be, but only slight. She was totally over Trevor now and determined not to let the absence of a husband prevent her from having the child she wanted.

She shifted her other bags, then tucked the flat parcel under her arm and carried it inside. She dumped everything on top of the dining room table before backtracking to the kitchen.

She opened the fridge, found a can of her diet soda next to the regular Pepsi her sister favored and popped the top.

Megan had been married for three months now, but Ashley still missed having her around. She certainly missed her more than she missed her former fiancé—she shook her head, pushing him firmly out of her mind. She wasn't going to ruin a perfectly nice day thinking about Trevor and what he'd done.

Instead, she carried her drink into the dining room, back to the mysterious paper-wrapped package. She couldn't remember buying anything that needed to be delivered, but the neatly printed label had her name and address on it, so she turned the parcel over and lifted the tape.

As she pulled back the paper, revealing a polished walnut frame and the edge of a cream-colored mat, she realized it was a picture. Tearing the paper further, she sucked in a breath at the image of herself wrapped in the arms of her supposedly devoted fiancé.

The frame slipped from her fingers and crashed to the ground.

The glass broke, a long jagged crack across the center, slicing neatly between the images of Ashley and Trevor.

She'd canceled the wedding and everything related to it. She'd made the phone calls herself to the florist and the caterer; she'd notified the band and the pastry chef. She'd been too late to stop the order at the printer, but she'd been certain to shred each and every invitation and response card and personalized thank-you note when they were delivered. She knew there was no way she would have forgotten to contact the photographer.

Then she spotted the piece of paper tucked into the bottom corner of the frame. She reached for it, frowning as she unfolded it. If it was an invoice—

No, it was a note.

From Trevor.

Ashley,
I just wanted you to know that I've been thinking about
you and missing you. I haven't given up hope that we can
find a way to work things out. I'm sending this picture to
remind you of the happy times we had together, and to let
you know that I want us to be together again.
I love you.
T xo

She tore the note into tiny pieces and let them fall from her
hands like confetti. Of course, thinking of confetti made her
think of weddings and that made her even angrier.

She picked up the broken frame and carted it to the kitchen
to dump it in the garbage where it belonged. She was over
him. She really was. Wholly and completely. But apparently
she wasn't over being mad.

She pulled the waste basket out of the cupboard and shoved
the picture in it, determined to put Trevor out of her mind. As
she pushed down on it, she felt a quick, slicing pain. She felt
the blood, warm and wet, dripping down her hand, before she
saw the streaks of red. And when she did, her stomach pitched.

She'd never done well with the sight of blood. Although
cuts and scrapes were common occurrences with first graders,
those cuts and scrapes could usually be fixed with a Band-Aid
or an ice pack. Ashley peeked at her hand again and didn't
think a Band-Aid was going to do the job. Not this time.

She grabbed a clean dish towel from the drawer and
wrapped it around her palm.

A quick glance at the clock revealed that it was almost five,
so she knew that the phones at her doctor's office would
already have been turned over to the answering service. But
she'd been a patient of Uncle Eli's since she was a child and
the duration of their relationship, combined with the fact that

he'd been a good friend of both of her parents, meant that she could show up at his office at this late hour and know that he would make time for her. Hopefully that would save her a trip to the emergency room.

Fifteen minutes later, she was ushered into an exam room by the nurse.

"The doctor will be in to see you shortly," Irene told her.

And Ashley, feeling a little queasy from the loss of blood, nodded gratefully, reassured that she'd made the right decision in coming here rather than the hospital.

An opinion that changed as soon as the doctor walked into the room.

Cam had been at the office since 8:00 a.m.

He knew that the nature of a family practice required a certain degree of flexibility with respect to unexpected emergencies, but as the day wore on and he worked through lunch, he wished that Courtney—the receptionist and general office manager—would show some appreciation of the same fact and schedule appointments with more than ten minutes between them.

By five o'clock, the number of patients in the waiting room had diminished sufficiently that there were enough chairs for those still waiting. By that same time, he'd managed to take half a dozen bites of the sandwich that Courtney had brought back for him when she returned from her lunch break. The thinning of the crowd combined with the silencing of his stomach gave him hope that he might actually get out of the office before he needed to return the following morning.

He was reaching for the file in the slot outside of exam room number two when Irene—Dr. Alexander's sister and longtime nurse—slipped out of room number four. The guilty flush in her cheeks warned him that she'd squeezed in yet another patient who didn't have an appointment.

He sighed. "I thought you wanted to go home as much as I do."

"You need a home in order to go to it," she said.

"I'll have one soon enough," he told her. "And you're not going to distract me that easily."

"I'm not trying to distract you at all." She took his arm and steered him towards the door she'd just exited.

"I thought Mrs. Kirkland was next."

"Mrs. Kirkland is a hypochondriac, but this patient is really bleeding."

He sighed again and took the folder she thrust into his hands, not even having a moment to note the name on the tab before he walked in the room.

And found himself face-to-face with Ashley Roarke.

He faltered, at a sudden loss for words since "Hello, Ashley, I'm Dr. Turcotte"—the standard greeting he'd given to Dr. Alexander's other patients—seemed a little ridiculous in light of their history.

But it was long ago history and he'd seen her only once since he'd left town more than a dozen years earlier—just a few months before at their high school reunion. Ashley had made it clear to him then then that she didn't forgive him for leaving her and that she had no interest in reminiscing with him.

She'd also told him that she was getting married in a few months, he remembered now. But her purse was clutched in her left hand and the impressive diamond she'd worn at the reunion wasn't on it.

Her other hand was wrapped in a bloody towel, and it was the blood that jerked him out of the past and firmly back into doctor mode.

He couldn't think of her as the first woman he'd ever

loved, the only woman he'd never forgotten. She was a patient, and it was his job to ascertain the nature of her injury and prescribe treatment.

"I, uh, came to see Eli," she told him, breaking the awkward silence.

"He's at the hospital."

"Oh. Well." She cleared her throat. "Okay. I'll go there then. To the hospital. To catch up with him there."

She was babbling, obviously not any more prepared for this unexpected meeting than he was. And though he was tempted to let her go, it was apparent that she hadn't come to chat with Eli but for medical attention, and he wouldn't shirk his duty.

"You're dripping blood," he told her.

She glanced down, and quickly averted her gaze again.

"I think I should take a look at that before you go anywhere." He reached into a box on the counter to pull out a pair of disposable gloves.

"I'd rather have Eli look at it," she said.

"Stop being stubborn, Ash."

"I'm not being stubborn," she denied. "I'd just feel more comfortable seeing my doctor."

Despite her close relationship with Elijah Alexander, she obviously hadn't heard that he wasn't doing patient rounds at the hospital but spending time with his wife, who was in ICU after suffering a near-fatal heart attack the previous evening.

So all he said to her was, "And I'd let you go if I didn't think it was likely you'd pass out while you were driving and potentially cause more harm to yourself and/or others."

He wouldn't have thought it was possible, but her face got even whiter. "Have I lost that much blood?"

He chuckled as he tugged on the second glove. "Hardly."

She scowled. "Then why do you think I'd pass out?"

"Because I was there when you fell off the stone wall at Eagle Point Park and cut your knee open. You said you were okay, then you saw the blood and your face went white just before your eyes rolled back in your head."

He shouldn't have mentioned the incident, because it was an admission that he still remembered that day, even so many years later. As he remembered so many things they'd done and moments they'd spent together. He had too many memories of Ashley. Memories that haunted his waking moments and taunted him in dreams.

"I was nine," she said, her indignant response forcing his attention back to the present.

"And you're as pale now as you were then," he told her.

Since she couldn't see her face, she really wasn't in a position to deny his accusation. Instead, she lifted her arm and thrust her towel-wrapped hand toward him.

"Fine. Take a look and give me one of those butterfly bandage things so I can go home."

Cam took her hand and carefully began unwrapping the towel. At another time, he might have lifted his brows at the parade of little goslings embroidered along the hem, but now it was the blood soaked into the fabric that held his attention.

"How did it happen?" he asked.

"Broken glass."

He was a doctor—he'd seen far worse than a three-inch gash in the flesh of a woman's hand. Except that this was Ashley's hand, and the gash ran down the side of her palm before abruptly detouring toward her wrist. Luckily, it stopped short of her ulnar artery, but his heart skipped a beat in his chest when he realized how close it had come.

"Must have been a big piece of glass," he noted.

"Eleven-by-fourteen."

It only took him a second to figure out the reference. "A picture frame."

She nodded, but kept her gaze firmly affixed to the opposite wall.

He tore open the packaging of a gauze pad, dabbed gently at the skin around the wound. "Well, I think it's going to take a little bit more than one of those butterfly bandage things to fix this up."

"How much more?"

"Probably ten to fifteen stitches."

He thought of the patients still in the waiting room and considered sending her to the hospital for the procedure. Now that he'd examined her injury, he was confident the repair was something any ER doctor could handle.

But she was already here and he had everything he needed on the premises to get the job done, and he would take care to minimize, as much as possible, any scarring.

"I was afraid you were going to say something like that." She sighed. "Okay. Let's just do it."

"Well, Ashley Roarke, I never thought I'd hear you say those words to me again," he teased.

That remark brought color to her too-pale cheeks and a flash to her lovely violet eyes.

Eyes that had haunted his thoughts and his dreams for longer than he was willing to admit.

"The stitches, *doctor.*"

He grinned, unrepentant. "Of course."

He released her hand and went to the door, poking his head out to ask Irene for a suture tray.

She must have anticipated his request, because she came in with the necessary equipment less than a minute later.

Her eyes grew wide when she saw Ashley's injury.

"Oh, honey, what have you done?"

"I lost a fight with a piece of broken glass," Ashley told her.

"Well, don't you worry. The doctor will have you fixed up in no time."

"But you're going to jab me with that first, aren't you?" she asked, warily eyeing the needle that the nurse was prepping.

"Actually, the doctor is going to jab you with it," Irene told her. "But you won't feel him poking at you after that."

Cam fought against a smile as Ashley's cheeks colored again.

He'd remembered so many things about her, but he'd forgotten how easily she blushed, how much he used to enjoy making her blush. But that was a long time ago.

Now he had to forget that they were ever lovers and concentrate on doing his job.

"There now. That wasn't so bad, was it?" Irene said.

"You wouldn't be asking that question if you'd been on the other end of the needle," Ashley told her.

The nurse chuckled. "You never did like getting shots," she remembered. "And your sister wasn't any better. How's she doing, by the way?"

He didn't know if Irene had asked the question because she was anxious to catch up on Roarke family gossip or if she was trying to distract Ashley from what he was doing, but since the patient wasn't paying any attention to him or the needle sliding through her skin, he was grateful.

"Meg's great," Ashley responded. "She seems to have adapted to marriage easily and blissfully."

"Good for her," the nurse asserted. Then her voice gentled when she said, "But I imagine it must have been difficult for you."

Ashley didn't move, but Cam sensed her tension.

"Megan getting married so soon after you ended your engagement, I mean," Irene clarified.

"I was—*am*—happy for her."

"Well, of course you are. And I have no doubt that someday you'll find a man who's perfect for you, too."

"I'm not looking for a man—perfect or otherwise," Ashley said.

She spoke with such conviction, he found himself wondering about the details of her broken engagement, and whether he might be able to subtly pry them out of the nurse at another time. Because he had no doubt that if there were details to be known, Irene would know them.

But for now, he clenched his teeth together to hold back the questions he wanted to ask. He had no business asking any questions, no business feeling anything for the woman who had once meant everything to him.

"Are you up to date with your tetanus shot?" he asked instead.

Ashley shifted her attention from the nurse to him. "I had a booster two years ago."

"Then you don't need another one."

"Must be my lucky day."

He smiled, appreciating that she could find humor in the situation.

"Since you're just about finished up here, I'll go check on Mrs. Kirkland," Irene told him. Then to Ashley, "Take care of yourself, hon."

"I will."

"How do they look?" he asked, after Irene had gone.

Ashley glanced down at her hand, at the dark thread that stood out in stark contrast to her pink skin. "It looks…good?"

He smiled again. "It looks raw and ugly, but it will look good when the wound has healed."

"How long?" she asked.

He tore open a sterile gauze pad, affixed it to her skin. "Seven to ten days."

"At least they'll be out before I go back to school."

"Too bad," he said. "I imagine fifteen stitches could be the object of intense fascination for a bunch of first graders."

She looked up, surprise evident in those stunning eyes.

He was suddenly aware of how close they were sitting. That he was still holding her hand. And that she had made no effort to pull away.

"How did you know I teach first grade?"

He shrugged. "It's what you always said you were going to do."

"I didn't think you would have remembered something like that," she murmured.

"You'd be surprised what I remember," he said. "What I couldn't forget."

Her gaze dropped away, and he cursed himself for speaking aloud a truth he'd only recently acknowledged.

He wrote her a prescription for some painkillers, tore off the page and handed it to her.

"Try to keep your hand elevated as much as possible, keep the stitches dry, and set up an appointment with Courtney to have them checked next week."

"I'll do that," she said. "Thanks."

Cam nodded and moved to the door, pausing with his hand on the knob.

"I never forgot you, Ashley. And I don't think you forgot me, either."

He walked out before she could reply. Because even if she denied it, even if she *had* forgotten about him, he was going to make sure she remembered him now.

This time, he wasn't going to walk away.

Chapter Three

Ashley didn't get the prescription filled.

She hadn't told Cam that she was taking Fedentropin because she didn't want him asking all kinds of questions about the drug trial she was participating in. It had been awkward enough when Irene had made reference to her broken engagement without getting into any explanations about her medical history or the experimental drug that was helping to manage her endometriosis so that pregnancy remained an option for her.

But her hand throbbed painfully as she tried to sweep up remnants of broken glass and wood with her left arm wrapped around the broom and the handle of the dustpan gripped with the thumb and two other fingers of her right hand, making her rethink that decision. She could call Megan, of course. Her sister had developed the drug she was taking and would know whether it was safe to take the painkiller she'd been prescribed.

But then she'd have to tell her sister about the fifteen stitches and Megan would insist on coming over to see for herself that it wasn't a fatal wound. And as much as she enjoyed spending time with her sister, she hated knowing that her family was still so worried about her. As they'd been worrying since she'd ended her engagement.

Because worrying translated into hovering, and while Ashley was still adjusting to living alone, she enjoyed having her own space. She ate her meals on her own schedule, watched whatever she wanted to watch on TV and generally came and went as she pleased without being accountable to anyone else.

Of course that would change when she had a baby, but she looked forward to the duties and responsibilities of motherhood. She wanted nothing more than to feel the stirring of a new life in her womb, and the warmth of a tiny baby in her arms.

Which was another reason she didn't want to fill the prescription Cam had written for her. Her appointment at the Pinehurst clinic was only a few days away and she didn't want anything to delay the start of the process. So she'd stick with her extra-strength Tylenol and hope that was enough to take the edge off of the pain.

Her stomach growled as she emptied the dustpan into the garbage, so she propped the broom and pan in the corner and moved to the fridge. Unfortunately, she found nothing that appealed to her. Or maybe she just didn't want to tackle putting together a meal with only one hand.

She could, however, dial the phone, and she was thinking about doing just that when the doorbell rang.

She'd never been the type to ignore a ringing phone and the echo of a bell had the same effect. She pulled open the door and, for the second time that day, found herself facing her past.

"Making house calls, Dr. Turcotte?" she asked him. Her

tone was deliberately casual, refusing to acknowledge the jump in her pulse.

For as far back as she could remember, her body had always instinctively reacted to Cameron's presence. Since she could do nothing about that response, she simply tried to ignore it.

But she couldn't deny that he looked good. His hair was as dark as she remembered, and still long enough to flirt with the collar of his shirt. His eyes were the same rich green that brought to mind the Irish countryside of her ancestors, and his gaze was just as intense. The shadow on his jaw attested to a long day at the office and gave him a slightly dangerous edge. Dangerously sexy, she mused, and immediately pushed the thought aside.

He had on the same shirt and khaki pants he'd been wearing earlier, but he'd loosened the knot in his tie and rolled up his sleeves, revealing darkly tanned and strongly muscled forearms. He used to be an avid tennis player and she found herself wondering if he still enjoyed pounding a fuzzy yellow ball around the court. It would certainly explain his trim and toned physique.

"Actually, I'm not here in my professional capacity," he told her, his comment drawing her back from her perusal.

"Then why are you here?" She knew the question sounded rude, but she didn't care. She was tired, her hand ached and she didn't have the energy or the desire to put a smile on her face, though she was suddenly experiencing an unwelcome stirring of certain other desires.

Cam lifted a flat white box that she hadn't even noticed he was carrying because she'd been too busy looking at him.

"Pizza delivery," he said.

"I didn't order pizza."

"And yet I've got a large double pepperoni and extra cheese in my hands."

It was her favorite kind. Of course, it had always been his favorite, too. Had he remembered her preference? Or had he just ordered it the way he liked it?

Not that it mattered. Even if he had remembered, their history was exactly that, and she wasn't going to let his sudden appearance at her door drag her down memory lane.

So all she asked was, "Why?"

He shrugged. "Because I worked through lunch and I was hungry, and because I figured it would be difficult for you to put together dinner for yourself with those stitches in your hand."

It sounded not only reasonable but thoughtful, and she was undeniably tempted to invite him in. There was something about Cam Turcotte that had always tempted her, but she wasn't a teenager anymore and she had no intention of letting down any of her barriers where he was concerned.

"I'm not hungry," she lied.

"You should eat anyway."

Still, she hesitated. "Contrary to whatever Irene might have told you, I don't need anyone looking out for me, Dr. Turcotte."

"It's just a pizza, Ash."

He was using his doctor tone again, patient and reasonable, and she knew that she was being anything but reasonable.

As he said, it was just a pizza. And she was hungry.

She stepped back from the door.

"Fine. Bring in the pizza."

Her welcome left something to be desired.

As Cam stepped into the foyer, he wondered again why he was there when it was readily apparent that Ashley wished he wasn't. He'd known he was taking a chance when he looked up her address in the file, but he'd never been able to think clearly when it came to Ashley Roarke.

"Nice neighborhood," he said, conversationally.

"We like it."

"We?" he queried, following her through to the kitchen.

"Megan and I bought the house a couple of years ago and lived here together until she got married. I guess I haven't quite got used to being on my own yet."

"I thought you were talking about the fiancé," he admitted, setting the pizza box in the middle of the table.

"*Ex*-fiancé," she clarified.

She opened the cupboard to get plates, but he reached over her head for them so that she didn't have to stretch.

"Yeah. I got that from what Irene said," he admitted.

"You mean she didn't give you the whole sordid story?"

"Is it sordid?"

She shrugged as she moved toward the refrigerator. "Let's just say he didn't think the act of putting a ring on my finger mandated exclusivity."

"Bastard," Cam said.

Ashley smiled, appreciating his unequivocal assessment and deciding that she might enjoy his company after all.

"The official term, at least among my friends, is 'cheating bastard,'" she told him.

"I'm sorry, Ash. You deserved better than that."

"Well, as Paige likes to remind me, at least I found out *before* we got married."

"I don't imagine that was much consolation."

"No," she admitted, peering into the refrigerator. "Beer, wine or soft drink?"

"Beer would be great."

She snagged a bottle for him and a soft drink for herself and carried the beverages to the table.

Again, before she could ask for help, Cam had both of the drinks open.

His unsolicited assistance reminded her of the days when they'd been dating, when he'd somehow been able to anticipate what she wanted without her saying a word. Like instinctively knowing the type of movie she wanted to see on a given night, or whether she preferred to stay home rather than go out. Bringing her flowers to brighten her day when she hadn't even known she was feeling down, or stopping by simply to spend time with her before she'd acknowledged that she was lonely.

Just like tonight, she realized now, and felt a funny little flutter in the vicinity of her heart.

She picked up the soda he'd opened for her and took a long swallow. She didn't want to be feeling any flutters, not now and definitely not because of Cam Turcotte.

"Premium beer," Cam noted appreciatively, picking up his bottle.

"My brother-in-law's company," she said, gratefully latching on to the neutral topic.

"That's right." He lifted a slice of pizza and slid it onto her plate before taking another one for himself. "Your sister married Gage Richmond. I read about his career change—and their marriage—in a business magazine somewhere."

"The Richmond name always makes good copy." She pulled a piece of pepperoni off of her pizza and popped it into her mouth.

"Megan works at Richmond Pharmaceuticals, doesn't she?"

She nodded. "Recently promoted to VP of clinical science."

"Impressive."

"No kidding. Whenever she tries to talk to me about something she's doing at work, my eyes glaze over."

"As I'm sure her eyes glaze when you want to discuss the intrinsic value of finger painting."

She smiled at that. "Very few people over the age of ten appreciate the intrinsic value of finger painting," she told him.

"But with Megan, it's not that she doesn't understand, just that she has an irrational fear of any human being less than three feet tall."

"I take it she doesn't plan on having kids then?"

"Not anytime in the near future," she said, then realized she was no longer certain it was true. After all, her sister was married now and starting a family with her new husband wasn't outside the realm of possibility. She pushed the thought—and the irrational spurt of envy—aside.

"I appreciate the pizza," she said. "But why are you really here?"

"I just wanted to see you, to talk to you, without an audience."

"Why?"

"For a lot of reasons," he said. "But primarily because we're living in the same town again, which means our paths are going to cross on occasion, and I don't want things to be awkward between us."

"Our paths are only crossing now because you showed up at my door."

He helped himself to another slice of pizza. "Actually, my door is just down the street."

She frowned. "Excuse me?"

"Number fifty-eight. The SOLD sign on the front lawn."

The pizza in Ashley's stomach suddenly felt like a ball of lead. "*You* bought that house?"

"The rent they were asking was astronomical," he said, as if that was a perfectly logical response to her question.

"I can't believe you bought it," she said.

But what she was thinking was that she was completely unprepared to be neighbors with her ex-lover. It was one thing to accept that he'd returned to Pinehurst—it was a big enough town that she wasn't likely to run into him at the grocery store very often—and quite another to know that he would be living just down the street and that she would have to pass by his house every single day on the way to and from her own.

"I thought you weren't sure this was a permanent move, that's why you wanted a one-year contract ..." She let the words trail off, realizing she'd already said too much, admitted too much.

"You asked Elijah about me," he guessed.

She shrugged, an implicit admission that she'd done just that after Paige had warned her of Cam's impending return. "I was curious about the rumors that you were coming back. It's not like he violated any doctor-patient privilege by confirming it was true."

"Curious in a good way?" he asked her.

She lifted her hand to brush her hair away from her face, winced. "Just curious."

Cam frowned at the expression of discomfort. "Are you still experiencing pain?"

"A little."

"You shouldn't have any with the meds I prescribed."

She didn't say anything.

"You did take the medication, didn't you?" he prompted.

"No," she admitted.

"Why not?"

She shrugged. "I don't like taking anything stronger than over-the-counter drugs."

"Honey, you didn't come into the office because you had a headache, you had fifteen stitches put in your hand."

"I'm fine," she said. "And don't call me 'honey.'"

"You didn't object to Irene calling you 'hon,'" he pointed out.

She didn't say anything.

"Or was that okay because she hasn't seen you naked?"

Ashley blushed at the reminder that *he* had seen her naked, as he knew she would, but tilted her chin. "Actually, Irene has seen me naked."

He lifted his brows.

"But not since I was in diapers," she admitted, and gave him a small smile.

She'd always been beautiful. But when she smiled, when the light of humor sparked in the depths of her violet eyes and those soft pink lips curved, she was absolutely radiant.

Sitting across the table from her now, looking at her over a pizza box, he wondered how he'd ever settled for anything less, how he'd ever believed that his feelings for anyone else could compare to the emotion that filled his heart when he was with Ashley.

His gaze locked with hers, held. And suddenly the air was sizzling with the attraction that had always sparked between them.

"Did you have those five freckles at the base of your spine when you were in diapers?" he asked.

He could tell by the darkening of her eyes that mention of those freckles had stirred memories for her, too.

"I don't know," she said softly.

"Do you still have them?"

"I don't know," she said again.

Obviously the ex-fiancé had never kissed each and every one of those freckles, as Cam used to do. But he wasn't going to mention the other man's name again. He didn't even want to think about her being with anyone else. He wanted—

The scrape of chair legs against the floor tiles severed his thought as Ashley pushed her chair away from the table. Which was probably for the best, because he had no business thinking about what he wanted to do with Ashley when so much of his life was still unsettled.

"I should, uh, clear this up," she said.

He carried the plates into the kitchen for her, and pulled out the waste basket to scrape them before loading the dishwasher. But he paused when he saw what was in the receptacle.

"I'm guessing this is the eleven-by-fourteen," he said.

"What?" She turned around, saw that he'd found the broken picture frame. "Oh. Yeah. It is."

"It's a good picture of you," he said. "You look happy."

She shrugged. "I was."

And the man in the photo with her looked happy, too. Of course, he had Ashley in his arms, so he had reason to be happy. Which made Cam realize her former fiancé wasn't just a bastard, he was an idiot. He'd been poised to start a life with this beautiful, vibrant woman, and he'd thrown it away.

Okay, so maybe he was being a little bit hypocritical. Because twelve years earlier, Ashley had wanted to talk about their future and he'd let her go. But he'd barely been nineteen years old, too young to be thinking in terms of "till death do us part" and too stupid to know what he was giving up.

Cam picked up his beer, took a long swallow. "Are you still in love with him?"

Ashley returned the unused napkins to the holder then leaned back against the counter. "How is that any of your business?"

"When a man kisses a woman it's important to his ego— crucial, in fact—to know that she's thinking of him and not anyone else."

She eyed him warily. "If a man doesn't know that about a woman, then he has no business kissing her."

"That's why I asked the question." He set the now empty bottle on the counter and stepped closer to her, bracing his hands on the edge of the counter so that she was boxed between them. "Are you still in love with him?"

* * *

Ashley didn't dare answer his question with the truth.

The truth was, she was no longer convinced she'd ever been in love with Trevor. Certainly she hadn't loved him as she should have loved the man she was planning to marry. But if she admitted that to Cam now, he would interpret it as an invitation and, as desperately as she wanted to feel his mouth on hers, she couldn't let that happen.

Because she knew that one kiss would lead to more, and she didn't want more. She'd meant what she said when she told Megan and Paige that she didn't want a man or a relationship. She didn't want to risk her heart again.

"Yes," she said.

"Yes what?"

"Yes, I still love…" Oh Lord, she couldn't even remember his name. She could only think of Cam. She only wanted Cam. "…I still love him."

"Liar."

The word was a husky whisper against her lips before he captured them with his own.

She couldn't stop herself from responding to his kiss any more than she could stop her heart from pounding or her body from yearning. His tongue traced over the seam of her lips, and they parted willingly, eagerly.

It seemed to her that they'd grown too far apart to fit together easily. The moment he slipped his arms around her and drew her against him, she knew she'd been wrong.

Cam had always been a fabulous kisser. When they'd first started dating, back in the early days of their relationship when they hadn't gone any further than kissing, he would hold her and kiss her forever. This kiss reminded her of that—as if it would go on forever, as if he could be content to just kiss her forever.

Ashley wasn't feeling content. She pressed against him, wanting to be closer, wanting more.

His hands slid up her back, his fingers tangled in her hair, and he drew her head back. His mouth trailed from hers to trace along her jaw, down her throat. His tongue stroked, his teeth scraped, his lips soothed.

He shifted, drew her nearer, so that she was nestled intimately between his legs, so that she could tell he wanted her as much as she wanted him. Desire—hot and reckless—churned in her veins, rushed through her body, making her feel as if she was seventeen years old again.

Of course, her teenage heart had been filled with more love than lust, and though she'd given herself to him willingly, even eagerly, she'd been unprepared for the complete and total heartbreak that was all he'd left her with when he went away.

A heartbreak that, at the time, she didn't ever think she would recover from. A heartbreak that she'd felt even deeper and sharper than the pain caused by Trevor's betrayal.

She'd loved Cam once and he'd trampled all over her emotions. She wouldn't let him do it again. She didn't want to feel anything for the man who'd broken her fragile heart so many years before.

But as she kissed him back, she couldn't deny that she was feeling something, though she didn't know how to define what that something was.

Attraction? Undoubtedly. Cam Turcotte had been a teenage heartthrob, and the years had added to rather than detracted from his appeal.

Lust? No doubt a healthy dose of that had been thrown into the mix. And maybe that wasn't surprising, considering that she was a twenty-nine-year-old woman who hadn't been on a date since the end of her engagement.

She'd had offers. When she'd gone out with Paige and

Megan or friends from work, she'd been approached by men who expressed an interest. But she hadn't even been tempted. In fact, she hadn't felt anything but numb for so long she didn't know what to think about the feelings that were spiraling through her now.

When would she ever learn?

Obviously the trauma of slicing open her hand had affected her brain. It was the only explanation for letting him kiss her, for letting the kiss go as far as it did.

He'd caught her in a moment of weakness, but she was drawing the line, right here and right now. She would not get caught up in the seductive magnetism of Cam Turcotte. Not again.

She had to end this now—that would be the smart thing to do. But it felt so good to be held and kissed and...cherished.

Except that he didn't cherish her. He never had. Because if he'd truly treasured her and what they had together, he wouldn't have walked away so easily.

Which was why, this time, she had to be the one to walk.

She tore her mouth from his and pushed against his chest.

Chapter Four

Ashley stumbled back and cried out in pain. The obvious distress in her voice effectively doused Cam's raging libido. He drew in a slow, deep breath then reached for her hand. She shook her head and took another step back, as if she couldn't bear to have him touch her.

He didn't know what he'd done to make her withdraw so abruptly and completely, but he wasn't thinking about that at the moment. He was thinking about the fact that her eyes were clouded with pain now rather than lust, and he worried that she might have re-injured her hand.

"I just want to make sure that you're not bleeding again," he told her.

This time when he reached for her hand, she didn't object. He carefully peeled back the gauze to check the wound, pleased to see that none of the stitches had opened up.

"It looks okay," he said, refastening the tape.

She nodded.

"But I want to know why you're not taking the painkillers when it's obvious that you're in pain."

"I told you, I don't like taking any medication unnecessarily."

Ashley had never been practiced in the art of deception, and the fact that she didn't look at him when she spoke told him more clearly than her words that there was something she was holding back.

"If you're hurting, it's necessary," he insisted.

"I'm fine."

"What medications are you taking that you didn't want to tell me about?"

The question was a stab in the dark, but her lack of response made him believe it had been an accurate one.

"We can argue back and forth for another few minutes if you really want," he told her. "But I'm not backing off until you tell me."

"Fedentropin," she finally said.

He frowned. "I'm not familiar with that one."

"It's an experimental drug to help alleviate the symptoms of endometriosis. I'm part of a clinical trial at Richmond Pharmaceuticals."

"I didn't realize…" He wasn't sure what he meant to say, what was the right thing to say. He'd had no idea that she had to endure what he knew was a painful and chronic condition for a woman, and he hated to think of her suffering.

But Ashley just shrugged. "It's not something that comes up in conversation."

"It should have been noted in your file," he said.

"Eli knows—I talked to him before I was accepted into the test group, but I haven't had an appointment with him since."

Cam believed there still should have been a note in her file, but right now he was more concerned about her current situation. "Is your sister running the trial?"

She nodded.

He picked up the cordless phone on the counter. "Call her."

"Why?"

"I want to know if you can take the medication I prescribed or if I should write a scrip for something else."

"Look, Cam, I appreciate your concern, but I took some Tylenol when I got home and I'm okay."

She wouldn't have cried out in pain if she was okay and since he figured they were both aware of that fact, he only asked, "Why don't you want to call your sister?"

"Why won't you back off?" she countered.

"Because I care about you."

Maybe he was surprised by the admission, but not by the feelings. He *did* care about Ashley. He'd always cared about Ashley.

She turned away from him, but not before he saw the glint of tears in her eyes.

"You have no right," she said, her tone laced with both hurt and anger. "No right to barge into my life after *twelve years* and make such a statement as if it gives you the right to interfere."

It was true. He'd given up any right he might have had when he'd ended their relationship a dozen years earlier. But his feelings for Ashley had never been rational, and even when he'd gone away, his feelings for her never had.

"I've always cared about you, Ash, and I always will."

She turned away to wrap up the leftover pizza, struggling a little because of her bandaged hand. "Thank you for your concern," she said, not sounding thankful at all. "Now go away."

He knew he should. But instead, Cam scrolled through the list of numbers stored in the memory of the phone still in his hand.

"What are you doing?" she demanded.

He found "Megan & Gage" and pressed the call button. "Calling your sister."

She stared at him, as if she didn't really believe he'd do it.

"It's ringing," he warned her.

She grabbed the phone with her uninjured hand. As obviously unhappy as she was about making the call, she seemed to accept that he would talk directly to Megan if she continued to refuse and had likely concluded that her sister would have fewer questions for her than she would for him.

After a brief conversation, during which she reassured her sister numerous times that she was fine and didn't need anyone coming over to check up on her, Ashley said goodbye and disconnected.

"*That's* why I didn't want to call her," she said.

"Because you knew she'd be worried about you?" he asked, wondering why her sister's concern should be a problem for Ashley.

"Because she's spent too much time worrying about me, and even more over the past four months."

"Since the broken engagement," he guessed.

She nodded, making him suspect that she might be more distressed over the end of that relationship than he wanted to believe. And though he was undeniably curious about the ex-fiancé, he forced himself to focus on more immediate concerns.

"What did Megan say about the medication?"

"She said it's fine. I just have to make sure that I inform the admin clerk of the dosage when I go in for my blood work."

"Except you didn't get the scrip filled, did you?"

"No, because I didn't plan on taking it."

He glanced at his watch. "I'll call it in to Brody's."

"I'm capable of taking my own prescription in."

"I know you are," he agreed. "I'm just not convinced that you'll actually do it."

"Fine." She thrust the phone at him. "Call it in and then leave me alone."

He dialed the familiar number, spoke to the pharmacist and made arrangements for the medication to be delivered, throughout which Ashley continued to glare at him.

"It should be here within twenty minutes," he told her.

"Do you plan on hanging around until it gets here?" she challenged.

"I don't have anywhere else that I need to be, and I have no intention of letting you push me out the door until we've had a chance to talk about what happened in the kitchen."

"There's nothing to talk about," she denied, but the flush in her cheeks told him otherwise. "It was a moment of insanity, that's all."

"The only insanity is in trying to pretend it didn't mean anything, trying to pretend that we aren't still as attracted to one another as we were twelve years ago."

She folded her arms over her chest as she lifted her gaze to his. "I'm not going to deny that there's an attraction, but I'm not looking to get involved with anyone right now."

A personal relationship was the absolute last thing he'd been looking for when he'd decided to move back to Pinehurst, but then he'd kissed Ashley, and he'd realized that getting involved with her wasn't a choice. But he understood why she was wary.

"You can't close your heart because of what your ex-fiancé did," he said gently.

"This had nothing to do with Trevor," she denied.

"I'd say the picture in your trash can suggests otherwise."

"You're right," she decided. "This has *everything* to do with Trevor. Because if he hadn't chosen to send that picture to me, I wouldn't have sliced my hand and you wouldn't have needed to stitch it up, and you definitely wouldn't be here right now."

"Then maybe I should thank Trevor," he said.

She glared at him. "In any event, I have no intention of picking up our relationship where we left off just because it's convenient for you now."

He felt his own anger stir. "My feelings for you were a lot of things," he told her. "But convenient was never one of them."

As soon as her prescription was delivered, Ashley took the requisite pills and sent Cam on his way.

From the moment she'd returned from her shopping trip earlier in the day, nothing had gone according to plan. Coming face-to-face with Cam had been unexpected, but it had also been unavoidable. Especially since he would be moving in down the street.

So while their meeting was inevitable, she'd been confident that when they did meet, they would simply exchange a few coolly polite words and go their separate ways. She certainly hadn't expected anything like the kiss they'd shared in her kitchen.

Because while Cam might have made the first move, there was no denying that she'd been an equal—and willing—participant.

Yeah, that kiss had definitely been a mistake, because now she was dealing with the aftermath—a jumble of feelings that she hadn't been prepared for and didn't know what to do with.

It had only been one kiss. Nothing that should have the power to turn her world upside down. But it felt as if that was exactly what had happened.

He'd been absent from her life for twelve years but somehow, after only a few hours, he'd managed to churn up all kinds of feelings and desires that she'd buried a long time ago. Or so she'd thought.

She sorted through the mail, opened the cupboard under the sink to drop the flyers into the recycle box and saw that a new bag had been put in the garbage can. Cam must have taken out the other bag for her—the one with the broken picture frame and her engagement photo in it.

Because he thought seeing the photo again might upset her? Or because he thought she was clumsy enough to injure herself again when she took the bag out?

She closed the cupboard and sighed. She had no idea what Cam's reasons were. She didn't know anything at all about him anymore. And yet, there was something still there between them. Something that both thrilled and terrified her.

It had been easy for her to toss the picture of her fiancé into the garbage, because she had closed the door on that part of her life with no regrets. She *had* been happy with Trevor, at least for a while, and she'd wanted the life they had planned to build together. But the truth was, she'd never loved him as completely and wholeheartedly as she'd loved Cam.

It was an unsettling realization, and one she wasn't ready to examine too closely. Determined to push the sexy doctor out of her mind, she went upstairs to get ready for bed.

The sun hadn't yet set, but she was exhausted—physically and emotionally—and she wanted nothing more than to crawl between the sheets and sink into oblivion where thoughts and memories of Cam Turcotte didn't exist.

Cam was surprised to find his parents' car in the driveway when he got back to their house after his detour to Ashley's. He walked through the back door and followed the trail of an enticingly spicy scent into the kitchen where his mother was stirring something on the stove.

"I thought tonight was your bowling night," he said in lieu of a greeting.

"Your dad spent the afternoon at Harry Reiner's, helping him lay patio stones," Gayle told her son.

"He screwed up his back again, didn't he?"

"He's in bed with an ice pack now," she confirmed.

"Why does he do things like that?"

"Because Harry helped stain our deck, and your dad insisted that this was his way of returning the favor."

"A paintbrush doesn't weigh forty pounds," Cam noted.

His mother smiled. "Which is exactly what I said to him. But then I made the mistake of noting that he's also several years older than Harry, which he interpreted as a challenge."

"Because it drives him crazy the way Harry flirts with you."

"Harry's been widowed for nearly ten years, he's lonely, and he flirts with every woman who crosses his path." She finished scooping chili into a bowl. "Do you want some?"

"Oh. No, thanks. I had a couple of slices of pizza earlier."

She carried her bowl to the table and sat down. "Is everything okay?"

"Sure. Why?"

"Because you're a lot later than usual getting home and you seem a little distracted."

"Busy day at the office." He helped himself to a bottle of beer from the fridge and sat down with her.

He'd moved in with them when he'd returned to Pinehurst because it was convenient and gave him the opportunity to look for a place of his own. What had surprised him was how much he'd enjoyed spending time with them. After living so far away for so many years, it was nice to reconnect again, and to realize that he actually liked his parents.

"That's why Elijah needed to hire you," she said. "So what was different about today?"

He took a long swallow from the bottle. "I saw Ashley."

She paused, her spoon halfway to her lips. "Ashley Roarke?"

He nodded.

"How did that go?"

He thought about their kiss—the soft responsiveness of her lips, the yielding warmth of her body—and her abrupt and complete withdrawal from him. "Better—and worse—than I expected."

"I'm…sorry?"

He smiled. "I guess I shouldn't have expected that she'd be happy about my decision to come back to Pinehurst now."

"I would think, if her feelings for you are well and truly gone, she wouldn't have much of an opinion one way or the other."

He mulled that over for a minute. "The implication being that if she cares, she must still have feelings for me?"

"Twelve years is a long time, and you were both so young when you went away. And yet—" she smiled "—a woman never forgets her first love."

"Spoken like a woman with fond memories," he noted.

"I fell in love when I was fifteen—much to the chagrin of both my parents and his. He was nearly twenty, already in college, and our families were united only in their desire to keep us apart."

"What happened?"

Her eyes sparkled. "I married him."

"Grandma and Grandpa disapproved of Dad?" He couldn't believe it. His father was the epitome of responsibility and respectability—certainly not the usual type that parents warned their daughters about.

"I was fifteen," she said again. "I don't think they would have approved of anyone I brought home at that age. And he was so…sexy. He worked in construction in the summer to earn money for college and he had all these rippling muscles and—"

"Please." Cam held up a hand, urging her to spare him the details.

"If I hadn't been attracted to your father, you wouldn't be here," she pointed out.

"Still, there are some things a kid doesn't need to know."

"Well, my point," she said, "is that parents always want what they think is best for their kids, even when it conflicts with what their kids want. That's why your dad encouraged you to go away to school, to put some distance between you and Ashley before you got too deeply involved."

"He knew how I felt about her."

She nodded. "And he was afraid that you'd give up your dreams to stay in Pinehurst with her."

"Why did he think that?" he asked curiously. "Was there something he felt he'd missed out on by getting married so young?"

His mother was silent for a long minute before she said, "He wasn't thinking about his own dreams, but mine."

It had never occurred to him that his mom might have sacrificed her own plans to be a wife and a mother, because she'd always seemed so settled and content in those roles. "What was your dream?" he asked her now.

"After I met your dad, I only wanted to be with him."

But he recognized the evasion, and his curiosity was piqued. "Before you met Dad?" he prompted.

"I was going to be a doctor," she finally admitted.

He shouldn't have been surprised, but he was. He couldn't believe that he'd never known his mother had once envisioned having the same career that he'd chosen for himself.

"A doctor," he echoed.

She nodded. "In fact, I'd just been accepted to medical school when I found out I was pregnant."

He set his now empty bottle down. "You gave up your dream because of me?"

But she shook her head vehemently. "No. By the time I got pregnant, my dream had changed. Finding out that I was going to have a baby was the most incredible moment of my life. I had no qualms about giving up medical school for motherhood.

"But when you first expressed an interest in becoming a doctor, your father was adamant that nothing would cause you to make the sacrifice he believed I'd made. But what he didn't think about—what neither of us really considered—was what would make you happy."

"You shouldn't worry about that anymore," he assured her. "I am happy."

"A parent always worries. Especially when her kids grow up and move away."

He knew she wasn't just thinking of him, but of his younger sister, Sherry, who was now married and living in Florida.

"Well, I have no doubt that you would have been a great doctor," he said. "But you made the right career choice, because you are definitely the world's greatest mom."

She smiled through the sheen of tears in her eyes. "And when a mother's grown son says something like that, she knows she's done her job well."

When Ashley returned to the doctor's office for her follow-up appointment, she was prepared to see Cam. Not just to see him, but to prove that she was completely unaffected by him, that the scorching kiss they'd shared in her kitchen meant nothing to her. Less than nothing, in fact.

When the door opened, however, it wasn't Cam who came in—it was Eli. She felt a slight pang but assured herself it wasn't disappointment. After all, it wasn't that she wanted to see Cam except to prove that he didn't mean anything to her. Not anymore.

But Eli meant the world to her, and her smile came easily for him.

"How's Ruby?" she asked, having learned about his wife's heart attack from Megan, who worked with one of the doctor's neighbors.

"She's doing well. Thanks for the beautiful flowers. She was so tickled that you remembered gerberas are her favorite."

"I was hoping they would brighten up her room and her spirits."

"The did both," Eli confirmed. "And remarkably well, I'd say, since she's scheduled to come home tomorrow."

"You must be so relieved."

He nodded. "We've been married forty-two years. After that much time, you start to take certain things for granted. But I'm not taking anything for granted anymore."

Ashley wondered if she would ever know that kind of deep and abiding love, and realized that she still hoped she would. She hadn't completely given up on the idea of finding someone to share her life, she'd just decided not to worry about doing so. And, in the meantime, she would happily lavish all of her love and attention on the baby she was going to have.

"But I know you didn't really come here to talk abut me," the doctor continued. "So tell me how you're doing."

"I'm anxious to get these stitches out," she admitted.

He scanned the notes in her file, closed the folder and reached for her hand. "Let's take a look then."

While he was bent over her hand, she stared at the calendar on the wall on the opposite side of the room, breathing slowly and carefully as she silently calculated the days and then the hours and minutes until it was time to go back to school. She felt a few little tugs, but no pain, and as long as she didn't think about the fact that he was pulling threads out of her hand, she didn't feel dizzy.

She hadn't felt anything when Cam put the stitches in, either. Of course, she'd been given an injection to freeze the site, but even without the artificial numbing, she knew her awareness of Cam would have eclipsed everything else.

"How does it feel?"

She glanced down, saw that he'd finished removing the stitches. She carefully curled her fingers into a fist, nodded. "It feels good."

"Cam did a nice job," Eli said. "In a few more weeks, the scar will barely be visible."

Ashley uncurled her fist and was pleased to note that there was no residual pain in her hand.

If only the same could be said about the scars Cam had left on her heart twelve years earlier.

Chapter Five

As a child, Ashley had always looked forward to the first day of school. As a teacher, she still did.

Maybe it would be different if she taught high school, where the students were more sullen and jaded. But for a group of five- and six-year-olds, entering first grade was as thrilling an event as Columbus's discovery of a whole new world. They were all so young and eager to learn, and Ashley found their excitement and enthusiasm never failed to recharge her own.

She didn't usually have supervision duty on Wednesday mornings, but like most other teachers on staff at Parkdale Elementary School, it was a tradition to meet on the play-ground behind the school so the students could catch a glimpse of their teachers before they entered the classroom, and vice versa. She knew most of the kids who would be in her class, of course, because the majority had attended kindergarten at the same school the previous year. But there were always a few new faces, children who had moved into the neighborhood over the summer and who were even more anxious about the first day because everything was strange and unfamiliar.

It was easy to spot the new ones, and Ashley liked to introduce herself before the first bell and to meet with the mother who was usually present and in whose hand a much smaller one would be tightly clasped.

She had three new students this year and she'd already made the rounds to say hello and invite the parents to come into the classroom. Some would accept her offer and, in doing so, would feel reassured about the environment in which they'd left their children. Others would decline, knowing that it would only make saying goodbye that much more difficult for the child. Ashley was supportive of either decision, trusting that the parent knew his or her child better than she did—at least on the first day.

She smiled at Adam Webber, one of the fifth-grade teachers and the boys' basketball coach, when he came out of the school with the ever-present orange ball tucked under his arm.

"Look at them." Adam shook his head. "So eager and enthusiastic."

"Don't worry, you'll beat that out of them soon enough."

He grinned easily at her teasing, because he knew he was one of the favorite teachers at Parkdale. "How does your class look this year? Or should I wait until the end of the day to ask you?"

"Twenty-three kids. Ten boys, thirteen girls."

"Twenty-four," he said.

"What?"

"Haven't you seen Wendy this morning?" Adam asked, referring to the principal's administrative assistant.

"No, I came directly around the back."

"She told me she has an updated class list for you."

"But I just picked up the list yesterday. And I did all of the name tags and locker magnets last night."

He shrugged. "I'm just the messenger."

Ashley turned to go into the school, and that's when she saw her.

The child looked the right age for a first grader, with long, dark hair and wide, terrified eyes. She was wearing a sleeveless pink dress with tiny white daisies embroidered at the square neckline and along the hem, with matching pink canvas sneakers embroidered with the same flowers on the toes.

Obviously the newest addition.

Feeling an instinctive stir of empathy, Ashley had already started forward when she glanced from the child to parent—and froze.

The man holding the little girl's hand was Cam Turcotte.

Ashley stopped by Wendy's office and grabbed the new class list before ducking into her classroom and closing the door at her back. She just needed five minutes alone. Five minutes to assimilate the reality that had been shoved in her face. Five minutes to accept that Cam had a child—that the baby she'd once dreamed of having with him had been born to someone else.

She didn't want to believe it. And yet she couldn't deny it was true. There was no doubt the little girl with the shiny dark hair and wide green eyes clinging to his hand as if he was the center of her world could be anyone but his daughter.

But how could she not have known?

Cam might have moved away more than twelve years ago, but his parents had remained in town. In fact, it had been from his mother that she'd heard about his marriage to Danica, and that news had hit her the same way.

Gayle Turcotte, apparently recognizing how much the

revelation had hurt Ashley, had been careful not to make any further mention of her son's life in Seattle whenever their paths had crossed. She'd certainly never mentioned the baby girl that Cam's wife had given birth to.

Madeline Carrington-Turcotte, according to the updated class list she'd inadvertently crumpled in her fist.

Cam had always been very traditional, so she would bet that the hyphenated name was his ex-wife's idea. Just because Ashley had been foolish enough to doodle "Ashley Turcotte" inside the cover of her notebooks when she was in high school didn't mean another woman would feel the same way about taking her husband's name.

In any event, she and Cam had broken up more than twelve years earlier, so she knew it was ridiculous to feel so hurt by the knowledge that he'd had a child with another woman. But that knowledge failed to lessen her sense of betrayal.

Because when Cam had left her, one of the reasons he'd given for ending their relationship was that he didn't want the life she'd envisioned for them—not yet.

"I've decided to go to Seattle," he told her.

Ashley stared at him, feeling as if the very ground beneath her feet had begun to crumble. "Washington?"

He nodded. "Their School of Medicine is one of the best in the country."

"But—" She didn't quite know what to say, how to respond to something that he'd obviously already decided upon, and without even discussing it with her "—but you have at least three years before med school."

"I know. But staying here, going to a university closer to home, it will only delay the inevitable."

Inevitable? What was it that he thought was inevitable?

Ashley didn't ask, because in her heart, she was afraid she already knew the answer. But she pushed aside her fears.

"There are good medical schools that aren't on the other side of the country. Like Northwestern and Cornell. Even Chapel Hill would be better than Washington."

"I want to go to Washington."

She'd heard the finality in his voice, and her eyes had filled with tears. "You're breaking up with me."

He glanced away. "This is for the best, Ash."

"Best for who?" she demanded.

"For both of us. Do you think this was an easy decision for me to make?"

"How would I know—since you never talked to me about it?"

"Because I knew you would try to convince me to stay. And because I was afraid I would let you." He reached out and took her hands. "Because there's a part of me that wants nothing more than to stay here with you."

The seemingly heartfelt words and the warmth of his touch failed to thaw the icy numbness that had taken hold of her.

She managed to speak, though she didn't manage to disguise the anguish in her tone when she asked, "Then why are you leaving?"

"Because we want different things, Ash. Being a doctor has been my dream for as long as I can remember."

"You said you wanted to get married."

"I do," he agreed. "Someday. But I'm nowhere near being ready to make that kind of commitment yet. I'm not even close to thinking about being a husband or a father."

As it turned out, that wasn't exactly true.

Because only a few years later, before Ashley had even graduated from teacher's college, he had married. He'd become someone else's husband. And now she knew that he'd become a father, too.

He'd had the family she always wanted, and she was still alone.

Ashley wiped the tears from her cheeks, reminding herself that she wasn't going to be alone forever. Despite her initial appointment at PARC having to be rescheduled, she *was* going to have a baby. And while she couldn't deny a certain amount of disappointment that her child wouldn't also have a father, she'd made her decision.

She wouldn't regret that the baby she'd so often dreamed of having with Cam Turcotte would never be. And she absolutely wouldn't let herself consider the possibility that his return to Pinehurst could change anything. Especially now that she knew he already was a father.

The ring of the bell jolted her out of her reverie. She hastily wiped the last of the moisture from her cheeks, pasted a smile on her face and opened the door to greet her new students.

She wasn't sure how she made it through the day, but when the bell sounded at three o'clock, Ashley nearly wept with relief.

It took a few more minutes, of course, to ensure all the kids had their agendas and the assortment of documents that always went home on the first day. But the halls eventually emptied and quiet descended, and Ashley sank back into her chair.

"One day down, only one hundred and eighty-something to go."

Ashley looked up, startled to see her sister in the doorway. Megan rarely ever came to the school to see Ashley, and the fact that she'd done so now indicated that she had something on her mind.

"One hundred and eighty-six," Ashley told her. "But what dragged you out of the lab in the middle of the day?"

Megan practically floated into the room. She wasn't usually the floating type, but she was obviously excited about something so Ashley tried to muster some enthusiasm for her.

"I had an appointment this side of town." Megan came

further into the room, some of the sparkle in her eyes fading as she looked more closely at her sister. "But let's talk about what's going on with you first."

Ashley shook her head. She couldn't talk about it. She didn't know what to say, how to explain.

"Come on, Ash. You love the first day of school. I thought you'd be ready to go out and celebrate the beginning of a new year with a great big chocolate fudge brownie sundae at Walton's."

"Let's just say that the day didn't go exactly as planned."

"I don't understand."

She sighed and pushed her class list across the desk. Megan picked up the page, frowning. Then her eyes widened.

"Madeline Carrington-Turcotte?"

Ashley nodded. "Cam's daughter."

"Oh, Ash."

"She's beautiful," she said softly. "And very sweet and shy. She doesn't say much, but she watches and she listens, her big green eyes taking everything in."

"Of all the classrooms in all the schools in all the world, she walks into yours."

Ashley managed to smile at the deliberate misquotation. "I just…I didn't know how to react. I was completely unprepared. I had no idea that he had a child, never mind one I would end up teaching."

"But he lives down the street," Megan reminded her. "You never saw her?"

She shook her head. "He only moved in on the weekend. I saw the truck, saw furniture being unloaded, but I didn't pay attention to anything else." And she was regretting that now.

"Chocolate fudge brownie sundae?" Meg prompted gently.

Ashley managed to smile. "That sounds like the perfect way to end a crappy day."

* * *

One of the reasons Cam had moved back to Pinehurst was to be able to spend more time with both his parents and his daughter. Another added benefit was that his parents were not just willing but happy to provide after-school care for Maddie on the days that he couldn't get away from the office in time to pick her up. But he refused to let her first day of school be one of those days, and when she came racing across the grass and into his arms, he was more certain than ever that this move was the best thing for both of them.

He felt a slight twinge when he recalled the shock—and the pain—he'd seen in Ashley's eyes when she saw him with Madeline that morning, and he realized the first-grade teacher might not agree. But he refused to worry about that while he walked home, hand in hand with his daughter, listening to her animated conversation the whole way.

He remembered her kindergarten teacher expressing concern that Maddie was too quiet in class, silent and withdrawn. But Cam knew it wasn't a character flaw, just her personality. She'd always been shy with strangers, but at home and with her family, she was quite the little chatterbox.

"Do you want a snack?" he asked.

"Ice cream," she said hopefully, hopping onto one of the stools at the breakfast bar.

"We don't have any."

She pouted. "You promised to get ice cream."

"I know I did, but I forgot."

His admission of guilt didn't appease her and though Cam knew the dangers of being over-indulgent, he figured the first day at a new school warranted an exception to the rules.

"So why don't you go wash up and we'll go to Walton's?"

"Who's Walton?"

He smiled. "Walton isn't a who but a where, and it's

where we go to get the very best ice cream in all of Pinehurst, New York."

"Really?" Her eyes were almost as wide as her smile.

"Really."

She hopped off of her stool and wrapped her arms around his waist. "Thanks, Daddy. You're the best."

Twenty minutes later, he handed a strawberry sundae to Maddie before accepting his double scoop of butter pecan from the teenager behind the counter and turned to look for a vacant table. A quick glance around the room revealed that there weren't any.

"There's my teacher, Daddy."

Maddie's words registered at the exact moment his gaze landed on Ashley, seated with her sister at a table for four on the other side of the room.

"Her name's Miss Ashley," his daughter reminded him.

Cam nodded.

"She's very pretty," Maddie said. "And she smiles a lot and she doesn't yell. Not even when the skinny boy with the curly hair forgot to ask to go to the bathroom and went pee right in his pants."

His lips curved. "Not even then?"

Maddie shook her head solemnly.

"So maybe first grade won't be so bad, huh?"

"Maybe," she allowed. "But it's really too soon to tell."

He was smiling at her comment as he guided her toward Ashley and Megan's table.

"Looks like someone else decided to celebrate the first day of school with ice cream," Ashley noted, her attention and smile focused on Madeline.

"It seemed appropriate," Cam said.

"We thought the same thing," Megan said, when Ashley failed to respond to his comment.

"But there don't seem to be any vacant tables," he pointed out. "So we were hoping you wouldn't object to us joining you."

"Of course not," Megan said, though she cast a worried glance across the table.

Ashley still didn't say anything to him, but she slid across the bench she was sitting on to make room for his daughter. Maddie smiled shyly at her and carefully set her dish on the table before climbing up beside her teacher.

"Thanks," Cam said, taking the seat beside Megan. "I don't remember it ever being so busy in here."

"A lot changes in twelve years," Ashley told him.

He met her gaze across the table and felt the zing of sparks that weren't entirely attributable to her obvious annoyance with him.

"And some things," he countered, "never do."

Ashley ate her chocolate fudge brownie sundae so fast she was surprised she didn't get brain freeze. But from the moment she'd looked up and spotted Cam in line at the counter, she'd wanted only to get out of Walton's as quickly as possible. Thankfully her sister had sensed her discomfort and quickly finished her ice cream as well.

It was only after they'd said goodbye to Cam and Maddie and were on their way out the door that Ashley thought to ask again about the reasons for her sister's unexpected midweek visit.

Megan dumped her empty dish and spoon in the garbage. "It really wasn't that important."

"Important enough to bring you to the school to talk to me."

Her sister sighed. "Because I wanted to tell you first, but you've had a lot sprung on you already today."

And Ashley knew her sister's news and why she was suddenly reluctant to share it.

"You're pregnant," she guessed.

Meg nodded.

Ashley sucked in a breath.

Her sister was going to have a baby.

She felt a tug deep inside her heart. A combination of excitement and envy. She wanted to be happy for Megan. She was happy for her. And yet she couldn't help but look at the life her sister was building with her new husband and wonder why all of the stars had aligned so perfectly for Megan and, seemingly at the same time, scattered everything in her own world.

A little more than six months earlier, she and Paige had struggled to convince Megan that she had nothing to lose by inviting Gage Richmond to be her date for Ashley's engagement party. Megan had finally agreed, only because she'd been sure that Gage wouldn't accept. But he had and, even on that first date, Ashley had seen the chemistry between them. Even more significantly, she'd recognized that there was a connection between them that she didn't feel with the man she was planning to marry.

But she didn't let that dissuade her from her plans, because she believed that there were more important things than connections. There were shared interests and common goals. Or maybe she'd deluded herself into thinking she and Trevor had shared interests and common goals because she so desperately wanted to get married and have a family of her own.

She wasn't so desperate, however, that she was willing to overlook the fact that he'd been sleeping around on her almost from the time he'd put the ring on her finger. She'd been crushed to learn of his betrayal. And maybe, just a little, secretly relieved.

Because the closer the date had come for their wedding, the more she had started to realize that she was making a mistake. That she didn't love Trevor as much as she should love the man she intended to marry. That she didn't love him specifically as much as she loved the prospect of being a wife and mother.

Now Megan and Gage were married and getting ready to have a baby.

The tug came again. Stronger this time, but she pushed it aside. "Oh, Meg. That's wonderful news."

Her sister looked uncertain. "Are you really okay with this?"

"I'm thrilled for you," Ashley told her, willing it to be true. "I was just caught off guard by your announcement. I didn't even realize you and Gage were trying to have a baby."

"Well, we weren't actually trying, we just weren't trying to prevent it." She blushed prettily. "In fact, I think Gage is a little disappointed it happened as quickly as it did."

"Obviously you guys are doing something right," Ashley said.

Her sister's blush deepened. "*Everything* is right with Gage. I never thought I would feel this way about anyone— or that anyone else would feel the same way about me. But he's just—" her sigh was filled with blissful contentment "—amazing."

"So are you," Ashley told her sister. "Which is why you guys are so perfect for one another."

"That's what I want for you," Megan said. "I know Trevor's betrayal hit you hard, but you can't give up hope that you'll find someone to spend your life with just because of CBB."

"I haven't given up hope," Ashley said, though she wasn't entirely sure it was true. "I'm just not willing to put the rest of my life on hold while I wait around for Mr. Right to show up, because the reality is, there may not be a Mr. Right for me."

"There is," Megan insisted, and smiled slyly. "And I think he might already have shown up. Or maybe I should say shown up *again*."

Ashley didn't bother to respond. Cam Turcotte was part of

her past, not her future, and she had no intention of arguing with her sister about that fact.

And no intention of letting herself yearn again for something that could never be.

Though it wasn't one of their scheduled evenings to get together, Ashley wasn't surprised when Paige showed up at her door Friday night. Or that she'd brought a bottle of her favorite merlot with her.

Ashley put together a platter of assorted crackers and cheeses and they took it out onto the porch with the wine.

"I don't know why you're paying rent on an apartment in Syracuse when you've been spending so much time in Pinehurst lately," Ashley said to her.

"I'm only here on the weekends," her cousin replied, glossing over the real issue. "Because it's too far to commute to the office every day."

"Seriously, Paige, what happened to your social life?"

Her cousin shrugged. "Things fizzled with Josh. Ben met someone else. As for Lucas—well, I realized I wasn't secure enough to date a guy who's prettier than me."

Ashley had met Lucas once, and while she had to admit the man was unbelievably good-looking, she knew that her cousin's serial dating was really a reflection of the nomadic childhood that had taught her, at an early age, not to form close attachments to people who wouldn't be in her life for very long. The pattern had changed only when Paige's father decided she needed more stability than his lifestyle afforded and finally left his daughter in the care of his sister and her husband. Ashley and Megan had forged an unbreakable bond with their cousin, but by habit or deliberation, she continued to keep everyone else at a distance.

"Is that why you're here?" Ashley asked her now. "Because

you had nothing better to do on a Friday night? Or because you were worried that I was going to fall apart?"

"You're not the falling apart type," Paige said, with such conviction Ashley almost believed her.

"Thanks for the vote of confidence."

"Seriously, you've dealt with a lot in the past six months and stood up through it all."

"I had a minor meltdown on Wednesday," she admitted, reaching for her glass. Thankfully the Fedentropin trial didn't prohibit the consumption of alcohol, and the wine she'd drank was already helping smooth the roughest of the edges.

"When you found out Cam had a child? Or when you learned that your sister's pregnant?"

"It was probably a combination of both."

Paige nodded and set a slice of blue cheese on a rye cracker.

"I'm happy for Megan and Gage," she said. "And I'm thrilled about the baby."

"I know you are," Paige agreed.

"I just want to know when it's going to happen for me. When is it going to be my turn?"

"What happened to your appointment at the clinic?"

"I got bumped," she grumbled. "The doctor had some kind of emergency."

Her cousin smiled. "I think that's the nature of the medical field."

"I know. It just seems like one more detour sign on a road that's been littered with them."

"What kind of sign is Cam?"

Ashley sipped from her glass again. "Dead end."

"Are you sure about that?" Paige asked. "Because if I'm not mistaken, that's him walking up your driveway."

Ashley set down her glass before she spilled the contents all over herself. "Don't you dare leave—"

But Paige was already on her feet, reaching for the tray of snacks. "I'll just go refresh this." She turned and smiled at the uninvited guest who had stepped up onto the porch. "Hello, Cam," she said, then slipped into the house before he could even respond.

Cam glanced at the closed door, then at Ashley. "Did I say something wrong?"

She didn't smile at his attempted humor. "Not yet."

He held up his hands in a gesture of surrender. "I just came over to apologize."

"What, exactly, are you apologizing for?"

"For not telling you that I had a child."

She lifted a shoulder. "You don't owe me any apologies, Cam."

"I didn't mean to blindside you."

"It doesn't matter."

"It does," he insisted. "Maybe I figured you would have heard about Maddie a long time ago, but I shouldn't have counted on that, and I should have given you the courtesy of an explanation."

"No explanation required. You dumped me, met someone else, got married, had a child."

"It wasn't quite that simple."

"I'd say it was exactly that simple."

"I'm not going to apologize for not wanting what you did when I was nineteen," Cam said. "Because any nineteen-year-old who wants to marry his high school sweetheart is either blinded by lust or completely without ambition. I'd apologize for hurting you because I was insensitive jerk, but I've already done that and I'm tired of trekking down the same path."

"Then you can just follow the path right back to your own house," she said coldly.

He shook his head. "That would be the easy way, and I'm not taking the easy way again."

"It's a way out," she said. "And that's all you ever wanted."

"Wrong. I wanted *you*, Ashley. I wanted you a hell of a lot more than I should have at that age, and it terrified me."

"Obviously you got over it."

"You'd think so, wouldn't you? But that's the real bitch of it—because I never did."

"You married another woman. Had a child with another woman." Her voice hitched, and she hated him for it. Hated him for the pain she felt every time she thought about the baby he'd given to someone else.

Cam lowered himself into the chair that Paige had vacated. "I married Danica because I thought we wanted the same things. By the time I realized I was wrong, it was too late. We were married, she was pregnant, and even knowing our marriage was a mistake, I wouldn't wish it away for anything in the world because I got Maddie out of it."

Ashley looked away. "It's ironic, isn't it? All I ever wanted was to get married and have a family, and you ran as far and as fast as you could from me because you weren't ready to make that kind of commitment."

"Twelve years ago, I wasn't ready," he agreed, then smiled wryly. "There are still days that I'm not ready, but Madeline doesn't really give me a choice in the matter."

Ashley didn't smile back, but she did ask, "So how did you end up with custody?"

Cam realized he should have been prepared for the question; Ashley certainly wasn't the first person to ask it. Because although the courts no longer awarded custody to mothers as a matter of course and shared custody arrangements were increasingly popular, it was still somewhat unusual for a father to be granted primary care of a child.

He'd always felt awkward explaining the situation, and he'd resented having to make excuses for what he'd believed for so long was simply his ex-wife's disinterest. He knew differently now, but he still didn't know how to make anyone else understand without sharing secrets that weren't his to share.

"Staying with me offered Madeline more stability," he finally responded to Ashley's question. "Especially since Danica was already planning to move to London."

Ashley frowned as she sipped her wine. "And she was okay with that arrangement? She just moved to another continent and left her child behind?"

"We agreed it was best for Maddie."

"Does Maddie see her very often?"

"Not as often, or as consistently, as I'd like," he admitted. "But she did spend the last month of her summer vacation in London with her."

"So why didn't you mention your daughter to me the night you came over here?"

"You mean the night I kissed you?"

"I mean the night you brought pizza," she clarified, as if the kiss was irrelevant.

But he could tell by the color that infused her cheeks that it wasn't irrelevant at all, and that she remembered that kiss as clearly as he did. And as much as he wanted to kiss her again, to prove that the attraction between them was still very relevant, his real purpose in coming here tonight had been to clear the air, not to cloud it further.

"I should have," he finally admitted. "But I don't talk about Maddie very much when she's gone. Not to anyone."

"Why not?"

"Because talking about her makes me miss her even more."

She seemed startled by his response, but then she nodded. "I guess I can understand that."

"She's the center of my world, the reason for everything I do."

"She's a lucky girl." Ashley's voice had softened, taken on

an almost wistful quality. "To have a father so committed to her best interests."

"Does that mean you forgive me?" he dared to ask.

"It means I like your daughter—she's a great kid."

"Her dad's a pretty good guy, too."

"I'm reserving judgment on that," she said, but the smile that curved her lips gave him hope.

Chapter Six

Over the next few weeks, Ashley crossed paths with Cam on a fairly regular basis. He came to school every Wednesday to pick up Maddie and when he did, he usually dropped in to the classroom to chat with Ashley and check on his daughter's progress. The awkwardness between them was fading and Ashley began to think that one day they might even be friends again.

And if Cam sometimes flirted with her, or dropped little hints that he wanted more from her than friendship, she didn't take him too seriously. She didn't dare.

She still thought about the kiss they'd shared in her kitchen, and she still got all hot and tingly when she did, but she had clearly established the boundaries for their relationship and she was determined to uphold them. But she was glad that her appointment at the clinic had been rescheduled. Even if it was still a few weeks away, it gave her something to look forward to and focus on. Maybe when she was finally expecting a baby of her own she would stop wishing she could be the mother Maddie needed so badly and the wife that shared Cam's bed every night.

Because as often as she reminded herself that there could be no future for her with Cam, she nevertheless found herself day-dreaming about the possibility. And as much as she'd always dreamed of having a child of her own, she knew that loving Cameron's little girl would fill the aching void in her heart.

But Maddie had a mother, and Ashley knew that letting her imagination create happily-ever-after scenarios would only end up causing more heartache for herself in the end. She knew it, and yet, when Cam came out of his house as she was walking past on her way home from the neighborhood market Saturday morning, she couldn't deny that her heart started to pound just a little bit faster.

"What perfect timing," he said by way of greeting.

"For?" she prompted cautiously.

"Apparently you mentioned to your class that you like to hike at Eagle Point Park," he said. "So Maddie suggested, as we're heading up there for a picnic today, that we should ask you to go with us."

"It was sweet of her to think of me, but I'm not sure that would be a good idea," she said, far more tempted than she ought to be by the prospect of an outing with Cam and his daughter.

"Why not?"

"I just don't think we should spend too much time together."

"Why not?" he asked again.

"Because," she said, unwilling to admit that wanting to say yes was proof enough to her that it was a bad idea. Because giving in to what she wanted where Cameron Turcotte was concerned had always gotten her into trouble.

"That's hardly a reasonable response," he chided.

"I'm sure it's one you use all the time with your daughter when it suits your purposes."

"Actually, I never say no to Madeline unless I can give her a reason for it."

"While I'm sure that chalks up extra parenting points for you, it doesn't change my answer," she said firmly.

But Cam wasn't dissuaded. "Come on, Ash," he said. "It's not as if we can get into too much trouble in the hills with a six-and-a-half-year-old chaperone."

"I'm not worried," she lied.

"No?"

It was more a challenge than a question, as if he was all too aware of the tug-of-war that was going on in her mind—the struggle between what she wanted and what she knew was smart.

"No," she insisted.

"Then why won't you come with us?" he challenged.

"Maybe I have other plans for the day," she hedged, mentally searching for some excuse, any excuse, that sounded less desperate than making a list of 1001 reasons that getting involved with Cameron Turcotte again is a very bad idea—even if that was exactly how she planned to spend her afternoon in order to ensure that she was clear on all of those reasons.

"Do you?"

"As a matter of fact, I was going to—"

She wasn't sure what she intended to say, because just then the front door flew open and Maddie came racing across the lawn.

"We're going to Eagle Point Park," she announced. "And I made samiches and Daddy packed juice and we're going to have a picnic. Are you going to come with us? Please, Miss Ashley. It's going to be so much fun, but it will be even more fun if you come, too."

And that quickly, all of Ashley's resolutions about putting

distance between herself and Cam and his little girl dissolved in the radiance of Maddie's smile.

"I think a picnic sounds wonderful," she said.

Cam never used to be the picnicking type, but there wasn't anything he wouldn't do for his little girl. So when Madeline suggested packing a lunch and taking it up to the park, it seemed like a relatively harmless request. It wasn't until they were putting together the sandwiches that his daughter mentioned Ashley, and he realized that he'd been set up.

Not that he minded, really. After all, spending time with Ashley Roarke was anything but a hardship. But he did worry that his daughter seemed to have become so attached to her teacher, and so quickly.

Part of it, he knew, was her desperate craving of female attention—something that he was simply incapable of giving her. Another part was Ashley's natural warmth and compassion, traits that made her such a great teacher and an easy target for his daughter's affections.

As they walked along one of the simpler trails, Ashley taught Maddie how to identify different kinds of trees by their leaves. She also pointed out various birds and the tracks of squirrels and raccoons and something that was—no, not a bear—probably just a big dog.

It was comfortable and easy, and Cam found himself wishing that they could spend every lazy Saturday afternoon together like this. Just him and his daughter and the woman he…liked?

The automatic mental pause nearly made Cam smile.

Of course, he liked Ashley. They'd been friends for a long time before they'd ever become lovers. They'd had a lot of similar interests, enjoyed the same books, music and movies. They liked the same kind of pizza, would both rather play baseball than watch it on TV, and appreciated walks in the rain.

In fact, Ashley had once been such an integral part of his life that, when he'd ended their relationship before going away to school, he'd lost not just his girlfriend but his best friend. It had been his decision to cut all ties between them, finally and completely, at least until he was finished college, but that didn't make it hurt any less.

He hadn't seen her again before their high school reunion in the spring, hadn't realized until then how much of a hole had been left in his life when he'd cut her out of it. But the worst part of seeing her again was realizing how much she still mattered to him, and learning that she was in love with and engaged to someone else.

He'd recognized that his feelings were more than a little hypocritical, considering that he'd already been married *and* divorced, but he just couldn't imagine her with anyone else. He didn't want to imagine her with anyone else.

Deciding to move back to Pinehurst when he knew she was planning a wedding to another man had been difficult. But in the end, he'd known it was what was best for his daughter. With Danica now living in London, there was no reason he had to stay in Seattle, and every reason to move closer to his family so that Madeline's grandparents could be part of her life.

"Hurry up, Daddy." Maddie's voice called back to him, prompting his feet into motion.

"Sorry," he apologized, when he caught up to them.

"What were you doing back there?" Ashley asked.

He shrugged the pack off of his shoulders, opened the zipper and pulled out the blanket they'd brought to spread out on the ground. "I thought I saw a…an owl."

"An owl?" She lifted her brow.

"Owls are…noc-tur-nal," Maddie said, carefully enunciating the word and looking to her teacher for confirmation. Ashley nodded.

"That means they sleep during the day and come out at night," his daughter informed him.

He shrugged. "Maybe it wasn't an owl."

"Owls eat mice and frogs and birds." She made a face after reciting that fact, as if the idea was as distasteful as eating peas or Brussels sprouts—her least favorite vegetables.

"Speaking of food," Cam said, beginning to unpack their lunch.

"I hope you didn't bring mice and frogs and birds," Ashley said.

Maddie giggled. "No, we made samiches." She took a plate and balanced it on her lap. "What kind of samich do you want, Miss Ashley?"

"What are my choices?"

"Peanut butter, peanut butter and jam, or peanut butter and banana."

Ashley mulled over the options, finally deciding, "Peanut butter and banana."

Cam watched as Maddie carefully selected three pinwheel sandwiches from the plastic container and arranged them in a semicircle on the plate. Then she added two cookies— peanut butter, of course—and a small cluster of green grapes.

"That looks absolutely delicious," Ashley said, accepting the plate.

Maddie beamed in appreciation of her praise, and Cam felt his heart swell. Until he'd started spending time with Maddie and Ashley together, he hadn't realized how much his daughter needed a woman's attention. She missed out on so much not having a mother involved in her life, and though *his* mother tried to spend as much time as possible with her grand-daughter, it wasn't the same thing.

Gayle had mentioned—several times in recent years—that he should think about getting married again, that he needed a wife as much as Maddie needed a mother. But even if he'd agreed with her assessment—and he was definitely on the fence about the wife part—none of the women he'd dated had tempted him to think any longer term than the next date. There certainly hadn't been anyone whom he'd wanted to wake up beside every morning for the rest of his life, and there hadn't been anyone who'd ever made his daughter smile as she was smiling at Ashley now.

Not that he was thinking in terms of marriage with Ashley. Definitely not.

And yet, he knew that if there was a woman who could tempt his thoughts in that direction, it was Maddie's first-grade teacher. Yes, Ashley tempted him. But he knew it was going to take some time to figure out if *he* could still tempt *her.*

Tearing his thoughts back to the picnic, he noticed that Maddie had taken a second plate and was loading it up with all of her favorites.

"What about my lunch?" Cam asked, indicating the last empty plate.

"Ladies always get served first," she informed him primly. "And you can get your own."

Ashley's cough sounded more like a laugh, and when he looked at her over his daughter's head, he saw the amusement that danced in her eyes.

Those beautiful, sparkling violet eyes.

The same eyes that had haunted his dreams for years, and that continued to haunt his dreams now.

He held her gaze for a long moment, a moment that spun out between them, until there were no birds chirping in the trees, until there was no wind rustling through the leaves.

Until there was nothing but the two of them.

Until Maddie broke the silence by asking for juice.

Ashley blinked and looked away, and the moment was gone.

* * *

Something had happened between them at Eagle Point Park. Ashley wasn't exactly sure what, except that something had changed. Until that moment, she'd managed to convince herself that the feelings she had for Cameron were only remnants of a long-ago attraction. And maybe there were still remnants of that attraction, but there were also new feelings stirring inside of her. Stronger and deeper feelings that she'd managed to ignore because they were only *her* feelings.

In the space of a heartbeat, with the heat of just one look, Cam decimated that belief. And the realization that there was still a connection between them, a simmering awareness that pulled at both of them, terrified her.

So when Maddie approached her desk at the end of the day on Monday, it was an effort to smile, to pretend that everything was the same. And then the child's question shattered even that illusion.

"Are you dating my daddy?"

The marker Ashley had been using to prepare a math chart for the next day's lesson slipped from her fingers.

She bent to retrieve it, wishing she could pick up an easy answer to the little girl's inquiry at the same time. Instead, she responded with a question of her own. "Why would you ask something like that?"

"Because I told Victoria that we went on a picnic on Saturday and she said that you must be dating my daddy and maybe you would marry him and be my new mommy."

She had worried that agreeing to go on a picnic with Cam and Maddie was a bad idea—she just hadn't known how bad. And the desperate yearning in the little girl's big green eyes nearly broke her heart.

Ashley carefully recapped the marker and set it aside so she could give Maddie her full attention.

"I'm not dating your daddy," she said gently. "But he and I are old friends and you and I are new friends, and friends spend time together."

The light in Maddie's eyes dimmed. "So you're not going to marry him?"

"No." She swallowed. "I'm not going to marry him."

"But if you're friends, you must like him," she insisted, with the unequivocal reasoning of a first grader. "And if you like him, then you should marry him."

"Lots of people like one another without getting married."

Maddie sighed. "But Grandma says that Daddy needs a wife who will make him happy and I need a mother who cares more about me than her career."

Out of the mouths of babes, Ashley thought, and cautiously asked, "She said this to you?"

Maddie shook her head. "She said it to Grandpa, but I could hear them talking."

"Sometimes adults have conversations that they don't mean for children to overhear, and what your grandma said probably wasn't intended to be repeated."

Maddie nodded. "But I think Daddy should get a new wife, too, 'cause then we could be a family."

The crack in Ashley's heart split open a little wider. "That's something only your daddy can decide."

Cam's daughter sighed again. "I need to go now. Grandma will be waiting for me."

"Okay." And because she figured they both needed it, she gave Maddie a quick hug. "I'll see you tomorrow."

Being summoned for a conference with the teacher wasn't quite the same as being called to the principal's office, but

Cam had an uncomfortable feeling in the pit of his stomach just the same when he heard the message from Ashley on his answering machine.

He glanced at the calendar before he called her back. "I have about an hour at seven o'clock tonight while Maddie's at ballet," he said. "Can I buy you a coffee at Bean There Café?"

"That works for me," she agreed, but still gave him no indication what it was she wanted to talk about.

So he worried about it while he cooked spaghetti for dinner, and though he gently tried to elicit details from Maddie about her day at school, his daughter was uncharacteristically close-mouthed, a fact which only increased his apprehension. They loaded the dishwasher together after they'd finished eating, then she washed up and went to get changed for her dance class, but there was no enthusiasm in her step and no sparkle in her eye.

When he got to the café, he noted that Ashley looked almost as apprehensive as he felt.

"What did she do?" he asked without preamble when he brought their drinks—regular black coffee for him, a cinnamon dolce latte for Ashley—to the table.

"She didn't do anything wrong," she hastened to reassure him. "I just thought you should be aware that your daughter is expressing an interest in you finding a new wife."

He exhaled a sigh of relief. "I thought maybe she'd stabbed that annoying Charlie Partridge with her safety scissors."

Her eyes flashed. "I'm glad you think this is funny."

"I don't," he assured her. "But I was envisioning so many worse things that the truth almost seems anticlimactic." He sipped his coffee, considering her revelation. "How did this come up?"

"She asked me—" her gaze slid away from his, her cheeks flushed with color "—if I was going to marry you."

Despite her obvious embarrassment, he couldn't resist teasing her a little. "Did you tell her that I hadn't asked you…yet?"

"Will you stop joking about this?" Ashley demanded, obviously not amused. "She's at an impressionable age and obviously looking for a mother figure."

"I know," he admitted. "I just didn't realize how much until recently."

Ashley sipped her latte.

"You told me she doesn't see her mother on a regular basis," she reminded him gently. "Is there anything you can do to change that?"

"Not likely. Danica comes to visit whenever it's convenient for her, and that's not more than two or three times a year. The four weeks that Maddie spent in London this summer is more time than she usually spends with her mother in a whole year."

And he wasn't entirely sure she'd spent most of that time with her mother, because she'd come home with a new handheld video game system and half a dozen games that Danica had bought to keep her busy while she "finished up some work."

"What about telephone calls?" Ashley prompted.

"Her mother tries to call once a week."

"Tries?"

He sighed. "What do you want me to say, Ash? I knew when I married Danica that she was committed to building her career. I didn't know that she was committed to her career at the expense of all else, but that's the way it is."

"Okay, so maybe she isn't a candidate for mother of the year," Ashley allowed, "but Maddie is her daughter and she needs her mother."

"Danica doesn't see it that way."

It was obvious that Ashley didn't understand. Hell, he wasn't sure he understood, but he'd long ago accepted that Maddie would never have a close relationship with her mother.

"The truth is," he heard himself say, "Danica never wanted to have children."

Ashley stared at him, as if she couldn't believe what he was saying. He could hardly believe he was telling her. But this was Ashley, and if he wanted a second chance with her—and he'd finally accepted that he did—he had to be honest with her, and he had to trust that she would understand.

"I've never admitted this to anyone else—not even my parents—but Madeline wasn't planned," he confided to her. "In fact, Danica wasn't very happy when she realized she was pregnant."

That was an understatement, but he couldn't admit to anyone, even so many years later, that Danica hadn't been happy at all. In fact, she'd been furious. Having apparently managed to put aside the grief of a previous miscarriage, she was too busy building a career to want to have a baby.

Cam had tried to understand. Maybe it wasn't what either of them had envisioned for a marriage that was barely into its sixth month, he'd admitted, but her pregnancy didn't change their plans, it merely accelerated them. Or so he'd believed, until he'd realized that, despite claiming to be pregnant when they married, Danica never really wanted to have children.

He'd been stunned by her attitude—and furious when she'd suggested terminating her pregnancy. She wasn't an unwed teenager, but a married woman and no way in hell was he going to agree to abort their child.

And so was laid the first brick in the wall that built up between them.

"But she fell in love with her baby when she held her in her arms," Ashley guessed, obviously unable to imagine any other possibility.

Which was exactly what Cam had hoped would happen.

But the truth was, Danica only agreed to have the baby so

long as he assumed complete responsibility for their child after the birth. And he'd gone along with her demands, certain that her attitude toward their child would change through the course of her pregnancy. But the distance between them continued to grow along with the baby in her womb.

"She tried to be a good mother," Cam said in defense of his ex-wife, because he wanted to believe it was true. And because, when he realized some hard truths about her own childhood, he knew she'd handled the situation in the way that she believed was best for their child. "But Madeline was a difficult baby and after working fourteen hours at the office, Danica didn't have the patience for a demanding infant."

"She went back to work right after having the baby?"

"Her career meant a lot to her," he said, all too aware that it didn't just sound like a lame excuse, it *was* a lame excuse.

"More than her family?" Ashley demanded incredulously. "And what about your career?"

"I was still finishing my internship."

"And taking care of the baby," she guessed.

"There was a retired woman who lived above us who helped out a lot, but I was happy to do as much as I could between shifts at the hospital."

"That couldn't have been easy."

"It wasn't easy," he agreed. "But I was happy to do it, to be the one who was there when she cut her first tooth, when she spoke her first word, when she took her first step." And each one of those precious moments was indelibly imprinted on his memory.

"I know I've said it before, but Madeline's lucky to have a dad like you," Ashley told him.

"And a teacher like you," he said.

She finished her latte. "I just thought you should know what was going through her mind."

"I'm a little surprised," he admitted. "She's never mentioned the possibility of me finding a new wife before."

"It might be a factor of her age," Ashley suggested. "She's making friends at school, and they talk about their mothers—it's not surprising that she might look for someone to fill that role for her."

"And that she would gravitate toward you." He reached across the table, touched her hand. "When I came back for the reunion, I was surprised to find that you weren't already married with the half a dozen kids you always wanted."

She pulled her hand away. "Life doesn't always turn out the way we plan."

A truth of which he was all too aware. And yet, coming back to Pinehurst had helped him to see beyond the boundaries imposed by the choices he'd made to the opportunities that might still be found.

"Do you believe in second chances?" he asked cautiously.

She was silent for a minute, and when she finally spoke, it was only to say, "I believe that Maddie's class will be finishing soon, and I need to get home."

Cam pushed back his chair to walk her out.

"Thanks—for the update."

She just nodded.

He watched her go, wondering why she'd refused to answer his question.

Because she didn't believe in second chances?

Or because she did?

Chapter Seven

The Fall Festival was an old but ever-evolving Pinehurst tradition. What had started as a single-day celebration of the harvest back in 1859, when most of the town's residents were farmers, had become a four-day mid-October event.

For Ashley and Paige, it was an annual ritual that brought back mostly fond memories of their teenage years. Because she'd been a bookworm rather than a social butterfly, Megan's memories weren't quite so fond, but they usually dragged her along to the fair with them anyway. And while Megan had critically assessed the engineering of the midway rides, Ashley and Paige were never deterred by her negative attitude.

They would save up their allowance for weeks in advance of the fair, happily giving up their hard-earned cash for a bird's-eye view of the grounds from the top of the Ferris wheel, the thrill of a spin around the Zipper or the heart-pounding fear of the haunted house.

Of course, the fair was more than just the rides and caramel apples and cotton candy. It included a livestock exhibition and agricultural displays with the fattest pig, prettiest flowers and biggest pumpkins proudly displayed with their award-winning ribbons. There were also cooking contests, with local chefs putting their pies and cookies and breads to the test of the judges, and offering samples and selling their wares to the public.

As Ashley walked along the well-trodden dirt path munching on a bag of fresh kettle corn, she had to admit that, at almost thirty years of age, she enjoyed the annual festival probably even more now than she had as a teen. She no longer stood in line for the Zipper, but she'd learned to appreciate the arts and crafts displays more, and she always bought a couple of jars of Mrs. Kurchik's homemade peach jam, winner of the blue ribbon every year for as far back as she could remember.

"You've got to see the baby pigs," Ashley told Paige, steering her cousin toward the barn. Having brought her class on a field trip the previous day, she'd scoped out most of the grounds already.

"It stinks in the barn," Paige protested.

"It smells like animals," Ashley allowed, breathing in the scent of damp earth and fresh straw with just an underlying hint of manure.

Paige wrinkled her nose but gamely followed her through the wide doors. "It smells exactly as it did fifteen years ago."

"Really?" Ashley was surprised by the comment. "We hardly ever came to see the animals when were in high school."

"I wasn't in here to see the animals."

Ashley glanced over her shoulder, saw her cousin smiling.

"Do you remember Marvin Tedeschi?" Paige asked.

She scrambled through her memories to put a face to the name. "Mr. Archer's history class?"

Paige smiled and nodded. "He got to second base with me, right here in this barn during the Fall Festival when we were in tenth grade."

"You went to second base with Marvin Tedeschi?" Ashley stared at her. "The quiet kid with shaggy blond hair?"

"That quiet kid had the lips of a poet and the hands of an artist."

"How did I not know this?"

"You were too busy lusting after Cam Turcotte to notice what was going on with anyone else," Paige said.

Ashley couldn't deny that was probably true, so she only asked, "And what happened after second base?"

Her cousin sighed. "Nothing."

"Nothing?"

"Well, he got to second base a couple more times after that, but we never took it any further." Her lips curved, her eyes glinted. "At least, not until I saw him at the reunion in the spring."

"You hooked up with him that night?"

"I was feeling a little…nostalgic."

"And he was feeling a little…Wilder?" Ashley teased.

Paige grinned. "I'd say he was feeling a *lot* Wilder. And left me feeling very grateful."

"So that was it? You had great sex, then just went your separate ways?"

"Neither of us wanted anything more than that."

"I don't know that I could ever be so casual about intimacy," Ashley admitted.

"Because you don't think about sex for the purpose of physical release but as an assessment tool in your search for a potential husband," her cousin pointed out.

"That's not true."

"It wasn't a criticism," Paige assured her.

Ashley frowned. "It's still not true."

"Have you ever had sex with a guy just because you thought it would be fun?"

Because she hadn't, she only said, "That doesn't prove anything."

"It proves that you're looking for a mate for life," Paige insisted. "And there's nothing wrong with that."

"I'm not looking for a mate at all, not anymore," Ashley reminded her.

"Then you should try sex just for fun," her cousin advised.

She shook her head. "I think I'll keep my expectations low, at least that way I won't be disappointed."

Paige stopped in mid-stride and turned to face her. "I can't believe it."

"What?"

"CBB wasn't even good in bed."

Ashley felt her cheeks flame as she reached out to rub the cow's head. The big, dark eyes closed and the animal seemed to sigh with pleasure. "Sex was…fine."

Paige lifted her brows. "Fine?"

"Look, if it's okay with you, I'd really rather not discuss this now." There wasn't anything she couldn't talk to her cousin about, but if they were going to perform a postmortem on her sex life, she wanted it to be in the privacy of her own home with a glass of wine in her hand, not in a public venue where anyone could overhear their conversation. Not that there were many other people in the barn, but still.

Unfortunately, Paige wouldn't be deterred. "I need to understand this."

"What's to understand?"

"You were going to marry him."

"And?" she prompted.

"And I can't fathom why you would want to marry a guy who didn't rock your world," her cousin told her.

"Maybe my world isn't capable of being rocked," Ashley said, aware that she sounded more than a little defensive.

"Are you saying…never?"

She looked away. "Never with Trevor."

"Sounds like a really bad slogan," Paige said. "Maybe you should suggest he put it on his business cards, as a warning to other unsuspecting women."

Ashley felt her lips curve, grateful that her cousin could make her see the light side of such a humiliating admission. "I'm happy just to move on," she said, doing so towards the pigpen.

"But—oh." Whatever else Paige was about to say was forgotten when she caught sight of the seven piglets, their round pink butts wiggling as they scrambled for position while nursing at their mother's belly. "Oh, they are so cute."

"My kids went crazy, oohing and aahing when they saw them yesterday," Ashley told her.

"Kind of like I just did?"

"Just like that," she agreed.

"Seven babies," Paige mused. "Can you imagine?"

Ashley would happily settle for one baby of her own. At least one at a time. But she pushed the pang of longing aside, as she'd been doing for months now, since the end of her engagement to Trevor and the realization that her dreams of motherhood were slipping further and further away from her.

"Mama Pig doesn't seem to be fazed," she said instead.

"That's because seven is actually a fairly small litter for a pig," a male voice informed her from over their shoulders.

A familiar voice that had Ashley's heart pounding too hard and too fast before she even turned around and confirmed the identity of the speaker. And when she saw Cam, her heart started to pound even harder and faster. He had his daughter with him, and obviously the little girl's infatuation with the piglets she'd seen on her field trip had compelled her to bring her father back to the barn.

"Someone's been doing his homework," Paige noted. "Trying to impress the teacher?"

Cam just grinned.

"Mother pigs can have between eight and twelve babies," Madeline said. Apparently she'd done the homework along with her father and wasn't going to be outdone by him. Then the little girl smiled at Ashley. "I had so much fun visiting the pigs yesterday that I brung Daddy back to see them."

"Brought," both Ashley and Cam corrected automatically.

"Sorry," Ashley said. "The teacher instincts don't clock out after hours."

"No need to apologize," Cam assured her.

From over her shoulder, Ashley registered the sound of a throat clearing. She sighed and turned.

"This is my cousin, Paige," she said to Maddie. "I brought her to see the pigs, too." Then, to Paige, "You know Cam, of course. And this is his daughter, Madeline."

Paige offered her hand to the girl. "It's a pleasure to meet you, Madeline."

Madeline took Paige's hand and shook it awkwardly. "Okay."

"She's six," Cam said, as an explanation of his daughter's response.

"She's adorable," Paige said, and he smiled like the proud father that he was, while Ashley tried to ignore the ache she felt whenever she looked at his little girl and the much stronger sizzle of attraction she experienced whenever he was near.

"There's cows, too, Daddy," Maddie said, tugging on his hand.

"Cows?" Paige interjected, as if they hadn't already come from that direction. "Can you show me where?"

Madeline looked to her father for permission. He nodded

and released her hand, and she immediately headed off for the bovine stalls, Paige trailing in her wake.

"Not very subtle, is she?" Ashley mused.

"You won't hear me complain about having some time alone with you," Cam assured her.

"We're not exactly alone."

"Close enough," he said, and edged nearer to her.

Too close, she thought, as her heart started to pound just a little bit faster. "Cam."

He ignored the warning in her voice and leaned closer. "You smell much nicer than the pigs."

She couldn't help but smile at that. "I should hope so."

"I like your perfume," he told her. "It's similar to what you wore in high school, but sexier."

"It's the same perfume I wore in high school," she admitted.

"Then it must be that you're even sexier now than you were then."

She swallowed and shifted away from him. "Why are you doing this, Cam?"

"What is it that you think I'm doing?" he asked her.

"Flirting with me."

He smiled. "Maybe to see if you'll flirt back."

"I won't," she said, a reminder to herself as much as a response to him.

"What if I took you for a ride on the Ferris wheel? Would you flirt with me then?"

She shook her head.

"How about a spin on the Zipper?"

"I'd be more likely to throw up on you," she warned.

"You used to love the Zipper."

"I used to love a lot of things."

His eyes locked on hers. "I remember."

The potent sensuality in his gaze had the nerves in her belly quivering and her knees trembling. She tightened her grip on the railing, holding on to the wood as she desperately tried to hold her hormones in check.

"And I can't stop thinking about that kiss we shared in your kitchen," he told her.

"It was just a kiss."

"A kiss that keeps me awake at night."

"A kiss that never should have happened," she said firmly, refusing to admit that the memory of that kiss had the exact same effect on her.

"We were always good together, Ash."

She swallowed. "*Were*—past tense."

"That kiss proves nothing is finished between us."

"I'm not going to get involved with you again, Cam."

He stroked the back of her hand, his fingertips tracing lazy circles over the soft skin. She wanted to snatch her hand away, but to do so would be to admit how much his touch affected her, how much he affected her.

"Because you're still hung up on your ex?" he asked.

"Because I have no interest in repeating the mistakes of the past."

"I made the mistake," he said, "when I said goodbye to you."

She couldn't stand here and listen to him sounding so sincerely contrite. She couldn't look into the fathomless depths of his dark-green eyes and not want to believe what he was saying. Because if she let herself believe he was sorry, that he really did want another chance, well, she just might be foolish enough to give him another chance. And that was something she couldn't let happen. She had an appointment at PARC and plans for her life now, plans that didn't include Cam Turcotte or any other man.

So she turned away and started walking in the direction Paige and Madeline had gone. She knew he would follow, but she also knew that he wouldn't continue whatever game he was playing if there was any danger of his daughter overhearing them.

"We have to run," Paige said, as soon as Ashley caught up with her. "I've got a client emergency and need to head back to the office, but I can drop you at home first, unless—" she looked questioningly at Cam.

"That's fine," Ashley said, wondering if her cousin had fabricated the client emergency in an attempt to drop her in Cam's lap.

At the same time, he said, "I can take Ashley home later."

She shook her head. No way was she going to spend a single moment more than was absolutely necessary with Cam Turcotte. "It's okay. I'm ready to go now."

"If Cam doesn't mind giving you a ride, that would simplify things for me," Paige said. "Since I'm closer to the office if I leave straight from here."

Ashley narrowed her gaze, more convinced than ever that there was no emergency. "Well, I don't want to inconvenience anyone, so I'll take a cab."

"It's not an inconvenience," Cam insisted.

"Great. Thanks," Paige said, then kissed Ashley's cheek, waved to Maddie, who had wandered over to look at the bunnies, and bolted from the barn.

Ashley bit back a sigh of frustration.

Cam smiled, as if he knew as well as she that they'd been played. The difference was, he apparently didn't mind, but Ashley vowed that she would have a serious talk with her cousin the next time she saw her.

"The bunnies are sleeping," Maddie announced to her father, her disappointment obvious.

"It must be past their bedtime," Cam said. "As it's also past yours."

"But I'm not tired," his daughter insisted, though the statement was immediately followed by a wide yawn just as an older couple entered the barn.

Cam's parents, Ashley realized, and wondered if this night could get any more awkward.

She'd spent a lot of time in their home and had grown to know Rob and Gayle Turcotte well while she and Cam were dating. But when Cam ended their relationship and went away to school, their paths had crossed much less frequently, and Ashley still felt awkward whenever they did. Maybe it was her own fault, because she'd loved them almost as much as she'd loved Cam and she'd mistakenly assumed they would be her family someday, too. Losing them, less than two years after her own father had passed away, had devastated her almost as much as being dumped by Cam.

"Looks like we're just on time," Rob said, scooping his granddaughter into his arms and making her giggle.

"I wondered where you two had wandered off to," Cam said to his parents.

"Your mother got waylaid by Ethel Mayer and conned into buying raffle tickets for a blanket we won't win and don't need even if we do," Rob explained.

"It's a quilt, not a blanket," his wife chided. "And a beautiful work of art." Then she smiled at Ashley. "This is a pleasant surprise."

"It's nice to see you again," Ashley said, and hoped she sounded half as sincere as Cam's mother.

Maddie, having been set back on her feet by her grandfather, reached for her grandmother's hand. "Come see the piggies, Grandma."

Gayle glanced at her watch. "Only for a quick minute, then we have to get you home to bed."

"But I'm not tired," Maddie said again.

"But Grandpa is," Gayle replied in a staged whisper. "And you know how cranky he gets if he stays up past his bedtime."

Maddie sighed. "Okay. But we have to see the piggies first."

"We'll see the piggies first," her grandmother promised. Then to the others, "Enjoy the rest of your evening."

"Hey," Cam called, as his daughter started to walk away with her grandparents.

Maddie turned and ran back to him. He squatted down so she could throw her arms around his neck and give him a loud smacking kiss. "Bye, Daddy. Love you."

"Love you, too, baby," he said, and something squeezed tight inside Ashley's heart.

Maddie raced back to her grandparents, turning to wave one last time, then Ashley was alone with Cam again.

Cam watched his daughter until she was out of sight before turning to Ashley. "Looks like it's just you and me now."

"Looks like," she agreed.

It was the first time they'd been alone together since their meeting at the Bean There Café, since she'd told him that his daughter was trying to find him a wife. He'd been thinking about that conversation a lot recently, and thinking that he might not object to getting married again.

Not that he was in any hurry to find himself standing at the altar, but he was no longer adamantly opposed to the possibility. Especially when he considered the potential benefits of making Ashley his bride.

Of course, thinking about marriage—even in the most abstract sense—was a little premature when Ashley was as skittish about being alone with him as the newborn foal was about the strangers hovering around her stall. First, they had to get to know one another all over again, and he would have to thank Paige for giving him this time with her cousin.

"So what do you want to do now?" he asked.

"I think I've had enough for tonight," Ashley said, making her way towards the doors. "So I'll just call a cab and—"

"I promised Paige I would take you home," he interrupted to remind her.

"You were conned by my cousin."

He shrugged. "Either way, there's no reason for you to take a cab when I'm going in the same direction."

"Fine," she relented.

"Are you really that opposed to spending time in my company?"

"I'm not opposed at all," she said. "I'm just not interested."

"You sure didn't kiss me like a woman who was not interested."

She glared at him over her shoulder; he just grinned.

"In fact, you kissed like a woman who enjoys being kissed, and touched and—"

"I was dizzy from the loss of blood," she said.

"You didn't lose that much blood." But he picked up her hand, turned it to the light.

"What are you doing?"

"It's called a follow-up exam."

Ashley was tempted to make some comment about playing doctor, but decided that any kind of sexual innuendo was inherently dangerous around Cam Turcotte. Instead she said, "Dr. Alex already checked it out and said everything's fine."

"It looks like it's healing nicely," he agreed. Then he dipped his head and feathered light kisses along the side of her palm. "How does it feel now?"

She felt all kinds of things she shouldn't be feeling, and none of them had anything to do with the fading scar on her hand. "Fine," she managed.

"No tightness? No pain?"

"No." *Not in my hand.*

He smiled, as if he knew exactly what she was thinking, but all he said was, "Good."

"Eli said you did an exceptional job with the stitches," she admitted. "That I probably won't even have much of a scar."

"You've always had pretty hands. I wanted to make sure they stayed that way." He lowered her hand but, instead of releasing it, linked their fingers together and led her toward the midway.

"The parking lot is the other way."

"I know. The Ferris wheel is this way."

"Aren't you anxious to get home to Maddie?"

"She's spending the night at my parents' house," he told her.

"Oh."

"Ferris wheel?" he prompted again.

She glanced up at the towering wheel, felt a quick jolt of excitement low in her belly, though she wasn't sure if it was anticipation of the ride or just the excitement of being with Cam. She decided not to question but to go with her instincts.

"The Ferris wheel sounds like fun," she agreed.

He must have purchased tickets earlier, because he pulled two out of his pocket and handed them to the attendant, and they joined the queue. There were only a few people ahead of them—most of the younger crowd preferred rides that offered more thrill—and it only took a few minutes before they were ushered into their car.

As she slid across the seat to make room for Cam, she thought it seemed smaller than she remembered. Or maybe it was that Cam seemed bigger. Or maybe it was just that her entire body was sizzling with awareness. Whatever the reason, Ashley found herself thinking that she should have nixed his suggestion. But the attendant had already secured the door and the wheel had shifted to load the next car.

They were only about halfway to the top, slowly making

their way round as the cars continued to load, but Ashley felt her tummy drop as she looked down at the crowds below. "I never used to be afraid of heights."

"Are you now?"

"I'm not sure," she admitted, but thought it probably wasn't the height so much as the possibility of falling and found herself wondering about maintenance schedules and metal fatigue and other things she'd never considered before. "Do you think this is the same Ferris wheel we used to ride as kids?"

"It might be," he teased. "Why—are you worried that the old wheel should be retired?"

"Maybe."

He chuckled and slid his arm across the back of the seat. "Do you remember how we used to ride it over and over again?"

She nodded.

"The first time I ever kissed you was at the very top."

She remembered that, too, and how she'd thought the drop in her belly was the car moving, until she realized it hadn't moved at all. That was the day she'd fallen in love with him.

"I think the local high school boys still lure their girl-friends onto the ride to steal kisses," she told him.

"I'm sure it's not a strategy exclusive to high school kids," he said, curling his arm around her shoulders.

She eyed him warily. "Don't get any ideas."

"Too late," he said, just before his lips touched hers.

Chapter Eight

She couldn't pull back—there was nowhere to go. She could have pushed him away—but she didn't want to.

His fingers sifted through her hair, cupping the back of her head, changing the angle of the kiss.

Her eyes drifted shut, her lips parted.

His tongue touched hers, lightly, teasingly.

Her stomach dropped, and this time she knew it had nothing to do with the ride and everything to do with the man.

When she was fifteen, she'd thought Cam Turcotte was a great kisser. Of course, her experience at the time had been extremely limited and Cam's technique had definitely been superior to that of any of the other three boys she'd kissed.

They'd both moved on since then, and though Ashley secretly hoped to find something to criticize so she could stop wanting him so damn much, she couldn't deny that his mastery was confirmed. Somehow he just knew how to do everything right. When to advance, when to tease, when to push, when to withdraw.

His lips were soft but firm, his taste both familiar and different, and altogether too tempting. It would be so easy to sink back into his arms, to pretend that the past twelve years had never happened. But no—she wouldn't let herself fall into that trap again. She wouldn't let herself forget anything of their past or delude herself into thinking they could have a future. She was just going to enjoy the moment for what it was.

When he finally drew back, they were both out of breath.

"This is crazy," she told him.

"I know," he agreed, and covered her mouth again.

She met him halfway this time, as eager and desperate as he. Maybe it was crazy, but it was safe. As long as she stayed on the Ferris wheel, there was no danger of this leading anywhere she wasn't ready to go.

Okay, so maybe she was more ready than she wanted to admit, but she still had no intention of succumbing to the desire that raged through her system. Then his hands slid beneath the hem of her top, his wide palms skimmed up her sides, over her ribs. His thumbs brushed over the aching peaks of her breasts through the satin fabric of her bra. She moaned, and he nibbled on her bottom lip while his thumbs moved back and forth over her nipples, the rhythmic motion shooting tingles through her whole body.

She arched against him, wanting to be closer, wanting to feel every inch of his body pressed against every inch of hers. But they were already as close as they could get in the narrow, swaying gondola of the rickety old Ferris wheel.

Her conversation with Paige came back to haunt her. It had been a long time since anyone had made her feel this good. Too long. And when Cam eased away because the attendant had started to unload passengers, she was undeniably disappointed that the ride—and this exquisite stolen moment—was over so soon.

Cam took Ashley's hand to help her out of the car. He'd been tempted to give the Ferris wheel attendant his last two tickets so they could stay on the ride, but then he'd had a better idea.

"Where are we going?"

"The haunted house," he said, thrusting the tickets at the bored attendant outside before he pulled Ashley through the strips of heavy black fabric that guarded the entrance.

It was pitch-black inside, illuminated by black lights that made her white T-shirt glow like a beacon. He took a moment to appreciate the curve of her breasts and the tight buds of her nipples before he led her through the narrow corridors and across shifting floorboards to his destination, ignoring the eerie moans and cackling laughs and other ghostly sounds.

"Maddie and I were in here earlier, and we took a wrong turn—" he pivoted, fervently hoping that he'd remembered correctly and was taking the right wrong turn "—and got shut in…here."

She moved ahead of him, and he guessed she took about three steps before bumping into the wall.

"Is this some kind of closet?"

"I don't know," he said. And he didn't care. All that mattered was that it was dark and private and that he needed to touch her.

He stepped up behind her, sliding his hands around to her front, under her shirt, over her breasts.

She moaned. "Cam."

"I need to touch you, Ash."

"I'm not having sex with you," she told him, though the tremor in her voice suggested her might be able to change her mind if he really wanted to.

"I didn't bring you here to have sex with you," he told her, and bent his head to kiss her throat. "I just want to touch you."

"You are touching me."

"All of you," he said, shifting one hand from her breast to her hips, pulling her more snugly against him. Her buttocks were nestled against his groin and there was no way she couldn't know how hard he was for her, how much he wanted her. But for now, he just wanted to pleasure Ashley.

His hand slipped lower, dipping beneath the waistband of her denim skirt. She sucked in a breath but didn't push him away, so he let his fingers dip lower, into the soft curls. She gasped, but shifted her legs apart a little more. He accepted the unspoken invitation, delving deeper into the slick heat. Her breath was coming faster now, quick shallow gasps that warned him she was on the edge. Just touching her had him trembling on the precipice himself, but he gritted his teeth and concentrated on her pleasure.

"Let go." He whispered the words into her ear.

She shook her head, denying what he wanted, what they both wanted. But he wouldn't be denied. He kept touching her, stroking her, kissing her neck, nibbling on her collarbone. He knew that she was close. Close but still fighting.

He turned her around, so that she was facing him, and captured her mouth with his own. He kissed her, hard and deep, and slipped his hand between her legs again. He swallowed her shocked gasps and blissful moans as he drove her harder and faster toward the edge, until he felt her tense and shudder and finally…release.

She trembled and sagged against him, burying her face in his shirt. He held her close, gently sliding his hand up and down her back and feeling just a little bit smug as he waited for her breathing to even out again.

"Well." She cleared her throat. "That was a new experience for me."

He tipped her chin up and brushed his lips against hers again. "A good one, I hope."

She sighed. "Oh. Yeah."

Though his own body was still aching with arousal, he managed to grin at the lazy satisfaction in her tone. "Imagine what we might accomplish if we ever found ourselves near a bed," he mused.

She pulled away from him, just a little, but the slight withdrawal was enough to make him realize he should have kept that tantalizing thought inside his head. Ashley had made it clear that she didn't want to get involved with him and what had just happened obviously hadn't changed her mind in that regard.

"As…interesting…as this was, it was a mistake," she told him. "And one I'm not going to compound by sleeping with you."

"It didn't feel like a mistake when you were trembling in my arms. It felt incredible. And right."

"Cam—"

Whatever she was going to say, he didn't want to hear it, so he opened the door and stepped back into the main corridor of the haunted house, where the noise and the dark made conversation impossible.

Because her knees were still shaking and her head was still spinning, Ashley took the hand Cam offered to her and followed him into the darkness. She knew they should talk about what had just happened, but she honestly didn't know what to say, how to explain her own outrageously reckless behavior.

She wondered if her conversation with Paige had lessened

her inhibitions, or if Cam's kisses had short-circuited her usually rational brain. There had to be some kind of explanation for what she'd just allowed to happen in a public place. The fact that they'd been behind a closed door and completely in the dark failed to lessen the shock she felt with respect to her own actions.

The intensity of her release was unlike anything she'd ever known. Or maybe it was the illicitness of the situation that had intensified the experience. Or maybe it was just that it had been far too long since she'd let herself go so completely.

And yet, her body still ached and yearned, wanting more.

Wanting Cam.

There, she'd admitted it. At least to herself. She wanted Cam Turcotte as much now as she'd wanted him when she was in high school. But she was an adult now, a grown woman, not an idealistic girl. A woman who had experienced love and heartbreak and who wasn't prepared to walk down that path again.

Paige had been right about the fact that Ashley didn't have sex for fun, and that was why she couldn't succumb to the desire that was coursing through her body. She didn't dare. Because she knew she would never be able to share her body with Cam without letting him into her heart, and she absolutely was not going to fall in love with him again.

No, she had plans for her life, and Cam Turcotte didn't fit anywhere in those plans.

He didn't say anything more as he led her across the still-crowded parking lot to his car. It obviously wasn't as late as she'd thought, but she was more than ready to head home, to say good-night and goodbye to Cam and crawl into bed alone.

Liar.

She scowled at the mocking voice inside her head.

Okay, so what she really wanted was to drag Cam into the

house with her and jump him. Because while her body was still humming with pleasure, she didn't feel completely fulfilled. She wanted him inside of her, moving with her, stoking the long-dormant fire that was suddenly roaring through her body.

I'm not having sex with you, she'd said, and she'd meant those words when she said them. Now, however, she wasn't feeling quite so adamant. Or maybe she was just feeling a little guilty that he had taken care of her needs and she'd done nothing for him.

Of course, he hadn't asked for or demanded anything from her. He never had. The first time they'd ever made love had been on her initiative and, even then, even when he'd had more enthusiasm than finesse, he'd tried to ensure she got some pleasure out of the experience.

While sex had never been an earth-shattering experience for her as a teenager, she'd loved Cam wholeheartedly and un-ashamedly and she'd enjoyed the closeness of being with him. It was a long time after he left before she'd dated anyone else, and longer still before she'd been willing to open up her heart again. But she'd never loved anyone else with the same unrestrained passion; she'd never loved anyone else as much as she'd loved Cam.

And that was precisely why getting involved with him again was a very bad idea.

He pulled into her driveway and cut the engine.

She wanted to protest that he didn't need to walk her to the door, but she knew he wouldn't listen. And maybe she needed to say good-night to him on the doorstep, to prove to herself that she was capable of sending him away even when she wanted to drag him inside.

He came around to her side and walked beside her up to the porch.

"You forgot to leave a light on," he noted.

"I do it all the time," she admitted, sliding her key into the lock. "Unless it's dark when I leave, I don't think about it."

"Then you should have sensor lights that come on automatically when you move in front of them."

She pushed the door open and hit the switch on the inside wall, spilling light onto the porch. "I'm a big girl, and this is a safe neighborhood."

"You're a single woman living alone. There's no harm in being cautious."

"I am cautious," she told him, then proved it by slipping inside before she could renege on her promise to herself that she wasn't going to invite him to come in.

"Lock the door," she heard him call from the other side.

She slid the deadbolt into place, and watched through the sidelight as he walked back to his car and drove away.

Cam slept like hell.

Or maybe it was more accurate to say that he didn't sleep at all. And when he finally caught a glimpse of the sun beginning to peek over the horizon, he gave up even pretending.

It was his own fault, he knew that. Just as he knew that he could take care of the ache in his body easily enough. But he also knew that any satisfaction would be both temporary and superficial. He wanted more than a physical release—he wanted Ashley. He wanted her naked body beneath him, her soft breasts pressed against his chest, her long legs wrapped around his hips—

He shoved the image out of his mind as he pushed back the tangled covers.

He needed a shower. A very cold shower.

And then he needed a plan.

Because he knew better than to think he'd made any

progress with Ashley last night. Sure, it might have seemed like they were on the same wavelength while they were in the haunted house, but he knew that she would do some serious backtracking in the light of day. Hell, she'd started backtracking even before they got in his car to drive home.

He firmly believed that the sizzling sexual attraction between them was proof that the chemistry had never died, but he knew that she still needed some convincing.

He turned off the shower and yanked a towel from the bar. It was early yet, but he would grab a cup of coffee on the way to his parents' house to pick up Maddie—maybe get there in time for some of his mother's buttermilk pancakes—then take his daughter to her ballet class and, afterward, for a quick trip to the hardware store.

Ashley was working at the computer late Saturday morning when the doorbell rang. She was tempted to ignore the summons. She wasn't expecting any company and, as a result of having gotten very little sleep the night before, she wasn't in the mood to chat with anyone selling anything.

But the bell rang again, as if whoever was on the other side knew she was home, so she finally pushed away from the desk.

Peeking through the sidelight and finding Cam on her porch only made her more wary. After what had happened between them the night before, she needed some time to figure out how to deal with him, and how to deal with her own mixed-up feelings.

How the heck was she supposed to carry on a conversation with the man who had taken her to heights of pleasure she hadn't experienced in a very long time? Especially when her hormones were already revving in anticipation of a return trip.

She wanted to pretend that last night had never happened,

but the heat in his eyes as they slowly skimmed over every inch of her body made that impossible.

"What are you doing here?" she asked.

"I need access to your electrical panel."

She lifted a brow. "That's one I haven't heard before."

He grinned. "It's not a secret male code, just a precaution to ensure that I don't get electrocuted while installing your new lights."

"I don't need new lights. And I thought you were a doctor, not a handyman."

"Actually, I'm a doctor who happens to be very handy," he told her. "And I picked up some motion sensor lights for you at the hardware store this morning."

"I don't mean to sound ungrateful," she said, all too aware that was precisely how she sounded, "but I didn't ask you to pick up any lights for me."

"I didn't do it for you, I did it for me."

She folded her arms across her chest. "How does putting up new lights for me benefit you?"

"It will ensure I worry less about you coming home after dark."

"There's no reason for you to worry," she insisted.

"I'm sure that's true, but I'll worry, anyway. So letting me put up these lights would be doing me a big favor."

"That is the most ridiculous argument I've ever heard."

"But creative."

Her lips curved. "I'll give you that."

"So—" he prompted. "Your electrical panel?"

"It's in the basement." She stepped away from the door so that he could enter.

"Was I interrupting something?" he asked, gesturing to the computer desk and the pile of notes she'd printed.

"Just lesson planning. We're studying the growth cycle of

the pumpkin this week in preparation for Halloween at the end of the month, and I was hoping to find some kind of art project that would reinforce the lesson for the kids."

"Don't you just teach the same stuff year after year?"

"I have to cover the same basic curriculum," she admitted, leading him down into the basement. "But I like to implement some new projects or approach the topics from different angles to keep the subjects fresh and interesting."

"I assume that's fresh and interesting for you, since you don't have the same group of kids for more than one year."

She smiled. "Yes, it's for me. I don't ever want to become one of those teachers who bores her students."

"I don't think there's any danger of that," Cam told her. "Maddie is always talking about school and she's always enthusiastic."

"Where is Maddie today?" she asked.

"She went back to my mom's after her ballet class. Whenever it comes to a choice between the hardware store with Daddy or the toy store with Grandma, she abandons me without a backward glance."

Ashley smiled as she gestured to the electrical panel. "Everything's labeled, so it shouldn't be too difficult to find the breakers you need to shut off."

He opened the panel, scanned the tags, flipped some switches. "That's it?"

"For now," he said, closing the panel door. "They'll need to be turned back on again when I'm done."

She nodded and followed him back up the stairs.

It didn't take long for Cam to install the lights. At least, it seemed to Ashley that not very much time had passed before he was back at the door to turn the breaker on again. She was making herself a sandwich and though she still thought it was smart to keep her distance from Cam, it seemed impolite not to offer him some lunch in exchange for the lights.

But if she felt awkward inviting him to stay for a sandwich, it was nothing compared to the discomfort she felt when he picked up the clinic brochure she'd inadvertently left on the counter.

She was dishing up potato salad alongside the sandwiches when she saw him reach for the pamphlet, the bold letters practically jumping off of the front: **PINEHURST ASSISTED REPRODUCTION CLINIC**

Cam looked at the cover, where the date and time of an appointment were noted, then at Ashley. She'd told him about the endometriosis and her participation in the clinical trial, so he didn't understand why she would have an appointment at PARC. Unless—

"Are you pregnant?" he asked her.

Her cheeks flushed and she snatched the pamphlet from his hand. "No."

He hadn't realized he was holding his breath in anticipation of her response until the air whooshed out of his lungs again.

Not pregnant.

That was good, because pregnant was definitely more of a complication than he was ready to handle at the beginning of a relationship—assuming that he and Ashley were at the beginning stages of a relationship. But if she wasn't pregnant—

"Then why do you have an appointment at PARC?"

"I'm keeping my options open."

"Options," he echoed, still uncomprehending.

"I want to have a baby, a family," she said, as if that should have been obvious. "I thought I was on track with Trevor, but obviously that train got derailed. Now I'm looking at some alternatives."

"Don't you think this…alternative…is a little extreme? You're only twenty-nine—"

"And I have endometriosis," she reminded him. "Before I started the drug trial, my specialist recommended radical surgery."

"A complete hysterectomy," he guessed.

She nodded, tears filling her eyes. For a woman who loved children as much as Ashley, that course of action would be devastating.

"Is the Fedentropin helping?" he asked her.

"It's bought me time, but it's not a cure."

Which he knew, of course. After she'd first mentioned the drug to him, he'd done some research. Because the drug was still in the trial phase, a lot of information was restricted, but he had learned that the medication was targeted specifically at women for whom more traditional treatments—usually birth control pills—were unsuccessful.

"But having a baby without a father—"

"Don't lecture me on the difficulties of being a single parent," she warned him.

"I wasn't going to lecture," he denied. "I was just going to suggest that you reconsider all of your options before you pursue artificial methods of conception."

"I have considered all of my options and I'm not rushing into anything. I'm only going to the clinic to get the information I need before making any final decision." She nudged his plate closer. "Now eat."

"You're always so gracious when we sit down at a table together."

"Must be your innate charm that brings out the best in me."

He picked up his fork and speared a chunk of potato. Ashley took a bite of her sandwich, clearly signaling that the conversation was at an end.

But Cam couldn't stop thinking about what she'd revealed. He wasn't surprised that she wanted a child, but he did wonder how far she was willing to go to get what she wanted—and if she was considering that another one of her options might be to find a ready-made family in need of a mother.

He munched on his sandwich and wondered if he'd completely misread the situation with her. Had he made a mistake in believing that he and Ashley were rekindling their romance? Was it possible that she didn't have any interest in a relationship with him and only wanted to be a mother to a little girl who desperately needed one?

It would be the irony of all ironies. The woman he'd married didn't want to have anything to do with her child, and now he was halfway in love with a woman who might only want to be with him because of his daughter.

Chapter Nine

Ashley always looked forward to Sunday brunch with her sister and her cousin. For the past several years, they'd met once a month at Michelynne's Café in the village to eat and chat and have what they fondly referred to as their girl time. Ashley had worried, after Megan and Gage got married, that her sister might start to skip out on their ritual gathering, but she was pleased that the tradition continued to endure.

Sometimes they celebrated, sometimes they commiserated, but always they supported one another unconditionally. So when Ashley announced that her appointment at the clinic hadn't gone quite as she'd hoped, that the doctor she'd met with had insisted she wait six months before pursuing intrauterine insemination, she was surprised by their responses.

"Six months doesn't seem unreasonable," Paige said.

"Six months is half a year—and two-thirds the term of a normal pregnancy," Ashley felt compelled to point out.

"But you're young," Megan said.

"I'm almost thirty," she said, and the knowledge of that birthday on the horizon taunted her. She'd had a plan for her life, and she'd expected to be a wife and a mother long before now.

"You just turned twenty-nine," her sister reminded her.

"And a lot of women today don't even think about having babies until they're in their forties," Paige added.

Ashley shook her head. "I don't believe this. I thought you would be on my side."

"We are on your side," her recently impregnated sister insisted.

"We just think you should take some time to be sure that this is what you want, that this isn't an impulse," her cousin added.

"When have I ever done anything impulsive?"

"Letting CBB put a ring on your finger after you'd been dating only a few months was pretty impulsive."

"Okay—so I made one mistake."

"The mistake wasn't yours, it was his," Paige said loyally. "But I still think, if you really want to have a baby, it should be with someone you care about—not a number and a description in a catalog."

"Since there's no one in my life who fits that criteria, I'll go with the catalog."

Megan speared a slice of peach with her fork. "What about Cam?"

"What about Cam?" Paige echoed, obviously intrigued by the possibility.

"I had a doctor's appointment last week," Megan said, "and ran into Cam at the office, and we chatted for a few minutes."

"And?" Paige prompted.

"And I got to thinking that there were still sparks between Cam and Ashley at the reunion, and that it might not take much to fan those sparks into flame."

"I didn't see them at the reunion," Paige admitted. "But I saw the way he was looking at her at the fair. He was making cow eyes at her over the cows."

Megan snickered.

"Yeah," Ashley said. "His feelings were so deep, he fell in love with someone else as soon as he left Pinehurst."

"I don't think that's quite how it happened," Megan chided gently.

Ashley shrugged. "It doesn't matter. Cam and I were over a long time ago."

"If that was true, you wouldn't be so determined to avoid the man who could give you everything you want."

"I don't want anything from Cam Turcotte."

"Then someone should call a doctor, because you obviously no longer have a pulse," Paige said. "And hey—Cam is a doctor, so maybe he can jump-start your heart."

"I'm glad you both find this situation so amusing," Ashley said.

"Only because you're so obviously in denial about your feelings for the man," her sister said.

Ashley picked up her cup and sipped her cappuccino. She'd already said more than she'd ever intended to say on the subject of Cam Turcotte.

"Think about it," Paige urged. "If you let Cam knock you up, at least then you'd know something about the father of your baby."

"Aside from a basic physical description and necessary medical information, I don't want to know anything about the father of my baby. That's why I decided to go through the clinic."

"Except that now you have to wait six months."

Six months seemed like an eternity when she'd wanted a baby for so long already, but she really didn't see that she had any other option.

"I'll bet you could have Cam in your bed in six weeks," Megan said.

"Six days," Paige interjected.

"Except that I don't want Cam in my bed."

"I'm starting to seriously wonder about your pulse," her cousin muttered.

"Because you're not attracted to him anymore?" Megan asked, ignoring Paige's comment. "Or because you *are?*"

Ashley frowned. "That's an odd question."

"Maybe, but I know how your mind works, and I know that, emotionally, you're still reeling from Trevor's betrayal, so the last thing you want is to stir up feelings for someone else."

Apparently Megan did know how Ashley's mind worked, and her sister's insight was more than a little unnerving. "Since when did you become such an expert on the human heart?" she grumbled.

"Since I was lucky enough to fall in love. I never imagined I could feel anything like what I feel for Gage, and I only want the same thing for you."

"I appreciate your concern," Ashley said. "And while there was a time when I wanted exactly what you have with Gage— and when I was engaged to Trevor, I thought I'd found it— I've since realized that not everyone finds his or her soul mate."

"You're certainly not going to find him if you keep closing the doors that are opened to you."

"Even if I was still attracted to Cam—and okay, I do have a pulse—I'm not foolish enough to get involved with a man who's already broken my heart. Besides, he has an ex-wife and a child, and that's more baggage than I'm willing to carry."

"An ex-wife who lives in another country and an absolutely adorable little girl," Megan clarified.

"Exactly how long were you chatting with him?"

Megan looked her in the eyes. "Long enough to figure out that the man still has a thing for my big sister."

Ashley was less concerned about Cam's feelings than her own, and she looked away before Megan could guess that her big sister still had a thing for the sexy doctor, too.

Nearly a week after he'd found out about Ashley's appointment at PARC, Cameron couldn't stop thinking about their conversation. He knew she would be a wonderful mother, so it wasn't her desire to have a child that unnerved him but her willingness to be injected by some anonymous donor in order to make it happen.

As a doctor, he had counseled patients with respect to all kinds of reproductive options. He had never recommended artificial insemination to a single woman under the age of thirty and he didn't understand why Ashley would choose that course.

But the more he thought about it, the more he thought that they each might be able to get what they wanted from the other. Of course, he first had to find a way to convince Ashley of that.

When he went to pick Maddie up from school the following Wednesday, he decided to put his plan into action. Leaving his daughter playing hopscotch with her friends, he dropped in to Ashley's classroom.

"How do you feel about dinner Saturday night?" he asked her.

"Actually, I'm in favor of dinner every night," she said.

"I meant dinner with me," he clarified.

She hesitated. "And Maddie?"

He shook his head. "Just the two of us, maybe somewhere with actual tablecloths and wine and candlelight."

"Sounds like a date," she said cautiously.

"That's the general idea," he agreed.

"And, for all the reasons we discussed weeks ago, not a good one."

"Forget about Maddie for a minute," he told her, even though he wondered if she could. "This is about us and whether or not you want to have dinner with me."

"I want to," she admitted, albeit with apparent reluctance.

"So why don't we discuss all the reasons you think it's a bad idea on Saturday night?"

Her lips curved, just a little, drawing his attention to that temptingly luscious mouth, stirring erotic memories of the kisses they'd recently shared, and churning up desires that were already almost out of control.

"What time are you suggesting that we have this discussion?" she asked.

"How about seven?"

"That could work," she finally agreed.

He took a step backward, determined to make his escape before she changed her mind. "Good. I'll see you then."

Ashley knew that going on a date with Cam was a bad idea. She knew it when he'd asked and when she'd agreed, but the sensible part of her had temporarily been overpowered by the sexually deprived part. Because while she'd been saying "yes, I'll have dinner with you" what she'd really been thinking was "yes, I want to get naked with you."

It was Megan's fault. She was the one who'd planted the idea of having sex with Cam in Ashley's mind. Okay, maybe the idea had already taken root, but both Megan and Paige had nurtured it so that suddenly all Ashley could think about was having sex with Cam. And as she was getting ready for her date, she did so knowing that she was probably going to be getting naked with Cam before the night was over.

She took a leisurely shower, rubbing scented lotion on her

skin when she was done, searching out her sexiest lingerie. The dress was a recent purchase from Chaundra's Boutique. She'd seen it on display in the window and knew she had to buy it, even if she'd wondered if she'd ever have occasion to wear it. As she wriggled into it, she was grateful she'd gone with her instincts because if there was ever a dress made to entice, it was this one that molded to every curve of her body like a lover's hands.

She'd never before set out to seduce a man. The fact that she was doing so now was both exciting and terrifying. The fact that the man was Cam was even more exciting and terrifying.

She gave a lot of thought to setting the scene. She straightened the bottles and pictures on her dresser, but she didn't set candles around the room or program soft music. She wanted cozy, not romantic. Nothing that would give him the impression that having sex was about anything more than sex.

She put fresh sheets on the bed, fluffed the pillows, then sank onto the edge of the mattress and wondered—for about the hundredth time—*can I really go through with this?*

Did she really believe she could have sex with Cam and not want more? And how much more did she want? Was she looking for a relationship with him—or did she want him to father her child?

And how could she explain to him what she wanted when she wasn't even sure herself?

Well, he knew she wanted a baby. But she'd let him believe that she wasn't in any big hurry to get pregnant and that she would be making an appointment at the clinic when she was ready. And, all things considered, that was still probably the best plan.

Except that the more she thought about having Cam's baby, the more she wanted Cam's baby, and that realization gave her pause.

Before she left the bedroom, she automatically pulled open the drawer of her nightstand, checking for the condoms she kept there. Use of birth control was a habit that she'd never disregarded, not even—thank goodness—with her cheating bastard ex-fiancé. Checking that she was prepared was simply another deeply ingrained habit, but one that introduced new doubts and questions.

She didn't think Cam slept around. She certainly hadn't heard any rumors of him being involved with anyone since he'd come back to Pinehurst. On the other hand, the lack of information might just be a testament to his discretion and not his morals. Although she honestly doubted that he'd have either the opportunity or energy for an affair with a young daughter at home.

But regardless of what she wanted to believe, the fact was, she really didn't know Cam any better than any man she might meet in a bar. And there was no way she would invite a stranger back to her home, to her bed, without gleaning some pertinent personal information about him first.

Could she trust that what she believed about Cam was true?

And could she trust that she was strong enough to share her body without giving him more?

When he'd left Pinehurst a dozen years earlier, he'd taken a good chunk of her seventeen-year-old heart and all of her silly, romantic dreams with him. Now that he was back, she knew she was in danger of falling into the same trap, of letting herself hope and yearn for something that could never be.

One of the reasons she'd decided to go the sperm bank route was that she hadn't found herself attracted to any man since she'd ended her engagement. She knew a lot of good-looking men, men with whom she'd flirted and laughed easily in the past. But Trevor's betrayal had cut deep, undermining both her self-confidence and faith in her own judgment.

If the man who'd claimed to love her and want a family with her could cheat on her even before the wedding, how was she ever supposed to trust anyone else? How could she know that the next guy she met and let herself care about wouldn't do exactly the same thing? How could she know that Cam wouldn't?

And the truth was, she didn't know. Except that she did trust Cam because he'd always been brutally honest with her. If he lost interest in her, he would tell her. He would end their relationship before he moved on, and if he broke her heart in the process, at least he wouldn't cheat on her.

She shook her head, pushing those thoughts aside. He wouldn't break her heart—not this time. Because this time, her decision to get involved with him had nothing to do with her heart. She wouldn't let it.

And yet there was a part of her that couldn't help but wonder if it wasn't already too late. If she was planning to bring Cam back here because she did care about him, because the idea of having *his* baby was one that she'd never completely relinquished.

She shook her head, reminding herself that she didn't want anything from Cam Turcotte except a single night of passion. She would never again make the mistake of loving him.

Considering Ashley's less-than-enthusiastic response when he'd invited her on this date, Cam didn't have high expectations when he went to pick her up Saturday night. Still, he figured her agreement, however reluctant, was the first step in the right direction. He knew exactly what he wanted—he'd figured that out even before he'd made the decision to move back to Pinehurst, in the moment that he'd seen her across the room at their high school reunion. He wanted Ashley.

Maybe the realization shouldn't have surprised him. It

seemed that, for as far back as he could remember, he'd wanted Ashley. There was something about her—her sweetness and gentleness and warmth—that made him feel as if he was the luckiest guy in the world when he was with her.

And he'd made the biggest mistake in his life when he'd walked away from her.

He thought about what his mother had told him, and about the role his father's warnings had played in his decision to go away to school, to leave Ashley behind. He didn't doubt his father's advice had been a factor, because he'd always listened to and respected his parents' opinions. But ultimately the final decision had been his, and the biggest factor in that decision had been his own fear that he loved her too much.

He'd been nineteen years old, with his whole life ahead of him. He'd had places he wanted to go, things he wanted to see and do, and Ashley didn't. Sure, she'd had plans for her life, but they were simple plans. Her career ambition was to be a first-grade teacher. Her personal goal was to get married and raise a family in Pinehurst. And when she talked to Cameron about her plans, it was all too easy to envision himself in the role of her husband, the father of her children, and it terrified him.

Knowing how she'd dreamed of a family, it seemed unbelievable to him that she hadn't married and had half a dozen children in the years he'd been gone. Unbelievable and unbelievably lucky for him.

He knew she wasn't ready to jump back into a relationship with him. After the way he'd walked out on her, she was understandably wary. He still wasn't sure if Maddie's obvious need for a mother figure made her even more so, or if his little girl was the only reason she was even giving him the time of day.

He knew she already loved his daughter. The question was, could she love him? Could she forgive the mistakes he'd made in the past and give him another chance?

That she'd agreed to this date tonight gave him hope that maybe she could.

And when she opened the door to greet him, he suddenly found himself hoping for a whole lot more.

He'd always known she was beautiful. The flawless ivory skin, stunning violet eyes and soft, kissable lips meant that she could be wearing ratty old jeans and an oversized shirt with her hair in a ponytail and she'd look beautiful. Tonight, wearing a siren-red dress and mile-high heels and the same scent that never failed to stir his fantasies, she completely took his breath away.

He closed his mouth, because he was seriously afraid he might drool. The sparkle in her eyes and the hint of a smile on her glossy lips warned that she knew exactly the image she presented and that she'd intended to bring him to his knees.

He was already halfway there, more than ready to beg.

The sound of the deadbolt clicking into place as she turned her key in the lock finally registered through the fog that had taken over his brain and propelled him into action. He took her hand and led her to his SUV.

"A friend of mine recommended a new place that recently opened up in downtown Syracuse, if you don't mind the drive."

"I don't mind," she said.

She stepped up onto the running board and slid onto the passenger seat, and as she did, the skirt of her dress slid up a few more tantalizing inches.

She'd always had incredible legs, and in that dress and those shoes, they were shown to full advantage. Long and lean and tanned and bare.

He forced his tongue back into his mouth and closed the door. It was going to be a hell of a long ride to Syracuse—and an uncomfortable one.

"You said you wanted to discuss all the reasons that this

date was a bad idea," he suddenly remembered, thinking that if he was focused on conversation, it would be a lot more difficult to imagine various and creative ways to get her out of that body-hugging dress.

"I changed my mind."

He glanced over at her. "You no longer think this is a bad idea?"

"I'm *sure* it's a bad idea," she told him. "But I've decided to go with it for tonight anyway."

There was something in her tone, something that tempted him to think that she was willing to go with it further than dinner. Or maybe he was letting his own desires influence his interpretation of her words.

One step at a time, he reminded his overly enthusiastic hormones.

She had agreed to a date, which he figured gave him permission to kiss her good night, but he wasn't going to think any further ahead than that.

And first, they had to get through dinner.

The little Italian bistro was both cozy and romantic and, as Cam had promised, there were neatly pressed cloths on the tables, candles flickering and wineglasses waiting to be filled.

The maître d' led them to a table for two tucked away in a corner, presented them with their menus, and wished them "buona sera."

Their waiter appeared almost immediately with a basket of warm bread, a pot of whipped butter and a pitcher of water. He announced the specials of the day—which included chicken, pasta and fish—and recommended wine pairings for each.

Ashley opted for the pasta, Cam chose the chicken and they both decided on wine.

Although the service was prompt, the atmosphere was relaxed and they chatted casually while they ate, first nibbling on the warm bread, then their salads and finally the main courses when they were delivered.

Ashley finished her second glass of wine before her tortellini, but declined Cam's offer of a third. The two glasses were hopefully enough to lessen her inhibitions about getting naked with Cam, but not so much that he would have qualms about taking advantage of a woman in a less-than-sober state.

There were still a few pasta crowns on her plate when she pushed it aside, but she was afraid that she would be testing the seams in her new dress if she finished them.

The busboy immediately whisked away their dinner plates and the waiter followed on his heels to deliver the dessert menu.

Cam opened the small leather folder.

"Amaretto cheesecake, cannoli, gelato, tiramisu." He read through the offerings, trying to tempt her.

She shook her head regretfully. "Not in this dress."

His eyes dropped, skimming over shoulders that were left bare by the halter-style top before dipping lower to follow the plunging neckline to the curve of her breasts. She felt the warmth of his gaze like a caress, and her nipples puckered instinctively. The flare of heat in his eyes warned that her body's response had not gone unnoticed, nor unappreciated.

His eyes shifted to hers again, his lips curved. "Did I mention that I like the dress?"

She swallowed. "Not in so many words."

He leaned closer and dropped his voice. "Did I mention that I'd really like to get you out of that dress?"

"Not in so many words," she said again.

"Do you still think being here with me tonight was a bad idea?" he asked, his voice thick with desire, his eyes dark with promise.

Ashley knew that if she told him yes, if she gave any hint that she regretted the impulse that had led her to accept his invitation, he would back off, he would give her space. But she didn't want space—she wanted Cam.

"I think," she said, keeping her gaze steady on his, "that being here with you might only be the first of several bad ideas we try tonight."

He closed the menu.

The waiter, obviously watching for his cue, immediately appeared. "Dessert, sir?"

Cam shook his head, his eyes never leaving her face. "Just the check, please."

And the tingles that had started low in her belly began to spread to her fingertips and her toes and all the erogenous zones in between.

He took care of the bill then pushed back his chair and offered her his hand. His grip was warm and strong, and Ashley's knees trembled as she thought of those hands moving over her body, touching her, teasing her, pleasing her.

She was so caught up in these erotic thoughts that she didn't even notice the other man until he stepped directly in her path.

"Hello, Ashley."

Her mood plummeted, and she silently cursed her ex-fiancé for killing the mood as she forced a smile to her lips. "Trevor. Hi."

Then Cam's hand squeezed hers, questioning, and the tingles surged through her blood again. And she knew that Trevor couldn't ruin anything else for her—and especially not her plans to be with Cam tonight. So she smiled back at her date, reassuring.

"I just finished dinner with a colleague," Trevor said. "But she had to run, so why don't you and your…friend…join me for coffee?"

If he was hinting for an introduction, he was going to be disappointed. Ashley had no intention of tainting her evening with Cam by bringing him into this confrontation. Instead, she lifted a brow and asked, "Is that the colleague you're currently sleeping with? Or have you made your way through the entire office staff already and moved on?"

Trevor's face flushed. "Really, Ashley, there's no need to be snide."

"I'd say there's every reason, except the truth is, I really don't give a damn who you're screwing anymore."

"I thought—I'd hoped—that we could have a rational discussion about our relationship, but obviously you're still hurting."

He stepped back so she could pass, but Ashley couldn't let him have the last word. "We don't have a relationship and I'm not still hurting, I'm simply over you. Completely."

She started to walk away then, but her hand was still linked with Cam's and he wasn't quite ready to go.

"I wasn't sure I'd ever have the opportunity to meet Ashley's ex-fiancé," Cam said to Trevor. "But I'm glad we saw you here tonight because I really wanted to thank you."

Trevor scowled. "Why are you thanking me?"

"Because you screwed up with the most amazing woman you'll ever know and she's going home with me tonight."

Ashley didn't bother to hide her smile as she and Cam finally exited the restaurant. "I can't believe you said that to him, but it was a great line."

"It was petty and mean, but I couldn't resist."

"It was also wrong," she informed him.

"You're not going home with me tonight?" he guessed, opening the door of his SUV for her.

She heard the disappointment in his voice and felt a surge of purely female satisfaction. Because she knew—despite her blatant invitation in the restaurant—that Cam wouldn't push her for more than she was ready to give. And maybe there was a part of her that was tempted to tease him a little more, but the temptation wasn't nearly as strong as the desire that was churning in her veins.

"No." She leaned in to kiss him, slow and deep. "You're coming home with me."

Chapter Ten

Cam blatantly disregarded the speed limit on the trip back to Pinehurst, anxious to get Ashley home before she changed her mind and reneged on her offer.

"Whose idea was it to go all the way to Syracuse for dinner anyway?" he grumbled, when he finally turned onto Chetwood Street.

Ashley laughed. "It was your idea. And it was a good one. Dinner was fabulous."

"There are good restaurants in Pinehurst."

"Maybe we'll try one of those next time."

He pulled into her driveway, shut off the engine. "Does that mean there's going to be a next time?"

She lifted one shoulder. "That depends on how the rest of the night goes."

He helped her out of the SUV and walked her to the door. "Is that a challenge?"

She turned her key in the lock before pivoting to face him. "Are you up to it?"

He pressed against her, reassuring her that he was very definitely up for the challenge.

Ashley responded by sliding her hands up his chest, linking them behind his head and pulling his mouth down to hers. She teased him with her lips and her tongue, with the fingertips that stroked the back of his neck, with the breasts that rubbed against his chest, until he was tempted to take her right here and now, against her front door, with her skirt hiked up around her hips and her legs locked around him.

The mental image, enticing though it was, forced him to take a step back.

"Give me five minutes," he told her.

She lifted her brows. "I was hoping it would take a little longer than that."

He chuckled. "I'm going to park my car in my own driveway so we don't give the neighbors reason to talk. And then—" he brushed his lips against hers "—we will have all night."

It was a tantalizing promise that made her heart pound and her knees weak, but Ashley wasn't looking for promises. She wasn't looking for anything more than this one night, even if she had slipped and mentioned the possibility of a next time. But more than one date constituted dating, and dating implied a relationship, and Ashley didn't want a relationship. She only wanted to ride the tide of euphoric lust that seemed to wash over her whenever she was with Cam.

The intensity of the desire was both reassuring and unnerving. Reassuring because it had been so long since she'd wanted to be with any man. And unnerving because she'd never wanted any other man as much as she wanted Cam.

When she'd met Trevor, when she'd decided to marry him, it hadn't bothered her that she didn't feel the same feverish excitement she'd felt with Cam. Because she'd attributed the intensity of her feelings for Cam to the hormones of youth and, by the time she met Trevor, she'd grown up. She didn't want or expect to be swept away by desire.

And yet, the most casual brush of Cam's hand against her arm had her feeling that same euphoric anticipation, and just the touch of his lips to hers inspired the same unrestrained eagerness to tear off his clothes and join their bodies together.

She stood at the door, watching for him. Waiting. Wanting.

And then he was there, and she was in his arms.

He flipped the lock as he pressed her back against the door. His mouth descended on hers again, his tongue sliding between her lips, teasing, tempting. She wrapped her arms around his neck, pressed her body closer. Her breasts rubbed against the solid wall of his chest, her nipples pebbling. She shifted her hips, angling them to meet his, and felt the hard press of his erection against the throbbing ache between her thighs. Fireworks erupted inside of her, little bursts of pleasure that left her gasping with shocked delight even as her body ached for more. So much more.

As if in response to her unspoken demand, his hands curled over the curve of her bottom, lifting her off the ground to press her more intimately against him.

Heat rushed through her veins, lust quivered in her belly. She felt hot and willful and reckless, and she didn't care. She only wanted.

Ashley's legs circled around his waist, anchoring her pelvis against his, and Cam realized that it was possible for the human body to go from zero to sixty in point-two seconds. And then she began rocking her hips, and the erotic motion threatened the already tenuous grip that Cam had on his self-control.

"If we don't find a bed soon, it's going to be too late," he warned her.

"Upstairs. First door on the left."

He pushed open the door but didn't bother searching for the lights. He let his instincts—and the thin sliver of moonlight that slanted through the open blinds—guide him.

Her bed was only a double, which might have disappointed any other man who was used to sleeping in a king. But it was Ashley's bedroom and he didn't plan on getting much sleep—two factors that more than made up for the narrowness of the mattress.

He laid her on the bed and sank down with her.

"I can't believe how much I want you," he admitted. "How much I've wanted you since I first saw you again at the reunion."

"I didn't invite you up here for conversation," she told him.

"And I'm grateful for that," he said. "But I can't help but wonder what changed your mind?"

She tugged his shirt out of his pants. "Do you really want to talk about this now?"

"No," he admitted, his breathing more than a little strained. "But something tells me that we should."

Instead, she leaned closer to nibble on his earlobe and whisper a very erotic suggestion to him. And all thought and reason drained out of his head along with the blood that surged quickly south.

He grasped the hem of her skirt and slid it upward, his hands guiding it over the curve of her thighs, her hips, her waist, her breasts. He stopped kissing her only long enough to tug the garment over her head and toss it aside.

He couldn't see much more than shadows, and he wanted to see her, needed to see her. So he reached for the lamp beside the bed and switched it on. Soft light spilled out from beneath the shade, illuminating her. And for the second time that night, just looking at her took his breath away.

He laid her back on the bed and took a moment simply to absorb the sight of her. From the golden hair splayed over the chocolate-brown pillowcase, to the graceful slope of her shoulders, the swell of her breasts covered in sexy black lace, and the indent of her narrow waist. From the subtle flare of her hips to a triangle of matching black lace at the apex of her thighs, and down the long, lean legs to sexy little toes.

She'd been too thin as a teenager, her curves barely existent. She was definitely a woman now, a little softer around the edges, her curves a little fuller, and his desire for her now even stronger.

He eased her over onto her stomach.

"What are you…." The indignant question faded on a sigh as his lips touched the base of her spine. "Oh."

He finished kissing each of the five freckles in turn.

"I had to make sure they were still there," he told her, and rolled her onto her back again.

"I'd forgotten about them," she admitted.

"I couldn't forget them…or you." He touched his lips to hers. "You were—and are—perfect."

Her lips curved, just a little. "And you're still dressed."

He stripped away his shirt and pants and socks, but kept his briefs on for the moment. As he knelt over her on the bed again, he had a sudden, disconcerting thought.

"I wasn't planning for this to happen tonight," he admitted. "And I stopped carrying condoms in my wallet a long time ago."

"I take care of myself," she assured him.

"You're on the Pill?"

He saw a flicker of something in her eyes, then she quickly looked away. Cam wasn't sure what to make of her lack of response, but then she drew his head back down to her.

"Don't worry," she said, and kissed him—long and slow and deep.

He sank down onto the bed with her. She was soft and warm and willing, and he wanted nothing else as much as he wanted to sink into the welcoming heat of her body. His body urged him on, clamoring for release of the tension that had been building for days, weeks, months. A release that only she could give him.

But she deserved better than that. Considering their history, she deserved a lot better. He'd loved her when he was a boy, but he hadn't been careful with her. He'd hurt her, and that was something he'd never wanted to do. And though he knew there was no way to make up for what had been done in the past, he could at least make sure this experience was a good one for her.

So he took his time, touching her slowly, carefully. His fingertips danced gently over her skin, tracing the scalloped cups of her bra, stroking the sides of her torso, the lace edge of her panties, the soft insides of her thighs. Then his lips followed a similar path, lingering here and there, letting her soft sighs and moans guide him.

He unhooked the clasp at her back and slowly pulled her bra off. As the lacy fabric slid across her breasts, over her nipples, her breath caught, her eyes darkened.

"Cam." It wasn't just his name, it was a plea.

"This is the first time we've actually made love in a bed. I don't want to rush it."

"I have no objection to rushing…the first time," she told him.

He chuckled. "I'll bet I can change your mind about that."

"Do you think you could forget about my mind and focus on my body?"

"Believe me, I'm focused," he told her, and dropped his head to take a turgid nipple in his mouth.

She arched instinctively, urging him to take more, to suckle deeper, and moaned when he accepted her invitation.

"Oh…my…oh…Cam."

He moved to the other breast, gave it the same thorough attention until she was squirming and panting.

"Cam, please."

"Tell me what you want."

She didn't hesitate to respond. "You. Inside of me. Please."

He nibbled gently on her bottom lip, teasing. "I don't remember you being quite so impatient."

"I don't remember ever wanting anyone as much as I want you right now," she admitted breathlessly.

It was gratifying to know that she felt the same way he did, but he continued his leisurely exploration, determined to show her how very much he wanted, and how much he wanted to please her.

His lips trailed down her throat, skimmed between her breasts, over her belly. He pushed her panties over her hips, and stripped them away. Then he spread her thighs and continued exploring her body with his mouth.

Ashley sucked in a breath.

"Cam." His name was both a reverent whisper and a heartfelt plea, and he responded.

His tongue dipped and dabbled. Slow, deep strokes alternating with short, rapid flicks that had her mind spinning and her body exploding like a Fourth of July fireworks finale.

She sobbed out his name as her body trembled and shuddered.

Finally he rose over her.

Her body was still quivering with the aftershocks of pleasure, but she suddenly felt cold.

She should have been filled with excitement and anticipation. This was what she'd been waiting for—not just the merging of their bodies but the potential merging of their DNA.

But as much as she wanted a child—as much as she wanted Cameron's child—she knew that going about it this way was wrong. She couldn't do it.

"Wait," she said.

His brows lifted. "*Now* you want me to wait?"

She reached blindly for the handle of the drawer in her nightstand, then fumbled around inside until her fingers found a small square packet.

Cam didn't ask any questions or make any protest. He simply took the packet from her hand, tore it open and quickly sheathed himself, and the icy numbness that had gripped her heart melted away.

"Am I still waiting?" he asked, his voice laced with both amusement and tenderness.

She shook her head and lifted her legs to hook them around his waist again. "No more waiting," she said.

He took her at her word and plunged into her.

She gasped and shuddered and clung to him as he moved inside of her.

She felt the pressure building inside again, a tight, spiraling tension deep in her womb, a sharp, aching need that grew more desperate with each thrust of his hips.

She wanted more.

She wanted everything.

And he gave it to her.

With his hands, his lips, his body, Cam took her to heights of pleasure she had never before experienced, could never even have imagined.

If she'd been able to think, she might have worried that she'd made a very big mistake by inviting Cam to her bed. But there was no thought, no reason. There was only layer upon layer of exquisite sensation, taking her higher and higher, until she flew apart in an explosion of white-hot light.

* * *

Ashley stared up at the ceiling, though she couldn't see anything through the tears that filled her eyes.

Nothing had gone according to plan since he'd shown up at their high school reunion more than six months earlier. Tonight, everything had spun completely out of her control.

"What's wrong?" Cam asked gently.

She shook her head. "It wasn't supposed to be like this."

"I'm a little out of practice," he admitted. "But I didn't think it was so bad."

She managed a smile. "It was supposed to be sex—primal and wild and meaningless."

He brushed his lips against hers.

"We could try again."

He sounded so hopeful she had to laugh, even as she shook her head. "I don't think so."

He kissed her again, and the touch of his mouth was so tender and affectionate she could hardly stand it. He was being so sweet and so kind, and she'd behaved so horribly.

"Tell me why you're crying," he said.

"Because I'm a rotten person."

"I happen to think you're an incredible woman," he told her, kissing her softly again. "Warm, passionate, giving."

She pulled away from him and slipped out of the bed as more tears spilled onto her cheeks. She swiped at them impatiently. "Do you know why I invited you to come back here tonight?"

"Because you were overcome by lust?"

She tugged on her robe, belted it at her waist, and turned to face him. "Because I want to have a baby," she said. "Truthfully, my decision had nothing to do with you aside from the fact that you were willing to get naked with me."

He plumped the pillow and settled back, apparently unconcerned by her revelation.

"Not just willing but eager," he admitted.

"I would have had sex with anyone. You were just convenient."

She'd thought he would be angry, insulted. Maybe she wanted him to be angry and insulted, to push his far-too-sexy body out of her bed, yank on his clothes and storm out of her bedroom and her life forever.

Instead his lips curved, and when he spoke, his words were tinged with amusement. "Do you think so?"

She frowned at him. "Why aren't you furious with me?"

"Maybe because I know you better than you know yourself."

"You don't know me at all anymore," she insisted.

"So tell me," he said, folding his hands behind his head in a casual pose that matched his tone, "why a woman who is desperate to get pregnant would suddenly, at the point of no return, thrust a condom into her partner's hand?"

She didn't know how to respond to that. She wasn't entirely certain she knew what had motivated her actions, whether it was deeply ingrained caution with respect to unprotected sex or an attack of conscience. She only knew that when it came right down to it, she couldn't deliberately deceive him like that.

"Okay, I'll tell you," he said, when she remained silent. "It was because you're *not* a rotten person. Because you're neither deceitful nor manipulative. Because you would never use someone else so callously."

"I almost did," she insisted. "The only reason you're here is because I wanted to trick you into getting me pregnant."

"And if you'd gone through with it but not ended up pregnant? How many times do you think you could trick me? How long do you think you could have continued the charade?"

"As long as I had to."

He caught her hand, tugging her back toward the bed. She let herself be drawn back down onto the edge of the mattress but held herself away from him. "Honey, you couldn't keep up the charade for one night."

"But I want a baby." Her voice hitched and her eyes filled with moisture. "I really do. I even had an appointment at the clinic, but the doctor there insisted that I wait six months."

He shifted slightly so that he was sitting with his arms around her, and his lips brushed away the lone tear that spilled onto her cheek. He didn't say anything for a minute, for several minutes, in fact, but he continued to hold her.

She let herself take comfort from his embrace, because she was sure that once he had a chance to fully absorb what she'd tried to do, he would hate her. And she wouldn't blame him if he did. What she'd almost done was unconscionable and unforgivable.

"It seems to me," he finally said, "that there's a relatively simple way to ensure you get what you want."

It wasn't so much the words as the tone that made her heart skip a beat. She swallowed, hardly daring to let herself hope but needing to ask. "What—" she licked her suddenly dry lips "—what are you suggesting?"

"That maybe we should replay that last scene—but forget about birth control this time."

Chapter Eleven

Ashley stared at him as if she couldn't quite believe what he was saying. Cam could hardly believe it himself. But it seemed to him the obvious solution to give both Ashley and him what they most wanted. She wanted a baby and he wanted her.

Of course, he knew it really wasn't that simple. Ashley wasn't looking for any kind of long-term commitment. The fact that she'd gone so far as to make an appointment at the reproductive clinic proved that she only wanted one thing from any relationship between them—a baby. He, on the other hand, wanted her in his life. Not just for one night, but forever.

So maybe their wants seemed to be at opposite ends of the same spectrum, but Cam believed they would find common ground with a baby.

Yeah, because that worked so well with your ex-wife.

Cam ignored the mocking voice of his conscience because

he knew the two situations were completely different. He hadn't known Danica nearly as long or as well as he knew Ashley, and he was confident that a pregnancy would bring him and Ashley even closer and help break down the barriers that she'd been working so hard to maintain.

"Why?" she finally asked, her voice tinged with both hope and wariness.

"Because that's the only way we'll make a baby."

She swallowed. "I mean, why are you willing to do this?"

"Because I can't imagine anyone who would be a better mother than you," he said. He'd spent enough time with her and Madeline to believe that if there was a woman who was meant to be a mother, it was Ashley. She had a natural warmth that children gravitated toward, and an innate gentleness that encouraged trust and confidence.

"But...what would *you* get out of this arrangement?"

He smiled. "I thought that would be obvious."

"Sex?" she asked skeptically.

"The value of which cannot be overestimated," he assured her. "But more than that, I get to spend time with you."

"I'm not looking for a relationship," she said, confirming his suspicions. "I'm not looking for a husband or even a father for my child."

"Just a not-so-anonymous sperm donor." He unfastened the knot at the front of her robe.

She nodded, though he thought he detected the slightest hesitation first.

Or maybe he was only hoping she hesitated. Just as he was hoping this little experiment of his didn't completely backfire. Because he wanted a lot more than sex from Ashley—he wanted her back in his life. But he knew that she wasn't ready to hear that, so he would play the game according to her rules for now.

He pushed the silky fabric off her shoulders. "And making love with me once or twice or even a dozen times isn't going to change that," he continued, wanting her to know that he understood the boundaries she was determined to set.

"*Having sex* with you a *hundred* times isn't going to change that."

"I got that," he said, and lowered his head to take one rosy nipple in his mouth, suckling hard.

Ashley moaned. "I mean it, Cam."

His tongue circled the moist, turgid peak. "I know you do."

"I just want to be sure there are no misunderstandings."

"None at all." He turned his attention to her other breast, confident that he understood her better than she understood herself. Because he didn't believe that Ashley could share her body without opening her heart, and he was counting on physical intimacy leading to emotional intimacy, and betting with his whole heart.

"Well, then." She sighed, arched. "What are you waiting for?"

He lifted his head to look into those stunning violet eyes.

"You," he said. "It seems as if I've been waiting for you my whole life."

Her brow furrowed. "Cam—"

He captured her mouth, swallowing whatever protest she might have made to the words he'd never intended to say aloud, no matter that they came straight from his heart.

Her lips softened beneath his, and she sank back onto the mattress, pulling him down with her.

His hands moved over her, skimming over the satiny smoothness of her skin, tracing the softness of her curves. His fingertips brushed the damp curls at the apex of her thighs, and she quivered.

"Cam." Not a protest but a plea this time.

He stroked her cleft, sliding two fingers deep into her silky wetness, and slowly withdrawing again. Her breath was coming in short, shallow gasps now, her hips instinctively pumping to match the rhythm of his strokes.

"Let go." He whispered the words against her lips, but she shook her head.

"I want you…inside of me."

It was a request he couldn't refuse.

He straddled her hips and, in one long, deep thrust, buried himself in her slick heat.

She gasped, as spasms immediately began to rock her body; he groaned, and held on while her muscles clenched him like a slippery fist.

They plunged into the abyss together.

Cam awoke the next morning to find Ashley's head tucked into his shoulder and her arm draped across his chest. She'd assured him that having sex wouldn't change anything, but he knew that it already had. Because she hadn't let herself cuddle up to him before she'd fallen asleep, but sometime during the night, her body had instinctively turned to his. He took that as a very good sign.

But for now, he reluctantly eased himself away from her and gathered his scattered clothing to dress. He considered using Ashley's shower but worried that the sound of the water might wake her. And though he wouldn't mind if she woke and decided to join him under the spray, the repercussions of that would definitely put him behind schedule.

But he took the time to put on a pot of coffee, because he desperately needed a hit of caffeine and because he wanted to show Ashley that he could be useful outside of the bedroom, too. When the pot was full, he poured a cup for himself and took a second into the bedroom. He set the cup on the table beside the bed where Ashley was still sleeping, and bent to brush his mouth against hers.

Her eyelids flickered, her lips curved.

"Hey, sleeping beauty."

"What are you doing up so early?" she asked him.

"I'm meeting my parents and Maddie at church," he told her. "It's become something of a Sunday morning tradition since we moved back."

"Oh," she said, but he was sure there was a tinge of disappointment in her tone.

"You could come with me," he suggested, but without much hope.

Her eyes widened. "To church? With your family?"

"Sure," he said, deliberately casual.

She shook her head. "I don't think so."

"You have something against going to church?"

"I'm not opposed to attending church in general," she said. "But with you—yes."

"Because?" he prompted, though he was pretty sure he already knew her answer.

"Because it would give your daughter and your parents and everyone else at Holy Trinity the idea that we're...involved," she told him, confirming his suspicions.

"Because we're not," he said.

"Right," she agreed.

"We're just having sex."

"Right," she said again.

"I'll keep that in mind," he promised, and kissed her again.

He left the house with a coffee cup in his hand, a smile on his face and the conviction that Ashley Roarke was the one who didn't have a clue what was really going on between them. And he figured it was probably a good idea to keep it that way, at least for now.

* * *

Every Wednesday afternoon, Cam left the clinic early so that he could pick Madeline up from school. On those days, he frequently popped in to the classroom to chat for a minute or two with Ashley, and she'd been impressed by the interest he took in his daughter's daily activities. He asked questions not just about her school projects, but about her classroom habits and interactions with other students.

On the Wednesday following the Saturday night he'd spent in her bed, Ashley didn't expect to see Cam because Madeline had happily announced to her that she was going to Victoria's house for a playdate after school. But when she exited the building, she found him waiting for her. Her pulse jolted, then raced, proving she was far more affected by his presence than she wanted to be.

"This is a surprise," she said.

He fell into step beside her. "Since Maddie was having a playdate at Victoria's house, I thought I'd invite you for a playdate at mine."

The invitation had desire churning low in her belly, but she shook her head. "I have some prep to do for the new science unit we're starting tomorrow."

"Do you have to do it now?"

She hesitated.

"Because if you're serious about wanting to have a baby, you should take advantage of opportunities like this."

Of course, she was still serious about wanting a baby, but she was also having serious doubts about the wisdom of enlisting Cam's assistance with her plan. "I'm having second thoughts," she admitted.

"About?" he prompted.

"Using you for my own purposes."

"It's demoralizing, but I think I can stand the humiliation."

The dry tone made her smile. "Or maybe you're just horny."

"That could be a factor," he agreed. "Although it's certainly one that works in your favor."

"I'm just worried that we jumped into this too fast, without clearly thinking it through."

"What's to think about? I want to have sex with you, you want to get pregnant, and having sex is a pretty good way to do it."

Her gaze narrowed. "It sounds perfectly logical and reasonable when you say it like that."

"So what's the problem? Because I thought the sex between us was pretty darn spectacular."

Her cheeks flushed. "Can we not talk about that here and now—where there are impressionable young children walking home from school?"

"None of those impressionable young children are close enough to hear anything we're saying," he assured her. "But if you prefer, we can finish the conversation at my place."

"I'm pretty sure if we went to your place, we wouldn't finish this conversation."

"Your choice," he told her, his tone serious now. "But I have a few hours free and I'd like to spend them with you."

"*That's* the problem," she told him.

He lifted his brows. "Wanting to spend time with you is a problem?"

"Yes," she said, all too aware that her response made her look as foolish as she felt. But she wanted boundaries—she *needed* boundaries. "Because you say things like that and it makes me want to spend time with you, and this—" she gestured between them "—isn't supposed to be about anything but sex."

"My initial offer was for sex," he reminded her.

She huffed out a breath. "Except that it's not that black and white."

"And the gray areas scare you," he guessed, the teasing glint gone from his eyes.

She nodded, though it was his insights that scared her even more and compelled her to remind him, "I'm not looking for a relationship. Not with you. Not with anyone."

"Because you're still getting over a broken heart—"

"Trevor didn't break my heart," she interjected. "He broke my trust."

"And that takes longer to heal," Cam acknowledged.

"But even if I didn't have questions or doubts because of what happened with Trevor, I still wouldn't want a relationship with you," Ashley told him. "Because you *did* break my heart."

"I was young and foolish," he said, and sounded genuinely remorseful.

"We were both young and foolish," she admitted.

"So why can't you forgive me?"

She sighed. "I have forgiven you; I just won't set myself up for the same heartbreak again."

"But we're not the same people we were then," he reminded her.

"No," she agreed. "And that's why you have even more reasons to be wary than I do."

"You're talking about Maddie."

"Of course I'm talking about Maddie. She made the mental leap from a picnic in the park to a potential wedding in less than forty-eight hours. Imagine what she would think if she knew we were actually involved."

"Maybe it's not Maddie's expectations that you're worried about," he said, stopping in front of his house. "Maybe it's your own."

He was right, of course, but that didn't alleviate her concerns. "Maybe it is," she allowed. "And maybe—"

"Maybe we should both stop worrying about what might

or might not happen and just let it happen," he suggested, and touched his mouth to hers.

Even as Ashley responded to his kiss, she knew that was exactly what she was afraid of. That if she just let things happen, she would end up falling for Cam all over again. But she wasn't yet ready to admit that to him, so when he finally eased his lips from hers, she only said, "This 'it' that I should just let happen…are you talking about sex again?"

"It's humiliating how easily you see right through me," he said.

They hadn't resolved anything, and she knew that the situation wasn't going to be easily resolved. But despite her concerns, she wasn't ready to give him up just yet.

"Well, it would be a shame to waste the next few hours," she said, and let him lead her into the house.

Ashley was on her way to Megan's for a scheduled Friday night get-together with her sister and her cousin when Paige called to let her know that she was stuck at the office and wouldn't be able to make it. Ashley didn't question what had kept her late because she understood that Paige's commitment to her clients was one of the qualities that made her such an effective advocate for them, but she couldn't deny that she was disappointed.

She'd been hoping to talk to both Megan and Paige, to get an objective assessment of the situation with Cam, because after only three weeks, she was afraid that she'd already lost all objectivity where he was concerned. Still, she was optimistic that Megan might be able to shed some light on things, if she could find a delicate way to broach the subject.

But when Megan asked her what was new, she responded by blurting out, "I'm sleeping with Cam."

Her sister's eyes popped wide, then her lips curved. "Oh,

Paige is going to be *so* annoyed that she didn't come tonight." She helped herself to another slice of pizza. "Since when?"

Ashley frowned at her sister's question. "Why does the when matter?"

"Because Paige and I made a bet about when it would happen."

"You *expected* this to happen?"

Megan smiled. "Honey, you're probably the only one who didn't. After seeing you and Cam together, it wasn't a question of if, but when."

Ashley huffed out a breath. "Three weeks ago," she admitted.

"Damn. That means Paige wins." She looked at her sister with obvious disapproval. "*I* thought you would hold out longer than that."

Ashley squirmed. "Well, it's been a long time."

"And Cam has always known how to ring your bell." Megan took a long sip of her Sprite, then looked across the table. "So—how is it?"

"Spectacular," Ashley admitted.

Her sister grinned. "Good old Cam."

"But I didn't want to be having great sex with him," Ashley told her sister.

"You wanted to be having lousy sex with him?"

She sighed. "I wanted to be having purposeful sex with him."

"Purposeful?" Megan queried skeptically.

"For the purpose of procreation," she explained.

"You want to have Cam's baby?" There was more than a hint of concern in Megan's question.

"No," she denied. "I want to have *a* baby, and Cam has agreed to help me."

Her sister frowned.

"You obviously don't approve," Ashley noted.

"I don't understand," Megan admitted.

"I thought it was pretty self-explanatory."

"And if you get pregnant?"

Now it was Ashley's turn to frown. "Why are you even asking that question? You know I'd be ecstatic."

"But what would it mean for your relationship with Cam?" her sister wondered.

"Well, that's what I'm worried about, because this was never supposed to be a relationship."

"Just sex?" There was skepticism again—a lot of it.

"Yes," Ashley insisted.

"And you expected that Cam would politely bow out of your life after his stud service had been completed?"

Her frown deepened. "You don't have to make it sound so crude."

"Using pretty words won't change the intent," Megan warned. "*If* that truly is your intent."

"I was clear about what I wanted and Cam accepted the terms."

"Do you really believe that?" her sister challenged.

"Why wouldn't I?" Ashley asked warily.

"Because you've seen that man with his daughter, you know how completely devoted he is to her, and yet you've somehow managed to delude yourself into believing that he would turn his back on another child.

"Or maybe," Megan continued, "you let yourself believe it because you want the forever kind of tie that having a baby together would create."

Ashley was stunned by her sister's conclusion and immediately opened her mouth to deny it. But then she found herself wondering—could it be true? Had she only been deluding herself about what she wanted from Cam? Did she really want a future with him, a family with him?

"I have been such an idiot," she said, reaching for her drink.

"Love will do that," Megan said consolingly.

Love?

She nearly choked on her Diet Coke. Though she'd acknowledged that there was probably some truth in what her sister had said, she hadn't yet made the jump from accepting that she had feelings for Cam to putting a label on those feelings.

"Oh. My. God."

Megan looked at her, silently questioning.

"I *am* in love with him," she admitted.

"Again—probably not news to anyone but yourself," Megan told her.

"I thought I was being so smart. So careful."

"Honey, this is a *good* thing, not a catastrophe."

"That's a viewpoint exclusive to the happily married," Ashley told her. "The perspective of a woman who was in love with the same man once before is a little bit different."

"You were both young," her sister said gently.

"I know." Which didn't alter the fact that he'd trampled her heart and shattered her dreams. He'd known what she most wanted and taken it away from her.

And now he's trying to give it back to you.

She wasn't sure where that thought had come from, but she realized it was true. Whether or not Cam's decision to help her have a baby was a conscious effort to make amends, there was no denying that he was offering her everything she'd always wanted.

Not just a baby but, if Megan's theory was right, a family. A life and a future with Cam and Maddie and any other children they might have together.

"Maybe you're right," Ashley finally said to her sister. "Maybe this is a good thing."

"Now that we've established that," Megan said, as if her

conclusion was never in question, "is there anything else I should know?"

"I think I've made enough potentially life-altering revelations for one night," Ashley told her.

But the truth was, there was one more.

Her period was two days late.

Chapter Twelve

Ashley woke early Saturday morning feeling tired and crampy, but she still didn't have her period. She poured herself a glass of orange juice and swallowed her daily dose of Fedentropin and the prenatal vitamins she'd been taking since she and Cam started sleeping together.

According to all the books she'd read—and she'd read a lot of them—it was important to take the vitamins not just in the first trimester of pregnancy but even before conception to ensure the mother's body wasn't lacking in any essential nutrients required for her baby's healthy development. She laid a hand on her belly and thought about the tiny life that might already be growing inside of her. Cam's baby.

She knew it was too early to make any plans. She didn't even know for sure that she was pregnant. She was only a few days late and she hadn't even taken a home pregnancy test, so sharing her suspicions with Cam might seem a little premature.

But when she headed out for her usual morning walk, she found herself turning toward his house. Her heart was pounding as she made her way along the interlocking brick path that led to his front door. She still didn't know what she was going to say, or even if she would say anything, she was suddenly just anxious to see him.

She pressed the bell and heard the chime through the partially open living room window, then the sound of pounding footsteps. Maddie, she thought, with a smile.

The little girl opened the door just as Ashley heard an unfamiliar female voice call out from the background. "Madeline, you know you don't open the door unless you know who it is."

"It's Miss Ashley," Maddie called back, and pushed the door wider, giving Ashley a clear view down the hall.

A view that included a stunningly beautiful woman who didn't seem to be wearing anything more than a silky robe that fell to mid-thigh.

Ashley felt as if the bottom had dropped out of her stomach.

The woman's silky dark hair, delicate features and slim build clearly identified her as Maddie's mother. And Cam's ex-wife.

"Miss Ashley?" Danica questioned, moving toward the door without any apparent regard for or concern about her state of undress.

"She's my teacher," Maddie announced.

The other woman's perfectly shaped brows lifted. "Oh. Well, I'll have to apologize, Miss Ashley. We had a late night and you've caught us before we're all up and about for the day."

"No, I'm sorry," Ashley said. "I didn't mean to intrude."

"Daddy and I are going to make pancakes," Maddie announced, oblivious to the tension between the adults. "Do you want to stay and have breakfast with us?"

Ashley shook her head. "Thanks, but I, uh, already ate."

"You're more than welcome to join us," Danica said, as if she had every right to be inviting guests for breakfast in her ex-husband's home. "Cameron should be down from the shower in just a minute or two, and he really does make fabulous pancakes."

"I'm sure he does," Ashley said, because she'd never actually tasted *Cameron's* pancakes. Because he'd never made breakfast for her after spending the night in her bed. Because that wasn't the kind of relationship they had. "But I really can't stay."

Those brows lifted again, and Ashley knew the other woman was wondering why she'd stopped by in the first place. So she made a hasty retreat before her lover's ex-wife could ask the question she had no idea how to answer.

Cam had become accustomed to changing his plans at a moment's notice, because he believed that it was important for Madeline to spend time with her mother. So whenever Danica contacted him to say that she would be in town— whether she gave him a week's notice or called from the nearest airport—he tried to accommodate her. That didn't mean he didn't resent it.

But he'd never resented it more than when he got the call Friday night and had to rearrange his whole weekend schedule. A weekend that he'd planned to include a sleepover for Maddie at her grandparents' and a quiet, romantic evening at home for himself with Ashley. He definitely resented having to change those plans.

After breakfast Saturday morning, he suggested that Danica take Maddie to her ballet class. He figured it would give his ex-wife the opportunity to see how well her daughter's dancing was coming along and give Maddie some time alone with her mother. But Danica balked at the idea, claiming she would love to see Maddie dance but that she was uncomfortable driving in an unfamiliar city. So the three of them had gone to Maddie's dance class, then to Walton's for ice cream, then to the grocery store to pick up a few things. By the time they got back home, most of the day was gone.

Cam checked the answering machine, listened to the three messages that had recorded. The first was from his mother, just checking in, the second was a credit card company wanting to share important information about his account and the third was Maddie's friend Victoria.

Maddie overheard the last message and insisted on calling her friend back right away. Cam recited the number for her to dial, while Danica set up her laptop at the breakfast bar to check her e-mail.

Cam put the groceries away while Maddie chatted to her friend and Danica clicked away on her keyboard.

Maddie hung up the phone and skipped back into the kitchen. "Daddy, I need you to take me to Victoria's."

"First of all, you *ask* if I can take you to Victoria's," he told her. "Second, you have to get permission before you make plans. And third, you can't go to Victoria's today because your mom is here to visit with you."

Maddie glanced at her mother, who was engrossed in her electronic correspondence and oblivious to their conversation.

"She's working, and I want to play with Victoria."

His usually sweet-natured daughter wasn't prone to temper tantrums, but Cam sensed that this was one of the rare occasions when she was heading in that direction. "I know you're disappointed, Maddie," he said reasonably, "but it's not often that you have the opportunity to spend time with your mom so you need to take advantage of it while you can."

"She doesn't want to spend time with me," Maddie said.

"Even when I go to London, she sends me off to museums and zoos with Peggy. I want to play with Victoria."

The mention of London seemed to catch Danica's attention, because she glanced over at Maddie and frowned, but she didn't dispute her daughter's claim. And while Cam was disappointed to learn that Maddie had spent her time in London with her mother's assistant rather than Danica, he wasn't really surprised.

"How about a compromise?" he suggested to his daughter now.

"What's a compromise?"

"It's when two people who want different things both accept that they can't have what they want but agree on something in the middle."

Her brow furrowed as she tried to follow that explanation. "What's in the middle?"

"Well, in this case, it might be Victoria coming over here to play."

She considered that for a minute before she asked, "But what if she doesn't want to come here because she doesn't want to intrude?"

He wasn't sure what had precipitated that question, but he answered it anyway, "If you invite someone, it's not an intrusion."

"But I invited Miss Ashley to stay for pancakes and she said she didn't want to intrude."

Cam frowned. "When was this?"

"At breakfast."

"Today?"

She nodded.

He looked at Danica, directing his next question at her. "Ashley was here this morning?"

"Did I forget to mention that?" Danica said.

Cam narrowed his gaze on his ex-wife, but she only shrugged.

"I didn't realize she was here to see *you*," she protested. "In fact, she didn't mention why she'd stopped by."

"Maddie, please call Victoria back and ask if she can come here to play."

Happy to accept his proposed compromise, she skipped off again.

"So who is Ashley?" Danica asked. "Because obviously she's someone more than Madeline's teacher."

"She's a friend."

"Our daughter seems quite taken with her," Danica noted.

"She's spent a lot of time with Ashley over the past few months."

"In the classroom—or here?"

He wasn't ashamed of his relationship with Ashley and he had no intention of hiding it from his ex-wife. On the other hand, he didn't feel as if he owed Danica any explanations, so he only asked, "Why the twenty questions?"

"I'm just curious about the woman you seem to have lined up to fill the role of stepmother in my daughter's life."

There was an unexpected edge to her voice, but Cam had learned a long time ago that Danica could manufacture whatever emotions were required to suit her purposes. "And I'm curious to know why you think spending maybe thirty days a year with your daughter gives you the right to turn everything upside-down when you do show up for a visit."

"If my being here is interfering with your life, I can go," she said coolly.

"You'd like me to say yes, wouldn't you? Then you could blame me for the lousy relationship you have with our daughter."

She looked away, but not before he saw her eyes fill with tears.

"Victoria's coming to play," Maddie announced, coming back to the kitchen. "Her mommy's going to drop her off so I'm going to sit on the porch to wait for her."

"Put your coat on, and make sure you stay on the porch." Cam reminded her.

"I will," she promised.

Danica watched her daughter walk away.

"No," she responded to his earlier question. "I know the lousy relationship I have with Madeline is entirely my fault."

He sighed. "You know it doesn't have to be like this. I would never deny you the opportunity to spend more time with Maddie."

"I know," she admitted. "But it's better this way. Really."

Cam didn't argue with her. He'd spent far too much time doing exactly that over the years and it had never changed anything. It made him wonder how he'd ever thought himself in love with Danica when it was apparent now that he'd never known her at all.

He pushed the thought, and the regrets, aside. He wasn't going to dwell on the mistakes of the past. He had too much to look forward to for the future—with Ashley.

Ashley was in the garage, up to her elbows in tangled Christmas lights, when Cam came up the walk. She'd been outside for a while, so her fingers were cold and struggling with the task. So far, she'd managed to untangle only half of one sixteen-foot strand.

Her frustration with the lights paled in comparison to her annoyance with him, though she wasn't entirely sure her annoyance was either rational or founded except that it was now after three o'clock in the afternoon and she'd been thinking about Cam being with his ex-wife for more than six hours.

He studied her for a moment, as if trying to figure out what she was doing, or maybe he didn't know what to say to her, either. But when he spoke, his voice was light, teasing.

"Jumping the gun, aren't you?"

Something she seemed to be doing a lot of these days. But all she said was, "I prefer not to be climbing a ladder when it's snowing."

"You shouldn't be climbing a ladder at all," he said. "I can do that for you."

"I appreciate the offer, but I don't need your help. I've been handling this particular task on my own for several years now and am more than capable of continuing to do so."

He tucked his hands in his pockets, rocked back on his heels. "You're annoyed with me."

She was, but she couldn't admit it because she had no right to be annoyed with him. So she shook her head. "No, I'm not."

"I heard you met my ex-wife this morning."

"Formal introductions weren't made, but yes, I met your ex-wife."

"What did she say to cause this mood?" he wanted to know.

"Nothing," she said, because it was true. "In fact, she was very pleasant."

He eyed her warily. "So why are you angry?"

She gave up trying to pretend that she wasn't. "Because she was in her robe and you were in the shower."

He took a moment to absorb her statement and the implications of it. When he responded, his tone was deliberate and even, as if he was trying to hold his own annoyance in check. "You don't honestly think I slept with Danica?"

She had thought that—if only for half a second. But that half a second had been long enough to make her question the relationship they'd only started to build, and make her wonder if she might lose him again.

"Ashley?" he prompted.

There was a definite edge in his voice, a dangerous glint in his eye, and she knew she'd been foolish to give in to her fears and insecurities for even that half-second.

"No," she finally responded. "At least, not when I think about it logically." Then she sighed and dumped the tangle of lights at her feet. "On the other hand, the door opens and there she is, and she's beautiful and half-naked and we never talked about exclusivity or lack of."

"I didn't think we needed to have a discussion," Cam said. "I thought the fact that we were sleeping together implied exclusivity."

"I don't assume anything," she said. "Not anymore."

His gaze narrowed. "Don't you dare compare me to that idiot you were engaged to."

"I'm not. At least, I'm trying not to. But I was the one who said this was just about sex, that I didn't want a relationship."

"Have you changed your mind?"

"No," she said, and immediately felt guilty for the lie. "Maybe. I don't know."

Cam picked up one end of a light strand and methodically began to unravel it. She wished she could do the same with the mess of emotions tangled inside of her. But every time she thought she'd figured out one thread, something happened to twist it up again.

"I just wish you'd told me that she was coming," she said, because coming face to face with the stunning woman he'd married had felt like a sucker punch.

"I would have told you if I'd known," he said gently.

She frowned at that. "You didn't?"

"Danica has a habit of calling at the last minute, showing up on a whim. And because Madeline gets little enough time with her mother, I let her."

She could hardly blame him for that, especially not after she'd encouraged him to facilitate more contact between mother and child.

"And then I showed up," she said, trying to look at the situation from his perspective. "How awkward was it for you to explain why Maddie's teacher was knocking at your door at nine o'clock on a Saturday morning?"

"Danica and I have been divorced for almost five years. She knows I've dated other women, just as I know she's dated other men. I don't have to explain anything to her."

Even so, Ashley knew the other woman had been curious about her visit. But she accepted his explanation for what it was, and tried to tamp down her own curiosity.

"Why did you come by this morning?" he asked her.

She couldn't—wouldn't—tell him the real reason. Not now. Not while Danica was in town and before anything had been confirmed.

"I was just thinking about you and Maddie," she said, because that was at least partially true.

He set aside one untangled and now neatly coiled string of lights. "And missing me?"

"No."

"I miss you," he said softly. "Whenever I wake up in the morning without you. Whenever I go to sleep at night without you. Whenever I think about you and you're not there, which happens about a hundred times a day, I miss you."

They were just words, but something about those words— or maybe it was the sincerity of his tone and the warmth in his eyes—made her heart soften, yearn. But all she said was, "Oh."

He smiled. "That surprises you, doesn't it?"

"A little."

"And scares you?" he guessed.

"More than a little," she admitted, but she knew that his feelings didn't scare her half as much as her own.

"Well, I just thought you should know," he told her.

She took the second string of lights from him. "It scares me," she said, "because I miss you, too. Sometimes."

Despite the obvious reluctance of her admission, he smiled, clearly pleased by her response. "That's a start." He touched his hand to her cheek, his palm warm against her skin. His smile faded. "You're freezing."

She shrugged. "I guess I've been out here for a while."

"Why don't we go in and put on a pot of coffee?"

She closed the garage door and followed him into the house.

Though she thought they'd cleared the air about his ex-wife's visit, mostly, there was still one specific concern gnawing at the back of her mind. She turned on the faucet and filled the pot with water and wondered if she dared ask Cam about it.

Paige had once told her that in relationships, as in a cross-examination at trial, you never ask a question you don't already know the answer to. Of equal importance was to never ask a question if the answer could hurt you. But she had to know.

When the coffee finished brewing, she poured two cups and slid one over the table to Cam before taking the seat across from him.

"Have you ever thought about getting back together with her?" she asked him.

"Danica?"

She nodded.

"No," he said.

The immediate and definitive response should have reassured her, but she wasn't able to relinquish her concerns so easily. "But she's Maddie's mother."

"Yes, she is," he agreed.

"And if she wanted to reconcile, wouldn't you want that for your daughter?"

"No," he said again.

"Why not?"

"Because we were never happy together, and that's not the kind of relationship example I want to set for my child."

She wanted to be satisfied by his explanation. It was logical and it answered her question, but for some reason she couldn't let it go. "You were in love with her once."

Cam set his cup down and met her gaze across the table.

She could tell he wasn't any happier than she was about the direction of their conversation, but like a train veering dangerously off-track, she couldn't seem to stop it.

"I wouldn't have married her if I wasn't," he admitted. "But, as it turned out, I didn't really know her and she didn't really know me, and when we finally got around to sharing all the intimate details that you should know about the person you marry, it was too late."

But whether he knew her or not, he'd fallen in love with her, and Danica was beautiful, sophisticated, ambitious—everything Ashley wasn't. "She obviously still cares about you."

"We have a child together," he reminded her. "That creates a bond that can't ever be broken."

Which was almost the same thing that Megan had said to her, but which took on a whole new meaning when applied to Cam and his ex-wife. And it made Ashley wonder if it might not be a mistake to tie herself to a man who was already tied to someone else.

Cam didn't know what else he could say to Ashley to alleviate the doubts he could see swirling in the depths of her violet eyes, and he mentally cursed his ex-wife again, adding bad timing to his usual complaints of selfishness and lack of consideration. Because just when he and Ashley had finally started to make progress in their relationship, Danica's unexpected appearance had put a damper on everything.

"But Maddie is the only reason we're still in contact," he continued his explanation. "There's nothing else between us anymore."

"I'm sorry if it seems like I was interrogating you," she said. "I was just caught off guard when Maddie opened the door and she was there."

"Does it bother you that she's staying at my house?"

"No," she said.

But he knew it was a lie. Because he knew that if Ashley's ex had suddenly taken up residence in her house, however temporarily, it sure as hell would bother him.

"It's only for a few days," he told her. "But I can check her into a hotel—"

"No," she said again. "If this is your usual arrangement, if it gives Maddie more time with her mother, then there's no reason to change it. But I have to admit, it bothers me that she'd rather be sleeping in your bed than down the hall."

"Whatever gave you that idea?" he asked cautiously.

"Are you going to deny that it's true?"

He wished he could. But he wouldn't lie to her and he wouldn't tiptoe around the truth. "She did imply that she didn't want to sleep in the spare room," he admitted. "But I clarified the situation for her."

"And why did it need clarification?"

He didn't know how to answer that question without landing himself in hotter water, so he said nothing.

"Because she's used to dropping in to your life when it's convenient for her—and back into your bed because that's convenient, too."

"It hasn't exactly been a pattern," he denied.

"But it's happened."

"I don't expect you to understand—"

"I do understand," she interrupted. "My friend Marilyn frequently has sex with her ex-husband because, to use her words, the itch needs to be scratched and it's safer to use a stick that's familiar for the task."

He winced at the harshness of the analogy, though he couldn't deny there was some truth in it.

"I haven't had sex with Danica in more than two years," he told her. "In fact, I haven't been with anyone at all in that time, until you. Do you want to know why?"

She shrugged.

"Because I got tired of sex that didn't mean anything. Because I wanted something more for myself." He slipped his arms around her waist, drew her closer. "Because I wanted to be with someone I care about."

"You're making this into something more complicated than it was supposed to be."

"So sue me."

"Paige is a lawyer," she reminded him. "Don't tempt me."

"Okay, I'll let you tempt me instead."

She tipped her head back so that her lips were only a whisper away from his. "Do you think I could?"

"You already have," he said, and carried her up to the bedroom.

Chapter Thirteen

Cam had told Ashley that Danica would only be in town for a few days, but at the end of the week, she was still there, still in Cam's house—sleeping down the hall from her ex-husband. And then one week turned into two, because—as she explained to Ashley when she came to school to pick up Maddie—she'd managed to settle a big case before trial, allowing her to extend her leave and spend more time with her family.

She hadn't said her *daughter,* but her *family.*

And the longer Danica stayed, the more Ashley worried that Cam might change his mind about wanting to reconcile with his ex-wife.

She knew she was being irrational, but from her perspective, Cam had chosen the other woman over her once already—when he'd left Ashley in Pinehurst and fallen in love with Danica.

Still, she had to give him an A for effort, because he continued to call her every night and to stop by whenever he had a chance. Of course, Danica kept him busy so that those chances were infrequent, but she didn't blame Cam for that. She knew he was only trying to facilitate the relationship between his daughter and her mother, but she couldn't deny that she missed spending time with him, and she missed making love with him.

She could call it having sex, but her conversation with her sister only a couple of weeks earlier had forced her to acknowledge the truth of her feelings for Cam. She was in love with him—and she was very much afraid that, for the second time in her life, she was going to lose him.

A fear that grew stronger every day through the week, until Friday night, when he showed up at her door.

"I thought Victoria was spending the night at your house with Maddie," Ashley said.

"She is," Cam agreed. "But it occurred to me that Danica should be able to handle two six-year-old girls for a few hours."

"Should?"

He shrugged. "They've got popcorn and movies—everything is good."

"So what are we going to do for a few hours?"

"We could make popcorn and watch a movie," he suggested. Which wasn't at all what she'd expected him to say. "Really?"

"Why do you sound so surprised?"

"I just figured you didn't come over here to watch a movie."

"I came over here to be with you, because I missed you."

And he sounded so sincere that her heart gave a little fluttery sigh, warning that she was in big trouble.

"I love making love with you," he told her, "but I love just being with you, too."

He'd used the word *love* three times in one sentence, but he hadn't actually said that he loved her. Of course, she hadn't said the words to him, either. Though she no longer had any doubts about the feelings in her heart, before she put it all on the line, she needed some more time to trust and believe that they could make their relationship work.

"In that case, I think I would enjoy watching a movie with you." She smiled. "Later."

When Cam sneaked out to see Ashley, he hadn't done so with the intention of getting her naked, but he sure as hell wasn't going to protest when things started moving in that direction. Even after several weeks, the attraction between them had not begun to wane and the intensity of their lovemaking had not diminished. And while he knew Ashley was hoping to get pregnant, he didn't believe her desire for a baby was the sole driving force behind her passion. No, the chemistry had been there twelve years ago and it was still there, and more powerful than ever.

But just as they were about to fall back onto Ashley's bed, his cell phone rang.

Cam swore under his breath as he released his hold on Ashley to reach into his pocket. CALL FROM HOME was on the display, and he glanced apologetically at her. "I'm sorry. I have to—"

"Don't apologize," she interrupted. "Of course you need to make sure everything's okay with your daughter."

He connected the call. "Maddie?"

"No, it's me."

Danica.

He frowned. "What's wrong?"

"Nothing. I just wanted to let you know that we're out of milk, so that you can pick some up on your way home."

He was silent, trying to decipher the hidden meaning behind the seemingly innocuous words.

"Cam?" she prompted, when he failed to respond.

"Yeah, I'm here. I just can't believe you called to ask me to pick up milk."

"Is that a problem?"

"No," he said, still not sure he wasn't missing something. "I'm just not sure when I'm going to be back."

"Oh." There was a not-so-subtle note of disapproval in her voice. "Madeline and Victoria wanted to make chocolate chip cookies, and we don't have any milk."

"You're baking cookies with the girls?"

"Is it so hard to believe?" she asked, the indignation in her tone confirming that he hadn't managed to hide the disbelief in his own.

"Actually, yes," he told her.

"Forget it, then," she said, obviously annoyed by his un-censored response. "I'll tell them that baking cookies will have to wait for another day."

"Have you even looked at the recipe?" he challenged.

"Of course I have."

"Because the recipe doesn't call for milk."

She didn't respond immediately, proving that she hadn't looked at the recipe, and that her request for milk wasn't the real reason for her call.

"Well, we want to drink milk with the cookies," she said.

"I'll pick some up before I come home," he told her. "But it won't be until later."

"Thank you," she said, and disconnected.

When Cameron turned around, Ashley had rebuttoned her shirt and was tugging a brush through her hair.

Obviously her mood had changed and the moment had passed.

"I'm sorry," he said again.

She just shook her head. "You don't even see what she's doing, do you?"

"Apparently not," he admitted cautiously.

She turned to face him. "She's playing the wife card."

"She's not my wife anymore," he reminded her.

"She called and asked you to pick up milk," Ashley said. "Which is the type of thing that a wife asks her husband to do."

"Even when we were married, she never made those kinds of calls. In fact, she probably wouldn't even have noticed if we were out of milk."

"And yet she called you now, knowing you were here, to ask."

"She doesn't know I'm here."

"You don't think so?" she challenged.

He frowned at the certainty in her tone. "How could she?"

"Your car is still in your driveway, which means that you didn't go too far, and, coincidentally, I live down the street."

"Danica doesn't play those kind of games," he said, but in the back of his mind, he wondered if he could be wrong.

"Neither do I," Ashley said.

It was the quiet resignation in her eyes that worried him more than the words or the tone.

"What are you saying?"

"I can't do this anymore, Cam. I won't be the other woman."

He was stunned. "Are you seriously asking me to choose between you and my ex-wife? Because if that's the case, let me remind you that she is my *ex*-wife."

Ashley took a step back. "I'm not asking you to choose at all. *I'm* making the choice this time, based on what's best for me, and that is to move on with my life without you in it."

"You don't mean that," he said, needing it to be true. Because to lose her again would be unbearable.

"I do mean it," she said softly. "Because you broke my heart once before, Cam, and I'm not going to give you a chance to do it again."

"What about the baby we were going to have?"

So much for Ashley's resolution not to let him break her heart again, because with only those words, it cracked wide open.

She looked away so he wouldn't see the distress she knew would be reflected in her eyes. Because having a baby with Cam had been her dream for so long, it broke her heart to admit that it just wasn't going to happen, that they were never going to be the family she wanted.

"Obviously it's a good thing I figured this out before I got pregnant."

"How do you know you're not pregnant?" he demanded.

"I got my period last week." She uttered the lie without compunction because she didn't want to put him in the position of having to choose—or maybe she didn't want to put herself in the position of being rejected again.

"Oh," he said, and she thought he sounded genuinely disappointed.

"It's for the best," she said, though it was another lie. Because she knew that if Cam even suspected the truth, he would never walk out the door. And she needed him to go. She needed to cut him out of her life so that she could get on with hers.

His gaze narrowed. "You expect me to believe that you've changed your mind about wanting a baby?"

She shook her head. "Of course not. I've just decided to revert to my original plan."

Because she'd jumped into this arrangement with Cam without thinking it through, without realizing that he already had responsibilities and obligations as a result of his first marriage. And she didn't want to spend the rest of her life in second place.

"You really want to have a baby fathered by a stranger?"

There was as much anger as disbelief in his tone, and it annoyed Ashley that he thought he had a right to be angry about anything. After all, she wasn't the one playing house with an ex-spouse.

"I'm not exactly planning on picking up someone in a bar," she reminded him.

"That would almost be preferable to having your baby's conception instigated by a catheter," he shot back.

"Then I'll be sure to keep that as a backup plan," she said coolly.

"Don't do this, Ashley." He sounded more worried than angry now, as if he'd finally realized that she meant what she'd said. "Don't shut me out of your life."

And she did mean what she'd said, even if the thought of watching him walk out on her once more made her heart break all over again. But she had to be strong—or at least make him believe that she was. It was the only way she would get through this.

"I was never looking for a relationship," she reminded him. "You were the one who tried to turn this into something more."

"Because I care about you." He took her hands, as if the physical connection would help her to believe the words he spoke. "I've always cared about you."

And she did believe that he cared about her. But she *loved* him, and she wouldn't settle for any less than being loved in return. Not this time.

"If you really care about me, you'll accept that this is my choice."

Cam had no intention of accepting Ashley's decision. At least not without doing everything he could to change her mind. But first he came to some conclusions of his own.

Before Danica left Pinehurst for Chicago, where she would be working on a corporate merger, he decided to set some guidelines and establish firm boundaries to govern future interactions with his ex-wife. For starters, he wanted Danica to commit to seeing Maddie at least four times a year on a regular schedule. He assured her that he would never deny requests for additional visitation, but he'd come to realize that one of the reasons Maddie was so despondent whenever she had to say goodbye to her mother was that she never knew when she would see her again. He also informed Danica that she would have to arrange for her own accommodations for future visits, with Maddie staying overnight with her mother if that was what they both wanted.

To his surprise, Danica didn't object to any of his terms. And when all was said and done, he felt good about the decisions they'd made. He only wished they'd made those same decisions six months earlier, or at least before Ashley had concluded that she didn't want to be with a man who was still struggling to fix the mistakes of his past.

As he sat with Maddie in the rooftop parking lot of the airport to watch his ex-wife's plane lift into the air, he was thinking of Ashley. Missing Ashley.

Apparently Maddie was, too, because he'd barely pulled out of the parking lot when she asked, "Can we go see Ashley now?"

"Oh, honey." He glanced at the clock on the dash. "It's too late to go visiting anyone tonight."

"But you're still friends with her, aren't you? You still like her, don't you?"

"Of course," he said.

But the truth was, he had no idea if he and Ashley were still friends, and he wanted to be so much more. And although he did like her, that word didn't begin to describe the depth of his feelings for her.

"Can we see her tomorrow?" Maddie pressed.

"You will see her tomorrow—at school," he reminded her.

"I like when she comes to visit us at home because then I get to call her Ashley instead of Miss Ashley."

The dropping of the title was something Ashley and

Maddie had decided, and though he worried that his daughter might slip up at school one day, so far she'd been careful. Probably because she was so thrilled to be on a first-name basis with her teacher outside of school that she wouldn't do anything to jeopardize the privilege.

Of course, she didn't know that her father had screwed everything up for her—and he was still hoping that he might find a way to fix it before she ever found out.

"But I am excited about going to school tomorrow," Maddie continued, oblivious to his inner turmoil. "Because we're going to make up our own fairy tales."

"That sounds like an ambitious project."

"Ashley—*Miss* Ashley—says the best stories are those that show imagination and heart. I thought she was talking about the pictures, and I asked her how to draw a picture of imagination, but she explained that imagination is making something up—telling about something that isn't real but that you can see in your mind.

"Can you see things in your mind, Daddy?"

"I guess I can sometimes."

"Then you know how to use your imagination," she told him.

Cam only wished he could imagine the right scenario to get Ashley back in his life.

Instead of their usual brunch, Ashley was meeting her sister and her cousin for a late lunch because Paige was babysitting while a friend went to an appointment. Since she had some time before she was due to meet them, Ashley decided to wander through some of the shops on Rockton Street.

She paused outside of Hush, Little Baby, her attention caught by the gorgeous cherrywood crib and dressing table on display. A recent visit to Dr. Alex had confirmed that the baby she'd wanted for so long would be a reality by the end of next summer, and though she knew it was too early in her pregnancy to think about making any major purchases, she couldn't resist browsing. Pushing open the door, she stepped inside and found that the store was a lot bigger than it appeared from the front and that the enormous space was divided into several distinctly themed rooms.

She walked past a hugely pregnant woman and her obviously adoring husband discussing infant car seats with one of the salesladies and tried not to think about the fact that, when it came time for her to pick out a car seat, she would be making the decision on her own. She would be making all of the decisions; she would bear all of the responsibilities. And that was okay, because it was her choice. But she knew that her child would miss out on so much if Cam wasn't part of his or her life.

Pushing the thought aside, she moved into the first room. This one had a sports focus, with dark furniture, bold plaid fabrics and an assortment of books and outfits for sale that continued the theme. She picked up a miniature baseball uniform displayed beside a board book version of "Casey at the Bat."

Beyond the sports room was a prehistoric setting, with everything and anything dinosaur. Then a vibrant circus-themed room, which she chose to bypass. Although she was sure the bright, primary colors would appeal to a child, there was something about perpetually grinning clown faces that had always creeped her out.

And then she discovered the fairy tale room, where everything was frilly and feminine—a little girl's dream. Neatly tucked inside the open drawer of a glossy white wardrobe was a frilly little tutu and a pair of tiny pink ballet slippers. She picked up the shoes, marveling at the detail and delicacy, and found herself thinking about Maddie, who loved to twirl and pirouette in her sock feet on the kitchen floor. And Ashley

wondered if maybe her daughter would display the same enthusiasm some day, inspired by a tiny pair of ballet slippers
just like the ones she was holding.

But it was too early in her pregnancy to begin speculating
about whether the baby she was carrying was a boy or a girl,
so it was more than a little premature to be thinking about
Little League and dreaming of ballet recitals. With a soft, regretful sigh, she put the shoes down and, turning, nearly
collided with Cam's mother.

"This is my favorite room in the whole store," Gayle told her,
her voice low as if she was confessing something she shouldn't.

"It's my first time in here," Ashley admitted. "But I'm
amazed."

"Then I know you'll be back," Gayle said. "Because every
time there's something new and different but always wonderful."

"I'll definitely be back," Ashley said, then felt her cheeks
color, a reaction that was more telling than her words. But she
recovered quickly with the explantion, "Because my sister's
pregnant."

"Ashley!" Maddie's voice rang out from across the room,
and the little girl skipped over, carrying a floppy-eared bunny
that had obviously caught her eye.

Ashley turned, grateful for the interruption that allowed her
to pull her foot out of her mouth.

"We're shopping for baby stuff," Maddie told her. "'Cause
my aunt Sherry's going to get a baby."

"Well, that's exciting news," Ashley said.

"Are you going to get a baby, too?"

Ashley sucked in a breath, caught off guard by the child's
innocent question. And she knew that's all it was—the simple
curiosity of a six-year-old. "Oh. Someday, I hope." She forced
a smile. "But before I have a baby, I'm going to have a niece
or a nephew."

"I'm getting a cousin," Maddie said proudly.

"A cousin who will be living in Florida," Gayle noted with obvious disappointment. "I don't know why it is that my kids had to go so far away to have their kids. I hate being a long-distance grandparent."

"Well, at least Cam and Maddie are home now," Ashley said, as the child wandered off again.

Gayle smiled as she kept a watchful eye on her granddaughter. "And I'm so grateful for that."

"Look at these, Grandma." Maddie was back again, this time with the little ballet slippers Ashley had recently admired. "Can we get these so the baby can be a dancer like me?"

Gayle looked at the price tag, winced. "Honey, she won't even be walking, never mind dancing when she's wearing shoes that size."

"But they're so pretty." Maddie stroked a finger over the satiny toe.

"And I am such a sucker," her grandmother laughed as she put the shoes into the basket she carried over one arm. "I can't tell you how much time—and money—I spent in here when Maddie was a baby. I don't think a week went by that I wasn't sending a sleeper or a dress or something out to her. Of course, Cam now blames me for his daughter being a clothes horse, but I figure it's a grandma's job to spoil the little ones."

"I take it Sherry's expecting a girl?" Ashley prompted.

"Oh, yes. She told me last night. I'd have started shopping as soon as I got the news, except that the store was already closed for the day," Gayle admitted.

"I'm glad it's a girl. Girls are better than boys," Maddie declared. "I think a sister would be better than a cousin, but I have to settle for a cousin because daddies can't have babies and my mommy isn't really the nurchring type."

"Maddie," her grandmother admonished gently.

"That's what you told Grandpa."

"I'm sure I did," Gayle admitted in an undertone to Ashley. "But I wouldn't have said it if I'd known she was within hearing distance."

Ashley smiled. "I teach first grade," she reminded the older woman. "Believe me, I understand only too well how they can forget direct instruction but recite verbatim something they should never have overheard."

"What's nurchring?" Maddie asked Ashley.

"I think you mean *nurturing,*" she said, scrambling to come up with a definition that wouldn't paint the little girl's mother in a completely negative light. "And it means to, uh, help grow or develop."

"Daddy says I grow like a weed, so maybe I don't need any more nurchring," Maddie decided. "Babies need help because they start out small, but I bet I could help."

"I'm sure you'd be a very big help," Ashley said, somehow forcing the words out through the tightness in her throat. And because she knew she would have a complete meltdown if she didn't get out of the store in the next thirty seconds, she said, "I have to run. I'm meeting Megan and Paige for lunch."

Then she fled, leaving Cam's daughter staring after her, and holding a huge piece of her heart.

Cam frowned at the stack of folders on his desk. It was almost seven o'clock, the last patient had walked out the door more than an hour earlier and he still had another hour or more of paperwork to finish. Thankfully his mother had agreed to take Maddie to ballet class so that he could stay late and try to catch up, but he refused to stay past eight o'clock—his daughter's bedtime.

He had been a part of her bedtime routine from the day she was born. Of course, the routine then had been much simpler:

a bottle and a cuddle—no snacks, drinks, checks for under-the-bed-monsters or stories required. But no matter how much the routine had changed and expanded over the years, Cam continued to cherish those quiet moments with his daughter.

On a few occasions, when Ashley had been over as Maddie was getting ready for bed, his daughter had asked her teacher to do story time instead. Cam wasn't really offended by her claims that Ashley told "the best stories" because he'd only had to listen to her once to know it was true.

He missed those story times. Or maybe he just missed Ashley.

Okay, no maybe about it—he *did* miss Ashley. And he was thinking, hoping, that if he gave her some time, she would soon realize that she missed him, too.

He opened the next folder on top of the pile, determined to push all thoughts of Ashley out of his mind and focus on his work so that he could be home for Maddie's bedtime.

Andy Robichaud was the name on the file. The elderly gentleman had come in a few weeks earlier, complaining of frequent and painful urination. Cam knew the cause could be something as simple as a urinary tract infection or as complicated as prostate cancer, so he'd ordered a series of tests to correctly identify the root of the problem.

The report from PDA Labs was on the top. He picked it up and skimmed the codes, the numbers, and struggled to make sense of the results. Because according to the paper, Mr. Robichaud was pregnant.

The report he was reading obviously belonged in someone else's file, not in that of a seventy-nine-year-old man—unless his patient was truly a medical miracle.

He was smiling at that impossibility when his gaze automatically shifted to the patient ID box at the top of the page. His smile slipped.

The test results were Ashley's.

Chapter Fourteen

When Ashley got home from her book club meeting Friday night, Cam was sitting in the dark on her front porch. If she'd been able to see him, she might have wondered why he was there. But she'd forgotten to leave the exterior lights on again and it was only when she stepped onto the path leading to the door that the sensor lights revealed his presence.

"Why didn't you tell me?" he demanded.

Her heart had jolted at the sight of him and now pounded crazily inside of her chest. It wasn't simply because she hadn't seem him in a while, but that she'd never seen him like this—his eyes hard, his jaw set, anger practically radiating off of him in waves.

And she immediately knew, without having to ask, what he was referring to. She swallowed. "How did you find out?"

"I hardly think that's the issue here."

Though her hands were shaking, she managed to slide her

key into the lock. "I assume you want to come in and talk about this."

"I'd say that a conversation is long overdue."

She dropped her coat and her purse inside the door, conscious of Cam following close on her heels as she made her way into the living room, turning on lights as she went and desperately trying to find the words to explain her deception.

"Did Eli tell you?" she finally asked.

"You know he would never breach doctor-patient confidentiality."

"Then how—"

"Your test results were misfiled. I might not have realized the error except that I've never known a seventy-nine-year-old man's blood work to reveal HCG."

"Oh."

"Now tell me why you didn't tell me," he challenged.

"I was going to," she hedged.

"When?"

"Even before I knew for certain that I was pregnant, I was so excited about the possibility that I wanted to share it with you."

"When was that?" he demanded to know.

She swallowed. "The day that I first met your ex-wife."

"That was almost three weeks ago."

"I know. But the longer she stayed, the more time she spent with you and Maddie, the more I started to doubt our relationship. Which I know doesn't make any sense," she admitted, "because I'm the one who said I didn't want a relationship and that Maddie should spend more time with her mother. But just when I started thinking that maybe we could be a family—you and Maddie and me and the baby—Danica showed up and reminded me that you already had a family."

"My marriage was never a secret," he pointed out.

"I know, but it was in the past and your ex-wife was on another continent. And then suddenly she was here and I decided I would rather raise my baby alone than let him know that he was your second choice."

"Why would you ever think something like that?" he demanded.

"Because I know what it feels like to be the runner-up. The bridesmaid instead of the bride."

"What are you talking about?"

"I fell in love with you when I was fifteen," she reminded him. "And during the two years that we were together, you told me you loved me, too. But when you graduated, you claimed that you weren't ready for a serious relationship, that you needed to concentrate on your studies. So I waited. You went away to college, then to med school, and I waited. Because I loved you. Then I found out that while I was waiting, you had married someone else."

"Because I was young and stupid and I foolishly thought that marrying someone else—someone who was completely unlike you—would finally help me forget about you.

"But it didn't work. I never forgot about you, Ashley. And I never stopped loving you. And when I agreed to go along with your plan to have a baby, it was only because I hoped that, by the time you got pregnant, you'd realize we should be together.

"Except that isn't quite how it happened, is it? As soon as you realized you were pregnant, you cut me out of your life. You never wanted me, you just wanted a baby."

His tone was so cold, so icily unforgiving, that she shivered. And because she knew that she was solely responsible for his anger, she didn't dispute his accusation. She didn't tell him that the truth was, she'd wanted everything.

Even if she hadn't realized it at the time, she'd wanted him and Maddie and their baby. But to admit that now would give him the power to destroy her pride along with her heart. And her pride was all she had left now.

"Because you were never going to let me be part of your family," she shot back.

"That's ridiculous."

"Every time I tried to include Maddie in our plans, you made other arrangements for her. Apparently I'm good enough to sleep with you, but you don't want me getting too close to your daughter."

"Maybe I just needed to know that you wanted to be with me for me, and not because of Maddie."

"You know me better than that."

"Apparently I don't, because I would never have expected you to keep the news of your pregnancy from me."

"Okay, I should have told you," she admitted. "Is that what you wanted me to say? Is that why you're here?"

"It's a start," he agreed.

"So where do we go from here? What are we going to do now?"

He didn't miss a beat. "Now we're going to get married."

She stared at him, stunned. "You want to get married?"

"Under the circumstances, it seems like a reasonable solution."

"Under the circumstances, it's completely ridiculous."

His jaw set. "Courts have pretty clear views on parental rights," he warned. "And I'm not going to let you cut me out of my child's life."

She managed to hold back the tears but couldn't hold back the words that were filled with anguish and torn from her heart. "You already took away my hopes and my dreams once, I'm not going to let you take *my* baby."

"*Our* baby," he said, but there was no warmth in his tone, only accusation.

She swiped a tear from her cheek. "Why are you doing this?"

"You can ask me that when you were the one who tried to trick me into getting you pregnant?" he asked scornfully.

She swallowed, but the guilt and the regrets stuck in her throat, practically choking her. "But I couldn't follow through with it."

"Except that you *are* pregnant," he pointed out.

"And I got that way with your consent and cooperation," she reminded him.

"Then you lied to me, telling me you weren't pregnant when you were."

"I didn't know for sure that I was!"

She was yelling at him. She'd never screamed at anyone before, and she was appalled by her behavior, ashamed of the out-of-control emotions that were churning inside of her.

"Look at us, Cam." She spoke softly, carefully, now. "We can't even have a rational conversation about this and you think we should get married?"

He took a step closer and cupped her face in his palms, his thumbs brushing away the tears she didn't even realize had spilled onto her cheeks. And then his mouth was on hers, and he was kissing her softly, slowly, deeply.

Her eyes drifted shut, her lips parted, her body yielded.

This was crazy. Complete insanity. She knew that, and yet, she couldn't seem to stop kissing him back.

She'd felt his absence from her life keenly in the past few weeks. And it wasn't just the physical aspect of their relationship that she missed, although there was no doubt she missed that as her pregnancy hormones seemed to have kicked into high gear, making her ache for him. But she'd missed so much more than that, too. The brief conversations they used to share when he picked Maddie up from school; their late night phone calls. Walks at Eagle Point Park; lazy Saturday mornings; Sunday afternoon matinees. In just a few short months, he'd become an integral part of her life again, and letting him go—even if it had been her decision—had ripped a hole in her heart.

But now he was here, holding on to her as if he never meant to let her go. And she was holding on to him, too.

When he finally eased his lips away from hers, he said, "Yes, I think we should get married."

"Wow. This is even better than last week's *Desperate Housewives*."

Ashley and Cam both turned to find Paige leaning against the doorjamb.

"I let myself in," she explained, "because it was apparent that nobody was going to respond to the bell."

Ashley didn't know if she was embarrassed to have been part of the scene her cousin walked in on or simply grateful that Paige had walked in. Because without the interruption, Ashley couldn't be certain she wouldn't have ended up back in bed with Cam—which is what had started this whole mess in the first place.

"I didn't think you were coming this weekend," she said.

"Change of plans."

"Well, your timing sucks," Cam told her.

She lifted a brow. "I really didn't mean to interrupt, but I thought you should know I was here before things moved beyond a PG-13 rating."

"Always happy to entertain you," Ashley said dryly.

Her cousin smiled, but Ashley noted the genuine concern and silent questions in her eyes.

"I should go," Cam said to Ashley, the focused intensity of his gaze warning that they still had a lot of unfinished business. "My mom's watching Maddie and I'm already later getting home than I told her I would be."

She nodded and followed him to the door, but it was only after she'd locked up behind him that she realized how much her knees were shaking.

"What was *that* all about?" Paige asked when she returned to the living room.

"I don't even know where to begin," Ashley admitted.

"Okay, let's start with Cam wanting to marry you."

She sighed. "Only because I'm pregnant."

Though Paige raised her eyebrows at that revelation, all she said was, "Knowing how much you've always wanted a baby, and how much you've always loved Cam, I'm not seeing a downside here."

"All I wanted was a baby. I didn't factor a husband anywhere into the equation, and Cam led me to believe that it would be up to me to decide what role—if any—he would play in our baby's life. And now that I am pregnant, he's changed his tune. Now it's all about his rights as the father. I didn't want a father—I wanted a sperm donor."

Paige didn't say anything.

Ashley swiped at more tears that had spilled onto her cheeks. "I can't believe I've made such a mess of everything."

"You only think it's a mess because it's not playing out the way you expected, because you didn't see that your plan was inherently flawed from the beginning."

Paige went to the freezer and pulled out a pint of Walton's chocolate fudge brownie ice cream. She got two spoons out of the drawer, then put one back when she peeled off the lid and realized there wasn't very much ice cream left.

Ashley frowned; Paige shrugged.

"I know pregnant women crave ice cream," she explained. "But sexually deprived women need chocolate. The fact that you are pregnant proves that you are not sexually deprived, ergo the pitiful amount of ice cream left in this container is mine."

"You can have the ice cream," Ashley said. "So long as you explain why you didn't warn me that this could happen."

Her cousin dipped her spoon into the ice cream. "Because you would have used it as an excuse to end your relationship before it had even begun, before you accepted that you never stopped loving Cam."

"Right now, I *hate* Cam."

"Love—hate." She licked the spoon. "Fine line."

Ashley shook her head. "I really hate him."

"You should have seen things from where I was standing. One minute you're spitting mad at each other, the next you're locked together in a steamy embrace." She fanned her face with her hand. "It was like watching a *really* hot movie."

"You're warped."

Her cousin grinned. "Seriously, Ash, that kind of passion is…inspiring. And all too rare."

"I don't want that kind of passion," Ashley lied. "And I sure as heck don't want Cam Turcotte barging into my life and telling me what to do."

"I could put up with some barging if it came with that kind of kissing."

"Then why don't *you* marry Cam?"

"He didn't ask me."

"And he only asked me because I'm going to have his baby."

"Congratulations, by the way."

Ashley allowed herself a smile. "Thanks."

"So when is due-day?"

"July twenty-ninth."

"Your mother will be happy."

"Why?" Ashley asked cautiously.

"Because she'll have a lot more time to plan your wedding than she had for Megan's."

"There's not going to be a wedding."

"That's not the impression I got from Cam."

"Well, Cam's already had one wedding, so that should be enough for him."

"Is that what this is really about? Are you still determined to punish him for finding someone else?"

"Do you really think I'm that petty?"

"I don't think you're petty at all," her cousin assured her. "But I also don't think you've ever been able to think clearly where Cam Turcotte is concerned."

"Well, forgive me for wanting to get married for reasons other than the fact that I'm pregnant."

"How about the fact that you love him?"

"I loved him once before, too," she admitted. "And he broke my heart when he left me."

And what she'd felt for Cam then was barely a shadow of what she felt now. Getting to know the man he'd become had forced her to let go of her infatuation with the boy he'd been and, in the process, her feelings had begun to change. The attraction was sharper, the chemistry stronger, the affection deeper.

And it worried her, that if she could love him so much more, he would have the power to hurt her even more. So she refused to give him that power.

Because Cam had moved away from home when he was nineteen, he'd learned at an early age to make his own choices and to live with the consequences—both good and bad—of those choices. Since coming home, he'd begun to appreciate the wisdom and experience his parents had to offer, and he'd found himself turning to them when he had questions or concerns about parenting or sometimes just to get a second opinion about something.

And that was why he went to his father's workshop Saturday morning.

Rob Turcotte was a finish carpenter by trade and by choice, and he'd taught his son that a job didn't feel like work if you loved the career you chose. It was a philosophy that was reflected in everything he did.

Cam mentally tried to assemble the various pieces of wood scattered on the table into some recognizable shape, then finally gave up and asked, "What are you making?"

"A cradle."

For half a second, Cam wondered if his father already knew what he'd come to talk to him about. Then he remembered his sister was expecting her first child—an exciting announcement but one that had been relegated to the back of his mind because he had more pressing concerns.

"For Sherry's baby?"

His father nodded. "Just like I made one for Maddie."

"She uses it for her dolls," Cam said, then wondered if he should have admitted that he let his daughter play with such a painstakingly crafted heirloom.

But his father, ever practical, said, "No reason to tuck it away in an attic to gather dust."

Cam watched him work for several minutes, checking edges, sanding rough spots. "It seems like a lot of work for a piece of furniture that's used for such a short time."

"It's a labor of love. And who knows? Maybe you'll have use for Maddie's cradle again someday."

"Maybe sooner than you think," Cam told him. "Ashley's pregnant."

Rob carefully set a delicate spindle down on the workbench before he met his son's gaze. "Is this what you wanted?"

Cam sighed. "It's what we both wanted. But now we can't seem to agree on where to go from here."

His father picked up a small sanding block and carefully began smoothing the rough edge of the wood.

"I want to marry her," Cam told him.

Rob nodded. "Seems reasonable."

"Ashley doesn't think so," he grumbled.

"She doesn't strike me as an unreasonable woman."

"About this, she's being completely unreasonable."

He paced the workshop while his dad sanded, and told him everything about their agreement.

"So you agreed, from the beginning, that you would make no claims with respect to the baby?" Rob asked.

Cam frowned. "I had to. It was the only way Ashley would include me in her plans."

"And now you want to change those plans?"

"She's carrying my child."

"I got that," his dad said. "But the fact remains that you set the terms and now you're pushing her to change them."

"Because I love her!"

His father lifted his brows. "Have you said those words to Ashley? And hopefully not shouted them at her."

Cam dropped his head into his hands. "I've really messed this up, haven't I?"

"It certainly seems that way."

"You know, that wasn't quite what I had in mind when I came in here for some fatherly advice."

His dad's only response was to ask, "When did you realize you were in love with Ashley?"

"When I saw her at the reunion," Cam admitted, though it had taken a long time after before he'd admitted as much to himself.

"So when you found out that Ashley wanted to have a baby, why didn't you just say, hey, that's convenient, because I'm in love with you anyway so we should get married and have a family together?"

"Because she would have thought I was a lunatic."

"Because she wasn't ready to accept your feelings?"

He nodded.

"And you knew that if you pushed her for too much too soon…." his dad prompted.

"I would push her away." Cam sighed as the point his father was trying to make finally became clear. "And that's what I'm doing now."

"Figured a man who graduated summa cum laude from medical school had to have at least half a brain," his father said.

"So what am I supposed to do—just back off and let her have this baby on her own?"

"That is what you said you'd do," his father reminded him.

"But—" Cam snapped his jaw shut as part of a long-ago conversation with Ashley played back inside his head.

"Trevor didn't break my heart. He broke my trust."

"And that takes longer to heal."

Cam had broken both her heart *and* her trust. Maybe Ashley did love him, but she was hurt and angry and scared, and if they were ever going to have a future together, he would have to earn her forgiveness.

And he knew that wasn't going to be easy.

When Greg Stafford showed up at her door the Tuesday night before Thanksgiving, Ashley wasn't just surprised, she was wary. She would say that she and the school principal had a friendly relationship, but she wouldn't say that they were friends.

Her trepidation increased when he said, "I apologize for bothering you at home, but I wanted to keep this conversation unofficial."

"Of course," she agreed, opening the door to invite him in.

She offered him coffee, which he declined, obviously not wanting to prolong his visit—the reason for which was still a mystery to her.

"I don't know how to delicately broach the subject," Greg

finally admitted, "so I'm just going to ask you point-blank. Is Cameron Turcotte the father of your baby?"

Ashley really wished he'd accepted her offer of coffee, because then she would be busy doing something and not just staring at him with a guilty flush staining her cheeks. "Where did you hear that?"

"It doesn't matter where I heard it," her principal said. "I'm asking you if it's true."

She'd told her principal about her pregnancy so that he would understand why she was taking a leave of absence at the end of the current school year, but she hadn't given him any details. And she swallowed nervously before answering his question now. "Yes."

"Are you going to marry him?"

She opened her mouth and, as if he knew that she was going to respond in the negative, Greg narrowed his gaze on her. "You might want to give that question some thought before you answer."

"We talked about the fact that I wanted to have a baby," she reminded him. "And you didn't express any concern about the fact that I wasn't married."

"Because you led me to believe that you were going to pursue alternate methods of conception."

"Why does it matter how I got pregnant?"

"It only matters if you're having an affair with the father of one of your students, which you just admitted that you are."

"Not having, had," she amended, though she suspected that the relationship being in the past wouldn't make a difference to her boss. "And we were both single, consenting adults."

Greg's sigh confirmed the fact. "Your personal life is just that," he told her. "Until someone brings it to the attention of the school board or the trustees. If that happens, it might be difficult for me to justify your position at the Parkdale."

She swallowed. "Are you threatening to fire me?"

"No." He sounded as shocked as she felt. "You have to know how much I enjoy having you on my staff, and how much the kids love you. But if the details of your relationship with Dr. Turcotte were revealed, the matter could be taken out of my hands."

"How did you find out?" she asked him.

"I got an anonymous phone call from someone. A woman. I don't believe your personal life is any of my business," he assured her. "But I couldn't ignore what she told me."

As soon as Greg said he'd spoken to a woman, Ashley instinctively knew it was Danica who had called. What she couldn't guess was why. What did the other woman hope to gain by exposing Ashley's relationship with Cameron? Or was it simply a power play—another chance to show Ashley that she still knew how to exert control over her ex-husband's life?

Ashley had the opportunity to answer at least some of her questions when she went to Walton's to pick up a couple of pints of ice cream the next day. It was her pitiful contribution to Thanksgiving dinner at Megan and Gage's house—a gathering that would include, in addition to the hosts, Ashley, Paige, Gage's parents, his brother and sister-in-law and their four kids, and Ashley and Megan's mother and her new husband.

When Ashley had commented on the size of the guest list, her sister had assured her that there was room for Cameron and Maddie, too. But Ashley knew that wasn't an option— not right now. She was still furious with Cam, still reeling from the fact that she'd barely had a chance to process the news of her pregnancy and he was threatening to sue for custody of a child who wasn't even close to being born.

Yes, she'd been furious and hurt, but she shouldn't have been surprised. Because, as her sister had so astutely pointed out, a man as devoted to one child as Cam was to Maddie would never turn his back on another. Maybe he'd misled her, but she was guilty of seeing what she wanted to see—or maybe not seeing anything beyond her own desires—and her reaction to his threat had been purely emotional and completely unreasonable.

Over the past couple of weeks, she'd finally accepted that she and Cam would need to find a way to work together for the sake of their child. And maybe they would find a way back to one another in the process. But first she had to get through the holiday.

While she was at Walton's, she ran into Danica, who was also picking up ice cream to go. It was ironic that, only a couple of months earlier, Ashley had suggested to Cam that Maddie should see more of her mother. Now Ashley was wishing Cam's ex-wife would just go back to England and stay there forever.

But she put a smile on her face and asked, "Are you in town to spend the holiday with Maddie?"

Danica nodded. "Just until Friday, then I'm back to Chicago, working on a corporate merger."

"I would have thought something like that would keep you so busy you wouldn't have time to stir up trouble for others."

The other woman shrugged, not even bothering to deny the accusation. "It seemed obvious to me that something had to be done to propel you and Cam forward."

"How does jeopardizing my job help either of us?"

Danica waved a hand dismissively. "They can't actually fire you."

"They could transfer me to another school."

"If you married Cameron, they'd have no reason to transfer you."

Ashley was as stunned by the suggestion as she was

annoyed by the other woman's machinations, and more than a little wary. The last time she'd been in town, Danica had focused her efforts on interfering in her ex-husband's new relationship. Was it really possible that she was now trying to push Ashley and Cam back together? And if so, why?

"You're assuming he's asked."

The other woman laughed. "I was married to the man once, remember?"

As if that was something Ashley was likely to forget.

"I know only too well how honorable and how committed to family he is," Danica reminded her. "And if I had to guess, I would say that 'marry me' were the first words out of his mouth when he learned you were pregnant. What I can't fathom is why you turned him down."

Ashley still wasn't sure that she should trust Cam's ex-wife, but the other woman's questions made her think, and made her wonder if she'd been too hasty in closing the door on a future with Cam. And though she'd had no intention of sharing her fears and concerns, she heard herself ask, "Would you want to marry a man who only proposed because you were pregnant?"

"I lied about being pregnant to get Cam to marry me," his ex-wife informed her.

Her shock must have been evident, because one corner of Danica's mouth lifted in a half smile. "He didn't tell you that, did he?"

Ashley shook her head.

"I was in love with him. Foolishly, perhaps, because it's obvious now that we were totally ill-suited for one another. But at the time, totally and completely. And when he started talking about coming back here and doing his internship in Pinehurst, I panicked. It was as if I knew, even without ever hearing him speak your name, that if he came home, I would lose him."

"So you told him you were pregnant?" Ashley was stunned by the audacity, then realized her own actions of late were hardly above reproach.

"And he, predictably, stepped right up to the plate," Danica told her.

She didn't know how to respond to this revelation; she didn't dare let herself think about how differently her life and Cameron's might both have turned out if Danica had never uttered those words. "What happened when he found out the truth?"

"He didn't—not for a long time. I told him I'd miscarried—" she looked away, and Ashley knew that Danica wasn't as blasé about her own behavior as she wanted to appear "—and he accepted that explanation."

"And then you did get pregnant."

Danica nodded. "And totally freaked. But he probably didn't tell you that, either."

She shook her head. "He said that the pregnancy was... unexpected."

"Unexpected," she agreed. "And unwelcome. I didn't want a baby. Not at that point in my life or our marriage, not ever."

"Why?"

"Long, boring story." Danica waved a hand dismissively. "My mother was unreasonable, demanding and abusive. My grandmother was the same, but also a drunk."

Ashley didn't have any trouble reading between the lines, and she felt an instinctive surge of sympathy for the other woman. "You were afraid you would continue the cycle."

"It just seemed smarter not to take any chances. And when Cam and I finally split, I knew the best thing I could ever do for Madeline was give custody to her father."

"You let him think you didn't want her."

"I didn't want her," Danica insisted.

But Ashley saw the pain in her eyes and she knew what it had cost Maddie's mother to give her up. She hadn't left her child because she didn't love her, but because she loved her too much to risk perpetuating the same kind of abuse she'd suffered. While the revelation didn't make Ashley like Danica any better, it did help her to understand the other woman. "Why are you telling me this?"

"Because I've finally realized that it's too late to undo the damage that I did to both Cam and Maddie, and I can see that you've helped both of them start healing."

Ashley wasn't entirely convinced of that, but Danica's words gave her hope that maybe she and Cam and Maddie could all do some healing together.

Chapter Fifteen

Thanksgiving dinner at Megan and Gage's was pure chaos, but in a good way. Having grown up with just one sister before Paige came to live with them, Ashley had never experienced a family meal that was quite so busy or loud or…fun.

She was immediately entranced by Gage's four nieces. Although the girls ranged in age from seven to twelve and had very different personalities, each one was charming in her own way. But Ashley enjoyed watching the interaction between Tess and Craig, too, observing the little touches and subtle signals that revealed a deep connection and enduring affection even after four kids. She saw evidence of the same bond between Megan and Gage and knew that her sister had truly lucked out when she'd fallen in love with Gage and married into the Richmond family.

Paige caught her in the kitchen, where she'd escaped on the pretext of wrapping up some of the leftover food but was really trying to fight the melancholic mood that had overtaken her.

"What's wrong?" her cousin asked, because she knew Ashley well enough to know that something was.

Ashley sighed. "I was just thinking about how lucky Megan is, to be with Gage, to be part of his family."

Paige opened her mouth as if there was something she intended to say, but closed it again without speaking a word.

"Come on, Paige. It's not like you to hold back if there's something on your mind."

"You don't want to hear it."

"I do," Megan said, coming into the kitchen with another armful of dishes.

"I just think that, instead of feeling sorry for herself, Ashley should go after what she wants."

"I'm not feeling sorry for myself," Ashley denied.

"Please—I can practically hear the violins."

"Paige," Megan admonished gently.

"I don't mean to be unsympathetic, but I had dinner last night with my friend Olivia—the one with the baby. She invited me over because she didn't want to celebrate the holiday alone but she has no family of her own, other than the baby, and she's had no contact with Emma's father since she told him she was pregnant. She didn't choose to be raising her child alone, but that's how it's working out.

"You made the decision to cut Cam out of your life, because I know that if it was up to him, he would be here with you right now. So if you're feeling neglected and alone, it's your own fault for not recognizing love when it's staring you right in the eye." And with that, she turned on her heel and stormed out of the kitchen.

"Well, that was quite a speech," Ashley said, as surprised as she was chastised by her cousin's outburst.

Megan slid an arm around hers sister's shoulder. "I think Olivia's really struggled with the adjustment from career woman to single mom, and it infuriates Paige that the father is doing nothing to help."

"Because it reminds her of her own father."

"Probably," her sister agreed.

"But she's right," Ashley realized. "And the truth is, I *don't* want to have this baby alone."

"I don't know why any woman in her right mind would," Megan said.

"But I'm scared," she admitted. "Cam and I have already screwed up our relationship twice. What if we try to make this work and screw it up again? Then we're not the only ones who get hurt—Maddie and her sister or brother will suffer, too."

"But what if you don't screw it up?"

And Ashley realized she'd been so focused on the potential negatives, she hadn't let herself fully consider the possibilities.

If she and Cam decided to work on their relationship and managed to succeed, then they could be a family. She would have everything she'd always wanted.

To say that Cameron was surprised when Ashley showed up at his door long after the turkey had been cleared away on Thanksgiving night would have been a colossal understatement. After their disastrous confrontation when he found out about her pregnancy, and his subsequent conversation with his father, he hadn't made any effort to see her or talk to her. He'd been clear about what he wanted, now it was up to Ashley to decide what she wanted.

As he put on a pot of decaf coffee, he wondered if her appearance at his door meant that she'd made a decision. But she didn't say anything until the coffee was made and he'd poured them each a cup.

"I thought Danica was in town."

Her mention of his ex-wife was another surprise, and definitely not a topic he wanted to discuss again.

"Yes, she is," he agreed.

"Is she here?"

"No, she's staying at a hotel downtown. We decided that would be a better arrangement from here on in."

"Oh."

"Did you come here to see me or her?"

"You," she said immediately. "And Maddie."

"She's in bed already."

Ashley nodded. "I didn't realize it was so late."

"It's not, really, but she had a busy day."

"Lots of turkey?"

"And too much pumpkin pie."

She nodded again, and he wondered if she felt half as awkward as he did. He wished he could go back a few months—even a few weeks—and change the way he'd handled things. Maybe then they'd still be together, looking forward to a future together.

"I've been thinking about what you said—the last time we talked," Ashley told him. "And I realized that I needed to clear up some of your misconceptions."

She wrapped her hands around the mug, stared into it. "When you found out I was pregnant, you accused me of only wanting a baby. But the truth is, after you came back to town, I never wanted *a* child so much as I wanted *your* child."

Her words, even more than the fact that she'd shown up at his door, gave him hope that maybe a future together wasn't completely out of reach, but he remained silent, cautious.

"And even if I hadn't gotten pregnant, I would have been happy. I *was* happy—with you and Maddie." She looked up at him now. "And I've been miserable without you."

"We've been pretty miserable, too," he admitted.

Those beautiful violet eyes filled with hope. "So…maybe… we could try again?"

It was what he wanted, what he hadn't dared let himself hope for when he saw her standing at his door, but as eager as he was to assure her, this time he wasn't agreeing to anything until he was sure they were on the same page.

"What is it, exactly, that you want to try?" he asked cautiously.

"I want us to be a family," she told him. "You and me and Maddie and our baby."

"Can I ask what precipitated this change of heart?" he asked, still cautious.

"I can't blame you for wondering, and I want to assure you that it doesn't have anything to do with the fact that I could lose my job, because—"

"What do you mean, you could lose your job?"

She flushed. "Oh. I thought you knew about that."

"About what?" He frowned.

"It doesn't matter," she said, opting not to mention his ex-wife's role in things. "My point is, deciding I wanted to be with you wasn't a change of heart at all. It just took me a while to acknowledge what was in my heart."

Which meant, if he was reading between the lines correctly, that she was—finally—admitting that she loved him.

"I would have told you about the baby," she continued. "I don't know how or when, but I never intended to keep my pregnancy a secret forever. I want my baby to know his or her father, and to know his or her big sister."

She pushed back her chair, stood up. "Anyway, that's what I wanted to tell you."

He stood up, too, and followed her down the hall. He didn't want to let her go, not with so much still unresolved between them. But he sensed that they both needed some time to assimilate everything before they moved forward, and he was determined to do better than an impulsive angry proposal the next time he asked Ashley to be his wife.

She paused at the door. "You once asked me if I believed in second chances."

He nodded. "I remember."

"Apparently I do believe in them after all."

"And third chances?" he prompted.

She smiled. "Maybe it's not the number of chances that matters as much as finally getting it right."

And as he watched her walk home, he was determined to ensure that this time they *would* get it right.

On Saturday, Maddie called Ashley to invite her to come over to for a movie marathon of *Shrek, Shrek Two* and *Shrek The Third*—her all-time favorite movies. Ashley wasn't sure what to make of the fact that the invitation had come from Cam's daughter instead of Cam, but she'd missed them both so much that she didn't hesitate.

They snuggled on the couch—Maddie tucked between her dad and Ashley—and ate popcorn and drank fruit punch. By the time the credits were rolling at the end of the second movie, Maddie was struggling to keep her eyes open.

"And now I think it's time for someone to brush her teeth and go to bed," Cam said, lifting his daughter up onto his shoulders and carting her toward the stairs.

"What about the third movie?"

"We can watch that one tomorrow," he promised her.

"And story time?" Maddie asked, not willing to relinquish that part of her bedtime routine despite her obvious fatigue.

"A short story," her dad agreed.

"Can Ashley tell me a story tonight?" Maddie turned to look beseechingly in Ashley's direction.

"Actually," Cam interrupted, "I had a story in mind for tonight."

Madeline frowned. "You only read stories from books."

"That's usually true," he admitted. "But I've been working on one that I thought you might like to hear."

"A made-up story? Is it any good?"

Cam's smile was wry. "I'll let you and Ashley be the judges of that."

So Ashley lowered herself onto the floor beside Maddie's bed while the little girl snuggled down under her covers.

"Once upon a time, in a land far, far away…"

Cam began his story in traditional fashion and proceeded to spin a fantastical tale about a beautiful princess who had fallen in love at a very young age with a handsome prince. And though the prince loved her, too, he had been given the gift of a magical sword and he wanted to travel the world and slay dragons, because he believed his desires and ambitions were far more important than a girl who had nothing to offer but all of the love in her heart.

"So the prince said goodbye to the princess and set out with his magic sword. And over the next twelve years, he slew more dragons than he'd ever imagined one man could slay, and he met many people and made many friends, but still there was an empty place in his heart. One of his friends was a very wise old man named Linus."

"Linus?" Maddie wrinkled her nose.

Cam scowled at the interruption. "What's wrong with Linus?"

"A fairy tale needs a fairy," she told him. "Preferably one with sparkly wings."

"Who's telling this story?"

"You are, Daddy, but—"

"One of those friends," he said again, "was a fairy named Linus—"

Maddie giggled.

"—who said to the prince, 'You have wealth and fame beyond your wildest dreams, but there is no love in your life.'"

"'That's not true,' the prince denied. 'I love Oscar, my loyal pet monkey, and I love all of my friends, and I especially love strawberry sundaes.'

"The sparkle-winged fairy shook his head. 'There is a different kind of love—the kind that a man feels for the woman who is his soul mate, the one who will stand by him and grow old with him—as he will stand by and grow old with her—until the stars fall from the sky. Have you never experienced this kind of love?'

"The prince was silent for a minute, remembering.

"'Once,' he finally said. 'A very long time ago.'

"'And did she love you?' Linus asked.

"'She said she did,' he recalled. 'But I thought she was too young to know what was in her heart, and I was too young to trust in my own.'

"'You are older now,' his friend pointed out.

"And so the prince strapped on his sword, tucked his monkey under his arm, and turned toward home. When he finally arrived back in the village, he was amazed to find that his feelings for the princess were even stronger now than they'd been so many years before.

"So the prince got down on one knee," Cam continued the story, but he was looking at Ashley while he spoke, and the intensity of his gaze stole all of the breath from her lungs. "And he took the princess's hand in his, vowed to love her forever and ever, and finally asked if she would do him the honor of becoming his bride."

"What did she say?" Madeline demanded when he fell silent again. "Did the princess agree to marry him?"

"What do you think?" Cam asked Ashley. "Would she accept his proposal?"

He wasn't asking about the fictional story, he was asking about their future. He was laying it all on the line right here in front of his daughter, showing that Maddie was part of the package that included his heart, his family, their future.

She had to swallow before she could speak, but then she assured him, "I think, if the prince really did love the princess enough to actually ask the question, she would most likely say yes."

"And then they would live happily-ever-after," Madeline announced.

"And then they would live happily-ever-after," her father agreed.

Maddie beamed. "That was a really good story."

"I'm glad you liked it," Cam told her.

"Will you tell me about Oscar tomorrow night?"

"Oscar?" He looked at her blankly.

"A pet monkey named Oscar should really have a story of his own."

"I'll have to think on that," Cam said, and kissed his daughter—first one cheek, then the other, then the tip of her nose.

Maddie giggled. "'Night, Daddy."

"Go straight to sleep now."

"Wait."

He paused.

"Can I have a drink of water? Please?"

"Didn't you have a drink before you got into bed?"

She nodded. "But I'm thirsty again."

"A quick drink," he reluctantly agreed. "Then no more stalling."

While Cam went to get her drink, Ashley pulled the covers up under Maddie's chin.

"Are you going to say yes?" Maddie whispered the question.

Ashley lowered herself onto the edge of the mattress. "Yes to what?" she asked cautiously.

The little girl rolled her eyes. "Didn't you pay any attention to his story?"

She couldn't help but smile at the indignant tone. "Yes, I paid attention to his story."

"Well, *he's* the prince," Maddie said, as if it was something Ashley should have figured out for herself. "And *you're* the princess. And if he loves you and you love him, then you should get married."

If only life was as simple as a fairy tale and happy endings were guaranteed, Ashley thought. But she'd learned long ago that there were no guarantees in life, and only more recently acknowledged that she was responsible for her own happiness.

And tonight she'd finally accepted that her greatest chance for happily-ever-after was with Cam, his little girl, their baby and the life they could build together.

"Would it be okay with you if we got married?"

Maddie's head bobbed enthusiastically. "Then you could be my new mommy."

"You have a mommy," Ashley felt compelled to remind her. Even if Danica had never been comfortable in that role, she was still the woman who had given birth to this amazing little girl and deserved to be acknowledged as her mother.

Maddie nodded again, with less enthusiasm this time. "But she's only a sometimes mommy, and I need an every day mommy like Victoria has."

"I kind of like the idea of being an every day mommy." She hugged the little girl, and though she knew she would have a baby of her own to cuddle in a few months, there was no doubt that Cam's firstborn would always hold a very special place in her heart.

When Cam came back into the room with a cup of water, Maddie took two tiny sips, then handed it back again.

"That's all you wanted?" he asked suspiciously.

She nodded.

He shook his head as he set the cup on the dresser. "Straight to sleep now."

She nodded again.

He turned out the light and led Ashley down the stairs and into the living room. Now that they were alone again, she worried that the awkwardness that had characterized their relationship of late might return, but then he took her in his arms, and she didn't feel awkward at all. She felt as if she was finally where she belonged.

"So," he said, pulling her into his arms. "What did you think of story time?"

She thought it was the most wonderful fairy tale she'd ever heard, but she wasn't quite ready to admit as much.

"Creative," she said. "But the magic sword? Talk about obviously and pathetically phallic."

"A dragon slayer needs a sword," he insisted, and tugged her down onto the couch beside him. "But if you think you could do better, you can help me with Oscar's adventures."

She shook her head. "His story line is entirely yours."

He shifted so that he was facing her, and stroked a finger gently down her cheek. "Actually, I was hoping we could work on it together. Maybe collaborate, over the next fifty or sixty years or more."

Her heart started pounding faster again. "That's a long-term collaboration," she warned.

"I figure it will take a while to get to the ever-after part."

"Is that your idea of a proposal?" she challenged.

"What do you think?"

As much as she wanted to throw her arms around him and

say yes a thousand times, she worried that giving in too soon would set a dangerous precedent for the next fifty or sixty years. She might finally be ready to admit that she loved him, but she didn't want to give him the impression that she was easy. Instead, she said, "I think you should stick to playing doctor."

He shifted closer, touched his lips lightly to hers. "Where did I screw up?"

"You skipped over the most important stuff," she told him.

He smiled. "You mean the stuff where I tell you how much I love you, have always loved you, and will always love you?"

"Yeah, that stuff."

"Okay," he said solemnly. "I love you Ashley Roarke, have always loved you and will always love you—until the stars fall from the sky."

"Ooh, that part about the stars…nice touch."

"Thanks." He took her hands, linked their fingers together. "Now would be a good time to tell me that you love me, too."

"I do love you," she admitted. "I always have and always will—until the stars fall from the sky."

He smiled. "So what do you say—will you marry me?"

"Will you slay dragons for me?" she asked him.

"Absolutely."

"Do I get to see the magic sword?"

"Honey, if you marry me, the magic sword is yours."

She leaned forward and touched her lips to his. "How could any girl refuse an offer like that?"

Epilogue

The night before Ashley and Cameron's wedding, an unexpected snowstorm blew through Pinehurst.

Being as it was the first Saturday in April, the bride had been prepared for rain—she hadn't anticipated snow. But even when she awoke to find the entire town buried beneath almost eight inches of fluffy white stuff, she wasn't concerned. She and Cameron had overcome much bigger obstacles to get to this point in their lives, and she knew that her husband-to-be wouldn't let anything get in the way of the ceremony, which was scheduled to take place later that morning.

Her mother wasn't quite so unruffled.

"It's April," Lillian Rolland fumed, stomping the snow off of her shoes inside the door. "There isn't supposed to be snow in April, and especially not on your wedding day."

Megan, who had managed to arrive even before the snowplows had been down the street, rolled her eyes behind their mother's back.

"You can't schedule the weather," Paige, who had driven in from Syracuse the day before, said philosophically.

"But I arranged for a horse-drawn carriage to take the bridal party to the church," Lillian reminded them.

She may have only had a few months to plan the wedding, but she hadn't overlooked any details. Since Megan had tied the knot with little notice and even less preparation at City Hall, Lillian had been determined to ensure that at least one of her daughters had a proper wedding, and she'd dragged her new husband away from their home in Europe and thrown herself into the preparations.

"If we can't have four horses, at least we have four-wheel drive," Ashley told her mother now.

"But I wanted to ride with the horses," Maddie chimed in.

Lillian brushed a hand affectionately over the child's hair. "At least someone here appreciates the details."

"Come on, Maddie," Paige steered the little girl toward the stairs and away from the battle she sensed was brewing. "Let's get you dressed."

"I appreciate everything you've done," Ashley assured her mother. "And I know that, because of all your careful planning, my wedding day is going to be wonderful. I just don't think anything—not my dress or flowers and especially not the weather—matters as much as finally marrying the man I love."

Her mother sighed. "You're right. Of course, you're right. I just wanted everything to be perfect for you."

"Everything will be," Ashley said, because she knew that being with Cam would make it true.

An hour and a half later, two horse-drawn sleighs glided to a halt in front of the Holy Trinity Church.

"It was just like riding in a fairy tale!" Maddie exclaimed.

"Personally, I would have much preferred a heated limo," Paige confided to Megan, as they followed the skipping child up the wide stone steps—which had been carefully shoveled clean and salted—toward the front doors.

Her cousin pulled her shawl more tightly around her shoulders. "Well, if we had to freeze our butts off, at least we did so in style."

As Ashley lifted her skirt to follow the others, she could barely feel her toes inside her satin pumps, but she didn't complain. Not just because she didn't want to offend her mother after she'd gone to such efforts to amend the transportation arrangements, but because she knew that Cam was waiting for her inside the church and that knowledge was enough to warm everything inside of her.

When the music began, Paige gave Ashley a quick hug—careful not to crush her flowers—before she started up the aisle. Megan went next, whispering, "Be happy," with a smile that assured her sister she knew she would be before she followed her cousin's path. Then it was Maddie's turn, and several guests would later remark that the little girl's smile was almost as radiant as the bride's.

For Maddie, this was the happiest day of her life, though she couldn't decide if it was because it was her daddy and Ashley's wedding day, or because she was getting a baby sister (she refused to consider that the baby might be a boy), or because she was going to Florida with Grandma and Grandpa for her spring break while the newlyweds went on their honeymoon.

It was the happiest day of Ashley's life, too, but she knew exactly why. Because she was finally married to the man she'd always loved. Because Cam and Maddie were now part of the family she'd always wanted.

And because her happily-ever-after was just beginning.

* * * * *

Helen R Myers is a collector of two and four-legged strays, and lives deep in the Piney Woods of East Texas. She cites cello music and bonsai gardening as favorite relaxation pastimes, and still edits in her sleep—an accident, learned while writing her first book. A bestselling author of diverse themes and focus, she is a three-time RITA® Award nominee, winning for *Navarrone* in 1993.

HOPE'S CHILD

BY
HELEN R MYERS

First published in Great Britain 2011
Harlequin Mills & Boon Limited,
Eton House, 18-24 Paradise Road, Richmond, Surrey TW9 1SR

© Helen R Myers 2010

ISBN: 978 0 263 88871 3

23-0311

Harlequin Mills & Boon policy is to use papers that are natural, renewable and recyclable products and made from wood grown in sustainable forests. The logging and manufacturing processes conform to the legal environmental regulations of the country of origin.

Printed and bound in Spain
by Litografia Rosés S.A., Barcelona

Prologue

"Would you hand over your truck keys, please?"

Right after sliding into the back booth of the Cedar Grove Bar and Grill, Hope Alessandro Harrell got the exact reaction she expected from her fiancé, Will Nichols. His baby blues widened, he reared back his blond head as though startled by an unexpected jab, and then he smirked.

"Now darlin', you aren't going to make a scene, are you?"

Blinking away tears of humiliation from what she'd witnessed upon entering the North Central Texas establishment, she enunciated softly to avoid being overheard by the diners around them, "You've put on enough of a show for one night, and I don't care to sit here a second longer than I have to being either pitied or gossiped about. Now, either pass me the keys to your truck, or I'll call someone to get a lift home…or ask Lyon to drive me." She regretted accepting a friend's offer to drop her off so she could drive back to her place with Will. What had seemed a good idea at the time—due to the weather—was suddenly a major error in judgment.

By "Lyon," she meant Chief of Police Lyon Teague still standing by the bar pretending to nurse a mug of coffee. Will's old schoolmate and best friend had stopped by to escape the May downpour that was making driving in their area treacherous. He had obviously witnessed what had transpired before her arrival, since he'd been standing beside Will when she'd entered. From the expression on his face, he, too, was wishing he was anywhere but there.

"And how am *I* supposed to get home?" Will asked. "I have two hundred head of cattle to transfer to the sale barns first thing tomorrow morning."

"Ask Rochelle Sims to give you a lift. I've no doubt as soon as I leave, she'll be all over you again anyway."

Will's bored expression spoke fathoms about how seriously he was taking this. "Rochelle is just...Rochelle."

Although there wasn't a hint of a slur to his speech to confirm that he'd been drinking for a while before she'd arrived, his attitude made Hope all the more offended and disgusted. "And that's acceptable behavior to you? Her hands all over you—in places no *lady* should venture in public?"

"Now you're exaggerating."

"I don't think so. I also don't think this was the first time she's been so familiar with you."

Aware that there were a good dozen people angling to see and listen to what was going on between them, Hope leaned across the table and extended her hand. "I'm dead serious, Will. Keys. Either way, I'm out of here."

Muttering, Will handed them over, but when she slid out

of the booth, she wasn't thrilled that he followed. At six-four he could pretty well go wherever he wanted to go, and being only five-seven in her highest heels, Hope felt compelled to pause by Lyon before exiting the grill.

"I'd just like you to know that we're leaving. I'll be driving myself home in Will's truck to my place. A friend dropped me off so I'm without a ride. Could you make sure he gets home okay once he takes possession of his vehicle?"

Shooting Will a grim look, Lyon opened his mouth to speak, then, paused and nodded once. "I'll do better than that, I'll be right behind you."

Hope sensed from Lyon's demeanor that what he really wanted was for her to let him drive her home. But she still had things to say to Will; they might as well get it over with than drag things out. Relieved to know that Lyon would be close, she touched the sleeve of his yellow police raincoat. "I appreciate that."

It was early May and spring was exhibiting its more serious side with a rock-and-roll thunderstorm. Lightning shot from black skies like laser guns in a sci-fi movie and the earth shook as bolts hit in frequent succession. The storm had stalled, so as soon as a bolt exploded in the east, another struck the pasture across the street, and before Hope could swallow her heart back down into her chest, the western sky lit followed by a hair-raising crack. Any thought of backing out of her decision to delay her departure was gone as the restaurant's door shut behind them indicating Will was blocking her retreat. Hope ran for the truck. Unfortunately, along with her high heels, she was in a pencil skirt, so when Will caught up with her and snatched the keys out of her hands, she could do nothing but shout his name in protest.

"Get inside before we both get fried!" he yelled back to her.

By the time she slammed the passenger door shut, she was as angry as she was drenched. Once Will climbed in on the driver's side, she snapped, "I swear, Will, this is it."

In truth, though, she was as fed up with herself than she was with him; after all, he was just being himself. She was the fool for believing that loving her would inspire some maturity and restraint in the man. At this point she had to wonder if he knew what the meaning of love truly meant? Even as he backed out of the parking slot and exited the lot, she could tell he was no less upset. But that was his perfect M.O. for being caught red-handed.

"The wedding is off," she continued, striving to keep her tone even.

Will's response was as if she'd thrown her engagement ring out the window. Swearing, he pounded the steering wheel with his fist. "That's not fair!"

"Oh, and playing touchy-feely with a woman who would lie with roadkill for a thrill is? What's unfair is that you've been misrepresenting yourself all along. How often did you cheat after dropping me off at home, or when I was out of town on business? Just count during this past year that we've been engaged."

"You can't expect me to answer such a lose-lose question. C'mon, baby, you know what happened back there was nothing."

"It was plenty something to me. Did you really think I was that desperate to get married that I would pretend to not notice your loose zipper mentality? Then you don't know me at all."

"Well, get it all out then and tell me what I need to do to

make you happy again because your father won't let you cancel the wedding," Will said, his tone resigned. "He wants Nichols land joined with Harrell land one way or another. Besides, I can't afford to pay him back what I owe him yet."

This second shock of the evening left Hope almost speechless. "You borrowed from my father knowing how he does business? When? How much?" The next troubling and infuriating thing to cross her mind was that her father hadn't said a word of this to her.

"Under the circumstances, it's none of your business, is it?"

He sounded more like a teenager focused on gaining the upper hand than an adult of thirty-four. "Right you are," Hope said telling herself that in the long run, she was about to get off easy. "Forget that I asked."

That indifference wasn't the reaction Will had expected. "Okay, so I goofed up and a couple of things didn't work out. The bank note was due last month, but cattle prices were too low to send them to market. Everything is fine now. I'll pay him back by Monday. You know, the bank was really impressed that I have you and your old man's support. They finally increased my line of credit, so I won't have to borrow from him again."

Hope experienced a new wave of revulsion for him. Why hadn't he let her see these anything-goes, means-to-an-end sides of him? Studying his profile for a few seconds, she announced. "I'm pregnant."

Will threw back his head and howled with glee. "Jackpot!"

That told Hope all she needed to know. She'd been taken off birth control by her doctor and Will had assured her that he would be responsible for taking care of things until she had made up her mind on the best means of pro-

tection, or was ready to start a family. They'd not had unprotected sex, so finding herself weeks late had rattled her,
especially since historically her menstrual cycle was as
regular as a government clock. "You tampered with those
condoms," she said voicing her worst suspicion.

With a shrug and self-satisfied grin, Will replied, "It all
works out. We wanted kids. I needed insurance in case
something like this sprang up before the wedding."

Amazing, she thought. He was disciplined enough for
all of these machinations, but he couldn't restrict himself
to one woman—let alone be truthful to her.

"I can't wait to tell Ellis," Will continued.

"You do that." Seething, Hope's hand shook as she
pulled off the engagement ring that had been feeling increasingly cumbersome and awkward on her hand. If he
was having financial troubles, she could only imagine what
he still owed on it. "And be sure to let him know that I'm
done with you and why."

When she pulled open the ashtray drawer and dropped
the ring inside, Will protested. "Hey! Put that back on!"

Hope couldn't believe when he began swatting away her
hand and grappling for the piece of jewelry. "Watch the
road, Will. *Will!*"

The big white dually pickup spun on the oil-and-water
slick county road. Uttering an explicit curse, Will jerked
on the steering wheel. That overreaction shot the diesel
truck down an embankment where the truck's right wheels
sunk quickly into ground already soft from two previous
flooding rains. The momentum sent the weighty vehicle
flipping into the pasture below.

As they rolled over and over, Hope screamed, first out of
terror, next from the pain as Will's much larger and heavier

body slammed repeatedly against hers. He'd been too agitated and too determined to get his way to fasten his seat belt.

When the 360-degree roller coaster came to a halt, they had settled upside down. Gasping to get air into her lungs as the seat belt threatened to slice her neck and crush her lungs from her body being forced against it, Hope's first thought was, *My baby!*

She knew she wouldn't be able to tell how badly she was hurt until she was upright again and prayed it was soon. Her body's blood was rushing to her head and she felt every heartbeat, the fresh night air rushing through all four shattered door windows reviving her more than she might have wanted. Then her gaze settled on the crumpled, still heap beside her.

"Will?"

He didn't respond, didn't move at all as he lay on the ceiling of the cab. In this rural field away from street lights, she couldn't tell if he was bleeding or even breathing. She reached for him.

"Will!"

"Hope—don't try to move him!"

The sound of Lyon's voice sent a wave of relief over her that brought tears to her eyes. She twisted what little she could to see him drop to his knees and lean down to peer at her. He aimed his flashlight all around her to gauge her condition, but tried to avoid getting the beam directly in her eyes. Grasping the hand she reached toward him, he squeezed reassuringly.

"Are you bleeding anywhere, sweetheart?"

"N-no. I don't think so. But Will—"

Lyon aimed the flashlight at him and after only three seconds, returned the beam to her. "Let's get you out first. I'm smelling fuel."

Come to think of it, Hope did, too. As a new wave of terror threatened to override reason, she repressed a whimper and wrestled with the seat belt.

"I've got it. Easy…"

Lyon opened a pocketknife and quickly sliced the belt. With his help, she slumped more than dropped to the padded ceiling. Then wrapping his arms around her, he eased her through the frame of sharp shards as quickly but carefully as he could.

"That's it," he said praising her instincts to fold into a fetal position to protect her face and extremities. In less than a minute from first arriving, he was jogging up the slope to his patrol car lighting the night sky with its own light show.

"Put me down, Lyon," she pleaded. "I'm okay and you need to get back to Will." But another close bolt of lightning made a liar out of her and she cringed into a tighter ball and wrapped her arms fiercely around his neck as she hid her face against him.

Lyon didn't put her down until he had her inside the backseat of his car. He quickly dragged off his raincoat and wrapped it around her. "You should hear an ambulance and fire truck any second now," he assured her. And with a tender caress of his fingers across her cheek, he was gone.

Before he reached the truck, Hope did hear sirens. The rain was easing up and the temperatures were milder than ever, but Hope hugged his raincoat closer, shivering. Shock, she realized.

She watched in dread as Lyon tried repeatedly to get Will to respond and then to drag him out, but ordinarily Will outweighed him by at least thirty pounds and in these circumstances that might as well be a hundred. As she concluded that she had to get back down there to help him, the truck turned into a fireball throwing Lyon yards back into the pasture.

Only yards down the slope, Hope froze clamping her hand against her mouth. *Dear God, no! Not Lyon, too!* she thought.

Amazingly, he scrambled to his knees and tried to reach into the truck again, but the flames forced him back—and that's what saved his life.

As firemen raced past her, two dragging a hose, another explosion flung Lyon even farther back.

Hope ran and stumbled behind EMTs to reach him. By the time she did, the EMTs were helping him up toward the street. They stopped and discreetly stepped aside and looked away as she and Lyon stared at each other. Then with a sob, Hope slumped against him. He quickly gathered her toward him, supporting her with his good arm.

"I'm sorry," he rasped.

Chapter One

The memorial service and funeral for William Jefferson Nichols II drew everyone who had ever met him or was interested in his highly publicized though short-lived pro-ball career—or was connected to the Harrells either socially, through business, or politics. With a crowd that size, the memorial service was forced to move to the high school gymnasium. Lyon had his entire department working and still had to ask for assistance from the Fannin County sheriff's department and the Texas state police.

Making things all the more challenging was the weather. Another drenching rain system was producing strong winds and adding to flood conditions. Culverts were overflowing from swelling streams and ditches making their countryside a maze of water and mud to navigate through—a challenge for locals, and a near nightmare for visiting out-of-towners in designer wear. So far, however, no deadly lightning had added to the situation, but after successfully navigating through town to the cemetery, Lyon knew better than to think they were out of the woods yet.

From his vantage point on the terrace, one block above the gravesite, he scanned the crowd below. He stood dressed in his summer uniform, the yellow rain jacket all but a fixture this week. His arms were crossed over his chest, so his right arm could serve as a rest for his bandaged left one. The tight fit of the jacket sleeve pressed on the bandages and added to the headache that had stuck with him since the night of the accident. But he couldn't complain and he had resisted the pain prescriptions written to him at the hospital. Things could have turned out much worse, and he wanted to remember that.

Only a fraction of those who'd been to the memorial service had continued over to the cemetery, but that was still too many to fit under the double tent tied to extra stakes due to the forty mph wind gusts. All four lanes surrounding the site where Will was about to join his parents, grandparents, and an aunt, created a vehicular fortress reminiscent of western movie scenes when wagon trains circled to protect the settlers from Indians. Having been born to a mother who was full Cherokee, Lyon saw the humor in that—especially since a number of these "wagons" were limousines, BMWs, Mercedes, and so forth. Lyon hadn't seen so much wealth centered in one place since Ellis had held a fundraiser for the current Texas governor.

He was doing his best to stay out of sight as much as possible and had been since the night of the accident when Rochelle Sims had burst into Emergency at Cedar Grove General and thrown her keys at him, slicing open his lower lip, which had earned him three stitches. Her subsequent tirade spread around town as quickly as the news about the wreck. As is always the case with gossip, there were a number of people willing to believe her accusations that he hadn't done enough to save Will, and by the funeral, a conspiracy theory had gained root—especially with Clyde and Mercy Nichols, Will's uncle and aunt, the closest remaining family he'd had left. There were several reasons for Clyde to show how devastated they were about Will— all of them having to do with financial profit—and so he was vowing to have Lyon's badge.

That didn't mean Lyon didn't feel some responsibility for what happened. No one could be harder on him than he was himself. If only he had made it outside of the grill in time to see it was Will behind the wheel and stopped him. While he hadn't felt a pulse when he'd reached for his old schoolmate and was fairly certain Will had broken his neck in the crash, the idea of him burning to death added to his sleeplessness. Making that all the worse was thinking how close beautiful Hope had come to dying, too. No, he wasn't going to make himself a target today for additional venting. Nevertheless, staying away hadn't been an option.

As he continued to scan the crowd, Lyon's gaze finally locked on Hope slowly working her way through a group of latecomers, thanking them for coming. She had been doing that since people had begun to arrive at the school gym almost three hours ago. Today her attire was tailored but sensible for the weather—black raincoat and tailored slacks, and boots that would have won his nod of approval if it hadn't been for the stiletto heels. She still stood out, though, among the silks and out-of-season leathers; she always did. Her other bit of fashion besides the sexy boots, was cultural, a black lace mantilla—no doubt her mother's—gracefully draped over her long black hair, the ends whipping in the wind behind her shoulders.

When the minister began to speak, she did not join Clyde and Mercy seated on the first row under the tent, unlike Ellis, who had unabashedly placed himself on their left. Instead, she stood out in the open, the wind alternately trying to push then pull her off her feet. Even from this distance Lyon noted her paleness. He fingered his radio, tempted to tell his people to get someone closer in case she needed their assistance. But knowing the audio noise would attract too much attention, upsetting her in the process, he sweated through the next few minutes, willing her to keep breathing and to stay on her feet.

Once the last prayer began, Lyon tensed. Hope started circling behind the crowd and walking toward him. With her every step, he felt a growing tightening in his abdomen as, one-by-one, people noticed her direction.

"What are you doing?" The question was whispered for his ears alone. It was pressure-relief for emotions reduced to scar tissue grown bow-tight by dread and desire for wanting the wrong woman.

Hope could have been homecoming queen, county Miss Whatever, Miss Texas and probably Miss America or Universe if that's what she'd wanted. She had what a movie producer would typecast as a smoldering sexuality, balanced by gentleness and sensitivity. What Lyon knew was that she was no stereotype and was as intelligent as anyone he knew and twice as smart as most. That made her highly attractive to ambitious men looking for more than a trophy wife. Her one weakness, however, was always siding with the underdog. Today that was apparently him.

When she stopped before him, he was unable to keep

the tenderness out of his voice or the warmth from his gaze. "Trying to earn me some loose teeth to go with this split lip?"

"I was suffocating down there. The air reeks with over-priced perfume and bad breath from money cancer." She took a deep cleansing breath. "Please don't be annoyed with me. I'm sick about what happened at the hospital, and speechless that you let Rochelle get away with it. If I'd been within hearing distance at the time, I'd have gladly decked her for you."

Lyon struggled against a choking laugh for that impos-sible image, as much as for her creative medical diagno-sis. "I appreciate the support, Mighty Might, but you let me deal with the rabble-rousers in this town."

While his rarely-voiced pet name for her drew a smile from her, it vanished as quickly as it appeared and she was all seriousness again. "Don't joke. We need to talk."

What he needed was for her to get home and go to bed and take better care of herself than it looked like she was doing. "Not today, Hope." He nodded to the scene below. "Your father has just noticed your whereabouts."

Without bothering to glance over her shoulder, she said, "He'll recover. He has plenty going on himself not to waste time figuring out what I'm up to."

For his sanity's sake, Lyon tried a different tack. "From the itinerary we received, the Nichols' reception follows this. Aren't you expected there?"

"I'm not going. I've extended my regrets to Clyde and Mercy. I've fulfilled my obligations to them and I don't think I can stomach one more minute of him pretending he's sorry for what's happened or watching her already putting on airs. I suspect my father will skip the reception, as well—or stop by only long enough to cull the people he wants to join him at the estate for aged liquor-of-choice and illegal cigars."

"Sounds like the place to be."

Looking like she didn't believe him for a second, Hope tilted her head as she studied him and replied, "If you're into buying favors, fixing elections, and various other offensive objectives during such grim circumstances. On the other hand, I've made my mother's tortilla soup, and we both need out of this weather."

While he'd never tasted the soup, Lyon had heard enough to know Hope had inherited Rebecca Alessandro Harrell's talents in the kitchen. Add that to his unwillingness to leave her to the vultures that had been salivating over her since learning she was a free woman again and he circled the white patrol car to open the passenger door for her.

Once he was seated behind the wheel, he finally noted, "What were you doing cooking when you look like I should take you back to the hospital instead of home?"

Hardly intimidated, she replied, "You're one to talk. How's the arm?"

"Most of the bandages should come off by Monday." He knew that before they'd entered the car, she'd been eyeing his singed hair and was kind not to bring up the lingering second degree burns on the left side of his face, some third degree ones particularly on the outer shell of his ear.

"You're still a quick healer, I'm grateful."

Was she remembering when he'd suffered a concussion trying to reach his parents after the tornado that had killed them, or thinking further back to when he'd cracked a rib during a football game at the beginning of his senior year in high school and continued to play through the pain?

Either way her compassion stirred a different hunger in him and he needed relief from it.

"Could we redirect this conversation to the person who matters?" Lyon replied just as concerned. "How are you—really? I'm sorry that I haven't been around as much as I should have…as much as I intended."

"You've been inundated with job responsibilities and the press when you should have been home recuperating and avoiding infection."

Her voice was naturally soft and soothing, not quite in the second soprano range, and yet more lilting than what an alto could achieve. If she had any free time, she could easily be an in-demand voice for audiobooks; a child with a scraped knee would yearn to sit on her lap. In that way she reminded him of her mother, and his.

"Hope?"

"Yes."

"Stop. It's over. Now tell me if it was as bad as it looked?"

"Being insulated by shock helps. You lost both of your parents, you know. One operates on automatic pilot waiting for privacy to come to terms with things—in my case, too many things that should already have been dealt with. But all that aside, I know I can't pretend that what was broken could be fixed."

Hoping that she intended to expand on that, Lyon eased out of the cemetery and headed for Hope's mini-ranch, a twenty-acre oasis barely six miles south of town, three if you were traveling by crow or buzzard. Although the property was just outside of Cedar Grove city limits, Lyon passed by there often enough to know that Hope worked hard on it when she wasn't busy with her small but increasingly prestigious consulting-investment firm that also involved some social service work, as well as arranging for legal advice for landowners trying to keep their property out of greedy opportunists' hands, including her father's.

There was virtually no traffic on the road for the moment, and except for calling into the station to tell his dispatcher that he would be taking a lunch break for an hour, there were no interruptions. That made the extending silence between them palpable.

"Okay, I'll start," Hope said. "As far as I'm concerned, you should have been the one to give the eulogy."

Something good *had* come from this mess—he didn't have to. "Kent Roberts did a good job."

"Kent's been the mayor for longer than you've been chief of police and he could eulogize every dog put asleep by the animal shelter. But you were Will's best friend."

"Not lately. Not for a good while."

Hope took a deep breath. "Thank you for opening that door. Did the trouble between you two have anything to do with what I witnessed that night between him and Rochelle?"

Lyon didn't want to add to her mental anguish. "You've been through enough, Hope. And, really, what does it matter now?"

"More than you know."

He didn't care for that answer, but since she shifted her gaze out the passenger window, he took the delay—undoubtedly a temporary one—as a welcome reprieve.

When he turned into the driveway of her property, she triggered the remote she took from her purse to open the electronic gates. The property was framed in front by wrought iron and in back by ranch wire for the quarter horses she stabled there. As a child, Hope had been trained to be an equestrian rider, but quit at eighteen after the death of her mother. Some said a fall during a cross country part of a competition had caused the heart attack that had claimed Rebecca's life. In any case, five years ago, her love of horses too strong to reject, Hope turned to the western saddle form of riding. At least she stayed out of any kind of competition, Lyon thought.

Her house was a white brick hacienda-style building complete with a stucco roof. The front courtyard was framed by a cactus garden on the west, and a rose garden on the east that the house itself protected from the killer Texas sun by midday. Beyond the back fencing, he could see a vegetable garden and behind it, a peach orchard.

"You've turned this into one of the prettiest properties around," he told her driving up the concrete driveway.

"I'm glad you think so. I've been trying to talk my neighbors into letting me buy another twenty acres, but my father has been doing his best to get their whole seven-hundred acres in a lot sum, so negotiations are in limbo."

Lyon didn't understand a parent doing such a thing—especially to his only child—but Ellis was a commodity known only to himself. "It seems to me that your father has gotten progressively worse since your mother passed away."

"Only at first glance. The truth is that while she was clever and could only curb a fraction of his ego trips—as she called them—she was better at keeping his missteps and embarrassments under the gossip radar. The robber baron impulses were there all along." Hope took out another remote and triggered the third garage door. "Pull in there if you don't mind."

Under different circumstances, Lyon would hesitate. In this day of endless sex crime litigation and personality smear campaigns, no law enforcement officer, let alone city or government employee, entered a situation that even remotely seemed like a set up. But this was Hope, and Lyon knew that she was trying to protect him from gossip should his car be spotted in her driveway for longer than a minute. When the skies opened to a new deluge any hesitation became moot. As he eased the police car in, he saw her cherry red pickup was in the first garage and her black Mercedes was in the second. She always looked capable of driving either, just as she looked tantalizing whether in a formal gown or worn jeans.

Exiting the car with a smoothness and grace that belied the fact that she'd been in a life threatening accident only four days ago, Hope unlocked the door leading inside and said over her shoulder, "Make yourself at home." She led him through the washroom to the kitchen-breakfast nook area. "That door on the left is a bathroom if you need it. I'd offer you a beer or drink, but I know you'd have to turn it down. Can I get you coffee, hot tea, or a cold drink?"

After setting her purse on the nearest breakfast nook chair, she slipped off her raincoat and draped it over the back.

"Nothing, thanks." Lyon eased out of his raincoat and draped it around the chair beside hers. Adjusting some of the layers of gauze that had gotten twisted gave him time to acclimate.

Despite their mutual long friendship with Will, this was his first time here and he found the kitchen warm and welcoming, despite the cabinets being in a dark tint and the appliances black. Two significant windows—the bay window in the breakfast area that faced the courtyard and the southeast, along with a double window looking out to the patio and the west—brought in enough light without having the need for lamps unless reading or precise measuring were required.

"You've been standing for hours. Have a seat." Hope nodded to the two stools at the breakfast bar. She was rolling up the sleeves of her white pleated shirt as she made her way to the sink to wash her hands. "This won't take me any time at all."

Wondering how she'd kept track of whether he'd been sitting or not when he had only caught her looking at him once, Lyon left the first chair for her and sat on the second. Yellow and blue cushions were adorned with a Spanish design and almost matched the placemats. He also noted the accent lighting below and above cabinets, and a potted herb garden out on the back patio—all to keep his gaze off of Hope as she dried her hands and got busy. Undeniably trim, she had curves where they counted and moved like a ballerina—probably from the riding lessons she'd taken as a child, Lyon suspected.

"If the rest of the house is like this," he noted, "that explains why Will had a hard time getting you to come out to a party once you were home."

She cast him a sheepish look. "I must admit that I am something of a homebody, especially when work can keep me away from here too many hours. Confession time—I'd begun to dread the thought of having to move from here permanently."

Lyon had wondered how she and Will would work out their future living arrangements. Will would never have given up the ranch, which had been in his family for three generations. Maybe Hope had been thinking they could live part time at one residence and part time at the other, but that didn't seem practical. Then again, Will had been willing to promise her anything to get and keep his ring on her finger. That was another thing that Lyon now knew Hope hadn't been aware of.

Taking a cheerful yellow tureen from the side-by-side refrigerator, Hope set it on the bar and took two soup bowls from the cabinet beside the sink. They were also blue, yellow and white. She ladled soup into the bowls, and put the soup into the microwave to heat.

"I made beef quesadillas, too. Do you have enough of an appetite to try some?"

Lyon sat back against the sturdy oak backrest. It wasn't that he couldn't eat; he couldn't believe that with all that had happened, she had the strength and was in the frame of mind to care. "Hope…you have to quit and sit down. Preferably lie down. Remember, I'm the guy who knows too well what you've been through and I'm not above calling my doctor to come check *you* for a slow-to-show-itself injury."

"Don't threaten, Lyon. Believe it or not this is soothing and stabilizing for me. I'll warm some for us."

She took out the plate of quesadillas, plates to match the bowls, and set out napkins and silverware on the placemats. By then it was time to get out the soup and put in the rest of their meal.

Leaning over his steaming bowl, Lyon moaned in pleasure. "The accolades don't do this justice."

Hope waved him on with a potholder. "Don't wait on me, dig in."

Tempting as the encouragement was, he did wait until the rest was on the counter and she was seated beside him. Finally, he lifted the first spoonful to his lips, mindful of the stitches. After a deep-throated groan, he said, "This is better than any pain medication, and perfect for this damp-to-your-bones weather."

"I'm so glad. If you'd like, I can give you a take-home container for your dinner?"

"You won't have to offer twice. It's good to see you use black beans instead of refried stuff and that you put corn in yours," he said holding up a last bite. "My mother did, too. It's depressing how often what you get in this town is taco filling. Taco filling and refried beans masquerading as a que-sadilla, taco filling as a Sloppy Joe, and taco filling as chili."

"I'll bet your mother is basking in your praise of her cooking," Hope said watching him devour the last bite and lick his fingers. "I used to buy strawberry preserves from her every year, and sweet onions. Our housekeeper could never find better."

"She told me." Lyon was glad she remembered that. He wondered if she had ever seen him watch her from the barn as she stopped at his parents' little fruit stand by the roadway in front of the farmhouse? "She said she couldn't believe anything as sweet and well-mannered as you could come from a man so twisted inside."

"No, no one will ever mistake my father for Santa Claus." Hope put down her spoon and looked straight into his eyes. "Lyon, I know you must miss your parents terribly. I still miss my mother although she's been gone years longer."

"I didn't mean to depress you further," he began.

"You aren't. But you'd make me feel much better if you promised that you aren't going to let some troublemakers chase you out of town?"

"Whoa," Lyon said slowly and eased the placemat further onto the counter so he could rest his aching arm on his good one. "That was a quick transition."

"I could tell by your eyes that you were getting impatient to know why I'd asked you here."

Lyon knew it would be a miracle in a community of less than five thousand people to avoid hearing when someone wanted your head on a platter along with your badge, but he'd hoped Hope had missed the ugly gossip nonetheless. "Not impatient," he replied. "Just concerned that something else was troubling you when you already have enough on your plate. Don't give Rochelle any more thought than she deserves."

"There are more people than Rochelle making accusations and demands," Hope replied in concern, "and you know it. I was appalled when I heard Clyde and Mercy say they agreed with her that you'd let Will die and told them so. All they had to do is look at your wounds…" Hope shook her head. "If anyone is to blame, it's me. I should have walked up to your car by myself and not allowed you to carry me. That would have given you more time to try and get Will out."

"You couldn't have walked, sweetheart. It was later determined that the truck rolled at least five times. The miracle was that you weren't killed, too, especially since the air bags didn't deploy."

Hope blinked clearly unaware of that. "They didn't, did they?"

"Your lawyer will need that information," he continued. "I can supply you with the paperwork whenever necessary."

"My lawyer—Lyon, I'm not going to sue," she replied her disbelief leaving her wide-eyed. "I wouldn't do that any more than I would blame you for Will dying." Hope swiveled her chair so that she was facing him and leaned forward to rest her elbows on her thighs so she could clasp her hands. "He had been drinking. You know that."

"That's why I'm loathe to absolve myself of all blame," he replied grimly. "If I hadn't delayed my following you outside to wait on George so I could let him know that I'd be back to monitor his locking up and escort him to the bank's night deposit, I wouldn't have missed Will grabbing the keys from you."

Hope smiled sadly. "I know. Things happen, Lyon. I was wrong for getting in the truck with him. But there were things that needed to be said."

Lyon had been haunted by the image of the empty parking slot ever since the wreck and by his imagination of how much worse things could have turned out. "If it's any consolation," he added quietly, "I'm sure Will was gone before the first explosion."

Although she closed her eyes, she nodded. "I think so, too."

Relieved that she didn't harbor any doubt, Lyon sat back in his chair slowly exhaling. "So let people say what they want. Things will calm down eventually."

Hope failed to look reassured. "Kent will stand by you, but only as long as it doesn't compromise his own political well-being. What I'm worried about is Clyde and Mercy agreeing with Rochelle, and more than that the talk of getting someone 'more dedicated' to take your place."

Wanting to make things easier for her, Lyon murmured, "I've heard what your father has been saying, Hope."

She bowed her head. "I'm so ashamed of him—he actually claims changing police chiefs would be good for the community. He means good for *his* position in the community. He just wants his own yes-man wearing your badge."

"I appreciate the concern, but if it comes to a question about the community's trust in me, I won't beg to keep the job. If trust in my work is so thin that one bombastic voice can oust someone with a proven record, then I don't want to be here."

Hope straightened, her expression growing anxious. "But we need you. You've seen how the population is growing—all that money coming from Dallas, people investing in gentlemen ranches, land prices going up when everywhere else it's a buyer's market. There's a power play going on and we need the rest of the community keeping a check on balance. I'm doing what I can, but…things have happened and I may have to cut back a bit on my pace."

Alarms went off inside Lyon. So his suspicions that she'd been avoiding him were true. Words came rushing out of him before he could stop them. "Damn it, Hope, I knew you were holding something in. What's happened? Did Will do something before the crash?"

"No. I mean it's not what you think. I'm sore, yes, but nothing else."

"Then what is it?" he demanded.

"I'm pregnant."

Thinking that she would be relieved to finally say it, Hope instead felt regret as she saw Lyon's shock, then his coloring turn ashen. His dark eyes inherited from his Cherokee mother lost all light and became like twin dark tunnels, an abyss to despair. When he covered his eyes with his uninjured hand, she felt her throat tighten with emotion. He was disappointed in her. He knew that Will had not changed and was wondering how she could stay with him, let alone get pregnant by him.

About to try to explain, she saw Lyon drag his hand down his face, rub his mouth, and clench his fingers into a fist.

"And you're telling me that you're okay?" he finally muttered. "How would you know? You left the hospital before I did having refused the tests that might have proved otherwise."

This was hardly what she expected him to say. Heartened, she impulsively touched his hand hoping to make him understand. "I needed to buy some time. I had to get through this week and today without all of the extra gossip and stares that would have occurred if I'd let them do what they would have done in ER....you know the lab results would have spread through town and points beyond faster than a Tweet."

"Are you saying Ellis doesn't even know yet?"

Hope made a ladylike scoffing sound. "If he did, that private reception at the ranch would be about buying me a husband before the family name is tarnished."

Lyon stared, incredulous. "Hope, the only one in danger of injuring your family name is the man who tries every day—Ellis himself."

She wanted to hug Lyon for completely disregarding the possibility that the baby was anyone's but Will's. His faith in her was a balm soothing her battered heart. "You're not thinking like my father does. Had I told him right away, he would be brooding over the lost opportunity of getting his hands on Nichols' property. Next on his mind, even before Will was in the ground, would be recovering some return on an asset, namely me. The fact that I'm as independent as I am constantly grates on his nerves, so he would never stand by and watch me get bloated like a beached whale without quickly trying to recoup some of his investment in me."

Veins at both of Lyon's temples grew pronounced. "Hope—that's outrageous."

The mere tip of the iceberg in her father's frozen-in-time way of thinking, she thought. "Sounds like something you're more likely to hear from the lands of lashings and stonings, isn't it? But sadly true. It wasn't too long ago that he genuinely mourned that he couldn't legally arrange a marriage for me. Mind you, I'd already been living on my own for a few years. He's entirely able and willing to try anyway. That's why I had to think things through first."

"How on earth did your mother manage to stay married to him?"

"She loved him," Hope replied with a shrug. "There were days when they barely spoke to each other, and I remember times growing up when she locked him out of their bedroom for days, but he was always allowed back in eventually. Without a doubt, the man was her Achilles' heel."

When Lyon failed to remark on that and remained silent, Hope caught on to what he must be thinking. "Yes, that's what I needed to discuss with Will and why I got into the truck with him. I told him about the baby. That's what led to the accident."

"You argued?"

"You know me better than that. But his adrenaline was flowing anyway—no doubt fueled by the alcohol. He pumped the air like a boxing champion and shouted, 'Jackpot!'"

"He said what?"

Hope nodded at his double-take. "I found that odd, too. Especially since he was responsible for protection because I was temporarily unable to continue with my birth control." Unwilling to let herself get upset again, she waved away all the negative baggage that flooded her mind like a bad dream. "Maybe that was too much information, even if the policeman is a friend," she said wryly. "I'm sorry."

"Stop that," Lyon replied. "You know that's exactly why I need to know. And as your friend I want to understand."

"Then let me get the rest out and I'll be happy not to broach the subject again." *Not even to my child when he or she is old enough to ask questions,* she promised herself. "When Will said and acted the way he did, I suddenly had a really bad feeling. I asked him if he'd tampered with the condoms." She turned to Lyon. "I was every bit as angry with what I learned as I was with what I saw when I entered the bar earlier. It turns out that he was in financial trouble and knew he might need my father's help if he couldn't repay the bank loan in time. My being pregnant was insurance to him. We were already having trouble in the faithfulness department. Correction, *he* was.

"When I heard his rationale for getting me pregnant, I told him regardless of the baby, the wedding was off. That's when I took off the engagement ring and put it in the ashtray. He got upset. He tried to make me put it back on and that's when he lost control of the truck."

In that instant Lyon looked more capable of violence than she'd ever seen him. But when he took her left hand with his right one, his touch was indescribably gentle. "If he'd hurt you more severely, I'd have ruined his pretty face for life. I'll never forgive him for what he did."

"Lyon—"

"Promise me that you'll call a doctor as soon as I leave?"

"Soon. There are a few more things that I need to resolve."

"What could be more important?" Lyon assured her, "I meant what I said. I didn't come here as a cop. Will used up my concern for him a long time ago. I came to see about you and find out what I could do to help."

"There is one thing."

"Yes, I'll drive you to the doctor. What else?"

"Marry me."

Chapter Two

Lyon's heart thudded as hard as it ever had on the football field. He was so burning mad at Will that he wasn't sure he'd heard Hope correctly at first, or was it wishful thinking? Had the big jerk survived the accident, he would have begged for the hereafter by the time Lyon finished with him.

Wherever you are, pal, you're getting off easy.

Hope was going to have a baby? His heart and stomach wrenched with dread. Granted, women did it every day and had since the beginning of time, but not Hope. She was too small, and she was virtually alone with no mother, no sister…zero close family to help in the ways that count. Fathers were useless at this stage and Ellis was ten times worse than that. Sure, she had friends…anyone with her type of accessibility and warm personality had friends. But Hope was so busy taking care of others, there wasn't much time left for enjoying

her property as she deserved, let alone nurturing those relationships. Add that for all of her compassion, she was
more like him—a loner who needed her private time to
stay balanced—and Lyon experienced a deep-seated
anxiety for her that he hadn't felt since hearing the
weather reports prior to the storm a few years back that
had killed his parents.

Marry me.

"You're right about your father descending on you like
an F-4 tornado once he learns your condition," Lyon said
finally. "But I'd only make things worse for you, Hope. You
said it yourself—people have me in their crosshairs and want
me gone." The irony didn't escape him in how quickly he
had gone from dismissing her concerns as unlikely to a de-
termination that she not get hurt from being too close to him.

"I think I can help make that a short-term threat. I'm a
believer in the safety-in-numbers theory. There are things
I can do and say to help word get out to residents who
wouldn't otherwise hear about the plan to get you fired
until it's too late."

"My denigrators will come after you for supporting me.
How in good conscience could I allow that, particularly in
your condition?"

"Maybe I can trigger a few consciences myself and
people won't allow themselves to say things to me that they
might to you—or the fact that I believe in you will make
them wonder how true the accusations are? And who says
anyone else needs to know about my condition? For the
time being anyway," Hope added at his arched look.

"Are you suggesting we pass the baby off as mine?" he
asked slowly.

"Maybe I'm splitting hairs, but I was thinking that if

we're not announcing a pregnancy, there's no deception. That's why I want to get a doctor out of town."

"Let me tell you the not-so-little flaw in your logic," Lyon replied, not unkindly. "There's going to be a bump where that flat tummy is now—and sooner than you think because with fate being as unkind to you as it is, that baby is going to take after Will. So much for any delay of full disclosure, unless you think it would work to suggest we'd had an affair behind his back—and you know that it wouldn't. You were about to be married to a local icon. As it is, I'd be accused of taking advantage of you while you're at your most vulnerable."

Raising her chin slightly, Hope replied, "I've been 'vulnerable' for months…if not all along. Did you catch sight of who else was at the funeral? Rochelle didn't try in the least to hide herself, and it wouldn't surprise me one bit if more of her type come out of the woodwork as time goes by." That was why she couldn't cry for Will and probably never would. He'd soiled any good memory she had of their time together and crushed any tenderness she'd held for him.

"Hope," Lyon reasoned drawing her attention back to him. "I'm not from the wrong side of the tracks, but my pedigree is nothing to the Nichols'. Marrying me is the one thing that might make your father disown you or have me murdered."

"That's not remotely funny, Lyon," Hope replied frowning. "What's more if my family's blood was ever blue, it was due to my mother." She softened her voice. "You're not going to choose now to tell me you're a reverse snob, are you?"

"What I am," he intoned, "is trying to save you from your own good intentions. You're trying to make me feel that I would be helping you as much as you would be helping me, and I just don't see it. I'd hurt you, Hope."

"No, aside from the mental pounding by my father, you'd give me protection from Clyde and Mercy."

"How so?"

"Technically Will's child would have rights to his estate, but I want them to have it."

"That alone would give your father a stroke."

"How else could I avoid them claiming visitation rights like some surrogate grandparents? I've seen enough this week to know they intend to stay close to the estate no matter who or what is in the way." Hope shook her head. "I refuse to put an innocent child into an atmosphere that makes him, or her, an obstruction."

Lyon looked torn, but when he spoke, all he said was, "When would you want to do this?"

Pressing her hand to her heart to ease the fluttering, Hope replied, "Could you check your calendar and let me know what dates you have free?"

"I'll also have to think a bit more on which explanation angle would work best for you. What if you have a blond-haired, blue-eyed baby next February or March? The nurses will panic at the first feeding time thinking there was a mistake made in the wrist banding."

He was actually going to do this, Hope thought. "My father has gray eyes and had dark blond hair before he turned gray."

Lyon cleared his throat. "People won't be thinking of your father, Hope."

"Maybe not. Or maybe by then you'll have found the love of your life and need your freedom back."

After staring at her for several seconds, he abruptly glanced at his watch that he was temporarily wearing backwards on his right wrist, and muttered an expletive under his breath. "I have to get back to the station. As good as this food is I can't handle more right now. Is that offer for a doggy bag still on?"

Although disappointed, Hope immediately went into action. "Absolutely. It won't take me a second to prepare things for you." But she wondered what had just happened. Of course he needed to get back, yet seconds ago he seemed willing to stay longer. Was it because of what she said? That understanding needed to be voiced. She didn't want him to think he couldn't be honest with her if he did meet someone. But if it happened…

As Lyon eased into his raincoat, she filled two plastic storage containers with aromatic food, then placed both in a brown bag. She couldn't deny that she was starting to get a queasy stomach—and not because of the baby.

Admit it. You don't want to think of him falling in love with anyone but you.

"These aren't throw-aways." She folded the top down on the bag. "Don't even worry about washing them. Just drop them back in the sack. Bring them anytime."

"Contrary to what you're suggesting," he replied drolly as he accepted the bag. "I'm not adverse to dishwashing detergent and water. In fact, I happen to be a decent housekeeper."

He proceeded to the door to the garage. Only when he realized that she wasn't following, did he turn around. Hope didn't have a clue as to what expression was on her face, but with a deep sigh, he retraced his steps until stopping before her.

"Forgive me," he began. "I'm admittedly tired, a little cranky and feeling way out of my comfort zone. Humor me and let me do at least one thing conventionally." Awkwardly shifting the bag into his bandaged left hand, he placed three fingers under her chin and tilted her face upwards. "Marry me?" he asked.

"Yes," she whispered.

Lyon didn't realize it hadn't stopped raining until he was a mile down the road. Uttering a self-deprecating oath, he turned on the wipers just in time to hit the brakes. He managed to miss hitting a mud-caked calf looking for dryer ground. As he and the young bovine with the guileless brown eyes studied each other, he burst into a brief but incredulous laugh. So this is what getting married was already doing to him.

Married.

He had begun to believe it would never happen. It certainly wasn't happening as he'd expected. Miraculously though, the woman was the right one.

Hope's face when he kissed the corner of her mouth would be imbedded in his memory forever. Hope in Hope's eyes was a mesmerizing thing. There was no denying that he'd wanted a different kiss, but he needed to be patient. He would be. Look what it had done for him so far.

Mind back on the job, he directed himself as he eased around the indecisive calf. The need to return to the station was real enough, but he'd had to get the devil out of there because of Hope's generous commitment to null and void their contract if "he met the love of his life." That had stung more than he could deal with in her presence because he didn't want to believe she could do it. If matters were reversed, there was no way in hell he could step back politely and say, "Okay, bye."

Back at the station he was greeted by the dispatcher, Buddy Yantis, who was the only one there at the moment.

The rest of the department was either taking lunch, or returning home until their night shift began, except for their one full-time detective, Cooper Jones, who was in court today. Despite the mild temperatures, Buddy was sweating and mopping his high forehead and balding head with a Dairy Queen napkin taken from around his Blizzard cup that one of the other officers must've dropped off. Usually calm and collected, that told Lyon that they had problems.

"What's happened?" he asked.

"Mr. Harrell." Buddy's hands shook as he held up three pink phone messages. "He expects you to call."

"I'm sure he does." Lyon took the slips of paper and nodded toward the door. "Take ninety minutes and go see your wife and baby."

"I'm okay, Chief. I can wait until I'm relieved."

Buddy was a war vet. He'd been serving in Iraq when a roadside bomb killed the three other soldiers in his armored vehicle and delivered a concussion so severe to Buddy that he was given a medical discharge. Several other police departments had rejected his application for employment, but Lyon had seen the desperation of a husband and father trying to rebuild his life and offered him the dispatcher's position on a trial basis. The last five months had been going well, until today.

"Yes, you could," Lyon replied calmly. "But you don't have to. I'll be fine until some of the others return. Don't let me see you back here until—" he checked his watch "—two o'clock. Understood?"

Buddy's bloodshot, green eyes grew bright with relief and gratitude. "Thank you, sir." He was out of the building faster than hurrying to a muster call.

Detouring to the break room, Lyon grabbed a pen from

the lunch table and wrote his name on the bag. Then he put his food from Hope into the full-size refrigerator. All the while he was thinking about Ellis and what the insensitive tyrant might have said to leave Buddy a step away from a mandatory visit to his VA psychiatrist. No wonder Hope's phone hadn't rung while he'd been at her house. Ellis had been having too much fun intimidating the least deserving person in his department.

Once in his office, Lyon took his time to check the rest of his messages. Then he downloaded his computer's Inbox. He sent notes of thanks to liaisons with the state police and county offices, and only then dialed Ellis' phone number.

"Harrell residence," a clipped voice announced.

"Chief Teague," Lyon replied. "I'm returning Mr. Harrell's call."

"I'll see if he's in, sir."

Lyon heard raucous laughter and male voices in the background. The party Hope had mentioned must be in full swing, he thought.

"Took your damned time," Ellis snapped instead of a greeting. "Did that idiot tell you that I called multiple times?"

"I have all of Officer Yantis' message slips in front of me, Mr. Harrell," Lyon replied mentally gritting his teeth. "And for the record, Buddy Yantis is a decorated war veteran. I'd appreciate you give him the same respect that he undoubtedly gave you. Now what seems to be your problem?"

"Where's my daughter?"

"At home."

"You drove her?"

"I did."

"I called there several times. I got no answer."

"Maybe she took her doctor's advice and pulled the

plugs to get some rest." Lyon could only hope that she did, but maybe her old man was bluffing. The phone hadn't rung while he was at Hope's.

After a weighty silence, Ellis said, "Let's cut through the sweet talk. I don't know what you're up to, but stay away from her."

"Excuse me?"

"You heard me. She's not herself right now and I won't have you taking advantage."

"Anything else?" Lyon asked keeping his tone flat.

"Yes. I want your badge. The more you annoy me, the sooner I'll get it."

"I had no idea you've filed for mayor," Lyon drawled.

Ellis slammed down the phone.

"By all means," Lyon murmured. Replacing the receiver in the phone's cradle, Lyon crushed the pink slips and dropped them into the trash can behind his chair. "Give it your best shot."

Not only did Hope lie down after Lyon left, totally exhausted and relieved, she slept until a mockingbird outside her bedroom window started its repertoire of impersonations at three in the morning. With almost fourteen hours of sleep to help her recuperate she soon made her way to the kitchen where she started a pot of coffee. She knew she wouldn't be able to go back to bed now that her mind had cranked into gear. Besides, there was plenty to do. She was checking the water in almost a dozen bouquets and that many potted plants scattered around the house—delivered since word got out about Will's passing—when the ringing phone startled her. Hope spilled a bit of water setting down the copper can and returned to dry off the antique oak chest with the remote to her ear. "Yes?"

"So you are awake. I saw the lights on and wondered if something was wrong, or you just didn't want to sleep in the dark?"

Hope immediately went to the breakfast nook bay window and angled to see the street. There she saw head-lights at the front gate. Her heart did a little skitter at the thought that Lyon was this concerned about her. "Hang on, I'm letting you in." Dashing to the garage, she also pressed the third door's button to open that for him, as well.

When Lyon untangled his long limbs from the car, Hope saw that he looked bleary-eyed and his hair was more than singed, it was rumpled from either tossing and turning instead of sleeping, or else raking his hand through it too often. Blood-shot eyes aside, his low-hooded caressing gaze made her feel a little underdressed in her white sports bra and shorts. She had been intending to work out to a yoga video right after she finished watering.

"You look like you need eyedrops as much as coffee," she said as she stepped back to let him enter.

"Too much paperwork to catch up on." Reaching the kitchen he sniffed the air and moaned. "Feel free to admin-ister that through an IV."

"It will be ready in two minutes," Hope said closing up after him. "Don't tell me that you haven't even been to bed yet?" While he didn't have a pronounced beard, it was obvious that he had shaved recently.

"I tried, but I gave up wrestling with the bed sheets."

"Oh, dear. And am I the cause of your unrest?"

"No, my other fiancée." Although his gaze was admiring, and he brushed a tender kiss on her cheek, he raised his eyebrows at her attire. "Please tell me that you weren't planning to head outside to jog?"

"Heavens, no. Yoga. I try to get in at least fifteen minutes most mornings and thirty on weekends. It's a wonderful stress reliever."

"That explains those fluid limbs and how you move like a dancer. You definitely look more rested than when I left you." He pulled out the same barstool and sat down.

"I wish I could return the compliment. Are you hungry? I can make you a skillet breakfast."

"Just coffee, thanks. I indulged myself with the rest of your lunch while watching the ten o'clock news. The bag with the containers is on the passenger seat. Don't let me forget to give it to you."

"Okay." Hope got another mug and set it before him on the placemat. It was a man's mug—big with a handle designed for man-sized hands, and no flowers, unlike her delicate sunflower one. When she poured the coffee and the aromatic brew wafted up to his nostrils, he closed his eyes and inhaled with appreciation.

"Lyon, I'm sorry that I'm giving you such a headache," Hope said filling her own mug. "Is this where you tell me that you've changed your mind?"

When he didn't answer right away, it was impossible for Hope to even think of tasting her own stabilizing but hot brew. Her heart tanked. After that sweet kiss, she'd assumed—well, hoped—that he would immediately reassure her.

"What I need," he said finally meeting her pensive gaze, "are some clarifications."

"About…?"

"How you expect this arrangement to work? I mean

technically we'll be entering into a marriage of conve- nience, only you have to admit it's going to be anything but convenient."

She understood. At least she thought she did. He was referring to this complicating his love life, even though he'd told her that presently there was no special someone. That didn't necessarily mean that he was celibate. But how could she give him her blessing to do what he needed to do when the mere thought nearly made the coffee she'd just swallowed rise back up her throat?

"Hope, what I'm asking is, you are wanting us to live together, right?"

"Well, we'll be living and working in the same town, so unlike some bi-coastal couples, I can't see a way around it," she replied curling the end of her ponytail around her right index finger. "It's not going to appear all that convinc- ing if you stay in that apartment while I'm over here." She knew that he lived in the two-story string of rentals three properties behind the police and volunteer fire stations.

Although he narrowed his eyes, the corners of his mouth twitched. "I was trying to be a gentleman and wait for you to invite me."

She hadn't actually done that, had she? They'd parted with so much yet to discuss, no wonder he couldn't get any rest. "You'd be doing me another huge favor and bringing me great peace of mind if you'd agree to live here, Lyon," she recited. Then she worried. "It's not too far from the station, is it? You're welcome to share my office. We might have to rearrange things if you have a lot of equipment."

"The distance isn't a problem and the only office stuff I have is a laptop and a four-drawer file cabinet. I tend to do my work at the kitchen bar, so you don't have to worry about being cramped at your desk. On the other hand if your guestroom is already furnished, I'll probably need to put my other stuff in storage."

Hope marveled at how he'd handled their sleeping arrangements so matter-of-factly. But in the next instant, she felt dejected that he hadn't needed clarification on *that*. Had she been way off on her hunch that he was sexually attracted to her?

"The room is furnished," she said determined to sound as normal as he did, "but there's no need for you to waste money on a storage unit. As you've probably noticed, there's plenty of room in the garage."

"You're sure? The money isn't an issue, but the amount of wildlife that often inhabits those places could considerably shorten the lifespan of my things."

"I'm sure."

Lyon took another sip of coffee. "All right then, how about your cleaning lady? Can she be trusted not to spread stories around town about us?"

Startled, Hope asked, "How did you know about Molly?"

"I met her in town one day when a couple of punks were taunting her as she tried to get into her pickup truck over by the farm and ranch supply store. They parked too close and she couldn't open her door. They wouldn't move. After I had a few words with them, I made sure she was okay. That's when I learned who she was and where she worked."

"Molly never said anything about that."

"She probably didn't want to upset you," Lyon replied. "She seems a sweet lady."

"Oh, she is. And as you probably surmised, she's not exactly like most people."

"Was she born that way or did an accident injure her mental state?"

Once again Hope was touched by the considerate way he posed his question. "When she was younger and living in Mississippi, she had an abusive boyfriend. That's how her husband Tan met her. He said the guy kicked her out of his moving car on a bridge. She not only hit the pavement, but fractured her skull on the iron bridge beams."

"Tan?"

Gesturing behind her toward the back acres, Hope replied, "Tan Lee. He works for me, too. He witnessed the crime and testified in court on her behalf. In fact, he'd seen her earlier in the day at a farmer's market. You might say that he fell in love on sight. When he saw what a jerk her boyfriend was, he was worried for her safety and followed them. I understand that he visited her in the hospital every day until her release."

"I think I've seen him a few times. Asian? Mid to late thirties?"

"Vietnamese. And, yes, he's about twelve years her senior, but that seems to have worked for them." She gestured toward the back again. "You haven't seen all of the property, but I put a camper by the pond in the north-west corner. I hope to build them a cottage by next year. Molly helps me with the housework and gardening. Tan is living his dream to be a cowboy on a Texas ranch—small though it is. He's doing beautifully with the horses when he's not costing me a small fortune in diesel fuel on the tractor. It appears that the one thing he likes more than animals is all things mechanical."

"Hope's Shelter for the Abused and Chronic Dreamers," Lyon murmured.

She gave a philosophical nod and shrug. "Guilty. At least you're kinder than my father about it. But they really have helped me more than whatever I've managed to do for them. To answer your question, though, both Tan and Molly rarely go to town except to run an occasional errand when I can't do something myself, and you'll find them too protective of me to gossip. Truth be told, Tan struggled to hide his dislike for Will. Having them here would have been the only good thing about having to move. I would have been able to keep this place and trust them to maintain things."

Lyon grimaced. "No telling how leery they'll be of me invading the place so out of the blue."

"They already know you saved my life," Hope said eager to assure him. "They're going to think you're as wonderful as I do."

The look she received for that had Hope all but weak-kneed. To keep from making a fool of herself, she spun away to grab the coffeepot and topped off both of their mugs.

"Are you telling them about the baby?" Lyon asked.

"It's the wise thing to do. Anything could happen—I could fall or have an accident…or something could go wrong early in the pregnancy. They need to know to get me help if I'm in no condition to do it myself."

"And to find me immediately."

Hope returned the pot to the machine and wrapped her arms around herself. His concern touched her deeply and his brushed-suede voice caressed her in places it was safer not to think about. "Thank you, Lyon."

"Can we talk like this if we cross paths in town?"

"As long as you resist offering to shake my hand," she quipped.

The mug was halted midway to his mouth. "Now when did I ever do that?"

"I'm teasing. At any rate, you've always been welcoming and make people feel like there's no one else you'd rather speak with."

"We're not talking about people," he replied with some weariness, "we're talking about—maybe I should get you an engagement ring."

"No! Oh, no," she said less anxiously. "Please don't go through that expense. What I would really like is a wedding band, not too wide, maybe with some delicate scrolling, nothing with stones, nothing square or rectangular so that there are edges. I don't want to constantly worry that a gem has come loose and been lost, or to keep getting hung on my clothes or scratching furniture."

Lyon frowned. "You're not saying that to protect my wallet or pride, are you? I may not have Will's bankroll, Hope, but that hardly makes me destitute."

"I'm not comparing. Besides, I told you Will wasn't as financially flush as he led everyone to believe. He was real estate rich, but cash poor. That ring he gave me was all for show. If it's ever found, it needs to go to Clyde and Mercy. They may need it to cover back taxes or who knows what else."

"That's extremely decent of you."

"It's the right thing to do."

"Well, I can tell you from what I've seen of relationships that have gone south, not every woman would share your perspective." Eyeing her hands as she toyed with her hair again, he relented. "A band it is. We could stop somewhere and look at some when we go for the license. I'd like one myself."

"Would you?" Hope couldn't hide her surprise and delight. "Why Lyon—thank you!"

Suddenly he looked less tired and far more pleased with himself. "I did check my schedule…what do you think about next Thursday?"

"That will work, provided we don't leave until afternoon. I have a consultation in the morning that could take a while. An elderly woman who was recently widowed. She knows nothing about her finances because her husband had always managed everything."

"Well, she's in good hands now," Lyon said.

"Would you mind us going down to Rockwall for the license? It's far enough away that we shouldn't run into anyone from here, and they have a nice historic courthouse. Lake Ray Hubbard makes for a scenic background, too." Just north of downtown Dallas in the last several years the area had mushroomed into its own not-so-little enclave of shops and restaurants, while elegant homes and condominiums lined the lake. "I know this is a marriage of convenience," she said wistfully, "but that doesn't mean we can't make the day enjoyable, even special."

His gaze dropped briefly to her lips. "We'll make it whatever you want it to be."

Heaven help her, Hope thought. Practically everything he was saying was rocketing her imagination into forbidden territory.

"This is all falling into place almost too easily," Hope murmured. "Lyon, I can't tell you how grateful I am for how agreeable *you're* being." To her surprise he not only dropped his gaze, his expression seemed guilty.

"You may take that back when I tell you that your father called me today," he said.

"Oh." Was that the real reason he couldn't sleep? Once again she wrestled with disappointment and guilt. Guilt won. Harrells were turning his world upside down and inside out. "I expected his first line of attack would be me and that my phone would be ringing off the wall," she said while wondering what Ellis had up his sleeve. "But it never did."

"He said he tried to reach you several times."

She shook her head slowly and went to the kitchen phone. Lifting the remote, she clicked the green icon, heard the dial tone and clicked on the red. Returning the remote to its cradle, she asked, "What did he have to say?"

"Nothing you haven't already heard or can't imagine. After warning me to stay away from you, he came right out and declared he was coming after my badge."

"At least now you believe me that he's serious."

"I believed you all along, Hope. I simply didn't want you worrying about me when you had enough going on."

"But can you see that my support of you will help thwart his plans and this proves he thinks so, too?"

"Maybe."

Hope accepted that.

"One thing," he continued, "and this isn't a negotiable issue. When you tell your father about us, I want to be there."

"But that will only encourage him to be all the more unpleasant. That's so unfair to you."

"How so if I'm half the man you make me out to be? We may not share a bed, Hope, but we'll be sharing vows. The responsibility that comes with them began when I agreed to this."

She had long thought him a principled and honorable man, but her respect and feelings deepened tenfold with that pronouncement. Coming at the end of a week of emo-

tional upheaval and psychological turmoil, her throat tightened, her eyes burned with unshed tears. She wished she
could articulate what she was feeling. Carrying the child
of a man she had stayed with longer than she'd loved him
left her with a sense of dues to pay and wrongs to be
righted. But she ached for how things could have been if
she'd made different choices sooner. All she could do was
try to get it right from now on.

"All right," she replied. "We'll face him together."

Chapter Three

As planned, on the following Thursday, Lyon and Hope drove down to Rockwall, the county seat of Rockwall County, which claimed the distinction of being the smallest county in Texas. It turned out that it was closer to three in the afternoon before they could get away.

With the sun nudging temperatures into the eighties and the medians along the north corridor of Interstate 30 changing from a flood of Indian paintbrush and crimson clover to summer wildflowers like black-eyed Susans and butterfly weeds, it was a perfect afternoon to be on the road. Hope had suggested they use her Mercedes for the trip and was glad when Lyon hesitated only briefly. Using his patrol car was a non-option, and their pickup trucks might still be considered the real Cadillacs by Texans, but neither would provide the right tone for this trip.

After a few years of seeing Lyon always in his uniform,

Hope couldn't help but admire him in his camel blazer, white dress shirt, and jeans. His black dress boots were polished to a military shine. She was relieved for him that his burns healed as fast as he'd assured her they would and that the doctors had let him remove the bandages on his left arm. He admitted his arm remained a bit stiff and the new skin felt a little tight, but it looked as though in time the scarring would be minimal. Yesterday's trip to his barber had eradicated most of the damage to his hair.

"You look like a very tough marine about to be deployed," she told him.

"I look scalped," he muttered.

Coming from him that was almost amusing, except that it made her think of how much worse things could have gotten. Grateful, Hope lifted her face to the warming sun. With the moon roof slightly open, her hair, feathered around her face, tickling her now and again, and she smiled feeling better than she had for some time.

She had chosen to wear a powder blue sheath topped with a matching bolero jacket trimmed with coffee brown lace. The lace collar stood up like gowns from the Elizabethan period and ruffled at her wrists. The earrings she brushed against as she smoothed her hair were turquoise in a squash-blossom design—another inheritance from her mother. She'd worn them and the delicate matching cross necklace hoping to feel her spirit—and she did.

"Where did you go just now to put that lovely, serene smile on your face?" Lyon asked.

"I was just thinking of my mother—and thank you."

"Would Miss Rebecca have approved of what her only child was doing?"

Hope considered the question for a few seconds. "She

would have worried, maybe, but understood. At any rate, what could she say considering who *she* married?"

"Good point."

"Then again, if she was still here, this wouldn't be necessary. She would have taken her riding crop to my father."

"And banished him from the bedroom."

"Exactly," she laughed.

After passing a USPS truck towing two trailers, Lyon continued. "Did you warn Tan and Molly that it might be dark before we get back?"

"Yes, Chief, *and* they have my cell phone number." At his sidelong look, she added, "It's all right, Lyon. I've been out after dark before."

"But you've never been pregnant before."

That was becoming his favorite mantra. Their engagement had tripped a protective switch in him, not that she really minded. She was also seeing how much more attentive Tan was growing since learning she was expecting. Suddenly, she couldn't get near the horses without him shadowing her, and now he insisted on unloading feed bags by himself. Molly was almost as bad; Hope could no longer carry anything heavier than a laundry basket. Climbing the kitchen ladder to dust the tops of cabinets and refrigerator was an invitation to hear Molly hum off key—a quirk she'd developed to help her cope when she became stressed.

"I have a feeling you're all going to get pretty annoying by the time I'm in maternity clothes," she told Lyon.

"Doesn't hurt for you to be the one being spoiled for a change. You do that plenty enough for others."

"Ah-ha…so being bird-dogged and shadowed is a gift."

It was a relief to see him relaxed and enjoying the drive,

as much as she was. The last several days had tested his resilience and commitment to the job.

On Monday, a "name withheld" Letter to the Editor had appeared in their weekly newspaper accusing Lyon of having something other than coffee in his mug at the grill the night of the accident. By Tuesday, rumor had it that seventy-five more people had signed the petition to terminate Lyon's contract with the city. Outraged, George Bauman, the grill's owner and bartender, had stormed into the newspaper's office and called Ted Pettigrew, owner and editor-in-chief of the *Cedar Grove Chronicle,* an enabler and idiot for allowing such libelous garbage to be printed and pulled his standing ad. But Ted remained unapologetic. He loved conflict wherever he could find it or stir it up, and gleefully informed George that he had two more letters critical of Lyon waiting for next week's issue.

Perhaps the most disturbing and disappointing occurrence was that one of Lyon's youngest officers, Chris Sealy, told him that his wife wanted him to quit and move to another town and police department because she "worried for his safety under Chief Teague." The embarrassed young officer acknowledged that his wife's cousin was Rochelle and that she thought she owed Rochelle her support. Nothing was set in stone yet, but it appeared Lyon would be looking for a new police officer before long.

That wasn't to say there weren't pleasant surprises to emerge like intermittent sunshine between storm clouds. Hope was learning that Lyon liked to call at least twice a day to see what she was up to—three times if he couldn't meet her for lunch or when a planned dinner together wouldn't work out. And so far they had only shared one dinner due to him trying to work ahead so that he could take a few extra days off to move once they were married.

As for her father, Hope had declined two of his dinner invitations. She'd cited her workload as her excuse. On a hunch, though, she'd driven past the ranch on the night of the first invitation and, sure enough, spotted Clyde and Mercy's aging Lincoln Towncar in the driveway. That made turning down the second invitation easier.

Before they reached Greenville, Hope winced and slipped out of the designer heels that matched the lace on her dress. "The Internet tells me that this embryo is the size of a pin head, but I've already gained two pounds and I think it's all in my feet! With my luck, I'll be wearing an NBA size by the time I deliver."

"What are you doing wearing shoes not broken in yet?"

"These aren't new, cowboy. I'm not so foolish and fashion crazy as to wear new shoes when I know I'll be on my feet for hours…but they are a half-inch higher than what I usually wear."

"No, not fashion crazy at all," Lyon drawled.

"Yes, you guys *hate* that we try to look our best for you."

"Can't stand it," he said agreeably. "By the way, what do you call that nail polish?"

"Iced Mocha." She wiggled her toes delighted that he'd noticed.

"That was my first guess, too." By now Lyon was almost sporting dimples. "What size shoe are you, a six?"

"Lucky guess."

"That's why they pay me the big bucks they do."

Leaning her head back against the seat, Hope studied him openly. "Lyon, why haven't you ever married?" It was a question she'd wondered about often, all the way back to when Will had suggested she play matchmaker for his buddy. But she'd never been satisfied with any of the potential partners Will had suggested.

When Lyon didn't answer, she waved away the question. "Forget that. I shouldn't have gotten that personal."

"We're about to live under the same roof. Something tells me we'll be hard-pressed to avoid getting more personal. Only…can I give you a rain check?"

"Sure, I'll be around," she quipped. But it wasn't all right and Hope immediately started speculating. Was he pining over someone? In a town their size, it was fairly easy to remember whom he'd dated and the ones who hadn't moved away appeared to be happily married. Had someone left Cedar Grove that she had forgotten about?

"Don't burn valuable brain cells."

Caught in the act, Hope stiffened to keep from squirming. "I'm not. I was about to ask how things went in court the other day? You never did say." Instead they had talked about the challenge of finding packing boxes and the most opportune time to transport them to an apartment when you weren't ready to tell anyone you were moving, or seem to confirm that an employment switch was looming.

"It turned out that I wasn't needed after all. I sat in the hall for two hours—the second lunch we missed—and then the guy accepted the plea bargain. He's already down in Huntsville. I'd rather talk about what you'd like to do after we get the license and rings. Dinner overlooking the lake might be nice. In fact I took a chance and made reservations at the Hilton."

Hope gasped with surprise and delight. Although there were some fun places with good food opening around the huge Bass Pro shop on the east side of the Interstate, the

Hilton provided more elegant, gourmet dining. *"Mistra's?"*

"I booked us for six o'clock. I hope that I left enough time to shop for the rings."

Hope couldn't believe he'd done this—actually wanted somewhere more formal. "I love that place. Have you been there before?"

"No, but I found it online. It seemed to suit you more than anything else I saw."

That was high flattery coming from a man who didn't seem to say anything that he didn't mean. "When I have a meeting with anyone in or around the city, I try to book it there. Not only does it split the driving distance, but the ambiance eases the tedium of talking numbers and growth patterns. It reminds me of Greece and the Mediterranean— open and airy, sun-bleached whites and cerulean blues. In fact that's where it gets its name."

"I wondered—or if it was named after the owner or chef?"

"No, for centuries, Mistra was a fortified city with quite a reputation for culture and philosophy."

"Have you been to Greece?" Lyon asked.

"Years ago, but not to the island, and I was quite young, so much of the art and history was wasted on me, but it's where I learned to love goat cheese—and probably cost my mother months off her life while diving from the cliffs. I really appreciate this, Lyon."

The courthouse was busy, but they waited their turn to fill out the application and then sat dutifully before the clerk and finished the paperwork. In less than forty minutes they were back outside, but that left them with the minimum time for ring shopping before their dinner reservations.

The first jewelry store had a beautiful selection, but

despite Lyon's coaxing, Hope held to her request for something simpler. The next store had a pair of bands they both liked and the inventory was such that they walked out with the small bag containing the symbols of their future.

At the hotel, they left the Mercedes with the valet and proceeded to the restaurant. As soon as the maître d' spotted her, his expression of cool reserve warmed to a wide smile. "Ms. Harrell! What a pleasure. I didn't realize you'd be a guest this evening."

"Thank you, Ivo. It's always good to see you."

"I would have thought we wouldn't be having the pleasure of your company for some time. My deepest sympathies for your loss."

Hope felt Lyon shift closer behind her and his hand go immediately to her waist. She appreciated that since she had completely overlooked that anyone here would have seen the obituaries, which was foolish of her. "I appreciate that so much," she replied. She stepped aside to gesture to Lyon. "This is Chief of Police Teague from my town. Lyon, Ivo Martini."

"Ah! Chief Teague, yes, we have the reservation. An honor, sir." With a bow he quickly stopped the hostess who was assigning a table and with a discreet few words did some hasty rearranging of her seating chart. "Please follow me," he said with menus in hand, then led them to the circular part of the restaurant where floor-to-ceiling windows looked out onto the pool and beyond it the lake.

"The best seats. You're already spoiling us, Ivo." Hope eased onto the chair that he held out for her.

"We will all do our best." He opened her leather menu and handed it to her and then did the same for Lyon. "We're featuring wines from South Africa this week."

"Thank you, but I can't this visit," she told him. "I'll just have water, thank you."

"I'll keep her company," Lyon said.

The slender man bowed again. "Medication, of course. I should have known better. But you look wonderful, Ms. Harrell. It's a blessing to still have you with us. I'll tell Martin and he will get your drinks and take your order. Enjoy."

"Amen to the blessing part," Lyon murmured once the dignified man was out of earshot.

Hope leaned toward him, distressed. "Lyon, I should have known he would have seen the papers. *The Dallas Morning News* did a sizable story on Will. I'm sorry that I didn't think to warn you as soon as you told me about the reservations."

"Never mind me, are you all right with this? It can't be comfortable. We can leave."

"No. I wouldn't do that to you and it wouldn't be fair to Ivo and the others." She just needed to keep her wits about her and not look too happy to be there with him.

"There you go thinking of everyone but yourself again. I hate that you won't relax now and enjoy yourself as you should have."

"We have the license, the rings, and we'll have a delicious dinner. Our cup pretty much runs over."

"Did Will ever come here with you?"

Having anticipated that question would be asked at some point, Hope realized that she didn't want to deceive him. "We stopped for drinks once on our way back from a Cowboy game. They were playing his old team and Will was eager to extend the night as long as he could to celebrate the win he had nothing to do with. Needless to say, I drove us the rest of the way home and never brought him again. Ivo was kind to forgive me."

"You have a distinct fan in him."

"The affection is mutual."

Lyon lowered his gaze to the menu. "So if we're staying, what do you recommend?"

After some discussion, Lyon ordered the warm Texas Gulf shrimp cocktail for an appetizer, while she revisited the corn-crusted scallops and oysters on a stand fork with grain mustard *mousseline*. Next Lyon chose the house salad, although he was skeptical about what the *manchego* cheese was and whether he would like the sweet sherry vinegar-mango dressing.

"That's Spanish cheese, made from sheep's milk instead of cows'," Hope told him. When his expression grew wary, she coaxed, "A former farm boy can handle that."

"I could handle a wedge of iceberg lettuce doused with Thousand Island dressing topped by a couple of cherry tomatoes, too."

Hope chose the baby spinach with Roquefort dressing, spiced pecans and strawberries. Lyon discreetly begged some of the pecans and she shared but wished she could have fed them to him with her fork. So much for the fantasy of a romantic pre-wedding dinner.

For their entree Lyon ordered the New York strip, while she had the lamb T-bone. Her meat was so thick she ended up giving him the entire rib portion and kept only the fillet.

"Just don't go around telling everyone back home that I prefer lamb to beef," Lyon warned when she looked too tickled at how quickly he'd devoured his food. "If those cattle ranchers hear that, you and the Four Horsemen won't be able to keep them from running me out of town."

"Until here, the best I've ever tasted was in *The Pink Adobe* in Santa Fe," she told him. "I remember it was

served with acorn squash and a black cherry sauce." Here
they'd served spinach and a goat cheese stack.

"My mother would have liked that. She used all of the
squashes."

"I'll attempt to duplicate it for you when the weather
cools."

The look he sent her left her as warm as the chiminea
did that night, but the sense of being closely observed by
the staff compelled Hope to keep her expression benign,
and she and Lyon stuck to impersonal subjects after that—
or remained silent when anyone was within hearing
distance. The strain took its toll and Hope passed on dessert
when Lyon asked what she would like. "If you don't
mind," she added.

"Not at all," he replied before the waiter could reach
them. "I'm ready to go, too. As lovely as you look framed
by these surroundings, I prefer the company of the woman
who took her shoes off in the car."

Hope coughed discreetly into her linen napkin to cover
a chuckle. But once they were in the Mercedes and Lyon
was pulling away from the valet station, she voiced her
true feelings.

"Did you at least enjoy the food? I'm so sorry this
wasn't the dinner you wanted for us."

"The food was terrific and any time spent with you
can't be a disappointment," he assured her.

How different he was from Will, she thought, although
she disliked herself when she made comparisons. But
Will's compliments tended to become like cold cream—a
little too thick, while Lyon's she could accept with pleasure
and not feel them linger uncomfortably between them. In
fact, they weren't on the Interstate but a minute or two

when she not only slipped out of her shoes, she was struggling to stay awake.

"This is crazy," she said after stifling a series of yawns. "I've had no alcohol or sugar. Why am I about to fall asleep?"

"I can think of a few reasons, not counting that you have a little package inside you gobbling up half of your energy. You'd better make that doctor's appointment soon and ask what vitamins you need."

"That's next on the list after the wedding."

"All the more reason to bump up the wedding. How does Tuesday sound for you?" At her startled glance, Lyon shrugged. "I have court on Monday, but it should be a one-day situation. Tuesday is free appointment-wise. I can either call a justice of the peace in Sherman or Gainesville. Both are sometime poker pals and would protect our privacy."

"Sherman," she replied without hesitation. "That's closer and we can get back sooner and have a celebratory dinner at the house."

"That's not fair, you cooking on your wedding day—even if it isn't a normal wedding."

"I told you, as much as I appreciate a good meal out on occasion, I'm a homebody at heart. I can prepare a few things in advance and you can grill the steaks in back while I finish up."

"That sounds better. I'll pick up the steaks over the weekend—and bring a suitcase with what I'll need to change into before we head off to Sherman."

"Perfect."

That was the last thing Hope remembered saying to him. The next thing she knew, she felt a warm caress on her cheek. When she opened her eyes, Lyon was leaning over and releasing her seat belt.

"You'll be more comfortable in your bed than spending the night in this car," he told her.

She glanced around and saw they were in her garage. All that time and noise of opening and shutting doors, too! "Good grief, Lyon! You shouldn't have let me sleep the whole way."

"I didn't mind. I'm glad you felt comfortable enough to sleep around me."

He was too dear to turn her rude behavior into a compliment. "Would you like to come in for a cup of coffee...or drink now that you're so close to home?" she asked as she got out and searched in her purse for her keys.

Lyon beat her to it using the keys she'd already given him, just as he'd used his own gate and garage door openers. "No thanks, I'm good. But if you don't mind, I'd like to make sure everything in the house is okay."

Hope didn't mind at all. She'd confessed that she didn't use her security system now that she had Tan and Molly around. Molly could forget about the alarm and it had upset her greatly once when she walked in and forgot how to turn it off. Although she could rely on Tan to keep an eye on the house during the day, by now he and Molly were in bed.

By the time he returned, Hope had placed her purse and shoes in her room and left her jacket on the chair by the closet. He took the small jeweler's bag from his pocket and set it on the kitchen counter.

"It's probably safer here than in an apartment that I'm rarely at," he said.

"I'll put it in the safe," she replied. "You're sure I can't get you anything?"

"A good-night kiss—and then you'd better get to bed before you fall asleep again this time while standing up."

When he lowered his head, clearly intending to kiss her cheek, Hope turned her head so that his lips met hers. His eyes opened and looked into hers, and then he slowly kissed her again. His lips grew firmer against hers and Hope felt something like champagne bubbles rush through her veins.

"Sweet dreams," he murmured against her lips.

"You, too."

When he closed the door quietly behind him, Hope leaned against the counter and covered her flat tummy with her hands. "Oh, baby," she whispered. "That was all the dessert Mommy needed."

On their wedding day, Lyon woke instantly alert and wishing it was already afternoon. When he'd called Ed Viney over in Sherman last Friday morning, the justice of the peace had enthusiastically said, "Marry you to Harrell's girl? And he doesn't know? Get over here! That'll be such a treat, I'm waiving my fee."

The support was more than welcome considering that Ellis had tried to get Hope over to the ranch on Saturday night to play hostess for what he described as a "friendly little dinner party." It turned out that one of the guests was to be Jack Nolan, who just happened to be one of Austin's most eligible bachelors. Hope declined and Lyon—having brought over that suitcase and several boxes of his things—got to hear Ellis' volcanic response even from several feet away. He'd known Ellis had a temper but never imagined he would treat a daughter and only child that way. It was all he could do not to take the phone from Hope and give the big bully a long overdue scare. In fact, Hope moved to the other side of the kitchen bar to make sure he didn't.

"Next time you suspect this wedding is only to help you

keep your job, remember that call," she told him after hanging up. "I know Jack Nolan a bit, and he would be like Will—placate my father to avoid the tirades."

Lyon looked from the phone back to her taking a moment to keep the fury out of his voice. "Once you're wearing my ring, I'd better not hear him tearing you like that again, or he'll be cooling off in a holding cell."

"You couldn't arrest him for bellowing like one of his cranky bulls," she replied with some anxiety.

"You're pregnant," he reminded her again. "You're carrying his grandchild. Would you have me wait for you to miscarry?"

After that call, a herd of feral hogs couldn't force him to leave her except when she was ready to turn in for the night. Hope made them a pizza from scratch, which they ate outside on the patio watching hummingbirds do dive-bomber acrobatics as they tried to claim one of the four feeders as their very own. Later they walked the twenty acres, chatted with Tan and Molly, and treated the horses to slices of apple. Lyon hadn't felt so content and aware of spring's promise since he was waiting for his high school senior year to start— and getting his driver's license and first car.

And now it was Tuesday and he was about to take himself a wife. He liked the old fashioned phrasing. It reminded him of how his mother and her people would speak. They were all gone now and he had been alone and lonely for too long. Saying I do would change that.

"I do," he said flinging back the sheet and launching out of bed. With a satisfied smile he began a mental list of everything he had to do before two o'clock when he was scheduled to meet Hope at her place.

Hours later, after Ted Pettigrew's call to the department

because someone had knifed all four of his car's tires—perhaps because his next Letters to the Editor column showed nothing close to "fair and balanced"—and after Ellis called complaining that a fifteen-thousand-dollar bull had been painted black and white like a skunk, Lyon made it to Hope's cozy haven. When he pulled into the third garage and saw that her Mercedes was there and the hardwood door was open for him, he felt an instant sense of homecoming.

"Hi, honey, I'm home," he called cheerfully hoping she'd heard none of the nonsense going around town and would be amused.

She emerged immediately from her room wearing a short, white satin robe with her hair up in a towel. "Are you all right?"

"Sure. I'm not late, am I?"

"Don't put on a front for me, Lyon. I heard about Pettigrew's tires and my father's bull."

"Since you didn't call me, I hoped you were buried in work and missed the commotion."

"The tire thing maybe…if Ted hadn't called my office and threatened that if he got one inkling of evidence that I was somehow behind that—"

"He did what?" Lyon interjected. "Why blame you?"

"The real reason? Because I joined Gus in protest and cancelled my ongoing ad in the paper, too. But you know Pettigrew, he would never come out and say that. He claims someone saw a lemon-yellow VW on the street where the paper's offices are located on the night of the alleged attack. Guess whose assistant drives a lemon-yellow VW?"

"Freddie." Fredericka Darlington was forty-something-year-old divorcée who wore drab clothes, sensible shoes, and seemed to never speak unless asked a direct question. The idea that Freddie would drive such a youthful, fun car, let alone be part of something so violent had Lyon shaking his head. "Did you ask her if she was involved?"

"Of course not. The post office is diagonally across the street. She goes there for me at least three times a day, often more. She has every right to be there." Hope pulled off the towel and fluffed her hair that she'd protected from the shower water. Then she blotted her face with the towel. "What I did do is ask for Ted's witness' name, which is supposed to be supplied upon request. Needless to say he demurred."

"Knowing how few friends he has, I'll bet he has his mother write the letters." But tired of Pettigrew interfering with their day, Lyon gave her a head-to-toe admiring look. "Interesting wedding dress…although I'm not sure I'm eager for anyone else to see it."

"Very funny. Bet I'm ready before you are," she said with all of the dignity her petite frame could muster.

She did beat him, too. When Lyon returned to the kitchen, she was already there and her lace-covered satin sheath made him stop in mid-step. "Stunning," he murmured.

"Thank you, but this bracelet has to come off," she said turning her back to him at the same time she tried to brush her hair to the side. "See this?"

"What?" he asked coming to her.

"My bracelet is hung on my dress."

"Hold still," he said carefully getting the fine threads freed from a bit of gold wire here and a hook there. When she was totally freed, he leaned closer and touched his lips to her nape. "Almost as good as new. There's just a tiny bit of threading pulled out of its weave."

"Thank you," she said again, this time more breathlessly.

She looked like she belonged on top of a cake and, yet, Lyon thought belatedly, they weren't even going to have a cake. She was being badly shortchanged on what should have been the happiest day of her life. Even those diamond and pearl earrings that matched the bracelet looked like serious heirlooms. They made him embarrassed for his simple band and he thought that he wasn't just marrying an heiress, he was marrying a goddess.

"Love the suit," she said taking in his newest purchase.

The gray silk had already been purchased for her wedding when he decided that he couldn't be the best man. He never got around to telling Will that and he saw no wisdom in explaining the particulars to Hope either. He simply said, "Glad you like it. If you're ready, we'd better get the rings and go."

He didn't want to hear his inner voice tell him to offer her a last chance to back out. Seeing her like this—radiant, her glossy hair almost as bright as her dark eyes, her perfect skin glowing—he had never wanted anyone more.

When they were westbound on the highway, Lyon noticed Hope fingering her small leather clutch purse a few times and smooth her skirt once too often. "Nervous?"

"No…well, maybe a little." She glanced toward him. "You?"

"Not a bit, unless you make a sudden grab for the doorknob."

She gasped and covered her tummy. "No worry about that. I'm just hoping you won't end up regretting this…or resenting me."

"Don't waste your time."

When they entered the outskirts of Sherman, Lyon pulled into a parking lot of a small strip mall and stopped in front of a flower shop. "Back in a minute."

"Oh, really?" Hope gave him a bemused smile. "What did you do?"

"Well, what's a wedding without flowers?"

He returned as quickly as promised carrying a bouquet of delicate, red tea roses framed by white lace.

Hope gasped, "How exquisite!" as she accepted the token. She lowered her face to the blossoms for several seconds. "Lyon, this is simply perfect."

He simply smiled, pleased that he had managed to make the occasion a little more special. She would have no family or friends. He hoped she understood that he knew what this was costing her.

At the courthouse, Lyon parked in the rear as Ed Viney directed and were met at the entryway by his secretary, who led them to his office. Grinning broadly, Ed shook Lyon's hand and kissed Hope's cheek. "My! I hope you two know how pleased I am to do this," he said.

His enthusiasm was contagious and Hope's smile deepened. "We appreciate you and your staff's time and discretion."

Ed was so committed to this little covert operation, he brought them into his office where his wife stood with his secretary to act as their witnesses. "I'll tell you how long I've know these two," he said as he introduced them. "My wife is Connie, and her sister is Bonnie, and I always get their names turned around, but Bonnie hasn't quit, and Connie hasn't filed for a divorce."

Lyon had discussed the ceremony with Ed and without explaining anything personal asked for the simplest service. So the older man had barely begun before he was saying, "Under the power vested me, I now pronounce you man and wife."

He could kiss his bride.

Looking down at her upturned face, calm, hopeful, so very lovely, Lyon framed her face with his hands and touched his lips to hers once, twice, and on the third time he kissed her wishing her to see his heart and offer him hers.

"Congratulations, Chief and Mrs. Teague."

The cheery greeting reluctantly brought him back to earth and they were instructed to sign the license, then Bonnie and Connie added their signatures.

"I so enjoyed this," said Ed's wife, Connie with merry eyes and a bubbly personality to match her every-which-way curls. "The way you two looked at each other and kissed was just like in one of my favorite romance novels." She brought out a camera from her legal-brief-size purse. "I see you didn't bring one to remember the day. Mind if I do that for you?"

"We completely forgot," Hope said, her cheeks still pink from Connie's effusive descriptions.

With Connie's direction, several poses were snapped. Lyon hoped the one with him standing behind Hope and his arms around her came out best; he wanted to set it on his desk in the office.

"It'll take a few weeks, but you'll receive the registered copy in the mail," Ed finally told them.

They didn't pass anyone on their way to the car and once inside, they were both silent. Lyon ached to reach for Hope and kiss her again, ask for her reassurance that she wasn't sorry, but all he managed was a gruff, "Too late now."

"Now it's time for the hard part," she amended.

Lyon frowned. "You weren't wanting to go straight over there and tell him, were you?"

"We should, but…would you mind if we waited until

tomorrow, or the day after? It seems so wrong to taint that ceremony."

"You won't hear any arguments from me." He would do whatever she asked to keep her looking as she was at her flowers and ring. It thrilled him to think that she was even fractionally as caught up in the moment as she appeared to be.

They talked and laughed all the way home. Hope asked for more stories about how he knew Ed, and Lyon teased her about how Ed's wife and sister-in-law tried to get her to throw her bouquet because Bonnie was presently single and wishing, but Hope couldn't make herself let go of it.

When they entered the house, they found another surprise—a one-layer cake with a bride and groom in the center. The frosting was cream cheese painstakingly spread, but the few crumbs around the plate suggested the cake was chocolate. What really had them chuckling was that Molly had used a black marking pen to try and color the bride's blond hair black.

"Now you know why I love her and Tan," Hope said.

"We should invite them over for some."

"They'd decline, but I'll call in a minute to thank them for us and promise to bring them each a piece in the morning." She gestured with her flowers. "Why don't you change and get the grill started? I'll see you in a few minutes."

While Lyon wished it was a real wedding day and that he could follow her to the master bedroom where they could help each other undress in the amber glow of the late afternoon sunlight, then make love until they knew each other by touch in the dark, he knew there were blessings to count with things as they were. At least she was bound to him now; all he had to do was build on his patience and her trust. He knew she considered him a friend, hopefully her dearest friend. Such friendships had been known to evolve into deeper love.

Only that wasn't enough.

There was great passion inside of Hope, and he wanted that, too. He'd seen it often enough to where it had fostered a gnawing hunger in him, saw it in those mysterious, exotic eyes, when she fought for others' rights, and spoke of protecting his job. How did he direct it at himself?

Show her.

The thought had him staring into space as in his school days when he faced a blank page when he was expected to write a term paper. English was his first language, but that didn't help the words move to paper. Adding to the challenge, he had always gotten along with women, but never had to woo one before. That wasn't arrogance; he simply had never had a relationship that interested him beyond that of mutual gratification. Like a lazy mind, an under-exercised heart was showing its disadvantages.

He knew one thing for certain—he didn't only want to seduce Hope, he wanted what his parents had found. Whatever happened, he decided, pulling at his tie, it mustn't be because he didn't try hard enough.

Chapter Four

"Are you sure about this?" Hope asked Lyon as he shut off the engine to his police car.

He'd picked her up ten minutes ago at the house for their ten o'clock meeting with her father, although Ellis didn't know the appointment was for both of them. Lyon had raised his eyebrows at the idea that a daughter was kept to such formal conditions, and she'd had to explain that there was no such thing as just dropping by. Ellis had made that clear when she refused to move back into the house after her mother's death. The protocol was fine with her, since it somewhat protected her from impromptu visits from him; however, she didn't doubt for a moment that he would show up at her front door if he was determined to see her. It was sad testimony to think that was the second, and not third or fourth, reason why she'd put in the electronic gate system.

"I told you," Lyon replied. "You handling this alone is not an option."

It wasn't that Hope wasn't grateful; she simply yearned for what they'd had yesterday—the peaceful atmosphere, the companionship as they'd cooked together and filled in the gaps of what life was like when each was away in school or jobs prior to their current work. It was hardly a conventional evening considering that they were supposed to be on their honeymoon, but knowing how her father was apt to react in a few moments made her yearn to turn back the clock for a few more hours alone with Lyon.

"I don't suppose you'd consider leaving your gun in the car?" she asked.

Lyon gave her a mild look. "Let's just get this over with."

Releasing their seat belts, they exited the car and walked together up the four stairs to the veranda of the two-story federal-style mansion that had been built less than two decades after the Alamo. The house was recognized by the state historical society and had been on the Cedar Grove tour of homes three times that Hope could remember. Two large concrete urns framed the front door bearing junipers trimmed into spiral topiaries. The structure could be a courthouse the way it looked now—well-tended, but extremely spare in adornment, and aloof, like the owner.

The front door opened before Hope could ring the bell. A slender man in a black suit and red-and-black striped tie about the same age and coloring as her father nodded his head in a nominal bow and stepped aside to let them enter.

"Miss Harrell, Chief Teague."

"Hello, Greenleaf," Hope replied to her father's longtime butler. "It's nice to see you."

"You as well, miss. You'll find him in the study."

That was as friendly as her father's employee was apt to dare get and she wasn't about to make things more difficult for him except for one question. "Is Mrs. Crandall okay? I haven't seen her in town in a while."

"She broke a toe almost two weeks ago, Miss. I'm doing the shopping and errands that I can until she can wear regular shoes again."

"I'm so sorry. I had no idea." Needless to say, her father hadn't shared that bit of news. "Please tell her that I asked about her and send my sympathies," she said. "And let me know if there is anything I can do for either of you."

"I will. Thank you, Miss Hope."

Greenleaf didn't invite warm fuzzies and using her first name was the only sign that he recognized her sincerity and concern, but Hope could never fault his service or discipline, and she felt much the same about Mrs. Crandall, although she barely knew her. Hope had moved out when their long-time housekeeper Naomi Jobs retired and Mrs. C had joined the staff.

As the butler stood back to let them cross the expansive foyer, Hope didn't attempt to explain or reminisce about the decor with Lyon, even though this was his first time there; however, she did pause so Lyon could get a closer look at the full-size portrait of her mother on her wedding day on the wall beside the study doors.

"She was beautiful," he murmured. "Except for the more formal gown, that could be a portrait of you."

Despite her awareness that Greenleaf was watching, Hope touched his arm. "You always say the right thing."

"Your hand is cold," he noted, covering it with his. He squeezed gently, his look reassuring.

Hope started to reply when the double doors swung open. She pivoted neatly, her hair and flower-print skirt flaring. Adjusting her red leather purse strap on the shoulder of a short white jacket, she settled her expression into a polite smile.

"Hello, Dad. How are you?"

"What's he doing here?" Ellis demanded, his gaze immediately narrowing on Lyon.

Hope suspected he'd seen them drive up and walk up to the front door, since the floor to ceiling windows in the study faced the circular driveway. But since he hated being caught unawares and she had refused to tell him what this meeting was about, he was at a disadvantage. A price was in the process of being exacted.

"We came to share a few things with you."

Not quite as tall as Lyon, or as toned, he remained an impressive physical specimen for a man turning sixty-two by Christmas. Even his lush head of hair still had some blonde in it. His tan sports jacket over crisp white shirt and pressed jeans might exude a casual first glance, but upon closer examination, they were undoubtedly tailored for him, and his black boots were sharkskin, not cowhide.

"You know perfectly well you made me believe my appointment was with you and you alone," Ellis replied, his baritone voice rough from shouting too many orders in corrals and meeting rooms than from scotch and cigars. "And you have ten minutes before I have to leave."

"Heading to the hospital?"

"What the devil for?" he asked, doing a 180-degree turn and retreating back into his office. His demeanor was such that he was giving notice that he didn't care if they followed or not.

"To purge whatever is making you sound like a stopped-up septic tank."

He spun around and looked like he was about to grind her into his lunch, but abruptly burst into a single bark of laughter. "Whatever it is you want," he said pointing at her, "that crack just cost you ten percent more than it would have."

"Then lucky for us that we're not here to negotiate," Hope replied. "How was your dinner party?"

"Fine, no thanks to you. Summer Isadore graciously agreed to take your place."

Summer was a dozen years her senior and so hardly what Jack Nolan might be in the market for, but always receptive to an invitation from Ellis, so Hope doubted there was no hardship involved. She owned *Summer's Ladies,* a boutique for women like her—affluent, discerning, and always on the prowl for greener pastures. As much as Hope tried to shop locally to support entrepreneurs, she wouldn't be crossing that threshold, unless she saw smoke billowing in the display window and had forgotten how to dial 911.

When Hope failed to take the bait, Ellis offered a cranky, "All right, so you won this round. I'll admit to being curious. What's up?"

"Lyon and I simply wanted to inform you before we make a formal announcement. We're married."

He looked from one of them to the other. "The hell you say."

Hope held out her left hand so he could see the ring. "And before you say something you're going to regret, you'd better know that I'm going to have a baby."

"His?"

"Careful," Lyon warned him.

Ellis turned away from them, his hands fisted at his side. "How dare you?" he finally rasped.

It was impossible to tell if that was meant for her or Lyon, but as far as Hope was concerned it was the same thing. "If you're accusing either one of us of something," she began, "please remember that we're both well over the age of consent and we hardly need the blessing of Vatican *West*. But if you're singling me out, consider that I could say the same thing to you for making a private loan to Will behind my back."

That startled her father and his about face wasn't smooth. "He told you?"

"Right after I broke our engagement."

A muscle under her father's right eye twitched. "Why did you do a fool thing like that?"

"Why is my not so subtle accusation so easy for you to dismiss?" Hope shook her head. "Mother would never have dreamed to give you cause to doubt her."

"Apples and oranges. Your mother was barely twenty when I married her. Will was a man, not a boy."

"You aren't going to claim age gives you the right to lie as well as cheat? Poor Mother," she said almost to herself. "She had it rougher than I even guessed."

Ellis circled his massive oak desk and sat down heavily in a burgundy leather chair. "That's not fair."

"Inconvenient truths, Father."

For several seconds Ellis looked out the nearest window, his jaw squared and his gray eyes hard. Hope once thought him as handsome as Robert Redford; however, while still in braids, she'd grasped that he had none of the actor-turned-director-turned renaissance man's finessed qualities. He remained handsome in his element, much the way a free predator could be artistically and scientifically mesmerizing, yet dangerous in the wild. Hope harbored a healthy wariness of that man.

When Ellis fixed Lyon with his gaze, he demanded, "And what do you have to say for yourself?"

"To you, nothing. But you might give your daughter your blessing."

"I'll take the H-brand to your cunning hide first."

"That would be fair if I thought you were concerned for her and her alone. But exactly how long do you think keeping your foot on her neck will work for you?"

"Why you—"

As Ellis pushed himself out of his chair, Hope stepped into his line of vision. "Lyon is the least manipulative man you'll ever meet. The least like you. Is that why Will had your full support? He was more of a son to you, a chip off the old block, than I'm a daughter?"

"You must be pregnant," Ellis spat. "You're getting emotional."

Lyon took careful hold of Hope's elbow. "We're done here, let's go."

Hope stood her ground. "This was a courtesy visit, but hear this—meddle in my private life or continue to support any of that nonsense going on in town to remove Lyon, and be assured—Clyde and Mercy aren't the only people who will know how Will was sweating to hide his business mistakes." Part of that was an educated guess, but it proved fruitful.

The arrogance of power was draining from her father's face. "You'd ruin the reputation of the man you were supposed to marry?"

"He was doing just fine on his own. But what is despicable is that you were willing to see me locked in a marriage that would break my heart. That I won't forget or easily forgive."

She let Lyon direct her out of the room and the house, grateful that there was no further sign of Greenleaf, although she suspected he wasn't far away. As for her and Lyon, they didn't speak again until they were in the car and almost at the end of the driveway.

"Remind me never to push you into a corner," Lyon said as though reciting the time and temperature.

Closing her eyes wasn't enough. Moaning, Hope covered her face with her hands. "He's right. I got emotional when I meant to stay so calm and focused. "

"You were terrific."

"You have to say that, you're stuck with me."

"No," he drawled. "I don't. A wedding vow doesn't mean unconditional support, especially for a bad idea—though I'm not saying this was. But it does mean recognizing what this meeting cost you. I admire your strength. You've lived under that roof for almost two decades and have seen the bodies of his enemies and victims pile up in bankruptcy court and cemeteries. I admit that once upon a time, I thought you were a bit of a Girl Scout. I'd already changed my mind since then, but my respect for you grew the width and depth of another ocean today."

Hope didn't want the compliment to matter so much, but she was feeling ultra exposed having said so much in front of him. "Girl Scout, huh? I guess a hug is a hug."

"I can do better."

They were well out of sight of the estate and Lyon turned into a wooded driveway where he shifted into Park and released his seat belt. Then he slid back the seat and released Hope's buckle and deftly lifted her onto his lap.

"Lyon…" she gasped. She found herself eye to eye with him. "This is crazy."

"Humor me," he replied. "It's either this or I take you to the ER to make sure your blood pressure isn't about to rupture a vein or hurt the baby."

With that he leaned her back over his arm and claimed her mouth with his, kissing her the way he'd been wanting for too long to remember. She was immediately responsive and pliant in his arms, her lips parting to his probing, her back arching as he coaxed her closer, as close as he could get her. She smelled like heaven, she felt like a dream, and her taste went to his head faster than any drink could. Craving much more, Lyon withdrew his tongue and slid his lips across her cheek to press against the side of her neck.

"Now you may need to get me to the hospital," she told him.

He was immediately contrite. "Did I hurt you lifting you over this confounded clutter?"

He was referring to the console where there was everything from more gadgets to communication gear. "No more than a bump or two. I was talking about that kiss."

"I'm breaking my own rule to not take advantage."

"You aren't. But you did say this arrangement could be anything I wanted it to be. I liked the kiss, Lyon. I liked it a lot."

His chest rose and fell as he breathed deeply, and he brushed his thumb against her lower lip. "I hope you mean that because I need to do it again."

Their second kiss had her wrapping her arms around his neck. That crushed her breasts against his hard chest, and she could feel their hearts leap and pound anew as his tongue coaxed hers to kiss him back in that steamy, languid way, as if they had all the time in the world. Hope felt her body heat as though the air conditioner wasn't running and it was triple-digit August instead of the middle of May. He made her wish they were home instead of here and that he would do more than run his hands up and down her back and torment her with only brushing the backs of his fingers over the outermost swell of her breast. She yearned to feel his skin touching hers, and his breath—

"I have to answer that," Lyon said sighing.

"Answer what?"

He grinned and his chest shook slightly from laughter. "Dispatch wants a check in."

That was when she heard a discreet clicking. Realizing it was a mic check, she tried to return to her seat, but he stayed her and just searched beneath the hem of her skirt to find the handheld device.

"Go ahead, Buddy. Over."

"Chief, Mr. Pettigrew is here."

Lyon exchanged looks with Hope, then he checked his dashboard clock. "I'm about twenty minutes out. Tell him I can call him later if he can't wait."

"Hang on. Over."

While Buddy conferred with the editor of Cedar Grove's newspaper, Lyon helped Hope back into her seat. His caresses left her ultra-sensitive to his touch and her subtle shiver and squirming to get her seat belt fastened must have telegraphed something to him.

"Are you okay?"

"Sure."

"That guy has the worst timing on the planet."

He sounded regretful, his voice as tender as his touch, but

she was thinking of how far she would have been willing to go. In who knows whose driveway? In broad daylight!

"I need to get to my office anyway." She smoothed her hair while he took the call back, and willed her heart to stop pounding like some over-wound toy.

Pettigrew would wait. Lyon said, "All right, see you eleven at the latest."

"Doesn't sound good," she said after he disconnected and replaced the mic. "Do you suppose my father called him the moment we left?"

"Not enough time for him to conjure a plan and order Ted to the station. This is something else. Please tell me you're okay?"

She gave him a bright look. "Fine."

"No, you're not." He placed his hand on her cheek to keep her face toward his. "What is it? Did I go too fast?"

"We're not preteens experimenting on a first date," she replied, her sardonic tone for herself, not him. So why did she suddenly feel so unlike herself, and wrong?

"No, thank heaven we're not." His focus was wholly on her lips. "I'll be hard pressed to listen to Ted let alone anyone else the rest of the day. All I'll be thinking about is you."

The push and pull of emotions continued to war within her until she groaned. "My father was right," she said with chagrin. "I'm all hormones."

"Forget about your father. He doesn't have a—" Lyon swore under his breath. "We can't have this conversation right now." He shifted roughly into reverse and backed out of the dirt driveway.

Hope grimaced at his rough handling of the car. She didn't blame him for being frustrated with her. She wasn't all that happy with herself, either.

"Do you *have* to go into the office?" he asked about a mile down the road. "It might do you good to take the day off."

"I can't. I have to prepare for a meeting right after lunch. It's a new client."

"Then at least promise me you'll call your doctor? The OBGYN you mentioned."

"I did before you picked me up. But Dr. Winslow can't see me until this time next week." She sent him an apologetic look. "I'm okay, Lyon. I'm sorry that I worried you."

But when he dropped her off at the house and he leaned over to kiss her goodbye, she turned her head in the last second and the kiss barely skimmed her cheek.

"See you later," she said and quickly jumped from the squad car. Seeing he was about to say her name or say something, she slammed shut the door and dashed to get her own vehicle.

Lyon turned the air conditioner on high for the trip back to town. If he had a cup with ice left over from a cold drink, he would have tossed that into his lap. Let Pettigrew and the whole office think what they would when he walked in dripping wet.

He ached and he worried and neither sensation was pleasant. Why had Hope gone—not cool, but distant and antsy on him? That wasn't hormones, or not all hormones. Had she been telling the truth that she was okay? She wouldn't have responded like she did if she wasn't.

Patience, he reminded himself. Married a day and already he had to remind himself about that oath. It was the delicacy of her clothes that had almost driven him crazy. Her blouse was as thin as a scarf, her bra as fine as her lace mantilla. Her nipples had been taut for him. When her jacket had parted, he'd seen that clearly. Whatever had made her not want to give him a real goodbye kiss, she wanted him as much as he wanted her. He had to take comfort in that.

Ted Pettigrew did not enjoy being kept waiting. When Lyon entered the station, he launched at him like a giraffe protecting a watering hole—narrow head and skinny neck first and lanky arms and legs playing catch up.

"There are allegations that you're using a city vehicle for personal use," he declared.

He was oblivious of Buddy, who gave him a pained look, since Pettigrew's voice was like a boom box and Buddy was trying to hear a radio call from one of the other officers in the field. Cooper Jones even leaned out of his office, and it took something considerable to tear him away from a forensics report.

One thing Lyon knew he was guilty of nothing—except to driving home and back to the station. "If this is a fishing expedition, you're wasting your time," he replied snatching up the pink phone message slips Buddy held up for him, and continuing to his office.

"It's been recorded that on the 5th, 7th, then the 10th through yesterday, either you didn't return to your apartment until late, or you didn't return at all." Pettigrew looked over his frameless lenses at him. "Can you prove these records are incorrect?"

Once behind his desk, Lyon glanced up at him. "Records? You mean notes, don't you, Ted? Or are you wasting the paper's money on a private detective?"

Only mildly set back by Lyon correcting him, Ted waved his pad dismissively. "It's been a hectic morning and

I misspoke. This is a personal log and, no, I won't share my sources."

"What did you do, plant your mother-in-law with a bag of cheddar popcorn in the parking lot of my apartment?" Once in a while, when all of the Letters to the Editor were critical of Ted's editorials, he would have his mother-in-law write something on his behalf. Who knew what else he'd asked of the poor woman?

"You'd be wise to take this seriously—and appreciate my attempt to give you an opportunity to defend yourself."

"I always take you seriously, Ted. That's why I'm telling you once and with complete frankness that my vehicle was not in use after hours on those dates."

"You haven't even checked your calendar or log."

"Don't have to. Those are memorable dates to me." He sat down and shot the disgruntled newspaperman a benign look. "Is there anything else?"

"You don't seem to grasp the importance of this—I'm going to be running an editorial on the critics who feel your job performance has left a bad taste in some people's mouths," Pettigrew replied.

An editorial, not a news article. "That's your prerogative, although I will say that I'm deeply disappointed."

"And I can quote you as not interested in helping yourself?"

Lyon pointed to the top envelope on his desk. "The autopsy report on Will Nichols came in this morning." He hadn't told Hope because he hadn't wanted to add to any nerves she was feeling before meeting with Ellis. "The medical examiner said that Will broke his neck during the rollovers. If he'd only had a partial break when I reached him and had I succeeded in pulling him out, I might have been guilty of involuntary manslaughter. As it is, all you have is the complaint by a woman who was messing around with an engaged man. You go with that and you're going to look pretty ridiculous. Anything else is criticism by people who don't care for me or for not signing on to their politics. That's not a firing offense."

"Can the press have a copy of that report?"

"Not before I share the results with his next of kin."

"What was his alcohol reading?"

Lyon winced inwardly, but enunciated slowly, "After I tell the family, Ted."

As soon as Pettigrew strode out of his office, Lyon dialed Hope's number. He didn't want to make this call—not after they'd parted so unsatisfactorily, but he was afraid Ted would call her wanting a statement. He couldn't not warn her.

"Harrell Consultants," a scratchy voice began. "May I help you?"

"Freddie, this is Chief Teague. Is Ms. Harrell available?"

"Oh! Yes, sir, she just walked in. Hold please."

It took Hope a good while before she picked up—long enough to make Lyon wonder if she was trying to avoid taking the call. Finally he heard a click and her soft voice. "Yes?"

"Sorry to bother you when you've only just arrived. Do you have anyone in your office?"

"No, why?"

"I wanted to beat Ted Pettigrew. I was afraid he would get hold of you before I could."

"Oh, God, what's happened?"

"Nothing you didn't know or suspect, but you'd still have been caught off guard. The autopsy report came in.

Actually, it was here early this morning, but I didn't think the time was right to tell you."

"I see."

Did she? Lyon prayed so. "Hope, his neck was broken on impact." A barely audible sound came over the line and his heart twisted. "Damn, I'm sorry for telling you like this. Are you okay?"

"Yes. You're right, I was prepared for that, but it still delivers a kick."

"It does. Pettigrew wanted to know his alcohol level. I told him that I wasn't releasing any other results until I reported to the next of kin. I'll call Clyde next."

"Yes, thank you. I wouldn't want to be the one."

"No, of course not." Lyon stared at the report. "He was well over the limit for alcohol, Hope. More so than I would have guessed, which means he'd been indulging elsewhere."

Hope drew in a ragged breath. "I can't listen to any more, Lyon. I—I have to get out of here."

"I'll be right there."

"No, you have work to—"

The phone went dead. Lyon's heart plunged, but he didn't give himself time to wonder if she'd done it on purpose or if she couldn't help it because she was about to be sick. He was out of his office and heading for the front door even as he gave directives to Buddy. "I'm out for anything but an emergency," he told him. "You can reach me by the radio."

"Do you need backup? Anything?"

"No. Tell Cooper the Nichols autopsy is on my desk—for his eyes only. If anyone else calls about it, delay them."

Lyon made it back to the house just as the first garage door was closing. He triggered the third one to open and saw Hope already at the storm door fumbling with keys. When she saw him, she covered her face with the tissues crumpled in her hand and turned away.

Lyon barely stopped the car before he was rushing to her. "Are you sick? Do you need the bathroom first?"

"No, I've already been there, done that. Now I'm just mortified."

"Don't be. You've been heading for this from the beginning and operating on sheer willpower. It's a wonder you've held it together as long as you did." His arm around her for support, he unlocked the door and helped her inside. Feeling how unsteady she was, once they were through to the kitchen, he took her purse and set it on the bar, then swept her into his arms and carried her to her bedroom.

She moaned and hid her face against his shoulder. "Please don't do this."

"Hush. It's going to be all right."

This was his first time coming to this side of the house. He barely noticed the pretty Santa Fe colors and elegant cherry furnishings, but the bright sunshine that was making the bedroom migraine bright immediately drew his concern. As soon as he laid her on the turquoise and green bedspread, he went to the windows and cranked the mini-blinds closed. That turned the room into a dusky oasis.

Returning to the bed, he saw that Hope had immediately folded into a tight fetal position. "Let's get you more comfortable," he said easing her up. He slipped off her red strappy heels and placed them on the far side of the night stand, then started on her jacket. "That's it," he said soothingly as she strived to help him. "Take your time. Should I call Molly?"

"No! She'd only get upset. I'll be fine as soon as I rest for a few minutes."

Lyon doubted it since she couldn't say that much without her voice cracking. He couldn't stand it. Settling onto the edge of the bed, he began coaxing her into his arms until he was cradling her. He thought things were going well…and then she burst into tears.

Lyon hated the ragged sounds that ripped through her. He couldn't imagine what she was feeling, caught in a world where she knew a fiancé hadn't loved her enough, a father she couldn't trust, and a mother long gone and unable for her to console or confide in. His words would be wholly inadequate right now. All he could do was rock her and hope that regretting their marriage wasn't part of her toppling world.

"You'll think this horrible," she said fighting for control, "but all I keep thinking is that…he could have killed both of us. All of us."

Lyon couldn't let his mind go there, and yet *she* had to. Her heart was shuddering in aftershocks for the tiny life she carried inside her, her body turning cold from the grim shadows that carried the echo, "What if?" She was right—as soon as he'd known her condition, Will should have driven like he had the world's most precious cargo in that truck. Better yet, Will should have pulled over and waited for him to get Hope home. The problem was Will couldn't deal with anyone coming before him. That character flaw would have ended his professional career if the injury hadn't, and it would have eventually killed Hope's love for him once she saw that even a baby came second to his own voracious ego. Hope was also right that Will Nichols would have been a perfect son-in-law for Ellis. Second to losing her mother, this was probably the worst day in her life.

"You have to take care now, too, sweetheart," he said

gently stroking her hair. "Making yourself sick can hurt the baby, as easily as anything else."

"You're right." She took a deep, sustaining breath. "I guess I just felt betrayed all over again, and then so angry. With myself, too."

Smiling to himself, Lyon kissed her hair. "Good idea. After all, you're the only one who was meant to have perfect judgment and never make a mistake."

That won a muffled laugh from her. "It's about time you noticed that."

Having stepped away from being trapped in that bad psychological place, she was sounding stronger. It was time to win another concession from her. "Are you going to reschedule that appointment you mentioned?"

"It wouldn't be fair to the poor woman not to. In fact, I may have Freddie close early and have her come over to tell her what's going on."

More good news, Lyon thought. "She's your right hand. She needs to know you're with child." That would also allow him to check on Hope without her knowing it.

"Freddie's a bit offbeat and hard to figure out, but even she will take this better knowing first that I'm married. I'll try to hold off the pregnancy news until next month."

That might be a good idea even if she didn't try to let it be perceived that he was the father. They were going to hear plenty of criticism as it was from the elopement announcement. "Then I'll start letting it be known at the office, too. Buddy looked like a grouper with his big eyes and working mouth when I left." He told her that he'd just stated he needed to go and to only radio if there was an emergency.

"You do need to get back, but I want you to know I appreciate this."

He stroked her back. "Just as long as you aren't upset with me—I mean about earlier."

Disengaging herself, Hope sat up and dabbed at the moisture still clinging to her lashes. It was a good sign if she was starting to worry about makeup damage, but not so good that she could only meet his eyes for a second before glancing away.

"I didn't mean to come off as a tease, Lyon."

"How do you figure you did?"

"I realized my, um, behavior had left you…uncomfortable."

"Aroused."

"It's only been a week since the funeral!"

He knew exactly what she was driving at—the same thing anyone who had faced life and death could have experienced. "What you're going through is natural," he told her. "Although I'd like to think that I had something to do with things."

"Of course you did," she said. "That's what made it worse."

"Worse?"

"More difficult to come to terms with. I value your opinion of me, Lyon. I didn't want you to think that despite feeling what I did, that I would have…you know."

"Let down your guard with anyone else?" If he wasn't so concerned that she quit beating herself up, he could have laughed at her cute way of trying to talk about sex without using the terminology. He folded her closer and laid his cheek on top of her head. "I knew that. But it's nice to hear anyway."

"That's good because I couldn't bear it if you—"

"I'm here for you. I know you're going to be going through changes and there'll be…"

"Struggles."

"I was going to say sexual tension, but wild woman that you are, I was concerned about triggering your libido and having to stop you from stripping off your clothes."

Hope gasped and pushed away from him, only to see his mischievous grin. "You are horrible," she said, although she couldn't repress a smile herself.

And she was beautiful even with a shiny, red nose and the hint of raccoon eyes. "Hope, promise me you won't keep me having to play twenty guesses? If you need to be held, I'll hold you. Taking a cold shower later is much easier than working up an ulcer because I don't know what's made you shut me out."

Her expression softened and she laid her hand against his cheek. "What did I do to deserve you?"

"Don't be too flattering, I do have my limits. Don't ask me to watch when you get around to craving pickles and ice cream."

"Yuck. That doesn't sound remotely appealing. Thank you," she added quietly. After she noticed his gaze lowering to her mouth, she leaned close and touched her lips to his.

"Again, please," he said keeping his eyes closed.

She did as he asked, this time lingering and gently brushing her lips back and forth against his. He liked the way their noses caressed, too, and wisps of her hair acted like fingertips stroking his face.

"Better." He had to swallow because even these sweet caresses were starting to raise his temperature and leave him parched. "I am, after all, the man who is going to endure watching you turn green from morning sickness and be asked for back rubs when you get geometrically imbalanced."

"Not necessarily, smarty. I've had a standing appointment for a few years with a massage therapist in town," she said against his lips. "Like the yoga, it's preventative care."

Before she could withdraw, he gave into the need to part her lips further and kissed her in a manner that caressed her the way he ached to explore the rest of her body. Her soft sounds of appreciation and yearning soon tempted him to lean her back against the bedspread and stretch out beside her.

"You're clicking, Chief."

Lyon realized he was being summoned. Buddy was giving his discreet indication requesting a check-in before he was forced to make a verbal request. With a sigh, Lyon pushed himself to his feet.

"Guess you know where I'm headed," he told Hope.

"Will you be home for dinner? I'm thinking of calling over Molly after all. We could make something nice."

She really needed to rest, but if some quiet time with sweet-natured Molly did the trick, that was good, too. "Short of a Caribbean cruise liner missing its dock and carving its way all the way up here, you bet," he replied.

"See you then."

Chapter Five

Hope didn't get morning sickness. What she did was develop an extreme taste for all foods with a Southwestern flavor and had to consciously work at not indulging three times a day. By the Fourth of July she had worked through her Rolodex of her mother's personal recipes, and the three other specialized cookbooks she owned. She was eyeing a recipe online when Molly entered the kitchen with a basket of roses from the front yard.

"How does grilled snapper stuffed with jalapeños sound?" she asked her. "My mouth is already watering."

Molly hugged the colorful blooms to her thin chest. "Jalapeños make my hands burn," she enunciated with care. Her expression reflected more than a little trepidation. "We can ask Tan to pick them. There are lots in the garden and they need to be picked, but he's been busy with the horses."

"Oh, sweetie, I can go pick them. I was just wondering

if it was just me and my crazy taste buds that thought the recipe sounded yummy."

She and Lyon were going to a town-and-church picnic in the city park and attendees were encouraged to donate to the buffet that would be open to the entire town. Lyon didn't want to go—he was already at the town's Liberty Parade and would be working tonight at the fireworks show. But while some people had taken their marriage announcement in stride—a few even relieved at what they saw as a better match—others had grown more negative than ever. Then, too, a client's freezer had gone out on them and they had several large red snappers that needed to be used up quickly.

"Let me put the roses in water," Molly said placing the basket on the counter beside the sink. "Then I'll go out with you and hold the hoe."

Bemused, Hope gave her a curious glance. "What for?"

"Tan saw a spread adder go in the garden yesterday. I'll watch and chase it away if it tries to come after you."

"I'm not afraid of a bluffing snake," Hope said with a laugh. But the thought of those critters meandering in her thriving garden did give her some pause. "You're sure he thought it was a non-venomous snake?"

"Oh, yes. He brought out his book and he showed me a picture. I hope it's gone. It looked like a cobra to me." Molly's expression grew vague and whimsical. "Tan is very smart. He reads all the time."

"And he's a good husband and groundskeeper. He wouldn't let a bad snake stay around here knowing you or I were going to be out there," Hope assured her. She squeezed the young woman's thin shoulder to bring her back from her mental wandering. If she didn't, sometimes

Molly could stay "gone" for minutes on end. "Okay, you see to the flowers and if you don't mind, wash the fish again that are soaking in the two big bowls in the refrigerator. I'll handle the pepper harvesting."

"Then I put the fish back in the refrigerator, right?"

"No, leave them soaking in the sink. We'll start the rest of the preparations as soon as I come back inside." The simplest tasks were sometimes a problem for Molly, but no one was more thorough and dependable when she got routines memorized.

Once outside, she saw Tan cleaning the hooves of Desiree, her gray pregnant mare. She let herself into the barn through a wooden gate and exited on the south side where he was bent over his task. "Good morning," she said. "I appreciate you getting that done today, Tan. But I hope you'll take it easy the rest of the day. It's a holiday."

Tan grinned at her, his eyes becoming little more than slits in his bronzed face. "Miss D follow me around all yesterday and paw ground. No more delay."

"I think she's training you as well as you're training her. Molly told me that you saw a spread adder in the garden. I just wanted you to know that if I yell, 'snake,' it's one of the more venomous varieties."

The slender, middle-aged man, who was her own height, shook his head. "No snake. I know you be coming out, so I look good. Find two fat tomato worm. Good fish bait. Molly and I catch dinner for later."

Luckily his wife loved fish. "Thank you, Tan. You spoil me. Are you and Molly going to come watch the fireworks tonight?"

He shook his head, then pointed. "Drive truck to middle of pasture and make picnic on back. Best view."

"How romantic. I'll envy you the privacy. I'm going to keep the chief company, since he wants to help his people monitor things. See you later."

She picked about a quart of peppers and returned to the kitchen where Molly was humming to herself and twisting a dish towel almost into a knot. Hope set her basket on the center workstation and peeled off her gloves.

"What's the problem, Molly?"

"I did wrong. I should let the machine answer the phone, but I wanted to help. You're busy and I was finished with the flowers and giving the fish a bath."

Oh, no, Hope thought. "Did the caller confuse you?"

"I asked the lady to not speak so fast. She got mad and called me the name."

Not *a* name, but *the* name. Hope immediately eased the towel from her hands and gave her a hug. She knew exactly what word the caller had used—*idiot*. Molly had heard it a great deal from her previous boyfriend even before the accident. Doctors had concluded it was the one thing she retained from that episode, although she had no memory of the man.

"I'm sorry, Molly, dear. That was rude of her. Can you remember who the caller was?"

"An M like me." Having no towel to twist, she began rubbing her wedding band like a worry stone. "I can't remember because it's not a real name. It's just a word."

Hope was getting as good as Tan at grasping what the young woman meant. She asked, "Was it Mercy?"

"That's the word!"

Why on earth had Mercy called here? Their last meeting in town, days after Hope and Lyon had made it public that they were married, had been stilted at best. Mercy acted as though she'd committed an offense against the entire Nichols family tree. Hope had clung to civility and lessons learned at her mother's skirt hem not to remind Mercy that until weeks ago, she had been the wife of a man who did little more than make excuses for why he couldn't find and keep gainful employment. While she'd taken in sewing and cleaned other people's houses, the senior-most Nichols strolled from store to coffee shop opining as to all that was wrong with this country. Only last year had Will succeeded in getting his deadbeat uncle a job with the city, but all that Clyde was qualified to do was burn gas driving around in a city truck. When the city was really shorthanded, he was the one holding the Slow sign at road repair locations. He couldn't even handle a Stop sign without causing a traffic jam. Most offensive was hearing through the grapevine that Clyde suspected the delay in getting the autopsy report on Will had been because Lyon was coercing the medical examiner to "doctor" the report in order to get attention off of himself. Hope fervently wished the Nichols to forget that they were once almost in-laws. What happened that Mercy should deign to phone here?

"Why don't you bring Tan something cool to drink?" she suggested to Molly. "He's almost finished making Desiree comfortable and even though it's still early, that sun has been baking him."

"He likes the lemonade you taught me to make. Can I take him some?"

"That's a great idea."

As soon as Molly shut the back door, carefully taking her husband the icy glass of lemonade, Hope hurried to her office and looked up the Nichols' number in the county phone book. Then she dialed it on the wireless phone. It rang twice before she received a recording that the number was no longer in service. The new number was the ranch one, which she dialed from her phone's directory, mentally reminding herself to remove it as soon as she finished with the call.

As she waited for the ringing to start, she thought how it hadn't taken the Nichols long at all to move in.

"Nichols residence."

"This is Hope," she said to Mercy. "I understand you called."

"How nice of you to call back so promptly," Mercy replied, her voice polite, but holding an unmistakable superior tone. "I wasn't sure you would get my message."

The woman was starting to get on her nerves. "You've probably forgotten my telling you about my helper Molly," Hope began, determined to keep her voice normal. "She was badly injured trying to escape a bad relationship. She had a difficult recovery and required much rehabilitation, but she is certainly capable of taking messages when given the chance."

After an awkward silence, Mercy said, "Now that you mention it, I do remember. I've had a great deal on my mind."

Disappointed that she wouldn't take ownership of her poor conduct, Hope replied, "Then don't let me keep you. What was it that you needed?"

"Well, as you can imagine, it's been nonstop stressful here since we probated William's estate. Since William was a bachelor and the place hadn't been given a proper cleaning in who knows how long, you can imagine the condition of the house."

Hope lifted her gaze to the ceiling and reached for more patience. Will had three sisters—one being the wife of one of his ranch hands—come by every week to clean and polish a different area of the house. In contrast, his uncle and aunt had lived in the same one-bedroom cottage in the oldest part of town since their marriage. And while the place was kept neat enough compared to some, during heavy rains a river flowed under the house that had no foundation and was precariously balanced on blocks. Hope remembered Will laughingly report that the floors were tilting more with each season and that one day the refrigerator was likely to end up on the back porch with the washing machine and probably finish turning that structure into a soggy pile of splinters and drowned termites.

"I don't know the name of the people who cleaned there regularly, Mercy," Hope told her. "I do know they were related to someone else who worked there. Ask Will's foreman. He'll know, but if you need me to refer someone, I can."

"First I need to inventory things properly. I can't allow strangers in here. But will your people have references that I can check out? I will require references."

Oh, my, Hope thought, she was certainly taking the Lady of the Manor role seriously. In fact, she suspected Mercy had known about the girls all along and had fired them the instant they came to the front door.

"I'm not sure," Hope replied. "You'll just have to ask them when the time comes. Is there anything else?"

"Since I have you on the phone, there is one small matter I wanted to clear up with you. Now that we have the court matters behind us, Clyde insists I get the Nichols family jewels."

Hope pressed her fingers to her lips. Did Mercy have any idea how the underlying excitement in her voice exposed her barely containable pleasure at the changes in their small lives?

"That sounds entirely legal and justified to me," she replied.

"You do? Well, thank you, Hope. Do you also understand that means if there's anything else found—I mean at the accident site or in the totaled truck at the salvage yard—it's to be returned here?"

What was obvious to Hope was that this entire conversation had been all a ploy to get to this subject. "Mercy, the authorities had my directives from the beginning for that to be the case, and if by chance someone forgot, I would have it redirected to you. Now I really must go and check on my oven. Take care and enjoy."

After disconnecting, she found herself feeling sorry for the woman. Her rudeness to Molly would not be forgotten, but Mercy undoubtedly thought money and property would open doors to a better society for her. She was about to find out it was far more complicated than that.

Once Molly returned smiling and happy again, she and Hope got the snappers stuffed and in the oven. They were just washing up when they heard the sound of the garage door opening. Lyon was home.

"Something smells mighty good," he said entering the kitchen.

As always when their gazes locked, Hope felt the world had righted itself somehow and a sense of peace and well-being seeped into her body. He looked hot and a bit tired, but his dark eyes sparkled as he gave her a discreet wink.

"Hot fish!" Molly declared wide-eyed for their achievement. "Not just hot from the oven. Hope picked every pepper in the garden—and all by herself. She cut them up, too, and never had to wash her hands once until the end. I couldn't do that."

Hope watched Lyon listen attentively and offer a comical grimace. "Me, either. I'd make a mistake and touch my eyes and the next thing I'd have my head under a faucet trying to cool off."

"Me, too," Molly echoed.

She looked pleased that she had something in common with a man who, until recently, she would never dare make eye contact with. Molly had believed the chief of police was way too important to speak to someone like her and Hope's own incomparable position in her world had risen to headier altitudes when she told Molly that she and Lyon were marrying.

"How was the parade?" Hope asked as he came up beside her and slipped his hand under her ponytail to caress her nape. That nominal touch sent a warm stream of pleasure down her spine.

"We had a stroller-motorcycle incident, but not much else."

"Goodness! I'd say that's enough. Was anyone hurt?"

"The bike. The stroller was empty except for a tote bag and canvas cooler full of baby bottles and water. The weight of that provided enough momentum to roll the buggy down a driveway ramp fast enough to knock over the bike and break a taillight. Otherwise, everyone seemed to enjoy themselves."

"That's a relief. You look ready for something cold to drink," Hope said.

"I brought Tan some of the fresh lemonade we made this morning," Molly said proudly. "Would you like me to pour you a glass?"

"Thanks, Molly, that would be great. But it sounds like Tan's the one who's been really working."

"Too hard," Hope said in agreement. "He didn't just

clean Desiree's hooves, he got all the girls fixed up. After you finish with that, Molly, I want you to head home and make sure he stays out of the sun until it cools off."

"Yes, ma'am." Once Molly poured the drink and set the glass on the kitchen bar in front of Lyon, who'd sat down on the first stool at the end of the counter, she began untying her apron. "Are you sure you don't need for me to wait with you until the fish are done?"

Hope shook her head. "No, since we bought throw-away pans, there isn't going to be anything to wash other than what you already did. Go and spoil Tan a little."

"I'll try," Molly replied, although she looked doubtful. "But he'll just spoil me more." She left the house shaking her head as though trying to resolve one of the world's most complex puzzles.

Hope pressed her hand to her heart. "Is that not the dearest thing you've ever heard? They so remind me of that O. Henry Christmas story, *The Gift of the Magi,* always putting each other first."

"Sounds like someone else I know," he murmured.

"What did you say?" Hope missed the first part of what he'd said and glanced back at him.

"I asked 'and how's Mommy and Biscuit?'" he added, nodding to the slight bump of her belly. It didn't show in her usual street clothes, but she was wearing a more fitted T-shirt this morning.

Hope got a kick out of his interpretation of the "bun in the oven" cliché. "Fine, though I did restrain myself to eating only one spoonful of the jalapeño stuffing, so the cooking smells are driving me crazy."

"You'll be like a rabid terrier before the picnic begins."

"That's better than being short stuffing for all of the fish.

As you can see, I was forced to use both ovens." She caught him stifling a yawn and was immediately concerned. "You didn't sleep well last night, did you?"

"Well enough."

"I think you should stay home and nap while I go to the picnic. After all, you have to stay up later to make sure everyone clears out safely after the fireworks display tonight."

"I'm not going to make you go to that alone."

"I'd miss you, but I'd feel better knowing you weren't jeopardizing your health—or safety." Lyon had been doing his share to make up for being short an officer since Chris Sealy got picked up by the Dallas PD. He and his young family had moved away two weeks ago and Lyon had been told by the mayor to delay hiring a replacement. Remembering that, Hope asked, "Any word on whether the city has removed the hold on hiring?"

Instead of answering, Lyon took a long sip of his lemonade.

The subtle evasion didn't fool Hope. "What aren't you telling me?"

"They're finally going to put my contract on the agenda for Monday's city council meeting."

"No!"

"So now you know why I didn't want you going to the picnic alone. I was hoping to delay you learning about that for as long as possible, and knew someone would be more likely to mention it to you if I wasn't around."

"Thank you for sparing me an ambush, but what about my right to hear it from you as soon as you got the news? Forget that." Hope circled the counter so she could put her arms around him. "Lyon, how can this be continuing when the autopsy report clearly vindicates you?"

"Your father's a stubborn old bull, you know that." He swung his chair a quarter turn to place her more comfortably between his thighs. "And our marriage has been sheer antagonism to him. Kent held him off as long as he could, but Ellis' man on the council is Dub Mooney and Dub is Ted Pettigrew's source for what's happening behind closed doors. Dub told Kent to either add it to the agenda or Ted was going to print an editorial about political subversion inside of city hall and go after *his* job."

They hadn't heard much out of her father lately, but Hope knew better than to think he'd been idle. "Dub can't get more than two votes against you," she declared after doing the mental calculations.

"Maybe not this time. But Ellis is patient. Next time it may be three, the next four. That's another reason for me to be visible as much as possible." His hands clasping her waist, he stroked her abdomen with his thumbs. "So next subject, please."

Hope wasn't as eager to move on. "You made me not want to attend."

"Don't say that. You know that would disappoint lots of people, particularly the seniors who just sit and watch and hope for someone to pause and give them a little attention. You're always very generous with them."

His suede voice and coaxing words took the edge off of her indignation and anger with her father. Sighing she hugged him tighter. "Thank you for reminding me there are more important things to focus on."

"Are you wearing that? Because if you are, the only thing anyone will be focusing on is how radiant and luscious you're looking."

Hope had been delightfully surprised herself at how

good she'd been feeling so far, and knew the pink-and-purple T-shirt's v-neckline was also exposing that she hadn't only rounded out a bit more in the tummy, but cleavage-wise, as well. "No, I'm wearing a patriotic tunic top with glitter and sequins. I'm not ready to announce anything until I'm through my first trimester."

"So this was all for my personal torment? Thank you."

"I'd planned to change before your return." Although there was a smile on Lyon's lips, Hope saw there was a slow burn going on behind those dark eyes and that made it impossible for her to ignore what that did to her libido and keep her own tone light. "Don't look at me that way."

"What way?"

The fact that he was willing to ante up the sizzle between them told her that he was disturbed about the upcoming meeting, too, and was in need of diversion. "Lyon, don't play with fire. You said it yourself—we have a busy day ahead of us."

"That's why I need a better hug."

Because of the entreaty she heard in his voice and yearning she saw in his eyes, she yielded to the hands that urged her closer. She knew what a risk it was and how the timing was all wrong. Painstakingly prepared food was expected…there were places to go…things to see to before that…but as soon as their bodies touched and he closed his mouth over hers, the desire that was never far from the surface short-circuited her ability to reason.

They had been navigating this sensual terrain with care, and yet not without a cost to their willpower. After weeks of living under the same roof, sharing meals and chores, they were growing more than comfortable in each other's company; their lives were becoming entwined—exactly as a married couple's should. Except that their unconventional marriage denied them the full, natural intimacy that would complete their union. Even the limited foreplay they assured each other was safe and helpful to ease sexual tension was having a counter-productive effect. It was evident in the deeper hunger of Lyon's kiss, and the intensity and possessiveness of his embrace. And when he slid his hands into her hair and all but feasted on her, she knew if he lifted her onto the counter, she would be hard-pressed to stop him.

With a groan, Lyon buried his face in the dark tunnel created by her hair and grazed the side of her neck with his teeth. "I've tried, but I can't stop wanting you."

And she wanted him. But the one thing that held her back was the commitment to herself that he could still get out of this union if he needed to. "I'm not being fair to you. Maybe you should…maybe if there's someone you're used to seeing—"

He recoiled as if he'd been struck. "Don't even go there."

"I'm being pragmatic," she entreated.

"We're married." Lyon looked so dumbfounded that he eased her aside and rose from the chair, paced several feet before fixing her with a stare as though she was suddenly a complete stranger to him. "I told you there was no one. Could *you* do that?"

"I'm pregnant!"

"And we're *married*." With a harsh oath, he headed for the back door. "I need some air," he muttered.

Hope watched him go, miserable and torn. She really had trapped him into a life of a celibate monk with this arrangement. It was so unfair, so unfair.

* * *

Hours later as night fell and the town collected to wait for the fireworks to begin Lyon was still stinging from Hope's suggestion. He couldn't believe that she'd all but encouraged him to be with another woman. Like a barbed hook caught in his flesh, he could barely breathe, let alone move, without sharp pain incapacitating him. Did Will do such a number on her self-esteem that she thought all men were capable and willing to behave like that regardless of commitment or respect for her reputation?

It had to be the pregnancy doing something to her logic. "Pragmatic" his backside. She wanted him every bit as much as he wanted her—and he was on the edge of eaten up with it. What was holding her back?

He'd never seen her more beautiful and desirable than she was now, blooming with the life inside her. He watched her yards away sitting on a blanket with Kent Roberts' two kids, trying to keep them entertained while wife Shana gave the new baby a bottle. Hope was routinely dipping a long-stemmed wand into the container of soap and blowing bubbles that the children were trying to make land on their hands and arms like resting butterflies, then squealing when they burst. With her white sparkly top and her gleeful smile, Hope outshined everyone in his range of vision—even the stars. He didn't want this relentless ache in his belly, but he couldn't take his eyes off of her.

"We lucked out all around this year, didn't we?" the mayor said coming up beside him and leaning against his patrol car as Lyon was doing. "Just enough rain this week to keep the fire threat minimal, but not enough to make the fair grounds a disaster for parking and picnicking."

"Uh-huh," Lyon replied.

"It was still a good idea to spray for mosquitoes earlier in the week. Glad you suggested that."

"Uh-huh."

"Of course, I'd feel a lot better if that herd of feral hogs wasn't getting too close for comfort."

"Uh—" Lyon turned his head and frowned at Kent. "What did you say?"

"Just checking to see if you were paying attention." His old schoolmate matched Lyon's stance—arms and ankles crossed—and nodded at his family and Hope. "Marriage obviously agrees with her. I don't know when I've seen her looking better, and that's no empty compliment."

"Can't disagree with you," Lyon replied.

"Does she know about the meeting on Monday?"

"Yeah."

"You going to let her attend?"

Hope was her own woman. The idea that he could order her to stay away was nothing short of ludicrous, and the look he gave his friend said as much.

The stocky man with the wavy brown hair shrugged. "She's your wife. I figured there were some things Miss Independent would now be willing to defer to you on."

"How's that working for you with Shana?"

Kent rubbed at his whisker-darkened chin. "Good point. But then you're still on your honeymoon. Shana hasn't forgiven me for getting her pregnant again before the other two were out of preschool."

Although Lyon winced inwardly at the word "honeymoon," he replied, "Bet your Italian mother and grandmother aren't complaining." He so wanted to get the conversation off of him and Hope.

"Mom's bringing Grandma Lombardo back from Italy on Saturday. I may be *persona non grata* in my own bedroom, but at least my stomach will be pampered for the next few months."

Lyon knew Kent was kidding about any marital stress. Earlier he'd seen Shana watching Kent with the baby and her sheer adoration was impossible to miss. In contrast, he and Hope hadn't said ten words to each other since arriving here in separate cars, since she'd been right about his responsibilities and needing to linger after she would be ready to return home. Of course, that was his fault. He was the one who had been keeping his distance and when they did speak, his answers to her attempts at conversation indicated his lack of receptivity. He didn't mean to be curt, let alone rude, but he was also in no frame of mind to pretend he wasn't troubled and wounded.

"It's going to be okay, you know."

Although he knew Kent was referring to the council meeting, Lyon's thoughts lingered on his relationship with his in-name-only wife. "I hope you're right."

"Well, it's time for me to get this show going." The mayor slapped him on the back. "See you later."

As Kent made his way to the flatbed trailer where several bands and singers had been entertaining all afternoon, Lyon saw Hope close the bubble container and put it in one of Shana's two totes. Then she made her way over to him.

"This is quite a turnout," she said in lieu of a greeting.

"Best we've had in a few years."

"We're almost not a rural community anymore."

"Have things been going well? I saw the ambulance rush to the pool area earlier.

"Did that teenager who hit the side of the pool with his ribs crack them?"

"Only bruised. The rest of the day has been okay. I'm sure we'll find some empty beer cans in the parking area later. If that's all, then we're doing good."

Lyon could feel her gaze on him but resisted looking down at her. If he did, he would be lost.

"Lyon, please don't be angry with me."

"I'm not." He wanted to be, that was the truth. Yet all he could manage was wanting her and aching because of it.

"I was only trying to be fair."

"What's more fair than being the man you need me to be?"

His quiet truth brought her hand on his bare arm and her forehead against the patch on his shoulder. He could smell her coconut shampoo and sugar body lotion seep through his senses and intoxicate him like a narcotic, but he didn't let himself touch her back.

As Kent took the stage and yelled, "How're y'all doing?" and the crowd erupted in cheers, Hope sighed and stepped back.

"I'm probably going to head home before the show is over. I'm more tired than I thought."

"Your cell phone battery still got a charge?" Lyon asked keeping his gaze on Kent.

"Yes."

"Okay. Take care and sleep well."

"You, too."

Freakin' fat chance, he thought in abject misery.

Chapter Six

By the end of the month, Hope knew two things: Lyon had almost forgiven her for what happened on the Fourth of July, and he still was Chief of Police of Cedar Grove. As a result, she should be as happy—or at least as content—as she'd been on July third, but it was now July thirty-first—Lyon's birthday—and nothing was going well.

She sat in Emergency at Cedar Grove General waiting on her father's doctor to report on Ellis' condition. He'd been admitted at eleven last night complaining of chest pains, and Hope had arrived shortly afterward when her father's butler, Greenleaf, called with the news that an ambulance had just carried him away. It had been a long night and thus far all she knew was that they were performing one test after another. Now it was almost seven o'clock and she'd hoped to be serving Lyon an extra special breakfast to start his thirty-sixth birthday off well. So far nothing else had helped to repair the chasm in their relationship. Instead she was sipping a diet soft drink because she needed the caffeine to stay awake, but her stomach couldn't bear one more sip of the tar they called coffee at the courtesy counter. Fortunately, she was the only one in the waiting room and didn't have to worry about making small talk when she least felt like it.

However no sooner did that thought pass through her mind when she heard the sliding doors open. Although he didn't look like he'd gotten any more sleep than she did, her insides melted at the sight of him, so handsome and official in his dark blue uniform. Belatedly, she noticed he carried a white sack.

"Hi," she said softly smoothing her hair and starting to rise.

"Stay put," he said. He set the bag on the coffee table, kissed the top of her head, and sat down beside her. "Any word?"

"Not yet." Hope felt a little dazed since that was the first time he'd voluntarily touched her in weeks. "They keep running tests."

"Maybe that's good news. If they'd found something, surely they would have told you by now."

"I hope you're right. It's so good of you to come, Lyon." She started to reach out, then checked herself and clasped her hands in her lap. She wouldn't make him uncomfortable, especially on his day. "Happy Birthday. I wanted to cook for you before you headed to the station, but—"

This time he kissed her silent. "It's a sweet thought, but don't worry about it. Did you get any sleep?"

"I rested a little here on the couch." She had folded up the blanket that had been given to her and returned it to the nurse over two hours ago. "Did you?" He certainly didn't look it. While appealing as ever and freshly shaved, his eyes were bloodshot and he had the same dark shadows under his eyes as she saw under hers in the bathroom mirror when she freshened up.

"Not much. I was worried about you."

He made her want to curl up on his lap and purr like a kitten. She had to look away until the burning threat of tears passed, then gestured to the clerk at Admittance, and to the security cameras. "It's perfectly safe."

"I meant worried about you and Biscuit being around all these sick people and not getting enough rest." He took both of her hands within his much larger ones and stared at that contrast as he stroked her with his thumbs. "The house has never been so quiet. It felt bereft."

That was not a tough-cop or football-jock word, but Hope knew Lyon used it with his own quiet truth because he was a reader. Not a latest *NY Times* bestseller aficionado, but someone who found moments in his life when education and experience had left him lacking in answers and he was seeking to fill those voids. Closing her eyes, Hope lowered her head until her cheek rested on his hands.

"Thank you." She could easily have fallen asleep like that—his warmth and strength her pillow.

"Don't get so comfortable that you go to sleep now, I'd be loathe to wake you up. Look what I brought you—your favorite French Vanilla decaf Cappuccino and a breakfast sandwich. You should eat while it's hot."

But before she could reach into the bag for the drink cup, Dr. Gandolf came around the corner looking more fatigued than either of them. "Hope…hello, Chief." He shook Lyon's hand and then focused on her. "I don't know what caused this episode. Let's get that out of the way first and foremost. As best as we can tell, he didn't suffer a heart attack or stroke, or angina attack. That's not saying that something isn't going on, but we'll have to get him to a different facility in either Tyler or Dallas for further testing to know for sure."

"But he was in pain."

Dr. Gandolf shrugged. "Maybe indigestion, although I listened to his stomach and there was no hint of distress there."

With a flash of intuition, Hope said, "He won't let you send him anywhere for tests."

"Well, then maybe you can talk to him because—"

"No."

"No?"

"Doctor, I believe you were right with your first guess. There's nothing wrong." Rubbing the kinks out of her neck, Hope gave the silver-haired, drained doctor an apologetic smile. "He pulled one over on you, Doc. He fooled all of us."

"You think? This is not something you play games with—and the bill doesn't come cheap, either."

"Make sure you tell that to the man who can buy you and all of your relatives several times over. I wouldn't blame you if you dropped him as a patient, but I'm telling you that the reason he pulled this is because he didn't succeed in getting Lyon fired earlier this month. He wanted to find out how willing I was to still come running if he wasn't well."

Vernon Gandolf shifted his gaze to Lyon, who shrugged and said, "It's possible. She knows him pretty well."

The weary doctor uttered a succinct reaction to that probability. "Okay, then if I can't get him to Dallas, I'll keep him monitored for another hour or so, and review my notes. If nothing changes, I'll have no choice but to release him."

"I'm sure you'll find him more than agreeable to that," Hope said.

Shaking his head Dr. Gandolf gestured for her to follow him back down the hall. "He's been asking for you every fifteen minutes since he knew you were here."

"I'll be there in a minute. Let me see Lyon out first."

As soon as the doctor was gone, Hope's slow burn intensified. "The nerve of the man!"

"Let it go. You've wasted enough energy on him," Lyon said. "I guess he's just running out of ideas on how to get me out of your life. Short of having me shot."

"Lyon! Don't even think such a thing."

He stroked her back. "At least you know that you won't be spending your entire day sitting here."

But so much time had been lost. "I didn't bake you a cake. You didn't get your present."

"You bought me a present?"

His bemused expression had her touching his chest in tenderness and reassurance. "Of course. I got you a hat and boots. I thought we could ride together sometime. I sneaked a peek into your closet for sizes because I didn't want to make a mistake." The last was a plea that he not get upset with her all over again.

"I don't know what to say."

"You're right, I should have asked for permission first."

"Hope." He lifted her chin so that she would have to meet his gaze. He started to say something, but instead leaned down and kissed her.

That communicated emotions that words couldn't. Hope let her body tilt into his, eager to absorb every sensation. How she had missed him and this, his tenderness and his strength.

Lyon was reluctant to sever their contact and lingered by touching his forehead to hers. "Are you going to be okay going in there alone?"

"Yes. I won't stay long. And I've already called Freddie to reschedule my meetings today because I didn't know what would be happening here."

"In that case maybe I'll take off early."

Hope loved how strong his heart beat against her hand. They made his words feel like a promise. "That would be lovely."

When he was gone, Hope collected her sack and went to find her father. He remained in an examination cubicle and didn't look happy about it.

"Took you long enough," Ellis grumbled as soon as he laid eyes on her.

"It could have been longer if I followed my first impulse to leave, once I realized what you'd done," she replied.

He shot her a dark look, but Hope remained unimpressed. He looked less threatening in that hospital gown. She did wonder, though, how they'd managed to get him in one of those. Probably only because he thought it would make him appear more convincing.

"What bull has that fool Gandolf been feeding you? He doesn't know what he's talking about. Can't recognize a sick man when he has one right under his nose."

His wild gesticulations sent the heart monitor going berserk, but although the nurses at the station were instantly alert, they didn't approach the cubicle.

"I'm sure he thinks your problem is nothing that the sight of an extra long hypodermic needle wouldn't cure." Hope didn't see an ounce of regret in his demeanor. "You should be ashamed of yourself wasting these good people's time. What if there'd been a real emergency here and you'd stolen priceless attention from someone?"

"Oh, stop the melodramatics. I don't have to listen to this."

"No, you don't. But you better have cried wolf for the first and last time. And understand this—" she took a step closer so she could keep her words strictly between the two of them "—you're not going to succeed in getting Lyon fired."

"We'll see about that."

"Then consider this—he's my husband. If he has to relocate, I'll go with him."

As she'd hoped, her warning left her father slack-jawed. Satisfied, she added with some reluctance, "Do you need a ride home or is Greenleaf coming to fetch you?"

Ellis ignored the question. Narrowing his eyes, he replied, "You won't leave. You're like your mother. You loved this place too much."

Although his pronouncement held its own shock, Hope managed to avoid flinching. But in that instant she did think him a particularly warped human being. "If that's the only reason you managed to keep her with you, I'm more disappointed in you than I can say. No wonder you thought I'd marry Will if he'd survived. But you're wrong about me. Maybe if Mother had lived you would have found out you were wrong about her, too."

Without waiting for a reply or to see if he did have that ride home, Hope left. She had to believe that her father was speaking from a point of loneliness and selfishness and didn't really believe what he'd said about her mother. It had to be terrible to have a lover and partner gone for so many years already. Maybe he was starting to feel abandoned by her. All she knew was that a year ago his surgically sharp words would have debilitated her; now she rejected them and returned to the property with a sense of excitement. Lyon had changed that for her.

She should have been exhausted, but as soon as she got home she was energized, and a luxuriating bath only added to that. Molly arrived shortly afterward and Hope had her starting on the cake while she blow-dried her hair. Then she put out Lyon's gifts on the breakfast table and helped Molly with the icing.

After the cake was on the racks cooling, they went outside and picked the garden. Although Lyon wasn't a fussy eater and seemed to like everything she'd made so far, she knew there was nothing like a thick, juicy steak dinner. The steaks were out on the counter defrosting, while a marinade was mixed together waiting in the refrigerator. Hope collected tomatoes, bell peppers, and had Molly retrieve the last of the hanging spring onions from the awning by the garden shed. They never used chemical fertilizer, but everything was still washed well and left to air dry in the dish drainer to go with the store-bought organic lettuce, since it was already too hot in Texas for lettuce to grow until October, when temperatures dropped permanently from triple-digit threats and even the 90s.

Once they had the cake frosted with a homemade mocha chocolate icing and chocolate shavings, Molly returned home and Hope checked in with Freddie again and returned some calls.

She was cutting zinnias and day lilies for a bouquet for the breakfast nook table when Lyon returned. It was just after three in the afternoon. Feeling as light-headed and hopeful as she did on the day of their wedding two months ago, she met him in the kitchen.

"Five minutes and I would have had these in water and

everything would have been perfect," she told him as he unbuckled his gun belt.

"I'll leave and come back," he said. He even did the side-to-side dart reminiscent of his old football days when he'd been Will's favorite receiver.

"No!" He might be teasing her, but she was taking no chances. "Come sit. Can you have a beer before you look at your presents?"

"I'll get it. You go ahead and try making those flowers look prettier than you."

Hope had changed into a gauzy poet's shirt that showed off her sun-kissed complexion to perfection. She could still wear her jeans, but they were low rise and she had to leave the top button open; however, the shirt hid that.

Returning with the beer he whistled at the cake. "You and Molly have been busy."

"A little bit, but I suspect they already OD'd you on sugar at the station, huh?" she asked.

"Hardly. I got a foot-long hot dog for lunch with a card that reads 'Dream on,' several other cards far worse that I won't describe or ever let you see, and we'll leave it at that."

"Ruthless bunch you work with."

"They're enjoying tormenting me about you whenever they get the chance."

"Because I'm Ellis Harrell's daughter?"

"Because you're the most beautiful woman most of them have ever seen, a little younger than they think I deserve and any one of them would have stuck a fork in my thigh to beat me in a race if getting you was the prize."

"Did I say brutal? I meant twisted."

"They're okay." He took a long drag on his bottle and sighed with pleasure. "The sign at the bank is reading 105.

I was going to suggest we go over to my family's farm so I can check on things and feed the horses, but you don't need the heat or the rough drive on the four-wheeler I keep there."

"But I'd like to see your horses. And you could start breaking in your hat and boots."

He looked pleased. "You're sure?"

"Let's give it a shot."

Lyon walked over to the table and looked at the boxes. Hope realized he was looking for a card, but she'd skipped that part of things, stuck on what the right tone should be given his reserve lately. After all, "To my darling husband" would have hardly fit how things stood between them.

Thankfully, he soon opened the hatbox and smiled at the beautifully woven summer hat with the rattlesnake-skin band and turquoise-and-silver buckle holding it in place. He whistled silently.

"That's a beaut."

He slid it onto his head with the casualness and confidence of a man well used to Western hats and would have had Tan mimicking in hero worship. Hope watched with the pleasure of having remembered the shape of the one he'd worn since he was helping his father on the farm; she'd managed to get the fitter her father always used to duplicate it.

The boots took a little more work to get on, but also fit like they were made for him. "I can't wear these on anything but pavement dressed in my good suit," he said in concern. "It would be criminal to make them dusty or muddy."

"It's not like we're going to be tromping through any lowland," she said delighted that he was thrilled with them. "Why don't you change and I'll pack some bottled water?"

Lyon stopped her as she turned to get the canvas tote in the washroom storage cabinet. "This is more than generous. More than I deserve," he told her.

"No, it isn't."

"Yes. Considering the way I've been acting—"

She rose on tiptoe and kissed his chin. "Happy Birthday, Lyon."

He started to reach for her, only to check himself. "I'll go change," he said.

Having missed his touch as much as their conversations, Hope felt a slight pang of disappointment; but she took heart: at least this was a step in the right direction.

Less than fifteen minutes later they were en route, driving Lyon's silver Chevy extended cab pickup truck, which he kept parked on the far side of the driveway since he'd moved in. Hope had offered the use of hers, but the farm had a dirt driveway and he didn't see a reason for her clean truck to get dusty.

"What did your father say?" he asked as he adjusted the air conditioner.

Hope didn't want to ruin the pleasant atmosphere they'd been enjoying but didn't see how she could refuse, so she relayed their conversation to him. As she feared, he didn't like what he heard.

"He's no better than a bully," he muttered.

"You wouldn't be in a very good mood, either, if you'd gone through the battery of tests he did."

"He wouldn't have had to endure them if he hadn't lied. You're the one who suffered standing watch all night and worrying. I'm sure that did the baby a heckuva lot of good, too."

"The baby has the best bed in the world," Hope countered stroking her tummy. Sighing she continued, "I'm not making excuses for him, but he's an empty, unhappy man."

"Mostly a result of his conduct and choices in life. Splitting us up would magically change things? Now that's twisted."

Hope enjoyed the scenery and let him vent. She'd done her own share in years past.

"Do you think your mother would have left him in time?" Lyon finally asked.

"If he'd spoken to her that way, it's possible. But he didn't. He was tough, yet ultimately he always could be tamed or toned down by her. Like I said, she's been gone too long and without her good influence, he's gone rogue."

As they turned into Lyon's family's farm, Hope looked at the remnants of where the house once stood. He'd done a great deal of cleaning up since the tornado. There was a new barn and a small trailer where he'd stayed on weekends when he was doing major projects that kept him working past dark and waking at dawn. The oak trees on the place were over a century old, but there were few of them. That's why the tornado had kept its strength and been so deadly.

"Is it hard to come back?" she asked.

"Sometimes. Does it bother you?"

She could see that he was sincerely concerned and shook her head. No one enjoyed going to a funeral home or cemetery, and coming to this site where loss had taken place brought its own vibrations. However, she felt no malevolence here, not like one would at a crime scene.

"It does make me sad for you," she admitted.

"That's why I haven't stayed in the trailer in a good while. In the last year I've been feeling my aloneness too much when I'm here."

Since about the time that she had gotten engaged to Will. Was that a coincidence? The thought made Hope's pulse leap.

Lyon parked in the shade of the barn and his two geldings, Big John and Dodger, left the shade of the nearest oak and wandered lazily over to them. Lyon brought out the bag of apples he'd sacked at the house and began slicing pieces for them. John wasn't the largest horse Hope had ever seen, although his withers stood inches higher than she did, but his attitude made you think he was. He made sure smaller but wily Dodger waited his turn for the treats and still sized up Hope all at the same time. He pawed the ground several times before he let her get close and stand next to Lyon.

"I'm honored, Big John," she said finally stroking the seriously alpha horse.

"Don't take it personally, you're quite a mystery to him," Lyon explained. "He hasn't been exposed to a female in some years and your scent combined with that of the mares' on your clothes intrigues him." He, too, stroked the snorting horse's nose and told the proud animal, "Behave. I know you're eating up her attention as much as you're salivating over the apples."

Dodger was all charm and mischief, at once skirting around Big John to appeal to Hope for his own TLC, then nipping at John's rump to get his attention off the treats so he could get his share. Invariably, he would have to dart out of the way of the larger horse's bared teeth.

"It may be hard to believe, but those two are usually good pals," Lyon said. "They're just showing off for you."

"Didn't you have some cattle?" Hope asked scanning the rest of the property.

Lyon pointed over a low bluff on the west that hid the pond and a larger grouping of trees. "They're probably staying close to the water and shade. I only keep about twenty head at a time. That's enough work for one man, although Tan said he would like to help out. Your few half-grown calves don't exactly fulfill his hunger for working with beef critters."

Hope laughed. "I suspect I'd better get more land fast."

Lyon got out the four-wheeler and gave her a slow and easy tour of the place. The cattle were exactly where he told her they might be. The pond was churned up to more resemble a mud puddle indicating they recently indulged in a dunking.

"The flies are getting bad," Lyon noted as the cattle swished and slapped their tails, then stomped their hind legs to chase off the pesky insects, especially from udders sweet from milk and sensitive from growing calves' teeth.

"Thank heavens for civilization so women don't have to go through that torture," Hope said wincing in sympathy. She caught a secret smile tug Lyon's firm lips and lowered the sunglasses she'd put on for the ride to give him a warning look. "Don't even think of going there."

"But it's my birthday."

It was wonderful to see his eye light with amusement and his broad chest shake with secret laughter. Except that her imagination went into overdrive, too, and that had her breasts growing taut and ultra sensitive to where the delicate satin and lace was unbearably uncomfortable. She slid her hands between her knees and clamped them tight to keep from fidgeting.

As they circled back toward the barn, Hope eagerly tried to change the subject. She pointed to the area behind the great oak where Big John and Dodger had returned. "If you were ever to rebuild, that would be the perfect spot for a house. There's not a good view of the road, but that grouping of cedars around your north property line would be a great wind barrier against the winter cold, and the oak would protect from the summer storms." She couldn't help but remember the tornado that had killed his parents and three others in town, as well as injured several more.

Lyon slowed to consider that. "I hadn't given it much thought, but you're right."

"Then again, you might not want to rebuild." She didn't want him to think she was suggesting that *he* live here again.

"Not for myself, no," he said. "I thought of putting up a house and then listing the property with a Realtor. I'd definitely have to if I was forced out of my job. But I guess I automatically thought of the existing home-site location, only there's no slab there, so you're right. I could build elsewhere, and your idea is a good one."

He circled away from the barn and stopped near the old home site. The surviving shrubbery that had once circled the house had gone wild and looked like the entryway to a secret garden. Lyon pointed to an open area. "That's where I found them. My mother was pulled from the house, then crushed by debris. My father survived long enough to crawl to her. He lay there with his hand covering my mother's. That was all of her that he could see."

Hope had heard something to that effect, but had never broached the subject not wanting to bring back the painful memories. "Everyone who has mentioned them always spoke of them as having a true romance until the end."

"You're right. I was always a little envious of them. Proud, but wondering where I went wrong."

Sliding over to him, Hope laid her head against his shoulder and her hand on his thigh. "Don't do that to yourself. You're on your own timetable."

Weaving his fingers between hers, Lyon squeezed gently. "You think?"

She could feel his melancholia as weighty as the heat. As still as it was there was barely enough air to breathe, and Hope swallowed as a droplet of perspiration trickled between her breasts like a lover's touch, another down the small of her back—unwanted stimulus when they were this close. Her breath shuddered as she exhaled and that drew his attention.

"It's too hot for you."

"I'm all right."

Clearly not convinced, Lyon drove back to the barn and parked the four-wheeler, securing it behind padlocked doors. Hope waited for him near the barn entrance. She leaned against a support beam and created an artificial breeze by fanning the hem of her gauzy blouse. A fluttering caught her attention and she looked up to see a pair of doves entering the barn and settling on the rafters to complete a mating dance they'd obviously started outside.

"You can't wait one more minute?" she muttered.

"Guess not." Lyon joined her, a wry smile curving his lips. He put his arm around her shoulders and led her to his truck where he opened the passenger door for her. As she climbed in and sat back against the seat, she gasped in pain and immediately leaned forward.

"What is it?" Lyon asked.

"Something stung me."

"Turn around, let me see."

"Ouch! It did it again."

She did and he lifted her blouse several inches and swiped his hand along her lower back.

"An ant," he said. "You must've picked it up while leaning against that beam. Hand me an ice cube from that tote bag on the floorboard. That should give you some relief and keep you from scratching and making the wound worse."

Hope pulled off her glasses and gave him an arched look over her shoulder. "Pain or no pain, you're not tormenting me with any ice cube!" She began to sit back in her seat, only to squirm and tug on her shirt. "Oh, blast—now my imagination is kicking into overdrive. Lyon, check and make sure there aren't any more crawling on me."

"Good idea. When has there been just one ant? Hold still."

She did as he directed sitting ramrod straight as he lifted her blouse even higher than before and brushed at the inside of the material. But when he did the same to her back, the strokes grew slower, until they were undeniable caresses.

"God, you have lovely skin," he murmured.

"Thanks. Did you—did you find any more?"

"No, although when I brushed the material I'm sure if anything was there it got knocked off. Do you want me to check your front?"

After a brief laugh, she said, "Nice try." But when she turned back to face him, she saw there was no amusement in the eyes shadowed by the brim of his hat. There was only raw desire. Her overactive libido needed no further stimulation and Hope dropped her gaze to the snaps on his light denim shirt. "Seriously, I'm sure I'm okay now."

"Are you?"

Two little words and yet spoken by Lyon they held a powder keg of meaning and emotion that had her trembling as though he'd just slid his hands under her blouse again.

"Hope…are you having one of *those* moments?"

She could have her own 1-900 number for what was happening inside her. But all she could do was nod in misery.

"Look at me."

That was so not a good idea, and yet she lifted her gaze to his anyway.

"Come here, sweetheart."

Bless him for understanding, she thought and with a sigh of relief, Hope wrapped her arms around him. Their initial body contact had her shuddering due to her body's aroused state. "This is insane," she whimpered. "I've loved being pregnant except for this. This is torture."

"What did your doctor say?" he asked, his breath tickling her ear.

"Ms. Helpful, you mean. She said it wasn't a problem, it was a gift, and to have all the sex I wanted. Hilarious, isn't it?"

"She doesn't know about us?" he asked stroking her from her hair to the small of her back.

"No. Lyon, that's our business, no one else's."

After a few seconds, Lyon said, "I think you should consider following her advice."

Somehow she'd known this would be his reply. "How can I? How fair is that to you?"

"It's not as though I wouldn't be getting something out of it."

Hearing the smile in his voice, Hope leaned back and met his concerned, compassionate gaze. How like him— he could find the humor in something like this and still understand this wasn't funny for her. She so wanted this. Him. If only he felt—or rather she wouldn't feel…

"Would it be easier if I decide for myself?"

She nodded.

Lowering his gaze to her lips, he said, "Don't end up hating me for this."

Then he tilted his head and closed his mouth over hers. When their tongues touched, she moaned with pleasure.

What started out as a tender probing soon grew intense as layer after layer of reserve and restraint yielded to repressed hunger. Hope couldn't hold still. Her hands had a mind of their own, at once clenching at his shirt, then wanting to explore the texture of the hair at his nape. His back muscles reminded her of her equestrian days when her highly trained mount's muscles flexed and strained as they flew over hazardous terrain during the cross country part of the competition.

Groaning, Lyon lifted her from the seat only to lean her against the cab door, and trapped her there with his body. "Wrap your legs around me," he said against her mouth. "I won't let you fall."

She had no doubt about that; she was worried about climaxing before he kissed her again. It was impossible not to be aware of how full and sensitive her breasts felt crushed by his chest, or how his arousal so perfectly fit against her core. If they'd been naked, she wouldn't have needed further foreplay; she was that moist and ready for him. Her mind showed her how it would be behind her tightly closed lids as he moved against her again and again matching the rhythm of a kiss gone out of control. And when she climaxed, he did, too, and they absorbed each other's whimper and moan just as they'd shared this incongruous ride.

Hope's body continued to hum with the passion he'd stirred in her, but finally, slowly, Lyon let her lower her legs to the ground. He didn't let her go altogether, though and they stood forehead to forehead panting as they waited for the world to stabilize beneath their feet.

"I thought that would take the edge off, but it didn't, did it?"

His voice sounded as dry as her throat felt. All she could do was manage a single negative shake of her head.

"We could go home," he added, his gaze holding hers. "Try again."

Hope had to moisten her parched lips. "I need a shower first."

"Me, too."

With that decision almost a palpable thing between them, Lyon drove back to her farm. He handled the truck as though he was carrying a load of nitroglycerin. They made no pretense at small talk, and yet it was clear that they'd never been more aware of each other.

Back at the house, Hope exited the truck with care upon discovering that her legs were still weak; she felt as though she'd been riding for hours. If Lyon could have that potent an effect on her after just a little heavy petting, what condition would her body be in when they truly became lovers? As a new wave of heat turned her forehead damp and cheeks hot, Hope blotted at her brow with the back of her hand.

Lyon came up beside her and slipped his hand under her hair to gently stroke the back of her neck. "Okay?"

There was a good chance that she would never be all right again. She was both excited and a bundle of nerves, but with an affirmative nod, she said, "Sure." She was determined to win some control over herself. That's the woman Lyon was used to seeing—calm, cool, collected Hope.

Once inside she set the canvas cooler on the kitchen bar.

That could be dealt with later. "Meet you back here in a few minutes?" she asked.

"Yeah, I'd like a drink. I know you can't have anything, but can I pour you a glass of juice or a soft drink when I get out?"

"There's peach tea in the refrigerator. That sounds good."

Lyon nodded then lightly stroked his thumb over her swollen lips. His Native American blood made it difficult to grow a beard, but her skin was so fine that what afternoon whiskers he did have had marked her. "I'd better shave again, too, because I'm damn well not done kissing you."

Calm, cool and collected...calm, cool, collected.

As Hope headed for her shower, she repeated that mantra over and over in her mind. What a fraud she was.

Lyon stood with his hands braced against the marble wall, his head thrown back willing the cool spray to ease the fever in his body. Ice chips as sharp as razors could have been shooting from the shower head and he doubted he would have felt them, nor would they have changed his condition. As long as his mind was on Hope, he was going to stay aroused. So be it, since there was no one and nothing else he would rather think about.

Her response to him had at once awed and humbled him; he'd never been with a more passionate woman—and they hadn't had intercourse yet. The way she'd clung to him with that elegant body, the way she'd whispered his name just before she'd climaxed as though in prayer had sent him over the edge, too. Heaven knew he was praying to be what she needed, all that she would ever want.

Shutting off the cold water, Lyon toweled off and eased into a fresh pair of jeans that he left unzipped for comfort as much as practicality. The white shirt he slipped into was left unbuttoned, as well. He'd already shaved so there was nothing left to do but go make that drink. His mouth was beginning to go dry in anticipation of what would follow—not that he needed any stimulant to make love with Hope. If anything he needed to slow down the flow of adrenaline in his body. He could not fail her.

He was only on his second long sip of a scotch and water when Hope emerged from the other side of the house. Already impressed with how quickly she'd achieved this transformation, her black spaghetti-strap sundress—constructed of just enough material to melt what was left of his ability to reason—had him putting down his glass to keep it from slipping out of his hand.

"Happy Birthday to me," he murmured.

She laughed softly. "I'm glad you like it. It's so much cooler. I should have worn this to your farm."

Hope had never flirted with him before; back in her Will days, that wouldn't have been right. Now, she didn't have to, her power over him was so strong that he was captivated by her. Nevertheless, he liked that she thought she needed to seduce him—and wanted to.

"If you had worn that," he replied, "we'd still be there."

She crossed to him, barefoot as he was. With that crazy Mocha-whatever nail polish, her feet were as pretty as her hands, and that dainty toe ring with the heart charm on her right little toe was ridiculously sexy, the impact of it going directly to his groin.

Feeling his tongue thicken, Lyon spared himself conversation by handing her the tea she'd asked for. Thanking him with that secret smile that drove him crazy, she took a long drink.

His own drink forgotten, he admired the graceful curve of her neck and the way she filled out the bodice of the empire-waist dress. Hope was no air-brushed magazine photo and was proud of it. He was simply and utterly grateful. "Want me to check your ant bites?"

"Only if you're prepared for what I'm not wearing underneath this." Her gaze slid over his exposed chest and belly, lingering at the gaping V of his jeans. "I'm glad we think alike."

He couldn't let her keep tying him into a sensual knot or he would explode just standing there. "Then you won't be disappointed if dinner is delayed?"

Slipping her left index finger into a belt loop on his jeans, she replied, "Come with me and you can atone."

As a seductress, she was adorable and he would have been well on his way to falling head over heels if he hadn't been living in that Purgatory for years. Now he just waited to show her that having freed him, his universe would forever begin and end with her—if she wanted it that way.

In the shadowy bedroom, beside the turned-down bed, she stopped and faced him again, this time slowly sliding her hands inside his shirt and inching upwards over his hard abdomen, his taut nipples, next caressing him with her breath, then her lips as she slipped the shirt off his shoulders. Sucking in a sharp breath, Lyon stroked her hair and watched with masochistic fascination as she duplicated those delicate ministrations to his right side, until he was forced to stop that sweet torture by framing her lovely face with his hands and urging her head up to receive his kiss of gratitude and ravenous hunger. He was determined to be patient and attentive, learn what else she liked and how many ways there were to bring her to the ecstasy he wanted for her. But he was only human.

"You feel so good." He drew her closer until the silk separating her feminine curves from his hot flesh was irrelevant. Her nipples were like sharp little needles tormenting him and, as he plumbed her mouth with his tongue, he ran his hands up and down the outer swells of her breasts, then reached between them to score the hard little points with the rougher pads of his thumbs.

"Lyon," she breathed. "Can't we lie down so we can feel all of each other?"

"First let's take care of this."

He slipped one strap off her shoulder, then the other, until the black wisp of fabric drifted to the carpet and she stood before him an exquisite, honey-skinned angel of temptation. The gentle swell where her child grew made his heart pound with barely containable emotions and he sunk to one knee and brushed a tender kiss on her flawless skin. "Little mother…"

"Lyon."

There was a hitch in her voice and his hands were a little unsteady as she stroked his hair. When Lyon rose he saw her eyes were over bright and dreamy. She'd never been more beautiful to him than at that moment.

"You, too," she urged her hands already at the waistband of his jeans.

Lyon shoved them to the floor and stepped out of them, achingly aware of her unabashed gaze.

"I'm glad that I can see how much you want me," she said slowly lowering herself onto the bed. "You've always been something of a mystery to me. So self-contained. Now I get to know at least one secret."

Stretching out beside her, stroking her from shoulder to hip, Lyon replied, "You'd be disappointed if you knew how few there are."

She reached down and closed her hand around him. "I don't believe that."

Having been flattened by three-hundred pound linebackers, kicked bloody by unruly cattle, and once even finding himself looking down the wrong end of a .12 gauge shotgun, Lyon didn't think there was too much that would make him beg for anything including his life, but this small woman with her fantasy body and sweet soul could. He knew it in that instant as she slid her leg over his hip and brushed his feverish length against her moist softness.

"Believe this," he said rolling her onto her back. Concerned not to crush her, he raised himself on his elbows and finished what she'd started. Thankfully, she was caught up in the same intoxicating cocktail mix of time-place-person as he was. Wet and hot as sin, when she tightened her inner muscles around him as tightly as she did her thighs, he knew this sharing was doomed to be over quickly, too. What saved his pride was recognizing that's exactly how she wanted it.

"Look at me," he rasped. When she did, he began moving inside her. "I want to see your eyes when it happens for you. I want you to know it's me."

She stroked his forearms and biceps the way she had his more sensitive muscles and raked her nails over his chest like a kitten flexing her claws. "I know it's you."

His muscles beginning to twitch from the sweet hell she was inciting in him, he asked, "I'm not hurting you?" He looked down at her so much smaller than him and that fragile little swell of her tummy, barely visible as she lay on her back.

"You won't...and the baby is well protected."

In the end it was her emotional discomfort and physical

need that allowed him to break a personal vow. All night, he had to remind himself. They had all night.

Lowering his head, Lyon promised as much to her. "All right, sweetheart, hold on."

Chapter Seven

Waking alone in the middle of the night with the room cast in a light as though there was a full moon outside had Hope spreading her arms wide across rumpled silk sheets and striving to remember if the soreness that came with well-used muscles and the images that flashed before her were real or was she caught up in a dream? Either way her bed was empty. Lyon was gone.

As the drug-like thick weight lifted a bit and her mind started to clear, she knew with certainty that the moon was in its final cusp and couldn't be so bright, and that she and Lyon had made love. *Three times?* Four if she counted that little appetizer at the farm. Because that had led to this, she most definitely would.

Shifting again to find his scent on the pillows beside her, she sighed as her body telegraphed sensations to her mind, surfacing memories of his exploration of her. Just as he was a man apart from others in his work and as a friend, he'd proven to be so as a lover. She'd learned there was much in him that was old-fashioned. *Traditional,* she amended, sensitive to the male ego. He was fair, poignantly generous, but even in his lovemaking reluctant to give up total control. She knew his work had forced him to see the worst sides in human nature, but who had made it difficult for him to trust a woman he took to bed? What woman had wounded his heart that he hid his vulnerability at the very instant his life's seed was pouring into her?

Hope opened her eyes. She was pregnant. She was the only one with whom it was safe to have unprotected sex. That would have made it all the more intense an experience. And yet he was gone. Why had he returned to his own bed?

Saddened, Hope buried her face in his pillow and soothed herself by stroking her only companion left in the room. Poor baby. Now she remembered. For an instant as Lyon began to climax that first time, he'd opened his eyes and she'd seen his total awareness that the baby she was carrying wasn't his. There had been a flash of pain in his dark eyes, and then he'd hidden it again and was all concern, all generosity.

Because despite everything, he wants you.

Wants being the problem. It was wonderful, of course; but it wasn't enough. Dear Lord, she had been a naive fool to think it could be, just as she'd believed helping to keep Lyon in Cedar Grove would be adequate penance for her stupid mistake with Will. Owning Lyon's gratitude was a reward for sure. But she wanted more. She wanted his love.

Oh, where was he?

Brooding about his whereabouts wouldn't help her to go back to sleep, but that didn't stop her from wondering.

Belatedly, Hope realized the light in the room was coming from another part of the house. And wasn't that talking she'd heard just now?

She slid off the bed and, on her way to investigate, grabbed an ivory cashmere throw off of the chaise lounge at the foot of the bed. Wrapping it around her shoulders, she continued out of the room, her bare feet almost silent on the wooden floor.

There in the lavender-blue glow of a plant's growing light, she found him standing naked, looking like some Sci-Fi movie's mouth-watering alien-who-fell-to-earth. With all that was going on, she'd forgotten to plug in the light, but he apparently had done it needing the added illumination to help operate the phone now held to his ear. Hope stood transfixed, admiring his broad shoulders, firm buttocks, and powerful long legs.

"Not at all, you did the right thing," he said to whoever it was that was on the other side of the connection. "Right, take it. You know where the keys are. Don't worry about it. Try to get some rest and I'll see you later."

Closing his cell phone, Lyon turned and saw her. His expression turned regretful. "I tried to be quiet."

"You were," she said coming to him. "I woke because I missed you." Parting her wrap like a butterfly spreading her wings, she then closed it around them both.

"Did you?" he murmured his tone as pleased as his expression.

With his erection pressing all the way up against her diaphragm, she managed a breathy, "Oh, yes."

Smiling ruefully, Lyon lifted one strong shoulder in a resigned shrug. "You'd think it would have developed some discipline in the last several hours. But then it's your fault for coming out here looking more incredible than anything I could dream."

Instead of an inadequate "thank you," Hope touched her lips to his chest and felt his strong-beating heart. "Did something happen at the station?"

"Cooper Jones had a spinout on one of the back roads trying to avoid a feral hog and her litter."

"Is he all right?"

"He's in better shape than the sow and three of the eight in her litter. But his SUV is scrap metal. I told him to take the patrol car that Chris used to drive."

Hope winced at the thought of the ugly scene. Those horrible creatures were nature's marauders, tearing up the land—when they weren't ravaging family pets or causing traffic hazards like what apparently had happened to Lyon's detective. Glancing at the microwave and stove clock, she frowned. "What's he doing working at almost eleven at night?"

"He's not. It happened at dusk. He was doing some follow-up work on an old case after hours. The exciting life of divorced cops," Lyon added with a sardonic twist to his lips. "It took him until now to get a wrecker out there and then to get his forensic bags out of the SUV and back to the station."

Hope couldn't help but think of repercussions, her protective instincts toward Lyon kicking in. "The expense of a new vehicle won't endear you to the city council."

"It'll be cheaper than a huge hospital bill if he'd been severely injured."

"Don't expect our fair-and-balanced local press to think that way. By the time Pettigrew finishes describing the accident, it will somehow reflect on you. You know it will."

Lyon stroked his free hand down her back to soothe her, but it became a sexual caress as he lingered over her bottom. "I never realized you were such a mommy. You can't worry over every little thing, especially as it relates to me and my job. Not when you have so much on your own plate."

How like a man—invincible and self-reliant prior to a tidal wave or hangnail. "Women come out of the womb multi-tasking. You never ate!" she declared immediately, proving it as she realized that she'd passed out from exhaustion and she never did make him that scrumptious birthday dinner.

"I ate. I feasted," he amended. "Breast of angel, leg of vixen…"

"If you say butt of Bambi, I promise somehow or other you'll hurt for a week."

Laughing, Lyon swept her up into his arms. "You do have a delectable tush. But the truth is that I ate a chunk of my birthday cake while waiting for Cooper to sign some forms for the wrecker driver. Sorry for the caveman table manners, but the cake is terrific. Did Molly help you?"

"Stop changing the subject, and put me down. I can have your steak in the broiler and be scrambling some eggs to go with them in nothing flat." But before she finished with that suggestion, they were back in her bedroom and Lyon was laying her on the bed. He trapped her there with his body. As good as that felt, Hope still protested. "Lyon, this wasn't the birthday I planned for you."

"Have you had the night I wanted for you?"

Despite the darkness, there was enough light that she could see his face grow somber. She laid her hand against his cheek. "You need to ask that?"

Lyon took that hand and planted a kiss in her palm. "I'd like to be sure before I dare ask to spend the night."

Was she that hard to read? "If I hadn't wakened, for all I know you'd still be here."

"That was the plan. Follow the strategy of a throw-away pup who lays low hoping that he won't be noticed and kicked out into the cold."

The comparison of a desperate, lonely pup to his superman self was laughable, but Hope couldn't bring herself to tease him. Come daylight, reality would burn off this sweet magic that protected their false marriage quickly enough. Where was the harm in lingering in this fantasy world for a little while longer—or as long as he was willing?

"Stay, Lyon," she said quiet but serious. "It feels good and right with you here." Glancing over his shoulder she added less confidently, "That closet on the left in the bath suite is empty, too. You could put your things in there so they would be closer."

It wasn't poetic or close to what she wanted to say, but at least she felt him relax beside her.

"Would you also let me spoon you while we sleep?"

We. The word filled her with something as poignant as when he'd slipped his ring on her finger. "I might. I don't know," she replied giving him the honesty the moment called for. "Is that actually comfortable? I've never been spooned before."

She sensed a dozen questions spawn, and then percolate inside him. Although his eyes grew troubled and a frown formed decisively cutting a lightning bolt line between his dark eyebrows, he voiced none of them, for which she was grateful. But slowly, with breathtaking tenderness, he eased his arm around her waist, then slid his body flush against her back. When he gently slid his left leg between hers, the rest of his anatomy voided any pretense that the night would be an ode to sleep and the recuperative powers of rest.

His breath was warm on her nape, his lips were hot against her skin when his teeth lightly scored her shoulder. The scent of chocolate had Hope licking her lips in anticipation.

"It's not only comfortable," he told her. "In some locations it's vital to survival."

He made her feel so protected and wanted that she closed her eyes to cherish this simple moment of sheer bliss. "I can see how this might make up for a shortage of fur pelts in cold climates," Hope said, dutiful student she was willing to be.

But when he slowly, carefully slid himself into her receptive body, Hope closed her eyes at this primal, yet natural way of tethering female to male. Nothing man could invent could compare with such a complete sense of well-being.

"Lyon…" she sighed.

"Yes, my dream?"

It was the last thing she remembered saying to him. The next thing she knew her clock was beeping her awake, and Lyon was already showered and making her coffee in the kitchen. What did or didn't happen remained a mystery to her, but his mysterious smile kept her blushing for days afterward.

When the promise of fall came in September, Hope's pregnancy advanced to where questions were impossible to avoid. Even so, she was carrying the child so high and totally in front that from the back she didn't look pregnant at all. The first time she ran into someone she hadn't seen

in a while, the startled look on his face when she turned
around to acknowledge his presence was priceless. It
happened at a Dallas charity event and the gentleman in
question just happened to be one of the men her father tried
to match her up with right before Will had proposed to her.

"Hope." The tall, dashingly attired man kissed her on
both cheeks in the European fashion that people in his
circles emulated with enthusiasm. "I didn't realize congratulations were in order. I saw nothing in the news and
Ellis didn't tell me."

"I'm not surprised. How are you, Reed?"

"Fine. Crushed to find you more of a vision than ever,
but I'll muddle on, dawdling tortoise that I am."

Reed Ames was no dawdling anything. A real estate
tycoon still in-between wives number three and four, he
was old enough to be her father, but a gentleman in the way
Golden Era film stars were heralded for their deportment.
His photograph was regularly on newspaper society pages
everywhere. Suspecting that this time would be no different, Hope reminded herself to warn Lyon in case that photo
included her and not the dazzling blonde who had arrived
on his arm an adornment like some men wore diamond
cufflinks and expensive watches.

"When is the baby due?" Reed asked.

"Late winter or early spring," she replied resorting to her
most vague answer.

"Who's the lucky father and—" Reed's eyebrows
arched as he examined her left hand "—mister?"

Focusing on the unspoken "husband," Hope replied
honestly, "A lovely man. You don't know him, but don't
speed if you come driving through our neck of the woods
anytime soon."

"It took a uniform to win your hand? I'm going to buy myself a yachtsman's jacket tomorrow."

Not everyone was as gracious. A week later at Cedar Grove's *Day to Give Back* event where residents were encouraged to take the initiative to clean up yards that had become an eyesore in town, paint someone's house that either couldn't manage or couldn't afford to do it themselves, see to repairs where needed, or fill in for those who were shorthanded in help, Hope was helping register animals at the pet-dipping vaccination tent at the city park. Two women who could certainly afford to take their toy poodle and Maltese to a groomer came up to register their pets for a free bath and flea-tick dipping. It was impossible for Hope to miss their smirks and blatant stares at her stomach as she worked in her increasingly snug red T-shirt. But she kept her smile intact as she signed in the eight animals in line before them.

"Aren't you the one who was engaged to Will Nichols?" they demanded when it was their turn to register.

"What can I help you with, ladies?" she asked.

"It is her," the other insisted. "My…look at you. Are you having a boy or girl? You know Rochelle is pregnant, too, only she's definitely bigger than you are. You must be carrying a girl because she's carrying a boy."

Hope kept her eyes down to prevent them from seeing her shock. "Can I have your dog's tag number for ID and your name and phone number, please?" she asked in her most business-like voice.

"How long a wait will it be?" the owner of the Maltese asked.

"As you can see, we have a great number of dogs in need. Some of them are seriously contaminated with fleas and ticks," she added in a stage whisper.

The owner of the poodle stared distastefully at the large tubs of treated water. "They do change that for each bathing and dipping, don't they?"

"Well, they do the best they can," Hope replied seeing a way of ending this humiliating experience. "I'd be sure to spray my clothes when I got home to rid myself of any infestation, and then wash them with bleach." She was going a bit overboard, but the ploy worked. The women quickly abandoned the line and their agenda on behalf of Rochelle.

Hope didn't feel guilty for scaring off the troublemakers, and assured the disapproving woman taking the donations beside her that she would make up the lost revenue herself. The wife of a Baptist church deacon, the older volunteer had heard enough to judge Hope guilty of something, if only bad taste in her connections, and wanted no contamination by association. She didn't speak to Hope again for the rest of the day.

As for the suggestion that Rochelle was pregnant and that the baby was Will's, Hope felt strangely apathetic. Will was fast becoming a sad mistake in her life and any results of those days were more the Nichols' business than hers.

It was a relief to be relieved by another worker and Hope continued around the park encouraged by the cooler but pretty weather. The cheers and applause from the big tent drew her attention. That was the wine and art auction, the proceeds being split between the town's library, food bank, and animal shelter.

A local DJ was acting as emcee and was luring more onlookers than there were tables and chairs, already claimed by Cedar Grove's most affluent. Despite her somewhat haggard condition after the long hours outside of the pet tent, Hope joined the outer rim of observers and was scanning the crowd when her eyes locked with Summer's. The ever-colorful forty-something divorcée was resplendent in the season's latest fashions. Hope bet that outfit would be returned to the rack at her store by morning and the sales tag reattached bearing the full price amount. Next to her, Hope's father was no shy mouse, irreverently dressed in white although it was weeks past Labor Day. A matching Western hat, pearl gray ostrich-leather cowboy boots and an obnoxiously large cigar completed his ensemble. When Summer pointed her out to Ellis, her father's gaze chilled as he focused on her stylishly form-fitting T-shirt. Without so much as a nod in acknowledgment, he turned away. Openly thrilled with his visible censure, Summer gave her a saccharin sweet smile followed by a "whatever" shrug and turned back to the auctioneer, too. Hope was used to her father's ways, but his letting Summer give the illusion to others around their table that she had tried to get Hope an invitation to join them was more than Hope could stomach. The final straw in the offensive day came as she found Summer bidding against her for a landscape painting by a local talent. The price had gone up to where she knew Summer would never risk her own money confirming her suspicion that this would be a gift from Ellis to his paramour. Summer failed in her plan, but it cost Hope twice what she felt was a fair price for the painting.

She was putting her purchase into the trunk of her car when Lyon pulled up behind her. He shifted into park and stepped out to inspect the painting.

"Nice," he said after a too-brief kiss hello. Except for a few waves and wistful glances from across the park, this was the closest they'd been to each other all day except when they'd dressed and he'd whistled at her scooped-neck top that showed off her improved cleavage as it did her pregnancy's progress. Then he'd buried his face against her and swore evening could not come soon enough.

"So this is what you were telling me that you wanted for the mantle for Thanksgiving," he said studying the painting. "This cropping of trees looks familiar to me. The artist is a nature-lover for sure. The wild turkeys can be that plentiful, but you have to be patient and wait for them to get over their skittishness."

She should have been pleased with his approval; instead, Hope found herself stinging after all from all that had happened today. "Ellis gave Summer permission to bid against me. My own father."

Lyon took a philosophical perspective. "That sounds like one of his tactics. Then he still makes things look like he helped charity. Forget it, sweetheart. You know he enjoys stirring things up for his own entertainment. And if he sees that he can get under your usual reserve with a woman who uses brighter eye shadow than most transvestites, he'll do it again."

True, but Hope wasn't in the mood to be reasonable right now. *"And,"* she sniped back, "Rochelle Sims is pregnant." Her annoyance with him was irrational as it was unfair. He would have to be a mind reader to know the real reason she was upset, but that didn't stop her.

She felt Lyon's gaze on her profile and knew he was waiting for more—particularly an apology. Hope hated conflict and went out of her way to avoid moments like this. She also knew that he was wondering when the day would come that she could stop thinking of Will and how much of a fool he'd made of her. It wouldn't be today. If he were alive, she would have unlocked her .12 gauge shotgun from her safe, driven over to the Nichols ranch, and emptied every shell into his dually.

"Is this where I'm supposed to ask who sired the poor thing? Because, frankly, Hope, I don't really see the point at this stage even if it is Will's."

So wrong an answer.

"The point is that what was once just a bad-joke rumor looks now to be the ugly truth. Do you think I want my child to know he has an illegitimate brother or sister virtually his own age?"

"I thought you had decided this was *our* baby?"

Hope clapped her hand over her mouth. She'd said it that way, hadn't she? When trying to convince Lyon that he should marry her. "Lyon, I'm sorry. Don't listen to me. I should just shut up and go home. That was just shock and hurt speaking."

Before he could answer, Lyon's radio triggered. He clicked the speaker he had tucked through his shoulder epaulet, but his gaze remained on Hope. "Teague, over."

"Chief, we have a situation in town. Disgruntled diner put his chair through the front window of Sally's Home Cooking."

Watching Lyon turn into the left-brained machine, Hope wondered what could have happened at the warm and friendly restaurant. Someone off of his meds, she surmised.

"Has he been contained? Any injuries?"

"Juarez has him. A kid on a skateboard was passing by at the same time and has some nasty cuts. Paramedics are on the scene stabilizing him for transport to the hospital."

"I'm on my way. Out." Wearily rubbing his face, he gave Hope an enigmatic look. "I have to go."

Feeling totally shut out of his mind and heart, Hope wrapped her arms around herself. "I hope the boy's injuries aren't severe. Be careful," she added inanely.

"There'll be statements to take and make, and paperwork." And they were still shorthanded.

"I don't know when I'll get through," he concluded.

He stumbled slightly with "through," which told Hope that he had intentionally avoided saying "home," a term he used with visible pleasure since moving into the master suite with her. That made her want to go after him as he headed back to his patrol car and wrap her arms around him until he understood her. "Lyon," she entreated as he paused and glanced at her over the roof. "I truly am sorry."

"I know. But it's what we say when we don't intend to that says the most about how we feel."

The disappointment flattening his voice hurt as much as his reluctance to hold her gaze, and he quickly climbed into his patrol car and drove off. Lucky man, she thought. He could escape her. How did she escape herself?

She had single-handedly brought an end to an idyllic few weeks. He had even been planning to go with her for the ultrasound in three days when she would hopefully be finding out if the baby was a boy or girl. This couldn't be the flip side of those raging hormones, could it?

Nice try, Hope. Wrong is still wrong.

Knowing it would be impossible to return to the festivities and pretend all was well, Hope returned home. The sun was sinking fast on the horizon and the air was progressively cooling, but she dreaded the idea of spending the next hours cloistered in the house surrounded by Lyon's possessions and scent when she knew how precarious she'd made things between them. After carrying in the painting and placing it on the mantle, she cut up some apples and walked out back to visit with the mares thinking maybe that pleasant task could distract her.

Desiree, the gray alpha female, was the first to spot her and trotted over with expectant enthusiasm for her share of treats. Black, mellow Bella, who liked to lay her head on Hope's shoulder to where you couldn't tell where her mane ended and Hope's hair started was heaviest with child and came more slowly. Saucy, the Dun, was the daintiest and least likely to behave with or without treats. An eye-catching gold with a white mane, she was mindful of Desiree's jealousy and impatience with her, but skirted around to get an apple slice at every opportunity.

Once she was out of treats, Hope walked over to the remains of the vegetable garden. She regretted not having had the time for a late-season garden this year, but promised herself that she would do better by spring. The baby would be here and they both would need the exercise and the fresh air.

Deep in thought, she failed to see or hear Saucy trying to sneak around Desiree, but apparently Desiree didn't and the incensed horse charged. Whether she meant to keep Hope's attention for herself or worried there might be one slice of apple left, the gray slammed into Saucy, who spun around screaming. She inadvertently struck Hope with her hind quarter knocking her off her feet as though she was nothing more than a bowling pin caught in a perfect strike.

Striving to catch her balance, Hope's aim was inches off and, instead of stopping the fall, she raked her left hand and wrist over the sharp edge of the garden's corner t-post and the overlapping cattle panels they used to keep the animals out of the plants. Hope knew even as she landed that she'd done more than scratch herself. Confirming that was a shout from far off. By the time the first blinding pain dimmed enough for Hope's vision to clear, she saw the horses were dashing away as Tan came chasing across the pasture yelling like he was performing a solo rendition of Pickett's Charge with a leaf rake held high instead of a rifle topped with a bayonet.

After her second attempt to get to her feet, she saw Molly was quickly catching up to him in their pickup.

"I come, Miss Hope!" Tan shouted as he neared. Then he went into a slew of Vietnamese that Hope thought sounded like a slew of kittens protesting as they were being dumped from a barrel. She didn't identify one of the half dozen words she'd learned from him so far.

"It's okay," she lied holding her abused arm against her belly as she bent at the waist and kept her balance by bracing herself against the cattle panels. She didn't care if the blood ruined her clothes or not. She'd already decided that she could never wear the thing again without being reminded of this awful day. "I just need to wash up and bandage it."

"Need ER," Tan enunciated carefully as he arrived beside her. Hardly breathing as she expected, he gently but firmly took hold of her arm to inspect the long, ugly wound.

Joining them, Molly was momentarily at a loss of what to do or say. "You—you need stitches. Tan stitches himself, but I think you need too many for him to do it."

Hope didn't need that visual in her mind what with her stomach going from queasy to openly in attack. One thing she knew for sure, she wasn't leaving here. "I'll settle for some disinfecting and pressure bandages," Hope replied.

"Call Chief," Tan directed his wife. "Maybe baby hurt."

Shuddering at the mere thought, Hope reassured them as she did herself.

"No," she said stroking her tummy with her good hand. "Things feel fine there, and Lyon is very busy with someone seriously injured in town today. Let's not add to his troubles."

Accepting that the Lees would not give up until they were convinced she was all right, she let them help her into the house and assist her in the clean up and wrapping of her hand and wrist. By the time it was done, under Tan's direction, Molly had her looking like she was preparing to be the understudy for the remake of The Mummy.

While Tan went out to make sure everything was secure outside and the mares corralled for the night, Molly warmed up a cup of homemade chicken soup for her.

Once she convinced her that all she needed now was rest, Hope got Molly to leave, too. She was tired, depressed, and totally disgusted with herself for getting herself into the predicament of letting herself end up between two argumentative horses. She knew too well that you never assumed anything with an animal regardless of how fond they were of you, especially when the critters were larger than some of today's hybrid automobiles.

She had been dusty before the fall and felt all the messier now. She should have asked Molly to stay and help her get undressed, but in the end, she had no reservations about taking scissors to her shirt. Once it was slit open like a gutted fish, she stripped out of it and the rest of her clothes. Getting her hair clipped on top of her head wasn't too difficult thanks to today's broad variety of hair accessories, and a plastic shopping bag served as adequate protection for her bandages from water.

A long soaking bath would probably have done her
more good, but Hope was afraid once she got in she would
fall asleep and sink underwater. She got into the shower,
she got out of the shower and, once toweled off, she collapsed into bed unable to summon the strength to bother
with a nightgown.

Despite her protests not to, she began to hope that Tan
or Molly did phone Lyon. But she fell asleep with a heavy
heart knowing he would not come if he could.

It was nearly dark when Lyon drove into the garage.
He was so tired and wired that he almost over-acceler-
ated instead of braking, then he had to punch the garage
genie three times to make it descend behind him. That
was warning enough to get a grip before heading inside
to face Hope.

Staying put and seeing things through in town had been
the hardest thing he'd done since challenging his mortality
against the flames burning up Will's truck. When Tan called
with the news about the horses and Hope's injury, he had
wanted badly to brush everything and everyone aside and
race home, especially since Tan hadn't been all that clear
or reassuring at first. But being right in the middle of that
fiasco at the community hospital, Lyon knew leaving
would have been the equivalence to handing his badge
away for good. Then what help would he be to Hope?

Tan had finally assured him that things were under
control and that the bleeding had stopped, so he had been
forced to put Hope's well-being on an emotional back-
burner. But that had been over two hours ago—when Tan
and Molly had been officially ordered home by Hope. It
took only minutes to bleed to death, and from what Tan had

told him, the worst of her cut had come extremely close to her most vital artery in her wrist.

Once inside, Lyon's devil's advocate kicked in stronger. It was so dark. That just wasn't right. Hope liked either the plant light or the stove light on. If she knew he was running late, she would leave some of the accent lighting on, then later tweak down to the subtler lights. Wasting no time on hunting for buttons or plugs, he flipped the nearest switch and the room blinded him with fluorescent brilliance. Thinking that enough to see to every corner of the house, he made his way to the master suite.

The stark lighting didn't wake her but he could see her clearly asleep in the bed. She looked so still and pale, and her injured hand lay across his pillow as though she was searching for him in her sleep. He didn't see any sign of blood coming through the bandages that mummified her from the beginning of her palm to above her wrist, but the amount of area covered made his stomach twist as hard as when he'd first heard Tan's voice on that incoming call.

The laceration had been *that* long?

He needed to see. Tan had some basic first aid knowledge—Lyon had inquired about that weeks ago after Hope had confided in them that she was pregnant—but that held less stock with him now when she suddenly moaned in her sleep. She was clearly feeling pain. And a wound that large would undoubtedly scar her permanently.

Feeling sick at heart, he eased down on his side of the bed. Yes, she was hurting; a small frown kept trying to etch a line between her eyebrows. Was that because of her hand alone, or was something going on in her womb?

He would go quickly and at least wash his hands so he could check her for fever and monitor her pulse. But before he could make good that intention, her lids lifted and he found himself looking into her eyes.

"You're home."

"Yeah." His voice sounded unfamiliar to his own ears and he cleared his throat. "How are you feeling?"

"Not great, and none too bright. You can save the lecture or brow-beating, whichever was the plan. I've already given myself several renditions of both."

The impulse to do either had vanished the instant he'd entered the dark house and thought the worst. "That's some bandage."

Hope glanced over at it as though that part of her anatomy belonged to someone else. She probably did wonder because she was careful not to move it.

"Overkill. The only reason Tan and Molly stopped was because they ran out of antibiotic ointment and gauze."

"That's not what I heard." Tan also assured him that he had come into town to restock on bandages and such while Molly had kept an eye on her.

Grimacing, Hope averted her gaze. "I should have known Tan would call you."

"You think I gave him my business card months back just to help him get out of a ticket?" When she briefly closed her eyes and compressed her lips, he knew she was feeling another throbbing or spasm and he wanted badly to sweep her into his arms and absorb the pain for her. Instead, he asked, "When did you last have a tetanus shot?"

As the moment passed, she opened her eyes to study the three-tiered ceiling. "Two years, six months and…I forget how many days ago. I'm safe."

"Being a wise guy isn't going to make me go away any sooner."

Her look was sheer confusion. "Why would I want you to do that? What I was saying was that's when I inadvertently ripped off half of this thumbnail." She held up the right one that had since grown back perfectly.

This time it was Lyon's turn to close his eyes. "How in heaven's name did you do that?"

"I'm not a princess, Lyon," she said with some indignation. "I did help create a good deal of what's around here. My nails get dirty. Sometimes I hurt myself."

He was upsetting her and didn't mean to, but didn't she see? They were married. She was his wife, and maybe the child wasn't biologically his, but it was his nonetheless, and she had to let him be upset and worried for her, for them, whether it was rational to her or not.

"I'm not trying to pick a fight," he said quietly.

Her gaze flicked to him, then away. "I tried to apologize. Now I'm scared and every time I open my mouth I seem to be making it worse."

On the contrary, it was getting a little easier to breathe. He had thought they'd experienced something earlier today that would make him lose everything that they had begun to create together. He didn't ever want to experience that feeling again.

"That boy in town?" he began sharing the other tiny slice of hell he'd lived in this afternoon. "His mother immediately threatened to sue the city as well as the idiot, who wouldn't restrain his emotions. Sue despite the ordinance against skateboards on the sidewalks—and you know what? I can't say that I blamed her. So I couldn't leave until the boy was out of danger and I talked the mother down from her hysteria in order for Kent to speak with her. The town isn't out of the woods yet, but the father finally arrived from a business trip out of state, and he talked with her, too. What you need to know is," he concluded searching her face as though memorizing each feature anew, "during all of that and watching how easily it is to have everything in the world and then almost lose it, I was worried sick about you. I don't know how much longer I could have stayed if the father didn't arrive when he did."

"Don't say that." Turning on her side so she could reach him with her good hand, she caressed the faint pink scars that remained on his ear, then brushed the backs of her fingers against his whisker-roughened jaw. "I'm proud you stayed. No one understands how hard it can be to do the right thing than you do, Lyon."

They sat there letting their words heal them, and bond them closer.

Finally with a sound of regret Hope added, "I overreacted about Rochelle. And I shouldn't have let those two women get to me."

"That would have been a good trick considering that they ambushed you."

"Whatever. The thing is that under normal circumstances Summer's behavior wouldn't have been a blip on my radar."

Lyon took hold of her right hand and touched his lips to it. "I know that. About Rochelle's news…do you think it's possible that the baby is someone else's besides Will's?"

"Clyde and Mercy will certainly be hoping so."

When their gazes met again, they burst into laughter. Just as quickly Hope gasped.

"What?" Lyon started to reach for her bandaged hand and then checked himself. "Do you need a pain pill?"

Hope stared at him, her eyes wide, her mouth a perfect

O. Silently, she pushed the sheet down past her waist, took hold of his hand and laid it on her stomach.

"Hope...sweetheart...what's wrong?" When she didn't immediately answer, his dread grew. "Don't do this to me. Are you cramping? I'll get a blanket and take you straight to the hospital."

"Ssh. Wait!"

Wait for what? he thought fearing the worst. Then he felt a bump beneath his fingers. "Whoa!"

Hope grinned through her tears.

"Oh, my." He had just witnessed a miracle and couldn't take his eyes off of her. "Biscuit's got quite a kick."

"You should feel it from this side of things," Hope mused.

Something quieted inside Lyon and he relaxed and stroked the spot over and over. "Do you think it'll happen again?"

"I suspect so."

"I shouldn't be doing this," he said as reason replaced wonder. She looked like a porcelain figurine, too perfect for him to touch. "Look at me, I need to shower."

"But I wanted you to experience this with me."

He met her radiant smile. "Is it the first time?"

She nodded.

When it happened again, he grinned like a fool. "That one wasn't as strong. I bet it's getting tired. Too much exercise for the first day." Filled with spiritual grace and unfathomable tenderness, Lyon drew the sheet back up over her. "You have to keep it warm."

Visibly tiring, Hope managed a chuckle. "You can't keep calling her 'it.'"

"Why are you calling her 'her'?" She couldn't know which she was having since the ultrasound wasn't happening for days yet.

"I've been praying while waiting for you to come home. It helped to ignore the deepest throbs." Her expression reflected both embarrassment and hope. "It struck me that it would be a blessing if the baby is a girl."

"I don't understand."

"It would be easier on you."

Easier for him to accept? Lyon was as blown away at her concern, but wondered, too. Didn't she realize that any tiny life that came from her body would be precious to him?

Unable to resist, he leaned forward and gently kissed her. "If she is a girl, I hope she's a perfect miniature of her mother."

"Gallant answer."

He kissed her again, but then forced himself to rise before he started to cry. "What can I get for you before I head for that shower? You have to have something for the pain, you were practically sobbing in your sleep."

"No, I'm afraid to. I don't have anything in the house except aspirin and acetaminophen and I've been reading that one can cause bleeding in the baby as well as me, and the other can cause wheezing in newborns. Imagine, simple over-the-counter drugs! I'm not taking any chances."

But Lyon could tell by her eyes that it had been and would be an ordeal. He only knew of one way he could help, minimal though it was. "Then I should go sleep in the guest-room," he told her. What if he accidentally bumped her during the night? They'd been together long enough now that his body automatically sought contact with hers even in sleep.

Hope looked instantly stricken. "Please don't. It would help having you close. We could switch sides."

Lyon eyed the queen-size bed. "There wouldn't be enough room for your arm to stay isolated like that."

"There would be if you spooned me."

Tempting as that—as well as the seductive look she gave him—was, he knew the extent of his own endurance. "We always get in trouble when I do that." Just the thought of her sweet bottom pressed into his lap stirred him to life.

"There, you see?" she coaxed. "The best kind of pain relief. Especially since Tan advised me to take off my ring because my fingers were starting to swell and he was concerned it would cause circulation problems. But now I can't even stroke it to pretend you're near."

Lyon had been unconvinced until she said that. She had just admitted to doing something he did all the time when they were apart. "Let me go get cleaned up," he said in surrender. "You scoot over."

Chapter Eight

On the first Tuesday in October, Hope and Lyon sat in the waiting room at Dr. Jacqueline Winslow's practice. They were her last appointment for the day, which gave them the privacy Hope had wanted for Lyon, since he hadn't had time to come home and change out of his uniform. They might be in the next county, but crossing county lines to transact business was a common matter in this sprawling state and one never knew who knew whom and would report a man in uniform from a distant town.

"Nervous?" he asked her as she reached over and gripped his hand.

Hope knew he had purposely positioned himself on her right so that they could do this. Her left hand no longer needed a bandage, but it remained sensitive. At least she was able to get her ring on again, she thought happily, fingering it with her thumb.

"I didn't think I would be, but I am." She rested her head on his shoulder. "It's not as though there's any pain involved."

"Good. Because you couldn't ask me to stand there and watch if there was."

He kept his voice low so that his words were for her ears only and Hope loved the way his breath caressed her hair. "But you've already signed up to be my natural childbirth coach," she teased.

"Under the condition that you understood I might not be able to go through with it on D-Day."

"B-Day," she amended, not at all worried.

"Stop being adorable when there's nothing that I can do about it in here."

Hope was giggling as the door opened and a nurse said, "Mrs. Teague?" She bounded quickly to her feet. "That's me."

To her surprise, Lyon held back. "Is something wrong?"

"Do you want some time alone first?"

"Don't be silly," she replied tugging his hand. "You know my body better than anyone here. Besides, with an ultrasound, all I have to do is raise my blouse."

"Thank you for sharing," Lyon replied, trying to ignore the smirking nurse.

Jacqueline Winslow was a tall, slender woman of forty with cropped blonde hair and kind gray eyes. She hugged Hope and shook Lyon's hand.

"Well, this is our big day, isn't it?" she said slipping on her gloves.

"One of them," Lyon muttered.

Hope grinned at her doctor. "Can you tell that we've been discussing the natural childbirth classes?"

"Is that what I was sensing between the lines?" Dr.

Winslow shook her head in bemusement. "It never fails that some of the strongest and bravest dads-to-be turn into Jell-O at the first sign of our mommies going into labor."

"I'm going to take that as confirmation that instincts still have value," Lyon drawled.

Hope shivered as the doctor put the cold gel on her stomach. "Sorry about that," Dr. Wilson said. "You'll get used to it in a second—or to be more accurate, totally forget about it. Watch that screen," she added placing the transducer probe onto the goo. She started easing the probe around, paused to type in some adjustments on the computerized part of the machine, then moved it some more. "Here we come…ah, and listen to that heartbeat. Best sound in the whole world until Delivery Day."

"D-Day. Told you so," Lyon said under his breath.

"Smarty," Hope replied, her gaze locked on the screen. Then her mouth fell open and she squeezed his hand even tighter. "Oh, my Lord! Is that her? I can't believe it." She had to blink furiously because tears were threatening to blind her.

"Her?" Dr. Winslow continued with her scanning. "It's a little late to put in an order."

"I know." Hope sighed. "But can you tell?"

"As a matter of fact, she's being very obliging this afternoon. I don't know how you knew it, but Mommy and Daddy had better start thinking of little girl names."

Hope dropped her head back onto the pillow and laughed with delight. "Thank you!"

Dr. Winslow reviewed Hope's chart with her, answered the questions Hope had brought with her, and gave her the contact information for the classes. The nurse printed a copy of the baby's image for Hope and also presented her with a DVD, too.

Hope was still staring at the picture as Lyon drove them home. "Isn't she beautiful?"

When Lyon didn't immediately reply, she turned to look at his profile in the dimming light of dusk. He'd been so quiet for the rest of the session. She thought she caught him gulping once, but with her own compromised vision, she couldn't be sure. That would be wonderful if he was as moved and thrilled as she was. Much stayed an unmarked road ahead of them. The most important things remained unsaid. That made it scary when she thought too far into the future, so she tried not to except when clients and black-and-white issues demanded it.

"She's going to be more than beautiful," Lyon said at last. "She'll be her mother's daughter. A single word won't ever describe her."

He always managed to move her with his simple yet almost romantic reflections. Why was she worrying?

Because *I love you* was simple and romantic, too.

She reached over and gently touched his nape. "Are you okay?"

"Watch the hand."

"I'm watching," she replied knowing full well what he was up to.

She accepted that he was going to make the most of Dr. Winslow's scolding; she knew it as soon as Jacqueline had spotted her injury and learned what they did not do that night. Although the wound had scabbed over and seemed to be healing, the doctor had demanded that if anything like that should happen again to get to the ER immediately. She spoke two words to make Hope realize her potential folly. "Staph infection."

In this day and age when germs could not only ignore

but outmaneuver state-of-the-art drugs and mutate, Hope had risked having a safer, healthier pregnancy. She'd learned that she was wrong to assume that being current with shots and careful with hygiene and medication that she was protected. And there was a danger of MRSA, which her doctor explained as "methicillin-resistant" staph bacteria. As a precaution, Dr. Winslow had the nurse take a blood sample to make sure there was no sign of infection in her bloodstream.

"I'm okay," Lyon said with a misleading nod. "Provided I can lock you in a safe place for the next four months where you only get out when I'm home to watch you."

"The concern is touching," she said playing along with him. "But what a caveman concept for such a respected women's advocate. Can't you see Pettigrew's headline? *Pregnant Sex Slave Discovered in Police Chief's Closet.*"

"I'm not talking as a law officer or the chief law authority. I'm talking as the concerned man in your life."

Hope looked out the passenger window at his careful phrasing. How could they be so free and open with each other when alone—particularly in bed—and hit this indescribable, unmovable mental glitch when it came to their public persona as a unit? Why not "husband and lover?" Was it because lover had the word *love* in it?

"I know you worry," she said this time touching his thigh.

"I like your doctor."

"Jacqueline lost her own baby and husband in a car accident ten years ago. She never remarried, but she adopted a special needs child."

"Lucky kid." Lyon folded his right hand around her fingers avoiding her palm that retained subtle swelling.

"Would you like to stop somewhere to eat? To celebrate? It would save having to fix something at the house."

"Are you hungry?"

"Not really, I had a late lunch. But if you are, I'd find something and keep you company."

"I had a big lunch, and—" with her right hand, Hope plucked at her red-and-black maternity top "—if you don't mind, I'd like to get home and wash off this gunk. The wipes the nurse gave me don't cut it."

"I had no idea. Of course."

They did reach home less than an hour later. It was dark and the lights that Lyon had set to come on by various timers since Hope's accident were working as programmed, lending a welcoming glow inside and out of the sprawling house.

As soon as they were in the kitchen, without even taking the time to remove her shawl or put down her purse and the DVD, Hope fastened the sonogram picture to the refrigerator with the service-number magnet from the side. "Ta-da!" she sang to the little being in the picture. "Your first piece of refrigerator art."

"Be careful what you wish for." Coming up beside her, Lyon put his arm around her. "Today a mesmerizing printout, tomorrow a wall-papered appliance—like a kitchen doesn't lend itself to being a fire hazard in a dozen different other ways."

"You cynic," Hope said laughing and threatening to punch his shoulder. "I bet your mother treasured your school drawings." She couldn't wait to see glimpses of what was going on inside her child's mind. "When I was growing up," she said to make Lyon understand, "the refrigerator was Mrs. Crandall's property. Don't get me wrong, she was a good woman, but she didn't want scribbles of stick figures with purple hair and eyelashes that resembled tarantula legs marring her everything-in-its-place territory."

"Poor rejected artist."

She supposed it must seem silly to anyone else. "How would you feel if your work was tucked away out of sight in a file?"

He gave the question about three seconds thought. "Confused. My stuff was used to start stove fires. Productive little guy that I was, I was instrumental in keeping us warm all that winter. After that I quit drawing and took up building ship models. They don't burn as well and the smoke stinks. I found out trying to have a Viking funeral in our stock pond. My dad gave me an earful when he came chasing out there thinking the pasture was on fire."

Hope gave him the arched Alessandro stare that Lyon recently told her made him almost hear flamenco music. "If you had said model horse kits, I might have believed you."

"Sissy stuff."

"You seriously did that?"

"Heck, no, there was no money for that. As soon as I was old enough, I got a paper route to start saving for college because I knew there was no way my parents were going to be able to afford to send me."

"Now that sounds like the Lyon Teague I know," Hope said over her shoulder as she moved on to the bedroom. She set her purse on her vanity in the bathroom, and folded the shawl and laid it on a shelf in her closet. As an afterthought, she slipped off her heels. They were low in comparison to what she was used to wearing, but they, too, made her back ache as if she wore them all day.

When she reemerged, she saw that he was removing his gun and the belt with the extra clip, and putting it in his closet. "I'm sorry that you had a demanding childhood."

He shrugged. "It kept me fit and taught me discipline. Let me help you with that." Coming up behind her, he moved her hair aside to unzip her top.

"Thanks." Hope watched him in her vanity mirror. "I guess we do need to start thinking of girl names."

Startled, he met her gaze in the mirror.

"What?"

"Well, I thought you'd want—" He shook his head. "Hope is what I would pick."

She made a face. "I like my name, but it would feel a little egotistical."

"Why?" Lyon scoffed. "Men do it all the time with the junior and second, third thing. It's a badge of honor. Let's get that left arm out of the sleeve before this knit material gets caught and rips off some scab prematurely."

"How lucky am I to have my own personal dresser," she said softly as she watched him focus diligently on his task.

"The official un-dresser." His secret smile suggested he enjoyed his own humor. "How about Rebecca Hope?" he added finally lifting the whole top over her head.

"Close!" She was delighted that they were almost on the same track. Watching as he laid the top on the edge of the garden tub, she said, "I was thinking Meredith. Meredith Rebecca Teague."

She watched as Lyon stared at the back of her head and then met her eyes in the mirror. "Our mothers would like that," he said quietly.

"I think so, too. I like the way Meredith flows off the tongue. It also makes me think of the lilt in inquisitive children's voices. You'll probably hate this, but we could call her Merri while she's little."

Lyon's eyes lit with humor as he took gentle hold of her shoulders. "Hope and Merri…doesn't that pairing demand it's own photo Christmas card?"

Dropping her head against his shoulder, Hope looked up at him. "Oh, you!"

She saw desire change the light in his dark eyes as he realized that she was wearing the red-over-black lace bra that had made his chest rise and fall the first time he'd seen her in it. Hope hadn't yet done more than finish unzipping her low-rise jeans but his glances down into that V indicated that he knew she had on the matching panties.

Framing her face with his right hand, he said, "Meredith or Merri, I can see I'll be quickly outnumbered and outvoted."

"No, you won't, but thank you for agreeing."

He stroked her high cheekbone with his thumb. "How could I not? I ache just looking at you," he said before lowering his head.

His kiss was possessive yet tender, hungry yet generous as he strived to give her as much pleasure as he was taking. When Hope reached up to slip her right hand to his nape to deepen the kiss, he groaned and gave her what she wanted, stealing her taste and then her breath with his tongue. Locked in this sensual prison, he slid his hands down her arms and over her breasts. Her sheer bra immediately exposed her arousal and he intensified it by circling her nipples, then raking his thumb nails over the ultra-sensitive peaks.

Hope's sounds of yearning abruptly ended in a choked cry and her body shuddered with the sexual need that remained close like a prowling predator whenever they were within sight of each other. Murmuring something she couldn't discern, he then slid his right hand into her jeans until he cupped her.

Her body jerked, defenseless against her own passion. When he drew her harder against his hips, it exposed the answer to an unasked question. Yes, he was as turned on as she was aroused.

Hope wanted to turn and wrap both arms around him, but she wouldn't even if she *could* free herself from his sensual vise. She would only get that awful gel on his uniform. As it was, he was probably getting some on his sleeve, but she could no more warn him than she could stop rocking against her hips in the erotic, age-old rhythm he coaxed from her with his hand.

The more the tension built, the more feral the bite of her fingers at his nape and the wilder his kiss. Then he tore his mouth from hers and with his teeth on her neck groaned in a quaking climax that thrust her into sensory overload, and she gasped from her own release.

Lyon wrapped both of his arms around her, clutching her to his chest and rocked them soothingly until his heart didn't beat like a jackhammer against her spine and neither of them was still panting like marathon runners.

"What you do to me," he said, his face buried in her hair.

Hope leaned her head back against his shoulder. "I want you inside me."

"In about five minutes," he said. "As soon as I shower." He kissed her hair before releasing her to start unbuttoning his shirt. "Come with me?"

Hope chuckled briefly. "Don't look at me that way. You'll get my hair drenched and I only washed it hours ago. Then you'll be lying in bed asking me what's taking so long to dry it."

"Not if you'd stand where I could watch you." He tossed his shirt beside hers.

"By the time I finish," she said ignoring that, "you'll be twenty minutes into REM sleep."

Glancing down at himself, Lyon muttered, "Want to bet?"

As he opened the shower's frosted glass door to turn on the spray, Hope turned away to the vanity to turn on the sink water and adjusted the wand to a comfortably warm temperature. Under her lashes she watched Lyon strip off the rest of his clothes. No, it wasn't likely that he would be asleep quite so soon. His provocative invitation and his own active imagination had sabotaged him. He may have climaxed two minutes ago, but his body was in denial.

As he closed the door behind himself, Hope exhaled a not-quite-steady breath and quickly stripped out of her lingerie knowing that he would waste no time in there. Reaching for the fluffy white wash cloth, she saturated it in the hot water and pumped some liquid coconut-scented soap onto it.

When Lyon shut off the bathroom lights and re-entered the bedroom he found Hope waiting for him resplendent in sea-green sheets. In the low light coming from under the dark shade of her bedside lamp, she looked as iridescent as the silk she lay between. As always, his heart clenched at the sight of her. He still didn't know what he'd done to deserve her, but tonight he was letting himself believe— at least a little—that this arrangement, legal though it was, wasn't temporary.

Hope's expression turned quizzical as he joined her. "That's an interesting look on your face," she said, welcoming him with her caressing touch. She lingered on the faint cropping of black hairs that reflected the other half of his ancestry. "What are you thinking about?"

"You."

"I wasn't begging for a compliment."

"It's the truth anyway. I was thinking of the kind of woman you are. How you heal your own wounds by easing those of others."

Her breath catching, Hope leaned over and kissed his chest. "Lyon…that's lovely. But sad, too. Is it because of what I asked to name the baby? If that's going to constantly remind you of losing your parents, we won't do it."

"No, I want to. I'm just floored at your generosity, making me more a part of this," he said gently stroking her abdomen.

Hope laid her head against him and stroked him with her cheek as she caressed him with her hands. "I always knew you as decent and different, Lyon, but when you say such things and show me more of who you are, I see something too tender to do the work you do."

"It's getting surprisingly easier," he said losing his fingers in her hair. "I have a little secret."

"You're going to say something sweet or too generous. Don't."

"A silken-haired seductress whose eyes forever tie me in knots."

Pushing him onto his back with a strength that shouldn't have surprised him since he knew what it took to handle animals ten and more times her weight, he was taken aback by the tears he saw in her eyes.

"Your soul touches mine," she whispered. "That probably sounds silly in this day and age, but it's the truth. Do you feel it?"

"You're precious to me."

She closed her eyes as though tasting the words. When she looked at him again, she asked, "Then why didn't you let me see who you were sooner?"

The question had been like a long-range missile, he'd known that it was coming, he just never knew exactly when. "You know why."

That grim reply silenced her because she clearly did. But he saw that she blamed herself for what didn't happen as much as for what did, and he didn't want that. "I'm no coward, Hope, but I'm not a big gambler. My assets limit me, and I'm not talking about finances. I'm talking about who and what I chose to be—as a son, a friend, and honorable cop. How could I tell you anything—a woman some elitists still believe I shouldn't touch?"

He'd noticed examples of the latter issue just recently. Every year Hope got invited to countless society functions, some of them touted pedigreed affairs. At the moment, one or two were not forthcoming. She gave no indication of being upset or even caring, but he was and did. Not for himself, but for what this could mean to her growing career in good works.

Hope, however, was shattered by what he'd shared. "If I hadn't proposed to you, you'd never have asked me out, would you?"

"It didn't seem like it would work in this lifetime." He held her gaze, but what he saw was what he'd expected his future to be—too empty and lonely to describe. Then he smiled and gave himself the gift of exploring her flawless skin. "But you're here now and as long as you are, I can't keep from reaching for you."

"Lyon…"

He silenced her by drawing her completely over him and

kissing her. His mood was as raw, his emotions as painful as an open wound. "Take me inside you," he whispered against her warm, pliant lips. "I need you."

For seconds longer he felt her resistance. She wanted to talk, to understand, to make him say things he had convinced himself that he had no right to say. But she was right—in the universe that housed their spirits, their souls had been designed to be as one. She'd recognized him before, and he was exposing himself to her now. With his searching kiss and his enticing touch he drew her away from this world of uncertainty, and into the bliss only they could create together.

Straddling him as she would one of her mounts, Hope accepted him slowly, even though she was already moist and ready for him. It just made the journey all the more poignant, a sweet torture that had him gritting his teeth and gripping the sheet to keep from leaving his imprint on her tender skin. She intensified the exquisite torment as she began caressing his chest, trailing her fingers along the collarbone he'd broken once during a game, over his hard nipples aching for her touch, down his rock-hard belly to his navel and then back up again.

When she leaned forward to wet his nipples and tease him with her mouth, he pulsed inside her, and the epithet wrenched from deep in his throat was both plea and prayer.

The movements of her hips were as graceful and smooth as though she was on a languid ride, her silken thighs holding him as firmly as she would her mount's flanks. Lyon opened his eyes wanting to watch her because that captivated him as much as her touch did. With her head and shoulders thrown back, her breasts were a superb offering and he worshipped her with his hands, then devoured her with his mouth.

Needing her liquid heat again, he drew her with him against the pillows and headboard, until her body rested completely against his. Pulsating deep inside her, he could feel her inner muscles clenching while her eyes grew low-hooded as she gave herself up to intoxicating lure of release.

"Kiss me," he said locking her against him with arms that ached to own and keep her.

"Yes," she whispered, her fingers moving over and through his hair. But her kisses were butterfly caresses that flittered over his cheekbone, along his jaw, between his eyebrows, and then the corner of his mouth. "Yes…yes…"

"For the love of heaven," Lyon groaned, *"Kiss me."*

Hope clasped his face between her hands and gave him what he wanted. With a groan of relief he drove into her. He couldn't hold her close enough, couldn't plunge himself deep enough to assuage the heavy ache. The desperation was upon him, but ecstasy was advancing. She rode them both to the edge and over and he heard her cry out his name and felt her shatter in his arms.

My heart. My life. My love.

They hovered in that place as long as possible, almost ceasing to breathe to prolong each delicious sensation. Then, although muscles relaxed and the fever ebbed, he couldn't bear to release her.

Coaxing her head onto his shoulder, he stroked her hair in apology. "Please…at least for a little while. You're comfortable, aren't you?"

"There are no words," she murmured against his neck.

As he felt her drift off to sleep, he drew up the sheet, extended his right arm and switched off her light. He lay there in the darkness a willing sentry guarding and warming what was most precious in his life.

His own lids were growing heavy when he felt a tiny kick against his abdomen. His heart swelled anew, his throat ached as emotion rose there straining for release. Slowly, with excruciating care so as not to rouse the dream in his arms, he reached down to lay a soothing hand over Hope's child. "Sweet dreams, little Meredith," he whispered.

Chapter Nine

For Christmas, Hope convinced Lyon that they should hold an open house. She explained that she always had one anyway, but at the office. Since her assistant Freddie would be taking her vacation over the holidays and would be out of the country, relocating made all the sense.

And then she got the idea that Lyon should invite everyone from the department. Lyon joked that while they were at it, they could invite the city council, too, but Hope thought it a brilliant idea. It would show how Lyon held no grudges, was well liked by his people, and that they were a happy couple.

Lyon asked, "Why can't we just send out smiling photo Christmas cards?"

Into early November, he kept trying to talk her out of it. At first he cited the strain on her pregnancy, and when that didn't do any good, he insisted that it was too much work for her regardless of how organized he had to admit she was—and, no, having Molly's able assistance didn't change his mind.

That's when Hope called upon one of her newer clients, divorcée Lara Conti. This was exactly the kind of exposure Lara's fledgling catering business needed to trigger word-of-mouth and get her more bookings. By the time their lunch meeting was over, Lara had the job and Hope knew she had gained another strong ally in town.

The open house was held the Saturday before Christmas and would begin at seven in the evening and would go until ten o' clock. By seven in the morning Hope, Lara and her mother Geraldine, and Molly were hard at it in Hope's kitchen.

Saturdays had become Lyon's indulgence time when he liked to linger in bed—preferably with Hope by his side, have coffee with her while reading the Dallas newspaper and Hope's *Wall Street Journal,* and basically play the day by ear in that give-and-take way they'd comfortably fallen into. But on Party Saturday, Hope was out of bed before the slightest hint of daylight peeked around the windows' mini-blinds. When he warily entered the kitchen at seven-thirty, the place looked like an understaffed soup kitchen.

Lyon politely greeted the ladies…and with papers under his arm, drove into town hoping the coffee wasn't already too thick at the station and that not all of the donuts were eaten.

Hope was in the bathroom putting the finishing touches on her makeup when he returned around five that evening. "Hey," she murmured as he stopped in the doorway to softly whistle at her.

"Woman, what are you on that you can look like that at seven months after being on your feet for ten hours?" he demanded.

"The vitamins Dr. Winslow put me on help, as does yoga, but—" closing the tube of mascara, she came to him and lifted her face for a kiss "—I highly recommend having a patient and understanding husband, too."

After a brief, but possessive kiss, Lyon said, "It would have been nice to hear *stud muffin* somewhere in all of that."

"I didn't want to get my imagination and hormones all hot and bothered when there's so little time," she told him in apology. "How was your day?"

"Far easier and less exciting than yours." Lyon took hold of her hands and held them out to inspect her dress. She wore a red velvet empire dress with long tight sleeves that ended in a point at her wrists. With the gold chain in her hair that dangled a teardrop ruby on her forehead, she looked like medieval royalty. Matching stud earrings completed the image. "You're breathtaking. I'm not sure I want my men within five miles of you, but like the rest of this place, you look like a fairy tale come to life."

Gently wiping lip gloss from his lower lip, Hope smiled. "I would have loved for everyone to bring their children, but with so many people, it would have been impossible to monitor them properly and to avoid accidents."

"Good point. We forgot just one thing—call for the EMTS to have a truck stationed outside. I glimpsed the food on my way through the kitchen and it's nothing short of a cardiac patient's last meal dream."

"Well, it's not a party unless the tummy gets pampered. I told you Lara is good. And wait until you see the heaping trays of shrimp and crab legs that are chilling."

When Hope met her, Lara had been an abandoned mother of three. The divorcée was living with her widowed mother Geraldine as she tried to dig her way out of debts and back taxes incurred by her two-timing ex-husband. No bank would touch her to help her launch a catering business, so Lara would bake in her mother's kitchen and go from store to office with her products, trying to garner enough interest to keep her family fed and clothed. Once she tasted Lara's quality product and saw how she paid attention to making packaging attractive, she sat the woman down in her office and said, "Show me your business plan." The rest, as the saying goes, was history.

"I'll have to arrange for a 211 call from the station to clear out my crew. It'll take at least a robbery to keep them from acting like they're at a feeding trough. You were too generous, sweetheart."

"There'll be plenty for everyone. But that reminds me— did you arrange for someone to bring your relief dispatcher a plate? Who's on duty this evening?"

"Maggie Greer. She all but begged for the job. She just lost over fifty pounds and wants to keep it that way."

Deep in thought, Hope tapped a red fingernail against her lips. "Then be sure to bring her one of the centerpieces afterward. She'll be able to use the crystal vase for years to come."

Lyon kissed her again. "As I said, too generous. So how many do you think will show? You have enough food for five or six hundred."

"Considering the list and add the spouses or dates…somewhere around 250-300."

"If they all come at once, Tan will have a nervous breakdown trying to keep parking under control."

"I know, but I've been to these kinds of events before and somehow it does seem to work out. You need to start getting ready and I need to get into the kitchen," she said

beginning to unbutton his shirt. "The girls will be returning at any minute to start the final preparations."

"I wish you would have saved yourself unnecessary
stress and not invited Clyde and Mercy," Lyon said.

Leaning forward to breathe in his male scene, Hope
then touched her lips to his chest. "I appreciate your pro-
tectiveness, but it was simply smart strategy not to snub
them, just as it was to send my father an invitation, too. I
doubt they'll come."

"You know I'll support you since at least he's a blood
relative, but if he marries Summer Isadore as rumor has it,
you can cut your ties with my blessing."

"He has a right to be happy I guess," she said. She took
his hand and drew him farther into the bathroom toward
his closet where she had a new sports jacket, dress shirt and
dress jeans hanging pressed and ready for him. "Do you
mind that I took the liberty?"

"Mind that you thought about me when you've been
working for weeks with this party and decorating on top
of your already busy schedule? Yeah, I'm ballistic."

Hope's body was humming with happiness when she
returned to the kitchen. As much as she was looking
forward to the party, she couldn't wait until tonight when
everyone went home and she could return to Lyon's arms.
They were growing closer with every day and becoming a
more intricate part of each other's lives. She couldn't ask
for anything more—except for the words a woman in love
had a right to own.

No, she told herself, she would not let herself get depressed or worry about that now.

The back door opened and a hesitant voice called, "Am
I too early?"

Molly entered and immediately took off her bright red wool coat exposing a green velvet dress with seed pearls sewn around the collar. It was Hope's Christmas present to her along with a set of pearl earrings.

"You're right on time and how lovely you look!" Hope said clapping her hands in delight. "What did Tan say when he saw you?"

"He cut me this from his greenhouse." She turned and pointed to the delicate gardenia in her hair above the bow that Hope had bought her so she could have her long hair tied back.

"Oh, how romantic. You're going to help the house smell so good."

Her blue eyes huge as she looked around, "It smells that way already. I told Tan—wait." Molly had to stop herself and think a moment. "Tan said to tell the chief that he will be outside at the front gate by 6:30."

"I will, and I'll remind Lyon that Tan needs the reflective vest he said he wanted to wear."

"He already did. He brought it to him last night—and the police radio and flashlight." Molly giggled, but looked proud, too. "You should see him. He's acting like it's the whole uniform, he's so proud."

Grateful to have such dear and helpful people in her life, Hope assured her. "Well, he's playing a vital role even if it doesn't get too crowded all at once out there. We've had a wet autumn and if people are allowed to drive anywhere they please, we'll have to start the landscaping all over come spring."

Molly looked stricken. "I didn't think of that—but I bet Tan did."

Patting her back gently, Hope redirected her focus.

"Let's start putting out the candles in strategic places, but we won't light them until we hear Tan on the radio Lyon put in the kitchen that he's taking his position. Do you know where your lighter is?"

Molly gave her a confident nod. "In my apron pocket in the kitchen."

"Wonderful. And while we're placing the candles, let's start plugging in the lights. This way when Lara and Gerri arrive, we can start setting out platters as they prepare them."

The slender woman headed for the kitchen repeating the directions to herself. Lara and Geraldine arrived about fifteen minutes later looking confident but excited and promptly put on their aprons bearing the Conti Catering logo.

By the time Lyon joined them, soft Christmas tunes were playing on the stereo, the tree was lit in the bay window in the living room, a small fire was burning in the fireplace, and Hope's lifelong collection of Christmas decorations created a fantasy world around the house.

"I hardly recognize the place," Lyon said planting a kiss just above the jewel on her forehead. "Where have you been keeping all of this stuff? The life-size, animated St. Nicholas at the front door for instance?"

"In one of the sheds behind the barn, carefully boxed and labeled," she added.

Rubbing his hands together, he said, "Shouldn't I be getting on with my job as the official food sampler?"

"If Lara or Gerri see you stick a fork in anything before the first guests arrive, they're apt to stick a fork in you. Go to the kitchen and they'll have you over your daily calorie limit before you know it."

The first to arrive were Lyon's people. Hope noticed that the men were a little reserved at first and, although the wives were wide-eyed and thrilled to be in what they considered a mansion, they were ready to find fault with her if they felt too awkward around her. Having traveled that road many a time since her school days, Hope welcomed everyone with the same warmth and enthusiasm. She'd made a point to query Lyon about each police officer's family and memorized names so that as she showed the ladies to the guest room to hang their coats and pointed out the guest bathroom, she seasoned her descriptions with, "How's your youngest, Elizabeth? I think Lyon told me that she needed tubes in her ears?" then "We thought about your Roger and some of the others being diabetic, Nancy. The dessert table has several desserts prepared for the no-sugar guests."

Kent and Shana arrived with the less-than-enthusiastic newspaper editor Tim Pettigrew in tow. That startled both Lyon and Hope, and they knew Tim had inveigled himself into an invitation when Shana rolled her eyes as she stood behind him. As they'd recovered, Gerri planted herself in front of Tim with her tray of hors d'oeuvres and with humor and southern charm declared, "Hello, Tall Drink of Water. You look parched with those pinched lips and in need of feeding."

Despite his sour-disposition, the newspaper man eyed the appealing treats with something close to lust. "If you think you can get free advertising out of this, you're sorely mistaken."

Nonplussed, Gerri batted her false eyelashes at him. "Sugar, what I was thinking is that if you ate one or two of these salmon-chive with fennel goodies right in line to the I in Conti—" she shimmied to indicate her right breast "—you'd trust me enough to show you some real treats in the kitchen we're saving for our favorite guests."

For a second, Tim looked as though he was about to charge for the front door, but suddenly he threw his head back and laughed. "Can't see how a bite or two would hurt," he said.

Teagues and Roberts exchanged bewildered looks as Gerri led Scrooge personified off to new experiences.

Within a half hour there were at least forty-five people scattered about, and at the top of the next hour three times that.

"I told you that you were spoiling everyone," Lyon said in her ear when they reconnected at one of the few vacant corners in the house. "No one wants to go home."

"It's Christmas and everyone is tired of politics and conflict." Hope eyed the crowd with pleasure. "Isn't everyone getting along nicely? It's been fun seeing chemistry in the works. See the forty-something Hispanic gentleman by the painting that I got at the auction?"

"The conspicuous guy standing alone and bored?"

"What's conspicuous about him?"

"He's the only person here that's in a full suit."

"Rafael Simone. My client, thank you. I've been meaning to introduce you, but we keep getting pulled in opposite directions. He manages the fish counter at the supermarket."

"There is no fish counter at the supermarket. There's some packaged stuff due to FDA laws about keeping beef, chicken, and seafood separate and most of it looks like it traveled to Texas via a rowboat from Australia."

"But he dreams of there being one, or a little shop in town. He dresses impeccably because five days a week he deals with fish in a place that really doesn't care about fish. We're working on his dream." Hope tightened her fingers on his sleeve. "I'm waiting for one of my widow ladies. They were talking earlier."

As Hope scanned the crowd, Lyon studied her. "Has it crossed your mind that he brushed her off and he's waiting for you?"

Frustrated, Hope directed his attention to the opposite side of the room where two people stood seemingly in rapt conversation over the igloo art beside the punchbowl. "Fine. Here's one you can't deny. Have you noticed your detective—"

"Sweetheart, you're allowed to look and sound like royalty from another era. I'm a chief not a chieftain. He's not *my* anything."

Hope stroked his shoulder. "I'm making a point. He's sought her out several times this evening. You said he's not much for mingling and prefers field work."

"His divorce was tough on him. He's probably intrigued with the physics of how she kept the ice clear so you could see the inside with the battery-operated fire display and the other figurines." Belatedly he allowed, "She's a pretty woman."

"He seems a very serious type. Look at how he listens to her. That's a plus."

"Hope."

"All I'm saying is that a nice-looking man, who seems to hang on her every word, is a nice change of pace for her. She doesn't need another 'Don't worry about it, honey' con in her life again. Nor do her kids."

"Table that." Taking hold of her shoulders, Lyon turned her toward the front entrance. "This requires your focus now."

Hope's gaze settled on what was getting him all tense. Her father and Summer had just entered the house. "I don't know how I can," she told him. "That image defies the logic of everything inside me."

Lyon slipped his arm around her waist. "Take a deep breath and know I'll be right beside you."

As usual, her father was his own fashion statement, wearing a black velvet tuxedo jacket and ruffled shirt over jeans and boots. Summer wore a black leather bomber jacket and pants with a red sequin tube top. Her ever-changing hair—today eggplant—was piled on her head with practiced indifference.

"Merry Christmas," Hope said as they reached them. "How nice of you to come, Father." Once he took the unlit cigar out of his mouth, she gave him a polite peck on the cheek.

"Hope, honey," Summer gushed. "Aren't you look-ing…ripe. When did you say you were due?"

Taking Hope's hand in his and giving it a gentle squeeze, Lyon said, "Her doctor is actually concerned that's she's on the lowest end for acceptable weight gain."

"You've never looked better," her father scoffed. "What's wrong with that doctor?"

"She's an excellent doctor and very dedicated to her patients' care," Hope replied resting her head against Lyon's shoulder. It had been dear of him to try and shut up Summer. "She did recommend I cut *one* activity from my routine for these last several weeks." She gave him a sidelong look because he knew exactly what that might include.

"I vote for shutting your office," he said keeping his expression blank. "The yoga and the rest are all good for you."

Clearing her throat, Hope redirected. "You're looking well, Dad."

"When my doctor told me to lose ten pounds, I cut back to two cigars a day."

The only person who seemed to think that was funny

was Summer. Perturbed, Ellis narrowed his eyes at Lyon. "Well, you're still here."

"Plan to keep it that way, too," Lyon replied with a feral smile.

"At least you don't scare easily, I'll give you that." Looking bored with the conversation, Ellis scanned the room. "Quite the turnout."

Looking unhappy with the way the conversation had been going so far, Summer sniffed. "But is there anyone here *we* can talk to?"

With something akin to a growl, Ellis pretended to flick ashes on top of her hair. "Well, hell, Summer, honey, you pretend to talk to me all the time. What's the difference?" He ignored her double-take and demanded "Where's the bar?"

"No bar." Lyon nodded across the room. "We have a facsimile of beer and a punch for the ladies with a touch of champagne. We want to make sure all of you make it home safely tonight."

Ellis looked like he smelled something bad and then patted his left pocket. "No matter. I always travel prepared." As he drew a lighter out of his right pocket, Hope grabbed it.

"Hey!" her father snapped.

"I don't believe you," Hope muttered. She directed both index fingers to her tummy. "Hello? Pregnant! I'll return it as you leave."

"Go find me a glass with some ice cubes," he told Summer. "Cubes, not that chipped crap. Don't crack the skin on that," he added to Hope pointing at the cigar she held out of his reach.

As he walked off, Lyon took a restless hold of Hope's shoulders. "Better hide that thing from me," he said. "I'm about to snap it into half a dozen pieces and toss it into the flowerbeds."

"Sure," she replied, "pollute my shrubs."

By 9:30 p.m., Lyon considered lighting the cigar himself—right under one of the smoke detectors. He was happy for Hope that things had gone as well as they did, but he was ready to clear everyone out. Attendance was down a bit from what she'd expected, but some of her older clients hadn't shown up. Considering the hours they'd scheduled, they'd known that was a possibility. The Nichols had stayed away, too, but that was fine. One thing Hope could take pride in was how people lingered, especially his crew. And maybe she was right about Cooper and Lara. The detective was spending as much time in the kitchen as in here with the other guests.

Laughter caught his attention and he saw Hope and Molly assisting one of the elderly clients up from a couch. Mrs. Dillinger, he thought, with an amused smile. Who was going to have trouble remembering a chauffeur-driven millionairess with a name like that? He went to offer his aid.

"It was delightful, Hope, dear," the woman said as she steadied herself with the help of several hands and her cane. "Next year a little less conservative with the champagne. I don't have to worry about driving."

Hope laughed then put a cautionary finger to her lips. "Not so loud, Mrs. D. My husband the cop is within hearing distance."

The wiry woman gazed up at him with bright eyes that declared she was free of cataracts. "Hello again, good looking. You don't have a twin brother, do you?"

Raucous laughter followed them out of the house. At the

sight of them easing down the sidewalk, her driver bolted from behind the wheel, opened the back passenger door and jogged up the sidewalk to take over.

"I have her, sir," he told Lyon.

"This is Wilmington," Mrs. Dillinger said releasing Lyon to pat the arm of the elderly chauffeur. "I've buried three husbands, buried two children, and made, lost, and made fortunes—the latter with help from your darling wife—but I've only had one chauffeur, eh Bobby?"

"Yes, ma'am. Good night, sir," he said to Lyon.

Wilmington wasn't much taller or younger than she was, but he was agile and caring, and clearly devoted to her. As they drove away, Lyon wondered if there was something more between them, then he shook his head. Hope's romantic nature was starting to rub off on him.

Although it was getting seriously cold now that the latest Blue Norther had pushed through, Lyon shoved his hands into the pockets of his sports jacket and walked down to the gate. Tan had slipped on the heavier coat he'd brought with him and wore a skier's wide headband, too.

"Come on inside," he said, shaking the shorter man's hand.

"I good, Chief," Tan replied, but he was bobbing in place like a boxer warming up for a fight. "I wait for all car to leave."

There were only five left and the catering van. "That's Hope's father's car, and the others belong to my officers. Even after they leave, it'll be another hour or more before the van leaves. Your work is finished. Come inside and let Molly get you a hot toddy or something."

"Thank you, Chief." As they walked together, Tan said, "Molly say party very good."

"She's right. Hope should be pleased. How did that radio work for you?"

Tan patted the handheld device with his gloved hand. "A-OK! Detective Jones teach Molly how to use. I think I get radio for us. Easier than driving across pasture. Good to check on Molly."

"You're right. It's a very smart idea. I'll tell Hope. We'll get them for you."

They had reached the sidewalk and Tan was thanking him effusively when they heard a scream from inside the house, then another and then yelling. Lyon's hand went immediately for his weapon, but, of course, he wasn't wearing a gun tonight, and with a house full of cops, he told himself it shouldn't have been needed. But what if Hope had fallen or been hurt somehow? He and Tan ran the rest of the way.

When they burst inside, everyone was still, but the tension in the room told Lyon what the screams had. Something had gone wrong.

His gaze encompassing, Lyon took in Summer Isadore cowering against one wall and looking like a train wreck with her hair falling, her mascara bleeding down her face and her nose bleeding. Buddy Yantis stood watching her as though ready to intercede if she threw herself toward Ellis. Ellis Harrell was being held against the opposite wall by Officers Juarez and Scott Laurie.

Cooper Jones standing between them had apparently started trying to gauge what had happened. Everyone else, including Hope, stood back, their expressions reflecting utter shock. As soon as Molly saw Tan behind him, she hurried to him. Lyon briefly glanced at Tan and motioned for them to get to the side and out of the way for precaution's sake.

Sobbing and clutching her hand to her chest, Summer shouted, "I'm going to sue you, you pig! You broke my nose and my w-wrist."

"It should have been your neck," Ellis snarled back at her.

"What happened?" Lyon demanded advancing toward them. He saw Hope begin to speak but gave her a look that stopped her.

Cooper situated himself on the other side of Summer to give Lyon clear scope, but gestured toward the master suite. "There was a scream from back there. As Juarez and I started to investigate, Mr. Harrell came barreling out of there dragging Ms.—" He glanced at Summer and then at Hope with uncertainty.

"Isadore," Hope supplied. "She was already bleeding from the nose," she told Lyon.

"She fell into the vanity," Ellis added.

"You hit me!" Summer declared.

"Come here and I'll show you the difference," he growled.

"Ellis!" Lyon's rebuke won his father-in-law's silence, although the older man continued to look like a predator unhappy with having only achieved half of his goal. "Did you hit her?" Lyon asked.

"Yes!" Summer declared. "I want to press charges."

"She fell."

"You pushed me!"

Ellis gave Lyon a satisfied smile. "Ah. Finally the truth from the alley cat's own mouth."

Pinching the bridge of his nose, Lyon asked wearily, "Why?"

"If your bulldogs would allow me, I'll show you."

"No stupid moves," Lyon said pointing into his face.

"You have my word." With that the two officers took a step back and Ellis slowly extended his clenched right hand, then opened it.

Hope gasped.

"Yes," Ellis said. "This diamond bracelet was my wife's and now belongs to my daughter. I gave it to Rebecca for our tenth wedding anniversary. When I heard that tramp complaining to Hope that she couldn't wait for the other bathroom to be free, Hope graciously offered her own." He gestured toward the master suite. "After what seemed like more than adequate time, I became suspicious and went to investigate. That's when I found her rifling through my daughter's things."

His speech was growing more slurred indicating to Lyon that as adrenaline faded, the effects of the alcohol he'd consumed became more apparent.

Turning to Summer, Lyon asked, "Is that true? Did you take it?"

"It was just lying there on the counter. I was only admiring it. The truth is, I thought it was fake."

"Liar!" Ellis roared. "You—"

"Easy now," Buddy Yantis warned. "You're in the presence of ladies."

"I think," Hope began slowly, "that if you will see to Summer's medical expenses, Father, that we can agree it was just a bad misunderstanding."

"No way!" Summer shouted.

Hope picked up several paper napkins from the nearest table and brought them to her. She said quietly, "The bracelet wasn't on the counter."

"Oh, fine. My word against the Chief of Police's wife. Talk about a stacked deck."

"If you want to keep up that attitude," Hope replied, "I think you should understand that I'm within my rights to have you taken down to the station and strip-searched by the department's female office, Maggie Greer."

"Miss Hope is right about the bracelet," Molly said clutching Tan as he held her to his side. "I clean for her. I mean Mrs. Teague. She keeps her jewelry just the way her mama did hers. She told me when she was teaching me how to do my job and where everything goes. Everything is boxed with the papers included. Nothing is ever left out. This way nothing can fall down a drain or get lost in the carpet."

Hope returned to Molly and touched her shoulder. "Thank you, Molly."

Seeing that she was trapped by her own lies, Summer started wailing. "That's not fair! Why should you get everything and I get crap? You don't even like him!" she declared pointing at Ellis.

"You're right," Hope replied. "Sometimes I don't like him at all. But he's my father, which is the only reason you were invited into this house. That courtesy won't happen again."

Lyon nodded to Juarez. "Can you and your wife take this woman to the hospital and either have her treated or admitted, depending on what the x-rays show? I don't trust her being alone with one officer in the car."

Juarez's wife stepped beside her husband. "We'll do it, Chief."

"I'll be his backup," Scott Laurie said.

Lyon thanked them all and while Vince's wife, Alicia, got their coats and Hope got Summer's things, he took the two officers aside and gave them additional instructions, then apologized for costing them additional hours away from home. But Scott reminded him that he was single, and Vince said his mother-in-law was babysitting and that Alicia would call once they got to the hospital and explained things to her.

"My things are at the ranch," Summer whined, annoyed at being virtually ignored. "I demand my things."

"I'll see you get them tomorrow," Hope said.

The party had officially ended. As soon as Summer was taken from the house, Hope went to her father and put her hand out for the bracelet. Ellis was slow to hand it over.

"I remember the night I gave it to her," he said. "I thought my heart would stop from looking at someone so beautiful." His gaze settled on Hope. "I know I've been a disappointment to you. It shouldn't make any difference to you, but I've come to realize that I'm a disappointment to myself."

Slowly, Hope reached into her father's pocket and took out the sterling flask. Shaking it, she found it empty. "Lyon," she said, "can you see he gets home, too? I'll call Greenleaf and warn him of their arrival."

"I'll do it," Cooper said.

Lyon said, "I'll follow in his car and you can drop me off back here."

Despite it only being a few miles away, it was a good half hour before Lyon and Cooper returned. Seeing the Conti van in the last stages of being loaded, Cooper said he would help them and then make sure the ladies got home.

Lyon went inside and found Hope putting out the last candles and pulling the plug on the Christmas tree. When she saw him, she came into his arms.

"Where's Molly and Tan?"

"I sent them home right after you left. I think she was as upset as I was." She sighed heavily. "Things had been going so well."

Lyon tightened his arms. "The party was a smashing success. Don't let what Summer did take away from that.

Maggie radioed me from the station and said the buzz was so cool she could kick herself for missing it. She asked if we'd do it next year."

"That's nice. But right now I don't think I'll ever want another party again."

"You're exhausted. Let's go to bed. The rest can wait until tomorrow and I'll help you."

But as they entered their bedroom, Hope held back. "I hate the idea of that woman being in our room."

"Let's change the sheets. That'll make you feel fresher." Lyon doubted Summer had done anything there, but knew she would be more comfortable.

While they worked, Lyon told her how wonderful the party had been, reported all of the compliments he'd heard, how much the wives liked her, how she was right about Cooper and Lara. She made polite responses and only displayed real emotion when she spoke of how Tan had cradled Molly against him when she had the courage to confirm where the bracelet was kept.

"What if Summer sues?" she asked abruptly.

"She won't," he replied. "In fact I'll bet she leaves Cedar Grove pretty quickly. Who's going to have anything to do with her if Ellis Harrell won't have her?"

"At least there's that. And here I was convinced she was about to be my stepmother."

"Your father apologized to you again."

"Okay." Suddenly she shivered. "I'm cold. I think I need to sleep in a warm gown tonight."

She went to get changed. Lyon followed and hung his things, then watched as she began spraying the counter and scrubbing at it with a washcloth. That was followed by her closing the sink drain and washing the bracelet with soap.

When she started at the closet doorknob with a sanitary wipe, he'd seen way too much.

"Hope." Taking the towelette away from her, he threw it into the trash and put the disinfectant spray under the sink cabinet. "That's enough. Everything is clean. She's gone."

Turning off the lights, he lifted her into his arms. "Come to bed, little queen." He carried her there and laid her between the fresh-scented sheets, quickly following. Shutting off his light, Lyon eased up behind her aligning their bodies and wrapping his arm around her to caress the firm mound where the child rested.

"Has Meredith been quiet tonight?" he asked, partly out of curiosity, partly to keep her from thinking of tonight's ugliness.

"Yes. Except when Summer screamed and my father roared. Then we both jumped." She covered his hand with hers.

Lyon thought she would drift off to sleep then, but he was wrong. Her breathing stayed the same and he knew she was staring at the closed mini-blinds, yet seeing the sad end to her wonderful party.

"You're not going to get any rest that way."

"I know." Sitting up, she tugged and wrestled with the gown. "This is suffocating me," she said. "And I can't feel you."

Lyon helped her and smiled as she flung the soft white flannel to the chaise at the foot of the bed. Then he let her show him how close she wanted him. When she lifted her leg over his and gently urged him to come inside her, he pressed an open-mouthed kiss to her neck.

"Are you sure?"

"Always."

He made slow, sweet love to her warming her from the outside until inside she burned with a fire of her own. He gave her all that he was because in giving, he received everything he needed in the world.

Chapter Ten

Christmas and New Year's passed quietly. Two days before the first holiday, Hope came down with a cold and stayed wrapped in a blanket on the couch sleeping most of the time. For New Year's, Lyon took his share of the shift work since there was a big party over at the grill, and several other bashes at some of the big estates in the area. He'd made sure Kent put announcements on the radio and in the newspaper that the department would be out in full force and that seemed to help keep arrests down this year. They ended up with only two DUI cases and one assault.

Hope spent New Year's taking down all of the Christmas decorations and wrapping and boxing everything. Tan and Molly offered to help but she insisted they spent New Year's Eve together. She did let them come over on New Year's Day and while Lyon caught up on lost sleep, they transferred the mountain of boxes to the storage shed for another year.

The next week she and Lyon began the natural childbirth classes held over at the junior college. There were seven other couples and Lyon got teased a bit for being the "senior" member of the group, but he took it good naturedly. He still wasn't too sure about being in the delivery room with her, though.

Summer didn't sue, although she continued to claim that she had a case to anyone who would listen. There were fewer and fewer of those, as the truth about what was behind her breakup with Ellis Harrell got around. Business at her store dropped, as well, which Lyon saw as indicative to how beloved Hope was in the community regardless of how anyone felt about Ellis or him. In the end, Summer sold her remaining inventory to another shop in town for pennies on the dollar, and Hope purchased the building that had been a divorce settlement from her third marriage. The last Hope heard, Summer moved to Memphis.

Hope was preparing to lease the building to Lara Conti for a fraction of the going rates in the area. They agreed to a one-year contract at which time they would review the books and see about what were the best options all around. Frankly, Hope was planning on selling her the building. Lara already was booked solid for Valentine's Day, had one Easter Egg Hunt Party, and one engagement party slated. She'd never looked happier, and Hope knew part of the reason was that Cooper was spending a good deal of his free time over there and Lara's boys thought the "CSI" man was super.

Gerri was having less success with Tim Pettigrew, but he didn't exactly run in the opposite direction when they happened to cross paths. "I'm giving him another month to play hard to get," she told Hope during their last chat, "and then I'm going to fish in friendlier waters. You'd be surprised how that can change a man's way of thinking."

Hope had heard that theory but was glad she didn't have to test it. She wasn't all that happy that Pettigrew might be who Gerri wanted; however, she was willing to play wait and see as Lara was resigned to.

There was no question that Lyon was right where he wanted to be. Three little words remained unspoken between them, and yet she was more content in her life than she'd ever been. She'd begun to conclude that maybe words were sometimes overrated. Almost.

During the second week in January, the steady pattern of cold weather intensified and Cedar Grove, along with all of North and East Texas suddenly found itself under a winter storm warning. It had begun to snow on the way to the office and by midday that had turned to freezing rain, then ice, then freezing rain again. Hope sent Freddie home only an hour after she'd arrived and was planning to lock up herself as soon as she finished the report she'd been working on. However, it was difficult to concentrate when her mind kept wandering to Lyon. He'd had to testify at the county court this morning and she wouldn't relax until he returned home.

When her phone rang, she grabbed it hoping it was him—and she wasn't disappointed.

"Hello, beautiful. Why am I getting you at your office? You should be home," he said.

"I'm not there because you're not here," she said looking out her office window. "Where are you?"

"Just now entering the city limits. Man, it's been rough. Some parts of the county have lost power and it's only a matter of time before we do. The ice is getting so heavy on trees and lines, when branches pop it sounds like gunfire, and the dead trees are wiping out pole after pole. If I passed one electric cooperative truck, I've passed a half dozen. You aren't wearing any of those sexy high heels, are you? One fall and you'd shake Meredith loose for sure. We'd never get you to Dr. Winslow's hospital on time."

She adored him for thinking of the baby as much as he did her. "I'm wearing my most comfortable Uggs with the nonskid bottoms," she assured him. "Not to worry. Are you coming by here or do you have to head to the station first?"

"We're going to get you home. I'll probably have to be out and about with the rest of the guys until this ends, so I want to see that you have a good fire going and that the generator is gassed up in case you do lose power over there."

"If you're pressed for time, Tan can help me do that," Hope replied.

"He would be proud to, I know, and I'm grateful for that. But he has Molly, and we need to rely on him to keep the horses fixed up with fresh hay, and—damn."

"What's wrong? Lyon?"

The phone suddenly switched to dial tone. Hope disconnected, too, and waited for the call back…and waited. When the phone rang again, she exhaled with relief.

"You scared me. What happened?" she asked.

"Hope? It's Buddy here at the station. Listen, the chief wanted you to know something's come up and he's going to be delayed. But he doesn't want you to worry."

If ever sillier words were ever spoken, Hope thought, her insides going from churning to clench. "Well, I can already hear trouble in your voice, Buddy, so you might as well tell me what's going on."

"Somebody's stuck on the ice and the chief needs to help him get out."

By now, Hope was out of her chair and moving from window to window to see what she could. When she got to the side window facing the south part of town, her heart shot up and lodged in her throat. "Oh, my God!"

"Blasted, Hope. You weren't supposed to go look."

Almost at the last traffic light a pickup truck was spinning and sliding sideways to try and champion the subtle slope in the road, but the thin ice was deceiving and there was no traction for the tires. To make matters worse, the power line could actually be seen starting to slowly tilt into the street. If the driver of the truck didn't move soon, he would be stuck under the downed pole and live lines—and the driver was her father!

Right behind him was Lyon in his patrol car striving to help him gain momentum and push through.

Hope hung up on Buddy and shut off her computer. Grabbing her coat and shawl, she locked up the office and hurried down the street as fast as she could given the weather and her own condition.

Despite the town being reduced to near ghost-town status, several people had already collected to watch the unfolding drama. When they saw her, she noticed winces and some grim exchanged glances.

"You shouldn't be out here in the cold," Matt Plummer told her. His barbershop was just to their right. "Come inside, honey. I'll get you a cup of hot tea."

"Thank you, Mr. Plummer, but I need to—" To do what? Wait and see? Watch the pole crush her father in his cab or electrocute him? "—I'll be fine," she said hugging herself as she began to shake from fear, not cold.

"There's no time, Chief! That pole's coming down," someone said.

"Look!" someone else said. "The chief's doing good. He's pushing him through."

Hope realized that was the plan just as the words were spoken. "Oh, no," she whispered pressing her gloved hands to her lips. They couldn't both make it. Didn't Lyon see?

Of course he did, she thought with her next breath. But that was his job—to help people, even if those people didn't like or even despised him.

In almost slow motion she watched with despair as Lyon eased back down the road and then shifted into drive. His chained tires would be useless on mere black ice, but on this composite mess the traction let him accelerate and using his reinforced bumper, he nudged the pickup into forward motion. But with every foot forward, the pole inched down.

Suddenly, the truck shot forward, but as Lyon tried to do the same, the pole landed with a sickening thud on the squad car's roof. The small crowd reacted with groans and one-line observations to relieve their own tension.

"Is the line touching the car?"

"Look at that! It's inches from the roof."

"Maybe if he could crawl over the seat and try to get out the back door…"

"I saw a spark from the transformer. He better not."

Hope had to shut out the voices. She would say something ugly or burst into tears if she didn't. She could see Lyon through his windshield and knew he could see her. She kept that eye contact as her lifeline.

Her father had parked a safe distance away and climbed out to see what had happened only to clasp his head with his hands.

Grateful that he understood the sacrifice on his behalf, Hope called, "Dad! Over here."

He slid and stumbled over to her. To his credit, he looked like he was about to have a stroke and Hope's heart softened toward him.

"I told him not to do it."

"It's his job," Hope replied her gaze back on Lyon.

Sirens sounded and Vince Juarez arrived to order people back to make room for the fire truck coming. He saw Hope and came toward her.

"Don't ask me to move, Vince," she said polite, but determined. "I'm not budging."

"I know, Mrs. Teague, but if I didn't at least try, the chief would have things to say if—"

Hope sent him a laser look.

"When he's freed. Sorry, ma'am."

"Are the electric people on the way?"

"Yeah. ETA maybe five minutes. They'll get him out."

Hope's hold on her emotions were slipping. "In time," she said forcefully. "I'd like him not to look like burned bacon."

Vince had to turn away. "Hurry up," she heard him mutter under his breath.

When Lyon indicated his cell phone to her, she showed him that she had hers and in a moment, it rang.

"Hey," he said his voice gruff. "What are you doing out here?"

"What are you doing *there?*"

"Guess my timing was a little off. Look, sweetheart, I'd feel better if you weren't watching this."

"Me, too. But do you think I can walk away?" Her voice cracked and she was ashamed because he didn't need the added pressure.

"Oh, baby…I know."

There was just silence for a minute and Hope watched him rub at his face and then check the wires again.

"Sweetheart, I need you to know something."

No! Not like this. But she forced herself to smile through tears and said, "Yeah, Chief, you do."

"Things have been getting pretty transparent—"

"A lot transparent."

"I know I've been holding out on you," he said with the same voice he used to tell her how he was going to make love to her before he did it. "But only for the best intentions."

"Don't you realize I don't want anyone but you?"

"So my skull is thicker than some. I just had to be sure, you know?"

"I know."

"And now I can't even say it with you in my arms."

"Please wait. Please tell me when you can do that."

As more ice fell, a larger spark erupted from the transformer at the top of the pole. There were several gasps and a scream. Hope knew it wasn't her because she had her hand clamped to her mouth and was gritting her teeth.

She heard Lyon breathing trying to control himself, as well.

"Hope," he said his voice almost guttural. "I love you. I love you with all I am and all I hoped to be."

Tears of joy and anguish washed down her frozen cheeks. "Come back to me," she whispered.

Then she felt a cramp that had her bending in half. "Oh! Lyon—oh, no…"

"What is it? Hope, is it the baby? Give the phone to Juarez. Hope!"

* * *

When Hope opened her eyes again, she was looking at a white ceiling that had a water stain in the corner. Something needed to be done about that, she thought drowsily wondering why she'd never noticed it before. Then a middle-aged man with glasses and wearing a white jacket blocked her view.

"There you are," he said, smiling. "How do you feel?"

Unless angels wore pens in their pockets, she told herself that she wasn't dead. "A little queasy. A little sore."

"You fainted."

It all came rushing back and Hope had the worst impulse to heave. "My husband! Lyon. I have to get back. Can you tell me—?"

The doctor vanished and an instant later, Lyon was hovering over her and lifting her into his arms. With a cry of joy, Hope hugged him fiercely.

"You're alive!"

He didn't reply right away. He was more intent on kissing her until they were both trembling. After that the first thing he said was, "I love you."

"I love you."

That required another long embrace until her machines and his racing heart settled down. During that time, Lyon made sure that he accounted for most of the hairs on her head, half of the bones in her body, and the peacefulness in her womb.

"The baby is fine," he said at last. "You just had a bit of system overload from the stress. You'll have to rest for a day or two to be sure, but we can get you home as soon as I sign your release."

"Home. Yes, please."

In barely an hour, Hope lay in Lyon's arms before a crackling fire. The world was right side up again and had never been more beautiful to her. She'd felt so blessed, she hadn't taken her eyes off of him the entire drive home.

Apparently the utility people had arrived just as she was fainting and had him out of the car before Vince and her father could carry her to Vince's patrol car. Lyon wouldn't wait for an ambulance and had held her in his arms the whole way.

Her father had stayed in the waiting room for news. When they emerged, he simply pressed his hand to his chest. But when he started to leave, Hope stopped him.

"Come here."

He stopped before her a tortured man. "I didn't mean to intrude. I just wanted to thank the chief again."

"His name is Lyon. He's your son-in-law."

"You must hate me."

It had been tempting at times. But Hope had new life in her—and love. She wouldn't let hate taint that.

"You can't talk the way you do, like you have done in front of me since as long as I can remember," she said. "I want Meredith to be a child, not an adult before her time like I was hearing things no child should hear. I want her to have a grandfather she can be proud of, not afraid or ashamed of."

Ellis had bowed his head both troubled and ashamed. "You're naming the baby Meredith?"

"Meredith Rebecca, after her grandmothers."

Her father nodded his head and his eyes filled. "Those are good names."

Touching his hand, Hope said, "We'll talk in a few days."

"I would like that," he said gravely.

Now, warm again and dry, having changed into a pink cashmere sweater and black jeans, she snuggled in Lyon's arms and kept stroking his chest to reassure herself that he was real and that this wasn't a dream her mind locked her in to hide from grief. He was here, strong and *alive*.

"Why did you make me wait so long to hear those words?" she said on a moan. "You knew how I felt about you."

He brought her hand up to his lips for a kiss. "I knew you liked me. I knew the sex was fantastic between us. I thought you might be falling a little in love with me, but…I worried that it was a rebound thing. Then, as I told you, I felt you deserved better."

"There is no one better, Lyon," she said before kissing him with all of her heart.

When he finally had to tear his mouth from hers and bury his face in the hollow of her throat, he apologized. "The doctor gave me strict orders," he told her. "We can't risk intercourse until you see Dr. Winslow next week."

"You're talking about sex," she told him. "We'll only be making love. Lyon, wasn't it that all the time?"

"To me it was," he said crushing her against his chest. "And I wish I had the words to tell you how that was a dream come true for me because it was always you, all along." He leaned back to stroke her face with his fingertips. "I was devastated when Will decided he wanted you. I even tried to hate you for not seeing what he was, but I couldn't."

"I'm glad."

"I knew that evening in the bar that I couldn't let you marry him. I don't know what I would have done, but you need that truth. Then when the truck exploded and you collapsed in my arms, I was too badly burned to do more than catch you for a second. The soul mates you spoke of—I saw mine in your eyes then. I wanted to carry you away from there and never let you think of him and your time together again." Lyon shook his head. "I'm not that different than your father, my love. There is and only will be one woman for me."

"I've been so blind. So foolish for not seeing how you felt."

"Why didn't you take a risk and ask—or tell me?" he teased.

Hope arched her eyebrows. "Lyon Teague, I am born and raised a southern woman. My mother came from Spanish nobility. We don't say it first."

Lyon's chest shook with laughter. "That didn't stop you from proposing."

She glanced at him from under her lashes. "Well, I didn't say we didn't know how to go about getting what we wanted."

His gaze fierce with love and dreams, Lyon leaned over to kiss the place where he last felt Meredith kick, and then lifted Hope against his heart. "Never let us go," he said.

"I promise, my love," Hope replied.

* * * * *

2 FREE BOOKS
AND A SURPRISE GIFT

We would like to take this opportunity to thank you for reading this Mills & Boon® book by offering you the chance to take TWO more specially selected books from the Cherish™ series absolutely FREE! We're also making this offer to introduce you to the benefits of the Mills & Boon® Book Club™—

- **FREE home delivery**
- **FREE gifts and competitions**
- **FREE monthly Newsletter**
- **Exclusive Mills & Boon Book Club offers**
- **Books available before they're in the shops**

Accepting these FREE books and gift places you under no obligation to buy, you may cancel at any time, even after receiving your free books. Simply complete your details below and return the entire page to the address below. You don't even need a stamp!

YES Please send me 2 free Cherish books and a surprise gift. I understand that unless you hear from me, I will receive 5 superb new stories every month, including two 2-in-1 books priced at £5.30 each, and a single book priced at £3.30, postage and packing free. I am under no obligation to purchase any books and may cancel my subscription at any time. The free books and gift will be mine to keep in any case.

Ms/Mrs/Miss/Mr _____ Initials _____

Surname _____

Address _____

_____

_____ Postcode _____

E-mail _____

Send this whole page to: Mills & Boon Book Club, Free Book Offer, FREEPOST NAT 10298, Richmond, TW9 1BR